W9-ATY-963

WITH
this
CURSE

AMANDA DeWees

ISBN-13: 978-1495934377

ISBN-10: 1495934373

Cover design by James T. Egan of Bookfly Design

Interior layout and design by Plaid Hat Books, LLC

Sign up for the author's newsletter at www.AmandaDeWees.com.

Acknowledgments

Tremendous thanks go to all of my writing friends and groups, but especially to Lisa Blackwell, Lesley and Maurice Cobbs, Jeanna Cornett, and Susan Goggins (Raven Hart) for their encouragement, enthusiasm, insight, and detailed feedback and suggestions.

And my sincere thanks go to all the readers who have embraced *Sea of Secrets* and proven that there is still great love for the traditional gothic romance genre.

About the Author

Award-winning author Amanda DeWees is a native of Atlanta and received her PhD from the University of Georgia. Learn more about her and her books at AmandaDeWees.com.

Books by Amanda DeWees

Cursed Once More
Nocturne for a Widow
Sea of Secrets
With This Curse

The Ash Grove Chronicles:

The Shadow and the Rose
Casting Shadows
Among the Shadows

Prologue
Cornwall, 1846

"The house is cursed," my mother said.

We stood at the edge of the circular gravel drive that led from the long approach to the house, walled in by beeches and rhododendron bushes, confronting for the first time Gravesend Hall. Stark white, square and unrelenting, with blank staring windows and sharply peaked gables, to my youthful eyes it was a building of grandeur unrelieved by beauty. Our new home.

"Why must we live here, then?" I demanded. I was nine years old.

My mother's lips compressed. She seemed often to have to make an effort to keep her temper with me. She was still pretty, with glossy dark hair smoothed back under a net, and her dark eyes were not yet strained and tired as they would become during our time at Gravesend. The wind plucked at our skirts and wrapped itself coldly around my legs. It was autumn, a clear day of crystalline blue sky and red and gold leaves in the wood that formed a burnished backdrop to the white stone mansion that was to become our home.

"You know perfectly well why we've come to Gravesend," she said. "With your father dead and my family not acknowledging our existence, we've no choice but to make our way in the world as best we can. Being housekeeper at Gravesend is an extraordinary opportunity." Her voice was emphatic, and I now realize, looking back from the remove of more than two decades, that she was attempting to convince herself of our good fortune as much as me. I have sometimes wondered why she did not secure our future by marrying again, but perhaps my father—whom she rarely spoke of—had been so dear to her that the idea of remarriage was repellent.

Now she looked down at me and frowned. I must have made an untidy sight, for we had walked the two miles from the railway station, and the brisk autumn breeze had made free with my hair, which was so thick and curly that it needed little encouragement to fly into disorder. She extracted a comb from her valise and set about the oft-repeated task of making me presentable.

"Why is the house cursed?" I asked.

I half expected her to tell me to hold my tongue, but perhaps she was not entirely unwilling to delay our arrival long enough to tell the tale. With only a slight hesitation she took up the story.

"Many years ago," she said, as she tugged the comb through my hair, "back in the days of Queen Anne it was, the first Lord Telford, who had just been given the barony, decided to build himself a fine new home suitable to his new rank. Lord Telford chose this spot for the house, less than two miles from the sea but with the loveliest gentle parkland surrounding it."

My mother's voice had softened as she settled into the telling of the tale, distracted from worry about the new position, about my being presentable. Too often mother's voice was stern, and furrows were drawn in her brow. There was little chance for her to rest; I always thought of her on her feet, directing me or other servants. But for the moment she seemed content to tell me the story.

"What was Lord Telford like?" I asked.

2

"Oh—young. Young and full of dreams." Her voice had sharpened again, I noted sadly. Why did she disapprove of him so, this young man she had never known? "He was but newly married, and he swore to his bride that their new home would be of a magnificence worthy of her. He consulted her on everything—the scheme of the rooms, the fabrics of the hangings, the furnishings to be crafted especially for their fine new hall. Even the color of the very stone itself was chosen with his bride in mind. Lord Telford let it be known that the white limestone was shipped in because it was as fair as his beloved's skin, and the mahogany of the doors and casements was as dark as her beautiful hair. And look there." Turning me by the shoulders, she nodded in the direction of the roof. Though she was in circumstances much reduced from those in which she had started life, my mother never forgot herself so far as to commit the solecism of pointing. "Do you see the leaded glass in the gable windows?"

I nodded. Even from this distance, I could see that there were colored panes in the high narrow windows. "It's blue," I said.

"The blue of forget-me-nots, and the very color of young Lady Telford's eyes, it is said." For a moment she was silent, and I shifted my weight restlessly. This story was not as interesting as I had expected it to be. I dug the toe of one scuffed shoe into the gravel, and the noise brought her to herself. "Be still, Clara," she said. "Those shoes must last you another winter at least."

"What about the curse?" I pressed her.

For a moment sadness flitted across her eyes. "The young baron died," she said. "Quite suddenly, and without having made any provision at all for his bride. The title, the lands, the hall itself all passed to his younger brother. And this brother did not care for the pretty young widow, indeed he did not. He made it plain that he did not trust her—even went so far as to suggest that she had taken a hand in her husband's death. And so instead of settling any portion of the estate on her, he bade her leave Gravesend Hall before another moon had turned."

"But it was her home," I said, stricken at the injustice of it.

My mother's nod was grim. "What is more, it was her husband's token of his love for her. She protested that every stick and stone of the hall spoke of her bond to her husband, and that it would be sacrilege for anyone to oust her from it. It's said that she pleaded on her knees to be permitted to stay in the home that was all she had left of her husband. 'Grant me but one wing of the house,' she begged. 'One room. I shall not disturb you further; only let me live out my life here in the home built by my husband's love. It would be a noble gesture.'

"They say the new Lord Telford laughed in her face. ''Twould be a foolhardiness, more like,' he told her. 'I'd not sleep sound in my bed knowing you were about, scheming to make an end to me as you did my brother. Begone, beldame, and let me not see your face more.'"

"I hope she refused to leave," I exclaimed. "I hope she spat in his face and—and—" But confronted with my mother's grave, steady gaze, I contained my indignation. No such satisfying ending to the story would fit with what she had told me already. "The curse," I said slowly. "It was the widow's doing?"

"It was indeed. And such a curse! 'For a house you have ruined me,' she told the heir, 'and the house shall be your ruin in turn. Live here you may, but you shall never know a day of peace within these walls. You, your kin, and your heirs are doomed to know the same fate that you have meted me: *you shall lose what you love the most.*"

I shivered and drew the thin fabric of my cloak more closely around my shoulders, even though the clear autumn sunshine lay warm upon my back. "And did they?"

"Oh, yes. The new master of Gravesend was restless in his magnificent new home. He was certain that the widow knew of secret ways of creeping into the house and that she shadowed him, always watching him, always wishing his doom upon him. Even after the lady made an end of herself—"

"What!"

A gentle sigh. "Yes, the poor creature committed that worst sin. One day she contrived to make her way into the house that should have been hers; bribed a servant, it is said, so that she might have one last look at the rooms that had been crafted with her delight as their purpose. When word reached the baron of this, he had her flushed from the house and pursued. She fled toward the wood and into the folly—"

"What is that?"

4

"A false ruin, another of the first baron's caprices. We cannot see it from here. If you wish me to continue, Clara, you mustn't interrupt."

"I'm sorry," I said quickly, afraid she would stop. "What happened to the lady?"

"The new baron's servants chased her to the folly, and she climbed all the way to the top of the tower. When the baron arrived to remonstrate with her, she said nothing—but flung herself from the tower."

Aghast, I stared with new dread at the house. I could imagine the widow, her beauty blighted by despair, her once dark hair streaked with white and tossed by the wind as she stepped up to the edge of the tower and leapt to her death.

"But even so, the new Lord Telford did not know peace," my mother continued. "He was convinced that, even though he had watched the lady die, she nonetheless roamed the manor, seeking to destroy him. He walked the halls every night, and his health began to fail. Finally his eccentricities grew so pronounced that his relatives had him removed from Gravesend to a quiet place of seclusion where his ravings would disturb no one."

"That means he didn't have Gravesend after all," I said triumphantly. "He lost it, just as the widow said."

"So he did." My mother picked up her valise again and took my hand. "Come, Clara, we mustn't dawdle here any longer; we shall be seen."

Our footsteps crunched over the gravel as we resumed our progress toward our new home, whose chilly white walls looked no less forbidding than before. "The curse should have ended then," I pointed out.

"Ah, but curses are not so easily done with," she told me. "The widow decreed that the baron's kin and heirs should also suffer. And so it came to pass that each resident of Gravesend sooner or later lost that thing that was dearest to them. The third Lord Telford, a brilliant athlete who was never happier than on horseback, was paralyzed in a terrible accident and never sat a horse again. An heir with a scholarly bent who knew no greater joy than when among his books was blinded one night in a fire that also destroyed his library." Reciting these horrors, my mother's voice was still calm, and that, if anything, made them more alarming. Were these such commonplace occurrences in this place we were to call home? She continued, "The beautiful Lady Alys was the toast of three counties until her maid ran mad and attacked her with scissors, leaving her face a scarred ruin."

"I don't want to live here," I burst out. "What will happen to us?" Then a comforting thought occurred to me. "We are not related to the family, though. We are safe—aren't we?"

My mother's smile was almost too hard and grim to deserve the name. "Gravesend's curse does not always make such fine distinctions," she said. "Innocent guests under this roof have been said to meet their doom here as well. You would do well to gather your courage and be on your guard, Clara. This house will take from you what you most treasure."

"From *me?* Are you not frightened, Mother?"

Suddenly her eyes looked like those of an old, old woman, someone who had seen more sorrow than I could ever guess at. "I am not frightened, no." Her voice was so low that I had to strain to hear her. "I have grown accustomed to having what I love taken from me." Then, as if coming to herself, she gave me a very different smile: warm, bright, reassuring. "But you are young, and even curses must sleep. Come, don't be frightened. Let us show Gravesend that a curse is no match for women of independent spirit."

Only later would I reflect that this resolve sorted oddly with what she had said before and realize that my mother was simply trying to assuage her young child's fears. She had truly meant me to fear Gravesend, to prepare myself for what it might deal to me, so that the doom when it fell would hurt that much the less.

Neither of us could have predicted what form that doom would take, or when the sword would fall. And it was only when I was tasting a happiness that I had never known before, when my future seemed cast in the golden radiance of hopeful love, that those fateful words came true. *This house will take from you what you most treasure.* My mother had spoken truly—but she could not have known that this treasure would be no less than a man's life.

CHAPTER ONE
London, 1873

He was not a ghost. I was certain of it. Very nearly certain, at least. The clean strong planes of his face were Richard's, and the arresting pale blue eyes. The fine-boned hand that had swept his high silk hat from his head as soon as I opened the dressing-room door. The cap of bright chestnut hair that gleamed in the light of the gas lamp. And the quick painful bound my heart gave at my first glimpse of the tall, broad-shouldered figure, even before I looked into his face: all of this cried *Richard, Richard.*

But he could not be Richard, for Richard was dead.

"I beg your pardon," he said, and the familiar warm, rich voice was another knife in my vitals. "The doorman—Harris, is it?—told me that this was Miss Ingram's dressing room."

"She'll not be here for another half hour yet," I said shortly. I knew him now, and the bitter knowledge that he still lived when

Richard did not brought a hot rush of anger to my heart. "You may return then, if you like."

Those disconcertingly pale eyes were gazing at me with such intentness that a cowardly impulse urged me to shut the door on him and blot out that scrutiny. Had he recognized me? Or had the more than eighteen years since our last meeting aged me to the point that he did not know me? Eighteen hard years they had been, and perhaps I had indeed changed that dramatically. And for that, too, I resented this visitor's presence. It was his family that had wrought the destructive change in my life.

Not just the family, whispered the cold voice of memory. *The curse.*

But he was speaking again. "In point of fact, it isn't Miss Ingram I came to see." He seemed to hesitate. "Am I correct in thinking that you're Mrs. Graves?"

"You are," I said. After so many years of owning to it, the alias was almost natural, but under that bright gaze I felt ashamed of the pretext, necessity though it was. But what could he want of me—the me that was masquerading as Mrs. Graves? "How can I help you?" I asked.

The lack of warmth or welcome in my voice did not deter him. "I'm Atticus Blackwood," he said unnecessarily. "My father is Edgar Blackwood, Baron Telford. Perhaps I might come in and tell you my business?"

Grudgingly I moved aside, permitting him to enter. I noticed the pale blue eyes taking in the dressing room, and for a moment I saw it as he must have seen it: the walls and furnishings of a soft salmon pink, the graceful feminine touches of pastel-hued prints and cushioned divan, the skirted dressing table with enormous gilt-edged mirror—all selected to create a setting that would frame its exquisite tenant as perfectly as the great seashell did Botticelli's Venus. But I was not the resident goddess, merely a functionary, and the feminine elegance of the room was at odds with my stark and stern appearance. My own domain could be glimpsed through the door opposite, which stood open just enough to offer a glimpse of the sewing machine.

A glance in the dressing-table mirror reassured me that I was tidy enough. My springy hair was subdued in a netted chignon, and my black bombazine dress, though unfashionable and severe in its cut, was free of the clinging stray threads and scraps that I seemed always to trail after me. Not that I felt any desire to impress my visitor, but I would have hated for him to see me at a disadvantage. His family had not robbed me of my dignity, whatever else they had taken.

At a nod from me, he took a seat on the divan, resting one hand on an ebony walking stick as he did so, and my eyes automatically went to his right foot. Possibly a stranger might not have recognized at once the deformity, so skillfully did he disguise it with a specially constructed boot, and his gait had seemed scarcely affected at all when he entered the room, but I remembered the brace he had worn in the earliest years I had known him, and how grotesquely he had lurched after Richard, unable to keep up.

He noted the direction of my gaze, and I quickly averted my eyes. It was not merely rude but quite improper for me to eye a man's limbs. When I had known him before I was a bold, reckless girl who thought little of such proprieties—but time had taught me the danger of that. "What business brings you to me, Mr. Blackwood?" I inquired. "Are you perhaps seeking a modiste for your wife?" If he had not recognized me, I would not help him to do so.

A faint, wry smile touched his mouth. It was a handsomely modeled mouth, I observed with some surprise. But of course—it was Richard's mouth. Strange, though, that every feature that had been handsome and distinctive on Richard had always seemed drab and homely on his twin brother. Identical though the two might have been in most ways, Richard had always been the one who took one's breath away, dazzling and reckless and athletic; Atticus had been the wan figure in the background. To realize now that the difference had never been in their physical appearance but in their personalities was something of a shock.

"My wife," he said, "is indeed the reason for my calling on you, but not in the way you suggest. I believe that you were once in my family's employ, were you not, under the name Crofton?" I nodded shortly. "I gather you've been married and widowed since that time."

9

"Neither," I said, more shortly still. "When I took employment with Miss Ingram and began traveling with her troupe, I found that it wasn't prudent to be known as an unmarried female. Becoming a widow has afforded some protection."

The intent scrutiny relaxed. "Ah, yes, I see. Some men will refrain from making unwanted advances if the object of their interest is cloaked in the solemnity of bereavement. It's unfortunate that you were forced into such a deception, but I salute the wisdom of it." The smile again, more relaxed and cordial now. "I must admit, though, that your alias substantially delayed my discovering your whereabouts. I've been searching for you for quite some time now."

"Indeed?" The thought made me uneasy. What further ill fortune was this family to visit upon me? My wariness must have shown in my face, for he was quick to reassure me.

"Don't be alarmed, Miss Crofton—or do you prefer Mrs. Graves?"

"If you please," I said, wondering if he had guessed that I had chosen the name for its similarity to the only place where I had known happiness . . . the same place that had destroyed it.

"Mrs. Graves, then. I've come with a proposition that I hope you will profit from." The pleasant richness of his voice wrapped around me like cashmere, disorienting me; it was Richard who had spoken like this, so that every word sounded like an endearment. Atlas—for that was the mocking nickname Richard had given his brother—had spoken rarely, and then almost inaudibly. The years had lent him eloquence and assurance, and I found myself resenting him for it. These things had been Richard's birthright; it was unjust that they should now have passed into the keeping of his unworthy sibling. If Fortune had been compelled to obliterate one of the Blackwood brothers, why could it not have been this one?

I ought to have been shocked at myself for so ruthless a thought. But it was not, I admit, a new one. In the terrible days and weeks after the news of Richard's death had reached me, I had thought it sometimes: *Why Richard and not Atlas? Why take the paragon and leave the ruin?*

"Pray go on," I said, to stem the tide of bitter thoughts.

He folded his hands on the ivory handle of his walking stick.

It was carved in the shape of a globe, and I wondered with a start if he somehow knew of the nickname Richard had given him. "My father is dying," he said bluntly. "He suffered a stroke some months ago and is not rallying as he should. The doctors believe he has little chance of seeing out the year."

I could not say I was sorry. Lord Telford had permitted his wife to throw me out of his house and into a world I was unprepared to navigate alone.

He continued, "In recent years my father has been much concerned with the future of the Telford title. In particular, it distresses him that I haven't married. He professes to be aware of the quite reasonable objections a suitable young lady might make to my deformity—and the very real possibility that it might be passed down to our children—but he's unaware of the other consideration that has prevented my marrying: the family curse, as it's known."

"You sound as if you do not believe in the curse," I said, curious in spite of myself.

He shrugged, and I noticed again the breadth of his shoulders; I had remembered him as a spindly youth, but perhaps my memory of him had been colored by dislike, either mine or Richard's. Or perhaps he had a tailor as clever as his cobbler. "My belief in it is immaterial," he said. "It's the fact that all of the marriageable ladies in my circle believe in it that presents the difficulty. And hence I come to you."

"How do I come into the matter?" I said, startled. "I'm not acquainted with any eligible young ladies to introduce to you, if that is your hope."

"This is my proposition." His blue eyes, icily pale, were once again disconcerting me with their intentness. "I'd like to ease my father's last few weeks or months of life by bringing a bride to Gravesend. If you will consent to be that bride, for as long as my father lives, I'll settle on you a sufficient income to keep you in comfort the rest of your days."

This effectively robbed me of speech, it was so unexpected, and perhaps to give me time to collect myself he continued, as calmly as if he had not just proposed marriage to me.

"My father's condition is so pitiable that I cannot imagine the term shall be very long. Perhaps we might extend it by a few weeks after his death, so as to forestall the worst gossip—although of course there will be talk. We may wish to spread word that your own health is delicate, so that when you depart from Gravesend to a healthier climate it won't come as a complete surprise."

Finding my tongue, I said, "Your father would be disappointed that you chose a bride too old to give you children. You would do much better to find a younger, ah, confederate for this scheme."

His gaze swept over me from head to foot, with a casual appraisal so like Richard's that I swallowed hard. "I think that in less severe garb than your widow's weeds, you'll look not much older than you were when you were put out of the house."

He had said it—voiced the great awkward unacknowledged fact of our acquaintance. And now that he had done so, I had a clue to help me toward an explanation for this bizarre visit.

"Are you attempting to make amends to me?" I asked. "Is that why I am the one you approached?"

"You are assuming that I haven't already approached and been rejected by other choices," he said, with amusement in his voice. "But yes, in fact, I have always felt that my parents were unduly harsh with you. You were little more than a child."

"I was seventeen," I said, stung, even though I knew I should accept his more flattering version of the past.

"Just so. Very young, very impressionable. And my brother would have made an impression on anyone."

There was sympathy in his voice, and that smarted worse than anything he had put into words.

"Thank you for the olive branch," I said crisply, "but I'll leave it to another young woman of reduced means to help you in your current difficulty."

"And what young woman would that be?" he asked wryly. "As I said, my deformity is a strong discourager of marriage. No bride wants a husband with a club foot, especially as the father of her children."

This was indelicate but honest, and I was forced to respect him for confronting the unpleasant truth. In return I felt compelled to be equally honest, even though that meant being equally indelicate. "So you approach me, a woman too old to bear children."

"That was not my reason," he protested. "Your age is immaterial, Cl—Mrs. Graves. I wouldn't expect you to bear lifelong consequences from a temporary domestic alliance. Our marriage would be in name only."

Our marriage. It sounded offensive coming from the lips of anyone but Richard. "How considerate of you," I said icily. "But you seem to have overlooked the other objection: the curse."

That made him blink in what seemed genuine surprise. "Mrs. Graves, surely you don't believe in servants' gossip."

He regretted the words as soon as they were spoken; I could see his brow contract in a wince. But I said mercilessly, "You forget, Mr. Blackwood, I *am* a servant."

"I sincerely beg your pardon. I meant no offense. Only—you must know the story to be nothing more than fantasy. You lived at Gravesend for years."

"Yes, and see where I am now." The bitterness in my voice was plain even to my own ears, and my hands had curled into fists. "Why shouldn't I believe in the curse? Can you not see that I am living proof of it?"

"Proof? I don't under—"

"I lost my love." My voice was shaking now, and I dropped it to a whisper. I would show no weakness before any of the Blackwood line. "I lost Richard." I stood abruptly, signaling an end to our meeting.

He leaned heavily on his stick as he got to his feet, but I felt no pity for him. "Please don't reject my offer just yet," he said. "Take a few days to consider it."

"As inviting as that sounds, Mr. Blackwood, I don't think there's any point in discussing the matter further." Three steps took me to the door, which I had left ajar, so I did not have the satisfaction of flinging it open for him now. Instead I stationed myself beside it meaningfully. His gait before had seemed almost normal, but now his bad leg almost buckled beneath him as he made his way to where I stood by the door.

"Clara," he said softly, "the furthest thing from my mind was to cause you distress. You have, as you say, lost something irreplaceable."

13

I would not look at him. Could not, when my heart ached at the sight of him, so like Richard—even sounding like him now, with his voice low and intimate.

"But don't you see," he continued. "That means that the curse, if it exists, has no more power over you." Before I could summon a response, he pressed a card into my hand. "I'll be in London all week, and I hope you'll consent to discuss the matter further. Send word to me at the Athenaeum Club, and I'll call any time you wish."

Still I refused to look at him. I sensed rather than saw his quick half bow, and then the sound of his footsteps receded down the uncarpeted passage, the gait with its slight unevenness accompanied by the tap of his stick.

"Who was that delicious man?"

Sybil Ingram's voice preceded the rest of her. The ringing mezzo-soprano tones struck my ear first, then her fragrance—a powerful amalgam of tuberose and violet—and finally the actress herself swept into view amid a rustle of taffeta skirts. She had the wide china-blue eyes and spun-gold hair of an ingénue, although I knew that she had passed her thirtieth birthday—a fact that would have been worth my life to divulge to any of her gentleman followers.

For once, none of these was in evidence, and this was perhaps the reason she felt free to question me at such indecorous volume. "What did he want?" she continued, sweeping past me into the dressing room and handing me her sealskin mantle without pausing. "I know he saw me, but he only tipped his hat and kept walking. Was he looking for Clement?" Clement Griffiths was her leading man, a far distant second in importance in the troupe hierarchy.

"No, Miss Ingram." The idea of anyone considering Atlas Blackwood "delicious" fairly stunned me. But then, she was not acquainted with the reality.

"Who, then?" It seemed her curiosity would not be satisfied without my going into explanations. I stifled a sigh as I hung up her wrap and helped her out of her dress, giving it a quick inspection as I did so. My employer was indifferent to such details as a drooping bit of lace or a loose button, so I had learned to stay vigilant for such small problems before they became large ones. But the smart chartreuse taffeta gown with its facings and edgings of lilac shot silk looked as pristine as it had when it first left my hands; the cartridge ruffles at the square neck and three-quarter sleeves were crisp, and the hem showed very little soiling. A few minutes with the clothes brush would prevent it from staining.

As I attended to this task, Miss Ingram slipped on a bright silk dressing gown and sank down onto the seat before the dressing table, unpinned the tiny saucer of a bonnet, and set about making up her face for the evening's performance. With its coating of face powder, its litter of bottles and jars, and the blonde wig on its stand, the dressing table was the only part of the room that was less than exquisite. "You haven't told me who the caller was," she reminded me. "Such a handsome fellow— one might run quite mad for eyes like those."

"It was Baron Telford's son, of Gravesend Hall."

"How interesting! If he didn't come to see me or Clement, what was his business?"

"He was here to see me," I admitted. "A small matter—a mistake, in fact. Nothing of importance."

"Indeed?" The actress looked more intrigued than ever as she picked up a rabbit's foot to daub rouge onto her cheeks. "I didn't know you had acquaintances of such standing, Graves." There was reproach in the words. My employer liked to believe that she was the most highly placed person in the troupe's world, the only one who had sufficient celebrity to be a household word among gentlefolk, and for the most part this was the case. The assemblage of actors, stagehands, attendants, and hangers-on that formed the theater troupe were all Sybil Ingram's vassals.

I most definitely counted myself among them. Ten years before, I had been working a sewing machine in a factory, a place of deafening noise and stifling heat, taking home finishing work to carry out by insufficient light in the rented room I shared with two other girls from the factory. One evening as the three of us were walking home, a glamorous figure had detained us. As one we gawked at the actress's shining golden hair, fine silk gown, and dainty features.

"What a charming frock," she said to me, reaching out boldly to grasp my collar. "Who made it for you?"

"I made it myself, ma'am." The piped scalloped trim that she was fingering had been a trial attempt before I cut into the more expensive goods of the dress I was trimming for a lady of fashion. "I'd be happy to make you one like it," I added daringly, for I was always seeking more opportunities to relieve the monotony of factory work with more interesting tasks—and to supplement my meager income.

"Hm." She did not answer at once. "And the color? Was that your choice as well?"

The bold greenish-blue woolen goods had cost me many a missed meal, but it was a color that lifted my spirits. "I wouldn't advise such a color for you, ma'am," I said, more daring every moment, for it was obvious from the woman's dress that she had plenty of money to spend on her own adornment. "With your complexion, I think a robin's-egg blue, trimmed in primrose and salmon. Or perhaps lavender with sea-green."

She laughed, not displeased. "You certainly do have a great many opinions about a stranger's ensemble."

"Oh, but you're not a stranger," said my friend Martha, whose eyes had gone as round as an owl's. "You're Sybil Ingram! I saw you in *The Prodigal's Return*. You were wonderful!"

Miss Ingram beamed at her, gratified at being recognized. "You're too kind," she said, in a tone of voice that indicated that it was her due. Though scarcely twenty, she was already firmly established as one of the most popular actresses in London. "I must admit I was fond of that particular role. But my gowns were sadly out of tune with the character. You, girl"—this was to me—"what would you say to coming to supper with me and giving me your thoughts on my gowns for the new tour? You seem to have a good head on your shoulders, a tumbled one though it be."

My hand went self-consciously to my curly hair, which I still had not learned to subdue. Later, when I had left the factory to work solely for Miss Ingram, she would show me how to tame it. "I'd be delighted, ma'am," I said. And thus our association began.

Becoming Sybil Ingram's modiste was the best thing to happen to me since my ignominious departure from Gravesend. It was exciting to be intimately involved in the life of the theater, to move among actors, who were, many of them, as entertaining off the stage as they were on it—but they could also, as I saw very quickly, put an unattached female in a compromising position. Partly for that reason, Sybil Ingram helped me construct the persona of Widow Graves, advising me on posture and vocal inflections to most effectively present a dampening effect on masculine ardor. "And I quite agree that you need some such armor," she said cheerfully.

"It isn't as if I were a young woman still," I had said.

"You look younger than you are, though. That tiny waist takes years off your age." She could say this without rancor, as her own waist was every bit as slender. Hers was the product of self-denial and tight lacing, mine of a life that had not permitted ample meals.

Now her voice brought me back to the present. "You're being quite mysterious about your gentleman visitor," she said as she settled the wig in place over her hair. "Did he wish to whisk you out of this sordid world of play-acting and into the rarefied sphere of his titled existence?"

This quip was so disconcertingly close to the truth that my clothes brush halted for a moment. What spirit possessed her to be so roguish today? Now that I took a closer look, I saw that her color was high—even apart from the rouge—and her eyes unusually bright. "Is something the matter, Miss Ingram?"

She gave a laugh that confirmed my suspicion. Some secret was energizing her, and now she sprang to her feet and darted over to grasp my hands, regardless of the clothes brush. "Graves," she exclaimed, "I'm to be married."

I stared at her. Never in the ten years that I had known her had Sybil Ingram breathed any intention of giving up the life of the theater for marriage. "Married?" I stammered. "To whom?" If only it were another actor, or someone well established in the theater world, perhaps she would not be abandoning us. But her next words shattered that possibility.

"To Alcott Lammle. You remember, from when we played last year in New York?"

17

Remember I most certainly did. Mr. Lammle, a prominent American hotelier, was among the most prosperous of the suitors Miss Ingram had collected during the tour, hosting lavish dinners in her honor and showering her with expensive gifts. "Will you be settling here in London?" I asked faintly. Perhaps her new husband would be expanding his business interests into England, and Sybil Ingram's vassals would not be disbanded after all.

This faint hope, however, was soon obliterated. "No, Graves, you don't understand," she cried, pulling me to my feet to lead me into an improvised waltz. "I'm leaving the theater. No more work for me. I shall grow fat and lazy and contented, and be 'that nice Mrs. Lammle,' and Alcott can spoil me to his heart's delight. I shall host society ladies at tea and throw the dullest dinner parties imaginable. And I shall revel in it!"

"And the troupe?" It felt churlish to question her decision, so elated was she, but I could not help but be anxious about the fate of those of us she would be leaving behind.

Such anxieties were clearly far from her mind, however. "Oh, Clement can take over quite easily. He can find some other leading lady—Narcissa Holm might suffice. The company will scarcely notice I'm gone."

This was unaccustomed modesty, and misplaced at that. But my most urgent thought was not, I admit, for the company. "And what of me?" I asked.

That finally brought her out of her fantasy. She looked at me with a little moue of dismay. "Oh. Graves, I am sorry, but I cannot take you with me."

"Cannot?"

"It is Alcott. He is quite determined that I leave all vestiges of my life in England behind once we are married. I believe it's a point of pride with him—he tells me that he has already hired a dressmaker who is quite in demand in New York." When I did not answer, she added, "Truly, if it were my decision, naturally I'd want you with me. But I shall need to dress in the style of the American ladies of Alcott's circle, and my dear, you're far too original for such drab work!"

I could not help but smile at her attempt to cushion the blow. "I fear that leaves me at a loose end," I said. "The fact is, the company won't need to keep me on. I've always worked for you rather than the troupe. They did for themselves before I arrived, and without you to pay my wages they'll not want the expense of a resident seamstress."

She bit her lip in the gesture she adopted on stage for vexation of thought. "You are right, of course. How too exasperating. What shall you do?"

What indeed? I could return to the factory. The thought of it made my stomach curdle. The long hours, from dark to dark, with only one day in every week to call one's own; the noise that seemed to batter at one's skull; the weariness that one wore like a heavy garment; and all for so little pay that a shared shabby room and three meager meals were all it would afford. And without another patron like Sybil Ingram, I would be likely to spend the rest of my life in such servitude. My very soul seemed to cringe. *Not that. Anything but that.*

But what else was there for an unattached female? I knew that the established modistes had no desire to take on a seamstress of my age; they preferred tractable younger women who were easily cowed and presented a prettier appearance to customers. Nor was I fit for work as a governess. My education had been a scanty, slapdash affair, doled out to me by my mother during her rare moments of leisure. Thanks to her, I had some fragments of learning beyond what was vouchsafed to many of my class, but it was far from the body of knowledge I would need in order to become a governess. Nor did I have the amiable disposition for such work—or for work in a shop, as I had proven. Was there no other course open to me?

Yes, one: become Atlas's wife.

I shrank from the thought. He was the worst match I could possibly have chosen. His face and form reminded me so strongly of Richard that I could scarcely bear his presence. It made my scarred heart feel the pain of breaking as keenly as if it had been only yesterday instead of more than eighteen years before. And this same man was the one Richard had seemed to despise above all others—the only person, in fact, who animated anything like hostility in him. It would be betraying the memory of the man I had loved to wed the very man he had held in contempt.

What other choice did I have, though? My thoughts flailed wildly. Miss Ingram was not unkind but completely engrossed in her good fortune. Even if I could rely on her to give me a reference, she was too absorbed in her own plans to be expected to seek out any of her acquaintance who might have the need— and means—for a personal modiste. Moreover, she would make every effort to prevent me from working for any of her professional rivals; just because she was leaving the theater did not mean that she would want any other prominent actresses to benefit from her departure. After ten years with Sybil Ingram, I knew that she would want her legacy to remain undimmed by comparisons to any other actress—even in as small a detail as their costumes.

My own circle of acquaintance was small and confined to the theater, so I could not rely on recommendations from them. As I mechanically helped Miss Ingram into her costume for the first act, I cudgeled my brains for another solution.

Finally, when the curtain had risen and all was quiet backstage, with only the occasional sound of the audience's laughter or applause to disturb the silence, I took pencil and paper and began to compose an advertisement.

Skilled seamstress and dressmaker of more than 15 years' experience seeks employment . . .

Chapter Two

I worked over the details and wording of the advertisement for half an hour before I was satisfied. Tomorrow I would send it to several newspapers. Surely I would be able to find something suitable by this means.

Nevertheless, the necessity of seeking work from strangers depressed my spirits. I could faintly hear outbursts of laughter from the audience from where I sat in the dressing room, but that served only to make me feel more isolated as I awaited Miss Ingram's first change of costume. There was no mending to do at the moment, no new garment to be sewn, and although I could have turned my hand to tidying the little room, I chose instead to indulge myself for a few minutes in memory.

Richard had been so easy to fall in love with. The golden son, cherished by his parents, doted upon by the servants. He excelled at everything he touched, it seemed, and perhaps that is what made him so reckless and daring: his mount was the wildest of stallions, his friends—so we heard—the most profligate and scandalous of men. Other stories circulated among the servants as well, of gambling losses, of duels, of debauches with fallen women and despoiled virgins, but these were easy for me to dismiss. Richard was not truly like that, I knew, and such gossip would have arisen about any young gentleman as handsome and dashing as he. I knew he was no rake. I knew it because he loved me.

This was still so miraculous to me that all these years later my breath still caught when I considered it. Desired by everyone, admired by everyone, this young man with the world at his feet had singled me out among all women.

We were discreet, of course—no other choice lay before us. At first it was merely glances held too long or given too frequently. Occasionally he would tease me by jerking the strings of my apron in passing, or winking at me when no others were around. Then it was murmured words and shared laughter. By the time of my seventeenth birthday we were meeting in secret. Nothing more untoward than kisses passed between us, although sometimes this was due to my strenuously resisting his attempts at further liberties.

"Anyone would think you a highborn lady, you're so careful of your virtue," he said once as I fended off his busy hands, even as a smile tempered the words.

"I am half a gentlewoman," I reminded him a bit stiffly. It was never pleasant to be reminded of the gulf between us. "My mother—"

"Yes, I know the story. Your worthy mother was gently born, and her efforts to foster the lady in you have been most effective." He grinned, and the sight almost made my heart stop its beating. "A pity, really. Such a fine tigress to be trained in timidity." With a fingertip he traced the line of my throat, and then downward over the bodice of my dress to my bosom, and I pushed his hand away.

"If you won't behave, I shall have to go."

He gave me a wounded look. It was those eyes that always came near to undoing me. His strong jaw, fine straight nose, and high, wide brow were formed with a strength that was almost overwhelming, like engravings of classical heroes. Indeed, strength was what I associated most with Richard—with both his body and his will. But his eyes, extraordinarily light blue, were unexpectedly candid and revealing. The rest of his form boasted of splendid vigor and energy, the pinnacle of man's fleshly self; his eyes, though, afforded a glimpse of his higher being. A man with eyes like those could not be a cad, no matter what gossip whispered, and I knew that as surely as I knew my own name.

"I'll behave, as you call it," he said, that rich voice like a caress. "But Clara, don't be angry. I can't help myself when I'm with you."

It was impossible to be angry with him, and I said so. For as exasperating as it sometimes was to be on constant guard against his hands creeping under my skirt or into my bodice, it was also, I must admit, flattering—and exciting. And in my heart I knew that these advances were more in show than in earnest, a game that we both enjoyed but whose unspoken rules he would not break.

There was one day in particular that proved the depth of Richard's feelings for me, and how much he valued what we shared. The memory of that idyllic afternoon had sustained me through all the years since. It was so perfect and so precious that I avoided recalling it too frequently, lest I wear its beauty thin like the fragile fabric of a gown worn too many times. Only when I was in the lowest spirits did I permit myself to recall the entire episode, as one would perform a ritual—and indeed, very nearly holy was the memory enshrined in my mind.

It was a Thursday afternoon in early summer, my precious half day free from my duties, and he and I had arranged to meet at the folly, as we often did when the weather was fair. From there we might wander through the woods, taking a nearly overgrown path where no one but us ever walked, or go to the old grotto, another architectural folly of the first baron's, where we would be assured of privacy. The ruin, with its two partial walls forming a right angle where they met at the tower, was on a rise that offered a fine view of the grounds and the back of Gravesend, so that we could see whether anyone was approaching. I had once tried to climb to the top of the tower, but Richard had hauled me down bodily, protesting that the old stairs were unsafe . . . or perhaps he merely wanted an excuse to pick me up and carry me, making me squeal in delighted indignation.

He had little love for the mock ruin, though; it was I who found it so fascinating and romantic. So I was surprised that day, when I arrived breathless from hurrying to find him lounging against the inner wall chewing idly on a blade of grass, that he was content to remain.

"I brought us a picnic," he said, gesturing to a bundle near him.

"Truly? You don't mind staying here?" I dropped down onto the grass beside him.

He smiled, looking as lazily contented as a cat lying in his pool of sunlight. Richard was usually happier in motion than at rest, but perhaps the beauty of the day had cast its spell on him. The sunshine filled up the little space inside the walls of the folly as wine filled a goblet, and it seemed to make everything more vivid than ever before. The grass was a tender new green, with violets springing up everywhere in little darts of purple and white. Auburn glints shone in Richard's hair, and when a cardinal alighted briefly on one of the arched openings in the wall it was as if scarlet had been invented just for that moment. But the most breathtaking color was the crystalline blue of his eyes.

"I know how you love it here," he said, reaching for the bundle and removing a bottle of wine and a meat pie, which he must have wheedled from Cook—or stolen when her back was turned. "It's picturesque, I must admit, even if its history isn't as eventful as it's said to be." He attempted to spread the cloth out on the ground even as the breeze tried to toss it back into his face, and I couldn't help but laugh at the sight of this most splendid of men confounded by domestic arrangements. I took over the laying of the cloth, and he seemed content to watch me do so.

As much in love as I was, I nonetheless had the appetite of a normal girl of seventeen, and he and I made quick work of our improvised meal. When nothing remained but crumbs, the joyous glow of the sunlight persuaded me to push back my bonnet, letting it hang by the ribbons tied around my neck. I plunged my fingers through my hair to free it from its pins and let it blow loose in the breeze.

"I feel so free," I said. "I love being here with you."

He reached out to twine one of my wild locks around his fingers. "And I with you, pet."

"What did you mean before, though, about the folly's history? Don't tell me the first Lady Telford didn't truly fling herself from the tower."

That won a laugh from him. "Are you so bloodthirsty that the idea disappoints you?"

I could feel myself blushing. "It is a terribly sad story, but you must admit there is a kind of—of splendor to it. That she and the first baron loved each other so dearly."

"It's too fantastical a story to be true," he said idly. He seemed more interested in playing with my hair than in the conversation, but this was what I was accustomed to in him. "When are property disputes ever so romantic? No, I don't think there was any suicide or any curse, either. I suspect the Blackwoods made themselves heartily disliked—as well as wealthy—simply by being the most successful smugglers in the region, not because of a curse."

"They were smugglers?"

"Indeed they were, and ruthless about it. They disliked competition and did their best to stamp it out."

"But how did they get away with it?"

The lucid clarity of his eyes kindled with his smile. My heart never failed to respond to that expression with a little leap in my breast. "Everyone smuggled in those days, pet," he said, his voice warm and caressing. "The Blackwoods were neither the first nor the last—they were just the most unpleasant. In fact, it wouldn't surprise me if they themselves invented the story of the curse to keep people from nosing around the grounds and discovering where they stored the contraband goods."

This was a new view of my employers' forebears, and I was not at all certain that I liked it. "That is so . . . sordid," I said.

"You prefer the romantic version, as tragic as it is?"

"It's far sadder to keep living all the years and decades after losing your love," I said positively. "A love that passionate is worth any sacrifice for. You always used to say the same."

"Did I? Well, a man may change his mind, after all."

"He may indeed," I said, and there was a wistful note in my voice. Never had Richard behaved in so polite and gentlemanly

25

a manner before, and I was, womanlike, contrary enough to be disappointed. He had not kissed me even once. I could not help but wonder, despite the thoughtfulness he had shown in bringing about this picnic, if perhaps his interest in me was ebbing.

My voice must have revealed my thoughts, for he put a hand under my chin and tipped it up so that I looked into eyes. That clear blue gaze had never seemed to read me so well, or with such understanding. "There's one thing you may rest assured I'll not change my mind about," he said softly. "I'll always love you, Clara."

For a moment I could not find my voice. I could only stare into his eyes, into that depth of understanding and tenderness so vast that it nearly swallowed up all thought. "You've never said that before," I finally managed to say.

The fingers beneath my chin moved to my cheek. "I know, and I'm sorry," he whispered. "You should scold me for that. But not . . . just . . . yet."

Even as my lips parted to upbraid him, he was kissing me. But this too was new. Instead of the fierce, swift kisses that seemed to insist on ever more intimacy, this was slow, tantalizingly so, as if he relished every moment and every shade of sensation that passed between us. Coaxing, almost teasing, but as leisured as if we had our whole lives to do nothing but this.

The effect was captivating. Under the magic of his touch I too found the pleasure in slow, drawn-out kisses that savored the warmth of his breath and the dizzying sweetness of his lips on mine. I could not catch my breath, but that seemed unimportant; my limbs seemed to dissolve so that I could no longer sit upright and sank backward onto the springy turf, and he followed after.

A tiny part of my brain whispered of the danger of this reclining position. Richard would seize upon this as an invitation; it was a move in our eternal game that put me at too great a disadvantage. But to lie on the sun-warmed grass with the man I loved drinking deep from my lips was a heady bliss I had never known before. He had unfolded his heart to me; perhaps this new stage of our game would take us to a place more beautiful and precious than the endless advance and rebuff that had constituted it up to now.

I opened my eyes when his touch left my lips and found him gazing down at me with an expression almost serious. The sun behind his head made a nimbus like auburn flame. Then I felt his fingertips at my throat, unfastening the top button of my bodice. His eyes were looking a question at me, and I knew, without a word being spoken, that he would stop the moment I asked him to.

A finger slipped between the parted edges of my bodice, and my breath caught at the touch of his fingertip on the sensitive skin there. His eyes, though, were still fixed on mine, still silently questioning if he might proceed.

It was the first time I had permitted such a liberty, but somehow I felt that I could completely trust him. With a sigh I closed my eyes. I would stop him soon. Just a minute more and I would stop him.

I felt another button gently released, and the touch of his hand, still light and gentle, proceeded down past the base of my throat. Another button. Still another. Where the edges of my bodice parted I felt the touch of the breeze along my skin, and the warmth of his fingertips. Then, making my breath catch in my throat, the warmth of his lips. A soft, lingering kiss, followed by more and more, proceeding unhurried along the sliver of skin he had bared. My heart was beating so quickly that I felt sure he must feel it as he kissed his way ever closer to it.

And then I felt a touch lighter still, a coolness that was neither hand nor lips, and opened my eyes in confusion.

He had plucked a violet from a clump nearby, and it was the flower's stem I felt as he slipped it beneath the top edge of my chemise to lie between my breasts. "To remember me by," he said, with the roguish smile that was so familiar, and to my astonishment he then began fastening my buttons up again, from where the violet lay hidden all the way back up to my throat.

I was so moved that I could not speak for a time. Something had changed. Sometimes in the past I had harbored doubts about the earnestness of Richard's feelings toward me; did he see as merely a flirtation the attachment that I felt so passionately? Today, for the first time, I knew. In words and deeds, Richard had shown me that he loved me. Let the world whisper about my foolishness, as I knew some of the other maids whispered. Let them giggle about how I was deceiving myself in mistaking his attentions for serious regard. Richard cherished me. I knew it now.

"You're very quiet," he observed, as the sun descended in the sky. He was once more sitting with his back against the rough stonework, and I nestled close within the circle of his arms, my head against his chest. "Are you happy?"

"Yes," I said, beaming up at him. "Happier than I've ever been. Thank you, Richard. You've given me the most perfect day of my life."

At that, he had to kiss me again, and consequently I was rather tardy returning to the house. I was scolded for truancy and sent to help the scullery maid wash dishes—an assignment intended to punish me, but I did not feel the sting of it because my thoughts were so full of Richard.

The next day the blow fell.

I was changing the linens in one of the family bedrooms when one of the parlormaids appeared at my side, her eyes wide with alarm or excitement. "You're wanted in the morning room," she whispered.

"By my mother?"

"By her ladyship."

I froze for a moment, then set aside the heap of bedclothes. "Thank you," I said with an effort, and set off for the morning room with what I hoped looked like jaunty unconcern. Perhaps her ladyship merely wanted me for some domestic chore, or to fetch her something. But why would she have sent for me specifically? This felt ominous to me.

When I reached the closed door, I took a moment to smooth down my apron and assure myself that my cap was straight. I took a deep breath in an effort to quiet my heartbeat, and rapped briskly.

"Enter," came the clear voice of Lady Telford. I pushed the door open and stepped inside, taking care to shut it behind me in case any of the other servants were about and of a mind to eavesdrop.

Lady Telford was seated behind the polished cherry wood desk where I knew she conferred with Cook and my mother on matters of the household. Her morning gown was sky blue festooned with ecru lace, and her lace cap with the pink rosebuds should have made her look sweet and harmless, but I knew that she was far from that. Her pale blue eyes, as pale as her sons', observed me coolly, and her small hands were folded on the desk blotter. She was not spoken of in the servants' hall as a kind or indulgent mistress but as a just if exacting one, and I knew my mother approved of these qualities; indeed, she did her best to emulate them.

A movement to the side caught my eye, and to my astonishment I beheld my mother herself, standing stock-still except for her hands, which fidgeted with the chain of her chatelaine. The ring containing the household keys—her charge as housekeeper—swung slightly, like a pendulum, and it seemed to me a kind of portent. My mother's face betrayed no sign of the business at hand, but I knew from her restless hands that she was worried. Evidently the matter that had brought me here was a mystery to her as well.

"Clara." The sharpness of Lady Telford's voice made me start and bring my gaze back to her. Her eyes had narrowed. "Do you know why I have summoned you?"

"No, ma'am," I said, casting my eyes down in what I hoped would appear to be a suitable meekness.

"Truly? You cannot imagine that you could comport yourself with such inappropriate familiarity with my son without its coming to my attention?"

My stomach seemed to plummet to my feet. I swallowed a sudden nausea and kept my eyes trained on the carpet.

"Clara, is this true?" my mother demanded. "Answer Lady Telford."

The anger in her voice was clear, but I heard an undercurrent that might be fear as well, and abruptly I recalled what had been all too convenient to forget before: that my behavior at Gravesend reflected on her as well as on me. My missteps would tarnish her standing in this most important post a woman could hold in a great manor house.

The nausea threatened to choke me, but I endeavored to speak steadily. "If my friendship with Mr. Richard was misconstrued—"

"Friendship!" Lady Telford exclaimed. "As if any such thing could exist between my son and you."

I risked a glance at her. She sat ramrod straight, and in each cheek an angry red patch was burning. "No impropriety has taken place," I ventured, but at this my mother flung up her hands in a passionate gesture.

"No impropriety, the girl says. Clara, don't you see that *any* familiarity between you and a son of this house is improper!"

I flinched. She had never scolded me before others, and that alone would have told me how deeply I had distressed her. She put a hand to her heart as if to still it.

"Tell me," she said, this time in a low, controlled voice. "Tell *us*. Are you with child?"

Heat rushed to my face. "Mother!"

"Your mother's question is quite reasonable, given the circumstances." Lady Telford's eyes were like two chips of ice. "Well, girl? Or is it too early to say?"

I stared from one to the other now, as if they might see reason and relent. "It isn't even a possibility," I stammered. "Nothing untoward—nothing of that nature—has happened."

Lady Telford sighed and closed her eyes briefly, as if my response had exhausted her. "Mrs. Crofton, is your daughter truly so ignorant of the details of basic husbandry? Or is she lying?"

"I am *not* lying!"

"I asked your mother a question, child. Don't interrupt your betters."

My mother's face was pale, and her dark eyes were haunted. However humiliating this interview was for me, for her it was equally bad. "I brought my daughter up to be truthful," she said, still in that terrible low voice. "And I endeavored to instill virtue in her as well. But with her father dead, and no man to provide the discipline she needs, I fear she's wilder than she should be." She looked at me now as if I were a stranger. "I shall always regret that my attention to my duties prevented me from keeping a more watchful eye on her."

But I'm *not* wild, I wanted to say, and then realized I wasn't certain whether it was true. Had I become a wicked woman? I didn't think I had, but I felt the memory of his lips imprinted on the skin beneath my collarbone and dropped my eyes, wishing

I could hide from the two accusing countenances. It was true I had not surrendered myself entirely to him. But I had permitted more liberties than were strictly in accordance with feminine propriety, and the memory made me unable to meet their eyes steadily and with conviction. I must have looked the picture of guilt, for Lady Telford clicked her tongue.

"It seems all too likely that the girl is *enceinte*. How vexing. Where may she be sent, Mrs. Crofton? Do you have family who can take her in?"

I was to be sent away from Richard? My heart gave a painful thud. "I don't want to leave Gravesend," I begged, but my mother gave me a hard look.

"What you want is of no issue. Lady Telford, I regret to say I don't have any connections to call upon." What she meant was that none of her family would receive either of us; they had cast her out when she married my father. That she should treat me so unjustly when she herself had been punished for loving a man of a different class outraged me.

"You can't send me away," I flared. "I've done nothing wrong. Ask Mr. Richard." My voice faltered there; if his mother did question him and he admitted that he loved me, would he too be cast off? I could not bear to be the cause of his ruin.

But it seemed that this was not to be my lot. "I'll not subject my son to such an indignity," said Lady Telford briskly. "He might produce some gallant lie to protect you, or, worse yet, decide to marry you to spite us all. He's quite impetuous enough to do it. No, my son shall not be dragged into this sordid business." She opened a drawer of the desk, removed a small pouch, and drew from it a few guineas. These she held out to me. "Take it," she told me, giving a little shake to her hand, so that the lace flounce on her sleeve fluttered. "This should more than pay for your remaining wages, with enough over for fare to London, I fancy."

"London," I repeated uncomprehendingly, as I stretched out numb fingers for the coins. "What am I to do in London?"

"That is not my concern. Your mother may be able to guide you."

If my mother had been pale before, now she looked little ruddier than a corpse. "Am I to accompany Clara?" she asked faintly.

For a moment our employer seemed to consider. "I think not," she said at length. "I'm far too busy now to set about seeking a new housekeeper. The house shall be discommoded quite enough by the loss of a chambermaid, and you shall need to set about finding a replacement and training her. I shall not discharge you, Mrs. Crofton, but your wages will be withheld this quarter. The morals of the female servants are your domain, as you well know, and I consider that you have let me down shamefully."

My mother bent her head in acknowledgment. "I apologize most sincerely, my lady. I shall see to it that nothing of this nature happens again."

"I should most certainly hope it doesn't." And with a whisk of her blue silk skirts Lady Telford rose from her seat behind the desk and left the room, not even deigning to look at me as she passed.

As soon as the door shut I turned to my mother. "It isn't fair," I protested. "It isn't true, what Lady Telford thinks. I'm not what she thinks I am."

But the expression she turned on me was grave and cool, and my protests died on my lips. "Don't you see, Clara," she said, and her voice shocked me with its weariness, "it does not matter. You have left yourself open to the suspicion, and that is enough." She sighed. "Was I so remiss in your education? How could I have let this happen?"

She had been too busy keeping a roof over our heads and food in our stomachs. As hard as she worked, little wonder that she had been unable to monitor all of my activities. And I had taken advantage of that. Tears blurred my vision, and my throat tightened painfully. "I'm sorry, Mother." *But I did nothing wrong.*

Her hand alighted briefly on my hair, a comforting touch that was gone almost before I felt it. "Let's get your things packed, and I'll have a groom take you to the station. There will be a train to London before the day is out."

I stared, aghast. "I'm to leave this very day?" How would I find a way to let Richard know—to say farewell until we could find a way to be together again?

My mother's nod was absent, her brow drawing into furrows. Her mind was already on the future. "I'm afraid so. I'll write some letters—Mrs. Laughton on Frances Street should still be taking lodgers and may have a room for you. But as for a situation . . . I shall have to put my mind to that."

The rest of the afternoon was a miserable confusion: collecting my belongings, setting aside my uniforms, which belonged to the Blackwoods; packing up the very few fittings of my shared room that belonged to me. My mother sat writing letters for me to carry to the few of her acquaintance who might be able to find me employment or take me in. Only once did I see her put a hand to her eyes and have to compose herself. Nor did she permit me any privacy in which I might have written a letter of my own. To be forced to leave in this manner, without seeing Richard once more or even sending a message to tell him where I was going, seemed the worst injustice of all. The sting of it grew until at last I was reduced to pleading with my mother to send word to him.

"He'd not want me to go without saying goodbye," I told her when she stood waiting with me at the servants' entrance for the groom who would bring the pony and trap to take me and my pathetically small bundle to the train station.

But she stood firm. "Has this sad business taught you nothing? Such impropriety is exactly what has been your undoing."

"If I *am* undone, then I ought to be able to pass a simple message to my partner in iniquity without further harm," I said, with a spark of rebellion.

Strangely, that made her laugh. It was a sad, low sound, but a laugh all the same. "My Clara," she said. "I shall miss you." A quick, fierce embrace, and she whispered, "Be better than you have been, and be safe." Then there was time for no more words, as the pony and trap drew up before us, with Sam, the groom, a study in curiosity. As we drove away, I twisted around to watch my mother as we drew farther and farther away from her. She raised her hand just once, perhaps conferring a blessing on me, and then swiftly turned and disappeared into the house.

CHAPTER THREE

T he years between my ignominious departure from Gravesend and my finding employment with Sibyl Ingram and her theatrical troupe were dark ones, and I did not linger long over their memory. There was the period of some eighteen months working for a martinet of a modiste, who dismissed me in a torrent of abuse. The even shorter period serving as parlormaid to the young couple who found me displeasing (the wife) and all too pleasing (the husband). The disastrous two months behind a piece goods counter, which ended in my dismissal for impertinence. And finally the garment factory, which made all before it look in comparison like an idyllic dream.

The curse seemed to have stored up all its malice to lash out on the occasion of my perceived fall from virtue. I was cast out of Gravesend, parted from Richard, and thrust into a nightmarish life of drudgery. At the time, though, the heartbreak of losing Richard felt like the worst thing that life had dealt or ever could deal to me.

Then word of his death came.

He had been restless, my mother hinted in her letter—she sent the news to me herself, a kindness I would not have expected. He and his brother had been on the point of departing for a tour of the Continent when Richard unexpectedly changed his plans. He wanted to see the fighting in the Crimea, he said, and had persuaded his father to purchase a commission for him. Within months of leaving Cornwall, he was dead. The curse had fulfilled itself: Lord and Lady Telford had lost what they most loved—their treasured whole son.

The shock, so I heard, nearly killed Lady Telford. It certainly left her in a weakened condition, so that when a wave of typhus swept through that corner of Cornwall, she was among the first at Gravesend to succumb. My mother held on for longer; she was among the last to die. I had only a last hastily written letter from her describing the inroads the illness was making at Gravesend, and then nothing. Finally I learned that she was gone. The curse had blotted out not just the person I most loved, but *all* those I loved.

It had not occurred to me then to wonder about Atlas, the son of the Blackwood line whom no one regarded.

I continued to put him from my mind as I set about looking for a new position. Marriage to Atlas was out of the question. But over the following days, which I spent walking from one modiste's establishment to another, seeking employment and finding none, I began almost to feel as if somehow he were working to force me to that exigency. I slogged from one establishment to another in the cold January rain, only to be met with refusals ranging from mere lack of interest to outright hostility. I could not understand it. I knew my manner was not as gentle and pleasing as that of many women, but I was civil, respectable, and well-spoken, with excellent credentials. Each night when I arrived at the theater, cold and discouraged, with my shoes caked in mud and the hem of my skirt and cloak soaked in rain, I felt a dart of fear that I might soon be bereft of options.

Miss Ingram, as I had expected, was so thoroughly occupied with her own arrangements that she did not seem to be aware of my endeavors; indeed, in addition to planning her relocation and wedding, she had a thousand details to attend to relating to her retirement and departure from the theater troupe. We scarcely saw each other now except when I assisted her during costume changes in her final performances, and we had little enough time on those occasions for conversation. "You look quite disheveled, Graves," she informed me one evening about a week after I had begun seeking employment. "Have you been standing under a gutter spout?"

"Not exactly, Miss Ingram." Even though I had money enough for a hansom cab, I had chosen to conduct my search on foot, knowing that with the future so uncertain I should save as much as I could of the little sum I had put by. But perhaps the reason I had found no success to this point was that my rain-drenched appearance was counting against me.

I received only two letters in response to my advertisement. One was from a new modiste just setting up her establishment and offering me a position if I could defer my wages for the first twelve months while the business found its footing; and the other was from Atlas. "The advertisement of a Miss Crofton seeking employment caught my eye," it read. I had decided to abandon my spurious widow's alias. "I am concerned that, if the notice was yours, it signals that your circumstances have altered, and not for the better. I hope you will consider again my proposal—"

I crumpled the letter in my hand and threw it into the fire in something close to panic. I could not marry Atlas. I simply couldn't. There had to be some other future for me.

The next day I humbled myself. I dressed myself with care and conquered my curls with a severely respectable coiffure, making certain that I looked at my most modest and proper. Then I hired a hansom cab to take me to the establishment of Mrs. Hill—the modiste for whom I had worked those miserable eighteen months, which ended when she had thrown me out. My sense of justice as well as my pride smarted at asking anything of this woman, but the time was past for such luxuries as pride.

Mrs. Hill had prospered in the years since we had parted, I found. An assistant answered my ring and showed me into a large, elegant fitting room furnished with large mirrors and comfortable divans. Mrs. Hill herself, who suffered me to wait a full half hour before she graced me with her presence, was impressively gowned in a silk rep day dress of rose trimmed in fawn soutache. Just as she had during our former acquaintance, she also sported a false front of glossy brown curls in the style of decades before. Her narrowed eyes and tight, mean little smile showed that she remembered exactly who I was.

"Why, Miss Crofton," she said in saccharine tones. "Such a surprise! I never thought to see you again."

I swallowed hard and forced a conciliatory note into my voice. "Indeed, I had not anticipated this pleasure myself until a recent turn of events."

She settled herself onto a divan opposite me, observing me at length, no doubt gauging the value of my gown and shoes. "You have done well for yourself," she said. "Personal modiste for the famous Miss Sybil Ingram, if you please! I am astonished that so important a personage as you have become would stoop to call on someone as obscure as myself."

My smile did not, I hope, look as stiff as it felt. "You flatter me, Mrs. Hill. I don't think of myself in such terms."

"No more should you," she said, an iron edge coming into her voice. I remembered that tone, and suddenly I was seventeen years old again, burning with helpless humiliation as she dressed me down before the other girls and lambasted me for faults both real and imagined. "It's clear that your good fortune has deserted you, or else you'd not have the gall to show your face here."

I tried not to let my smile falter. "I hope that the circumstances of our parting will not count against me," I said, forcing the words out even though they turned my stomach.

"Circumstances!" she spat out, all pretense of politeness gone. "You dare speak to me of circumstances! Don't think I've forgotten you, miss, with your insolent tongue and headstrong ways. It was only my soft heart that made me tolerate you for as long as I did!"

Soft heart? Hard business head, more like. *Don't let her anger you. Be composed.* "I trust that in the years since our parting I have learned to comport myself in a more—"

A shrill laugh cut my words short. "Pretty manners don't fool me, Miss Crofton. I shan't be taken in by you again.

You should have been thanking me on your knees every day for a situation with me, and instead you treated me with such insolence—and before a customer, yet!—that I had no choice but to dismiss you."

"I remember it differently," I said shortly. My transgression had been pointing out to the customer that the peau de soie she had requested had been replaced with cheap cotton sateen. This had been Mrs. Hill's method of maximizing profits: switch cheaper fabrics for those the customer had selected—and if the customer noticed the substitution, blame one of the seamstresses. By scolding us in front of the customer for our supposed deception, she often earned the client's respect . . . and future custom. I took a deep breath and strove to prevent my anger from showing. "You said that I had cheated the customer, and I defended myself against that misapprehension"—*lie,* I longed to say—"as any wronged party would."

That brought her to her feet. "The only wronged party, miss high-and-mighty, was me! And you may be sure that I let all the other modistes in London know it. Oh, yes, you imagined you could simply knock on any door and be welcomed with open arms for your association with the great Miss Ingram, did you? Well, I'll wager you've found your reception to be quite different!"

"What do you mean?" I asked, a premonitory chill creeping across my neck. "Have you been prejudicing the other dressmakers against me?"

"Warning them, my girl, as was my duty!" The false curls trembled with self-righteous indignation. "I couldn't let any of my sister modistes be taken in by you. 'Don't expect loyalty from that one!' I told them. 'She'll steal from you, mark my words, and will lie to your very face if you tax her with it!' Oh, they were most grateful for the warning, I can tell you. And I've been cautioning all of my customers as well. Word has no doubt spread as far as the Hebrides by now." Her self-satisfied smile made my hands itch to shake her. "I saw your advertisement, Miss Crofton. My memory is not so poor that I had forgotten you. You may be certain that I wasted no time in notifying everyone that they should be on their guard against you!"

"You poisoned everyone's mind against me," I exclaimed. It made sense now, the fact that every door had been closed to me. The absence of responses to my advertisement. "After all these years, to think you could be so spiteful!"

"Insolence and ingratitude will always reap their due punishment," she snapped, planting her hands on her hips. "You'd do well to learn that, girl—and learn some humility as well. And I fancy that's just what's in store for you! Now, leave my establishment at once, and don't set foot on my doorstep again."

I rose from the divan. I had the advantage in height, and sudden uncertainty flashed into her eyes when I glared down at her. She must have expected retaliation, but at that moment I realized that I had none. She had won. It was as simple as that.

I turned and walked out. A kind of hollowness had taken the place of the anger and dread. She had walled up every door for me, and there was nothing I could do to change that.

For a time I walked aimlessly, trying to awaken my numbed brain. The blow Mrs. Hill had dealt me seemed to have stunned all thought. *What now?* I asked myself again and again, but no answer came.

I walked until there was scarcely any feeling left in my feet. When the sun began to dip toward the horizon, I came to myself to find that I was in a shabby, congested area of the city that I remembered well from ten years ago. Without conscious intention, my feet had found the way back to the district in which lay the garment factory where I had once worked.

The racket of the machines was audible from a block away. It made my head throb and set my teeth on edge, and as I unwillingly drew nearer to the source, it stirred the beginnings of nausea in my stomach. I paused for a moment by the door of an apothecary to gather my courage. *You can do this,* I told myself. *You must. You have no choice.* Memories clogged my brain: the way my legs had trembled when I stood after working the treadle for long hours. My eyes burning from straining them and my throat burning from breathing the lint in the air. The ache in my neck and shoulders from bending over my work for hour after hour, day after day. And always the anxiety lest some unexpected problem prevent me from reaching my quota and reduce even further the pittance I earned.

Some men at the alehouse across the street called something to me, and I was thankful that I did not catch the words. Behind me, a bell jingled, and automatically I moved away from the doorway to permit whoever was exiting to pass. Then a woman's voice said, "Clara? Is it you?"

It took me a handful of moments to recognize my old friend, so changed was she. "Martha?" I exclaimed, my tone too astonished for courtesy, but she smiled. She had lost a front tooth, which gave her expression an air of gruesome whimsy.

"It's me, right enough," she said. Her voice was loud, and I wondered if she had lost some of her hearing, as so many workers did over time at the factory. "I'd have known you anywhere. You don't look a day older than when I last saw you."

I could not say the same, sadly. Martha looked as if she had aged more than twenty years for my ten. She was dangerously thin, with spots of rouge on her sunken cheeks, and her hair was tinted a garish red. A certain fixed brightness in her eyes made me wonder uneasily what she had been purchasing at the apothecary's.

"How wonderful to see you," I said. It was a lie, for I hated to see her in this condition, but I would lie from one end of London to the other rather than hurt her feelings. "You're still at the factory, then?"

Her laugh was bitter. "No, they had no use for me after—well, have a look yourself." She stripped the worn cotton glove from her right hand, and I smothered a cry as I saw that her thumb was gone.

"What happened?" I exclaimed. "Did you injure it sewing?" From time to time an unlucky girl would run the needle into her finger, and I had heard of at least one case in which the wound became so infected that the entire finger had to be removed.

"I was working one of the cutting machines," she said offhandedly. "I couldn't see so well as I used to sewing, so they moved me to cutting. It wasn't but a moment that I looked away—but it was enough." She pulled her glove back on, dropping her eyes.

"They couldn't find anything for you to do after that?"

She shrugged. "Oh, they set me to sweeping up for a time, but it didn't pay enough to keep body and soul together."

"Then how do you manage?" As soon as the words left my mouth I longed to call them back, for Martha merely smiled—a ghastly, humorless smile—and I felt my face burning with shame at my clumsy naiveté. "Here," I told her, fumbling in my purse for the few coins I had with me. "Take this. Buy yourself a hot meal—or a warm cloak if there's enough."

"I don't want your money," she said roughly.

"Please take it. For old friendship's sake, Martha."

For a moment I thought she would refuse again. Then her hand—her left hand—closed around the coins, and she favored me with a grin. The gap left by her missing tooth gave it a grotesque quality. "Right you are," she said cheerfully. "But it's gin I'll be buying with your charity—if it please your ladyship."

A mocking curtsey was her farewell. Struck dumb, I could only watch as she sauntered across the street toward the alehouse, where the men welcomed her so warmly that I gathered they were already acquainted. In a moment she had vanished inside the dim interior.

I turned so quickly that I almost collided with someone behind me, and at a pace that was almost a run I made my way home, with Martha's worn, rouged face and marred grin hovering before my eyes at every step.

Chapter Four

Atlas accepted my invitation to call on me the following afternoon. My landlady was kind enough to provide us with tea, bread and butter, and the use of the front parlor. After bringing in the tray she retreated to an armchair at the other side of the room with her knitting, close enough to keep us in view but distant enough that our conversation would have a certain degree of privacy.

"I see we have a chaperone," Atlas observed as I poured out the tea.

"So much in our acquaintance is unconventional, and likely to become more so," I said, handing him his cup and saucer, "that I hope you'll indulge me by observing a few of the conventions." It was still a bit difficult to look at him directly, so striking was his resemblance to Richard, but I was trying to accustom myself to him. In the clear sunlight shining into the parlor that afternoon, his handsomeness was all the more vivid; I had seen my landlady herself, a prim virgin of some sixty

42

summers, widen her eyes and grow pink in the face when the tweeny first ushered him into the parlor.

It was odd for me to think of Atlas—Atticus, rather—as handsome. True, the resemblance between him and Richard had always been there, but where Richard always seemed dazzling, his brother seemed dull; lacking Richard's gifts of charm, athleticism, and confidence, Atticus had been in comparison slight from lack of exercise, pale from time spent indoors over his books, shy and stammering and anxious. It was that air of earnestness that had earned him his nickname. Richard said laughingly that his brother looked as worried as if he carried the weight of the world on his insufficient shoulders, and Atlas he became.

It had not struck me as cruel at the time, but now I shifted uncomfortably in my chair at the recollection and hoped that Atticus had not heard about the jest.

"You look ill at ease, Mrs. Graves," he commented, as if reading my thoughts. "Is something troubling you?"

Why, yes, in fact: being put to the extremity of marrying you. "I was just reflecting on how much you've changed since I left Gravesend," I said.

That brought a surprised lift of his eyebrows. The sunlight streaming through the window picked out red glints in his chestnut hair and brows, and the contrast with his startlingly pale blue eyes was arresting. "I can't say I'm aware of it."

"If you'll forgive me for mentioning it, it seems you no longer wear a brace."

"I was able to cast that aside by the time I turned sixteen."

"Oh. I hadn't realized." That would have been well before I was turned out of the house, as he and Richard had been my elders by some two years, and I was embarrassed that I had not even been aware of the change.

"Well, our activities didn't bring us much into each other's sphere," he said. "I'm not surprised you did not observe every detail of my toilette." His expressive mouth curved in a smile, which astonished me.

"You are able to find amusement in reflecting on the disadvantage to which your—your condition put you?" I could not keep myself from asking.

43

That brought a full-blown smile, and for a second it was as if I were sitting across from Richard, who was so often smiling or laughing in my memory. The impression robbed me of breath. I dropped my gaze to my cup and saucer as I fought for control over my emotions, and he said, "I discovered some time ago that if I couldn't laugh at myself, every burden that life handed me would be all the heavier."

This made my thoughts turn again to the uncomfortable memory of his nickname, so I said, "I hadn't remembered you and Richard as being so similar, that's all."

"I see. Well, it's true that when we were children Richard and I were easily distinguished. I think I closed that gap as I grew older. Once the head groom began training me in bareknuckle fighting, I put on a bit of muscle and became able to borrow my brother's clothing." Then he stopped abruptly. "Forgive me, this must be painful for you. I've been tactless."

"No, it's I who brought up the subject of your brother. But I mustn't waste any more of your time. I asked you here to discuss your offer."

He nodded and waited for me to go on. He seemed remarkably at ease; his broad shoulders—definitely broader than I recalled—were relaxed and did not disarrange the lines of his grey wool sack jacket. His fine-boned hands held cup and saucer without fidgeting or self-consciousness. This, in short, was an Atticus I did not seem to know after all.

"If I'm to accept you," I said, "there are some areas of concern that I'd like to discuss."

"Naturally," he said politely, but interest had quickened in his eyes. To avoid that penetrating gaze I turned to the teapot and refilled my cup.

"First among these is my lack of plausibility as a member of your class, or indeed a sufficiently elevated position to marry into the Telford line."

He shook his head. "My dear Cl—Mrs. Graves, as far as your bearing and speech are concerned, you'll move freely among my circles without detection. As a matter of fact, if you'll forgive me, I'm curious as to how you came to speak so little like a servant."

"My mother's doing," I said, my throat suddenly tightening as I remembered her intent, serious face as she tirelessly corrected my pronunciation and vocabulary. So much patient effort, and all for naught—or so I had thought up to now. "I believe she wanted me to retain as much gentility as she could pass on to me."

"A thoughtful and most maternal impulse."

"A burden and a curse," I snapped before I could stop myself. The other servants had thought me pretentious and stuck-up, and they had made a point of treating me with exaggerated deference. "It made it much more difficult to get along with the other servants."

"Ah, I can see how it would. They must have thought you were mocking them by speaking like your . . . I suppose they would have said 'your betters.' But now it's most convenient."

"Please tell me the truth," I said. "Don't spare my feelings. If there are small ways in which I reveal my origins, better to know them now and contrive some explanation."

"That's a wise precaution, Mrs. Graves. It seems I'm to have a wife who is clever in more ways than with her needle." He saw that the pleasantry sat ill with me, however, and without comment moved back to the topic at issue. "If there are any small differences that occur in your speech, we may explain that with your time in America. The peculiarities of speech there have no doubt influenced your own."

"And that's another difficulty," I said. "My past. We can scarcely acknowledge that I was a servant for your family, nor that I have been earning my keep as a seamstress with a traveling theatrical troupe."

"A widow who traveled a great deal with her American husband," he said promptly, making me wonder how much thought he had already given the matter. "A railway magnate, shall we say? They seem to proliferate in America. Apparently one can scarcely take two steps down any major thoroughfare without colliding with a captain of industry. They are a bigger nuisance than pigeons, I hear."

I laughed before I could help myself, and his cup paused on its way to his lips.

"Your whole demeanor changes when you laugh," he said thoughtfully. "I should like to see you smile more often . . . by which I mean at all."

Discomfited, I stared down at my lap. "One certain way to prevent my doing so is to make me self-conscious about it."

"My apologies. That was not my intention."

"To return to the subject at hand," I said, grasping after a less uncomfortable topic, "such a story may indeed allay suspicions when I betray my unfamiliarity with your social customs. But will there be anyone among your acquaintance who is familiar enough with American society to recognize that my story is false? That could be disastrous."

He set down his cup and looked at me quizzically. "Mrs. Graves, I understood that you summoned me here with the idea to accept my proposition, yet you've put forth nothing but objections. Which of us are you trying to convince that marrying me is out of the question?"

The direct gaze of those piercing pale eyes was a challenge, and I summoned the fortitude to meet it, although I wished to avert my own eyes—to hide, were it possible.

"I do accept the offer," I said. "It is only that—"

"I'm delighted to hear it." The smile struck again, and I blinked; he seemed genuinely pleased, but why I could not fathom. "You have made me the happiest of men, my dear Clara. I may call you Clara?"

"I suppose, if you must. But—"

"Thank you, Clara."

"You are welcome. But—"

"I hope you'll call me Atticus."

"If you insist. *But*," I repeated, "it would be foolish not to examine every area where my imposture may be exposed."

He considered this as he helped himself to more bread and butter. His appetite seemed to be improving now that he had his answer. I, on the other hand, felt some queasiness now that I had committed myself. "A very sensible attitude," he declared. "I'm doubly fortunate in having won a wife as intelligent as she is lovely."

I gave him an even look. "Do you have many such pretty compliments memorized for this occasion, or shall I be spared further sallies? I'm well aware that I am not your first choice . . . or, indeed, any man's." Any man since Richard.

The blue eyes and warm, resonant voice were all innocent concern. "Clara, the furthest thing from my mind is to injure you. I meant what I said. But if it makes you uncomfortable for me to voice such sentiments . . ."

"Thank you for your understanding."

". . . then I shall have to accustom you to accepting compliments."

Exasperated, I directed at him a look that no prospective bride should level upon her intended husband. "Must you make light of my feelings? I don't think it unreasonable of me to expect some consideration from my . . . from you."

That sobered him. Before I knew what he was about, he had reached across the table and taken my hand in a firm clasp. "Clara," he said in a different voice—a voice pitched so that my landlady would not hear, "if I seem flippant, it's merely that you've made me very happy. I'm delighted that you'll be returning to Gravesend with me and that I may offer you—I don't think I'm boasting to say it—a far pleasanter life than what you've been forced to endure to this point."

He raised my hand to his lips and kissed it before I knew what he was about, and this surprised me into forgetting the rejoinder that had been poised on my lips. It was the first gesture of tenderness that anyone had shown me in . . . how long? The light pleasant impression of his lips seemed to have been imprinted upon my skin, and I was aware of it still as he continued, "I intend to quash all of your doubts and convince you that you've made the right decision."

"I hope you're right," I said, coming back to myself. "But permit me to ask something. You've spoken of your wish to make your father's final days easier by presenting him with a wife. You have been good enough to say that you want to make amends to me for being turned out—something that was not of your doing." Or could it be that he really was culpable, but in a way I was not aware of? That was a thought worth contemplating more at another time. "What is it that you yourself gain from this scheme?"

"I'm anticipating a great deal of pleasure from being a sort of Father Christmas to you. And I regard you highly. I know that

I shall enjoy your company and that your presence will make Gravesend a far more cheerful place."

"And that is all?" My skepticism was plain in my voice.

At first I thought he would turn the question away with a glib pleasantry. Then he seemed to reconsider. In repose, without the smile, his face was surprisingly stern: the sharp, strong line of his jaw lent a grim cast to his expression, and with his eyes fixed on the distance I realized how much older they looked when he wasn't merry. Not just older . . . sadder, perhaps. Or wiser.

"Masculine pride is a terrible thing, Clara. Knowing that wherever I go in society people are thinking, 'Ah, there's the Blackwood cripple who couldn't get a bride . . .'" He drew a hand down over his face as if to wipe away the grimness and favored me with a wry twist of his mouth that was not a smile. "I do not wish to have married any of the empty-headed misses I've met in society. But it's nonetheless a rather jarring feeling to know that they are even more grateful not to have been forced to marry me."

"But you are not a cripple," I said. It was the only point on which I felt I could offer him any reassurance. "You scarcely even have a limp now, unless one looks for it."

"It comes and goes. When I'm tired—or self-conscious under the stare of a passel of busybodies—it sometimes gives me trouble. But you're right, of course; I don't think of myself that way. I just see it so often in the eyes of people I'm speaking to." Abruptly he said in a different voice, "That is quite enough about me and my motives, I think. In any case, one must leave something to come as a surprise."

"I dislike surprises," I said. "In my experience, they are rarely pleasant. Perhaps you'd best warn me."

"No, no; it will keep." His brief grin made him suddenly look like an impudent schoolboy. "But we were speaking of your concerns, earlier. Your anxiety about being caught out as an impostor."

Those had not been my words, but they captured my unease. "I do think there is a substantial risk."

"There shall be far less of one once you have been kitted out with a new wardrobe." His glance swept over my dress.

"Anyone who might remember you as Clara the housemaid won't connect you with her once you've changed those widow's weeds for something more becoming to your new station. I hope it is agreeable to you, but I've made appointments for you tomorrow with three of the modistes that come most highly recommended. With all of them working on your new things at once, they should have you newly outfitted in short order, and I should like to return to Gravesend before the end of the month."

"Appointments? You assumed I would agree to your proposal, then?"

The broad shoulders moved in a shrug. "I hoped, merely. And I believe in planning ahead. I have started a list of clothes you'll need—naturally you will see things I've omitted and can fill them in. Visiting dresses, dinner gowns . . . you'll need a great many, I think."

Suddenly all my doubts and fears were replaced by a glorious vision. No more eternal black bombazine in dour unfashionable styles. I saw myself in bronze shot silk with the skirt trimmed in pleated purple ribbon and drawn back over an underskirt of cream moiré. A reception gown of forest-green satin, trained in back, with a deep square neckline and lace festoons at the elbow sleeves like Marie Antoinette. A claret-red velvet evening dress like the one I had made up for Sibyl Ingram for one of her roles—knowing at the time that it would have suited me far better, with my olive complexion and dark hair. Elegantly fashioned high-heeled slippers and cunning boots instead of my clumsy, much-scuffed shoes . . . fine silk and cotton lawn chemises and petticoats instead of coarse homespun . . .

I realized I had been staring into space for some minutes, and when I came to myself and found Atticus watching me I felt a blush rising to my cheeks. "I beg your pardon," I said in mortification. "You must think me just as shallow as your society misses for losing my head so at the prospect of pretty clothes. I confess I have the weakness of my sex for adorning myself, and I have been unable to indulge that vice until now."

His chuckle was reassuring. "I think no less of you for having an eye for beauty. And every jewel deserves a fine setting. I believe the modistes will be able to guide you toward what is most suited to your new standing, but don't let them bully you.

49

A touch of originality will not come amiss. The future Lady Telford need not follow fashion blindly; she may set it."

Lady Telford. How astonishing to realize that this would be my role. Not that I would inhabit it longer than was strictly necessary before going into retirement in comfortable independence. But I wondered how my mother would have felt had she known what position I was being singled out for, and I swallowed hard. She might have been pleased by this windfall, and it struck me as terribly unjust that she would never know of it.

My mother . . . an unresolved anxiety darted back into my head, routing sorrow. "What if your father recognizes me? And the servants? There must still be some remaining from my time there, and I'll have been fixed in their memory because of the circumstances of my departure, I've no doubt."

"The solution is simple: you must purchase a wardrobe so fine as to dazzle them into gazing only at the clothes and not on your face. The tactical deployment of taffeta, aided by the strategic implementation of satin and ribbons."

"You are teasing me."

"A husband's privilege, surely. But I mean no offense by it." His merry expression grew thoughtful. "To be honest, I suspect that my father would have difficulty dredging up the memory of any servant's face save his valet's, and then only after strenuous thought. He shall have no reason to associate my new bride with anyone on his staff, especially when she is turned out like a woman of wealth and birth. I'm entirely serious about your providing yourself with all the appropriate adornments. I have a substantial line of credit, and I wish for you to avail yourself of it without hesitation."

"You are too kind," I said awkwardly. I was not sufficiently accustomed to kindness to know how to accept it gracefully. "Oh, but there is one person who won't be swayed by fine feathers. I shall need a maid—and if anyone is situated to know all of a lady's secrets, it is her personal maid. How are we to prevent her from giving it out below stairs that her mistress's marriage is no more than show?"

This was clearly a new idea, and he frowned over it. "I'll give the matter some thought. Have you no acquaintance we could hire, someone whose loyalty will be with you rather than the household?"

I sifted through my small catalogue of acquaintance who might be suited to such a role. Perhaps one of the lesser handmaidens in the theater, or my landlady's younger niece, might do—but could I rely on either's silence and loyalty? I was not much given to close friendships, after having been so roundly snubbed by my own set at Gravesend and having held back from what seemed to me the dangerously unrestrained camaraderie of the theater, so the question was a perplexing one. As I considered it, Atlas's voice broke in on my thoughts.

"I must be off, I fear; now that you have so amiably consented to be mine, there is much I must attend to. A license, for a start."

"Of course," I said, hiding the frisson of doubt I felt at that reference to the scope of the new life upon which I was embarking. I rose to my feet, and he followed—again with the aid of his ebony walking stick, which I gathered was his constant companion. I led the way to the vestibule, where he retrieved his hat and gloves, whistling, and again I felt a strange irritation at his obviously buoyant mood, because I did not understand it.

"You are doing me a great kindness," I began, returning to the question he had not answered.

"And am overjoyed to do so."

Clearly—but why? "And you are doing your father an even greater kindness. I cannot imagine that you would go to such extreme means—shackling yourself to an inappropriate wife, lavishing money on her—without there being any benefit to yourself."

He looked at me quizzically. "Do I seem that selfish, Clara, or are you attributing to me qualities of other gentlemen you have known?"

"I am merely trying to understand your motives. Marriage is a tremendous step unless you're gaining something by it."

"Do not expect to fathom all of my mysteries at once, my dear Clara." Then he seemed to think better of his levity. "Since it troubles you, yes, I do act partly out of my own interests. It will give me peace of mind to know that I can make my father's last days better. I'd like to know that I did all that was in my power to ease his going and give him the assurance that he need not consume himself with anxiety over what will happen to the estate after his death."

I felt rebuked; but still, there was something else he was not saying. "And nothing else?" I asked, not trying to hide my skepticism.

"I have my reasons," he said only, before bringing my hand to his lips for a brief kiss. Something about his expression then, as he bent over my hand but kept his eyes on me, was so enigmatic that I felt a chill of sudden doubt whether our life together was truly going to be as idyllic as he portrayed it. There was much that Atticus was not telling me, and I wondered uneasily what might lie ahead.

CHAPTER FIVE

I confess that the first dressmaking establishment to which I directed the carriage was Mrs. Hill's. It gave me a mean-spirited satisfaction to inform her of my engagement—and consequent need for fine new clothes—and send her scurrying about in an effort to satisfy my whims.

"I have such a passion for bottle-green peau de soie," I confided, glimpsing a bolt of this fabric at the very bottom of a stack, and watching in satisfaction as she struggled to unearth it. "It would go so nicely with that figured velvet . . . earmarked for Lady Carstone, you say? Such a pity. I suppose I must go to another establishment for something similar . . . oh, it's truly no trouble for me to have it? How charming. See that you don't try to fob me off with some cheap velveteen in its place, mind! Now, on this bonnet, can you take all the trimmings off and change them?"

I ordered her about until I wearied of the game and departed for the next modiste on my list, where I would order the bulk of my new wardrobe. My conscience could not reproach me very severely, though, since I had ordered a gown from Mrs. Hill, and one that I was paying her all the more generously for due to the haste with which my order would be filled. I would be recompensing the woman quite well for my small revenge—or, rather, my husband would be.

My husband. This, like the title to which I would eventually succeed, had such a strange sound in my mind that I stopped to examine it further, in as gingerly a fashion as one might approach a spider whose bite might or might not prove poisonous.

Not for many years had I considered that I might marry. As a lovestruck girl I had spun farfetched dreams around Richard, but at this remove it was difficult to believe that I had ever been so naive as to think they might come true. After the cruel blow of losing him twice, I had felt for a long time that I would never consider marriage. And if once in a while in later years my certainty relaxed into curiosity, I was always driven back into the resolution of solitude by what I observed—and experienced—in the company of the theater and its followers. Actors, I determined, were an unreliable lot, charming and full of blandishments but slipping easily out of any suggestion of marriage. And my standards were all the higher after having known a true gentleman. Held up against my memories of Richard, even the kindest and most sincere of the men in the troupe might have come up wanting.

And Atlas? Was he kind and sincere? I had seen enough to realize that the man with whom I was linking my life bore little resemblance to the boy I remembered. I should have felt little surprise there; with Richard the shining sun in my eyes, his less fortunate brother was always eclipsed. It spoke well of Atlas that he cared so much that his father's last days be comfortable, but the mysterious other motive to which he had referred so obliquely would trouble me until I knew what it was.

No one else, I observed, harbored any such doubts. My landlady was delighted with my luck, especially (she did not quite say) considering my advanced age. She suggested that her youngest niece, a girl of fourteen, accompany me as my maid, but I had noted the girl's shy, uncertain demeanor and knew she would be too easily influenced by her superiors into giving up my secrets. I needed an experienced, unshakeable veteran of below-stairs politics, not a well-meaning innocent. I thanked my landlady but assured her that I could not yet part her sister from her youngest chick.

My thoughts then turned to Martha. It grieved me to see her in such a life as she was now living, but I knew that her pride would not permit her to accept employment with me even if she had been suited to such a position. When I asked Sybil Ingram if she could recommend anyone, her response astonished me.

"My dear, as happy as I am that you are marrying, I cannot in good conscience send anyone to that house."

"Whyever not?" I exclaimed, and then light dawned. "The curse."

"Indeed yes. I'd be far happier were you and Mr. Blackwood to settle elsewhere." She gave a little shudder that might not have been affected; like many in her profession, I knew, she was distinctly superstitious. "I'm astonished that you aren't doing your utmost to persuade him to make some other home. The baron has plenty of money, I've heard; if he doesn't already own properties elsewhere, it would be of little difficulty to him to have a new home built for his only son and daughter-in-law."

"Setting aside the trouble and expense," I said, "my betrothed does not wish to be separated from his father during what will surely be his final illness. In any case, he does not fear the curse, and I have nothing to fear from it."

Putting her head on one side, she narrowed her eyes in a long, searching look at me. "No, it is something else you fear, is it not?"

"I never said that." To avoid that close scrutiny I turned away and resumed packing up my sewing things. Atlas—Atticus—was having my few belongings sent ahead to Gravesend, my sewing machine among them, and I was clearing out the little sewing room in the theater. Sybil Ingram settled on the sewing chair, arranging her skirts so that they would fall becomingly, and watched me.

"You do not have to say it. Your shoulders are drawn almost up to your ears, and you won't meet my eyes. It isn't fear of the marriage bed, surely, with so handsome and amiable a gentleman as Mr. Blackwood. And he is hardly the sort to beat you, I should think. What is it you're afraid of?"

The bluntness was, in a way, a relief. I stopped plucking at a mess of spools that had become entangled and turned to face her. "I used to be a servant at Gravesend," I said frankly. "My betrothed knows this, but no one else must. It seems I'm not truly leaving the theater after all, Miss Ingram, for I must become an actress."

That brought a smile that softened the shrewd gaze. "Determination is half of it, and you seem to be well equipped with that. But you must work without a script, and that can be nerve wracking. I shall give you a piece of advice: make your lies as brief as they can reasonably be. If you must concoct a story, make it a simple one; it is when you go into too-elaborate detail that a story becomes implausible." She rose to depart and twitched her canary-yellow overskirt into place over the cerise skirt. "I shall miss you, Clara. Write to me if you wish." She embraced me lightly, and added with her lips close to my ear: "No matter how foolish you may think me for saying so, do try to influence your husband to leave Gravesend. Take the old baron with you if need be, but don't stay a moment more than you must." Drawing back, she looked into my face and gave a troubled shake of her head. "Obstinate girl. Trust an experienced trouper, my dear, and believe me when I tell you that my intuition is not wrong on this. Gravesend will place you in danger."

Atticus and I were married on a bleak morning in late January. When he came to fetch me, he gave my ensemble a look of approbation. "I see I was right to trust your eye for fashion," he said, after greeting me with a kiss on the hand that I did not even feel, so distracted was I.

"You approve, then?" I asked. I was far more nervous than I had expected to be. In his morning suit and high silk hat my soon-to-be husband looked both familiar and alarmingly alien. His likeness to Richard was a constant distraction rather than a reassurance; each time I saw him my heart would lift for one delighted instant before being cast down again as memory took hold. I was full of dread that I would say "I take thee, Richard" instead of "I take thee, Atticus." Or even "Atlas." I was still finding it difficult to stop thinking of him by that old nickname.

Unaware of my turmoil, or else tactful enough to ignore it, he said, "The dress is lovely, but it merely underscores what I already knew, which is that my bride is a most handsome woman."

I did not know what to say to that. "I hope dove gray is appropriate," I finally replied. "It may be a trifle young, and goodness knows with this weather we hardly need *more* gray. I look like a cloudbank settling over the Thames."

"Clara," he said gently, and waited until I stopped fussing with my gloves and gave him my attention. He was watching me gravely. His voice was very quiet when he said, "If you wish to change your mind, now is the time to say so."

Yes, I've changed my mind. Part of me wanted to say this— wanted it desperately. But what would happen then? I had seen what life in the factory—and out of it—had done to Martha. I could never become like her and the others like her, women who had grown old in that life, turning to laudanum or gin to make their existence bearable, sometimes to the extent that their habit had to be funded by gentleman "admirers." Anything rather than that.

Yet when I met that icily pale blue gaze, with its mysteriously pensive quality, I was not certain I could take this course either. At Gravesend I would have no allies save this man, and I did not even know to what extent I could trust him. I would be cut off from the world, surrounded by strangers, and living in the constant fear that someone would reveal my true identity.

Mother would not have run, I thought suddenly. She had taken that position at Gravesend to support us, believing all the while in the curse. Trying to keep me on my guard against it. Had she lived in dread? Or had she, having lost my father, felt that the curse had nothing more to use against her—except me?

"I haven't changed my mind," I said through dry lips.

His taut, listening posture relaxed, and he smiled. The same mobile, expressive lips, but so different a smile from Richard's: understanding and kind instead of knowing and devilish. A pale shadow of the man I had lost, but he was doing me a good turn—an extraordinarily good turn—and I owed him a debt of gratitude for that.

All the more chafing that I hated to be in anyone's debt.

The ceremony itself proceeded with a kind of hazy unreality, as if I were watching it through a fogged-over windowpane. The vows I spoke sounded muffled in my own ears, and with my thoughts full of Miss Ingram's portents, I half expected Atticus to say "With this curse I thee wed." Even the ring my new husband placed on my finger—an heirloom of rose gold set with opals—did not make the event any more real to me.

This would not do. Once we were settled in the railway carriage and hurtling away from London, I asked, "What is our story?"

Atticus, fortunately, did not need me to explain the question. That was pleasant to see: he was more intelligent than I had expected, given my impressions of him from our younger days.

"I think it would be convenient for us to have met through a mutual acquaintance of your late husband's," he suggested. "An American businessman, let's say, interested in expanding his reach to our shores." He seemed thoroughly at ease now with the wedding behind us, his arms crossed over his chest, the ankle of his good leg propped on the opposite knee. I, in contrast, was sitting primly straight in the seat across from him, not yet accustomed to the rattling, shaking rhythm of our passage; it had been months since I had last been on a train.

"And you met him how?"

"Through a . . . charitable institution that I'm developing. A genuine one," he added, seeing the question in my eyes. "That work will occasionally take me away from Gravesend, I should mention."

"Oh?" Uncertain though I was at how enjoyable married life would be with my new husband, the prospect of being left alone at Gravesend was perhaps even less appealing. "Will you be gone for long periods?"

"Not at first, no. And I won't be traveling to France as often as I used to, certainly. Now that you and I are married, my ward can come to live with us."

"Your ward," I repeated blankly. This was the first time he had mentioned such a person.

In his enthusiasm he seemed handsomer somehow, younger; closer to my memory of Richard. "Her name is Genevieve Rowe. She's of English parentage but has lived in France since before she learned to speak, and she's far more French than English now. Sometimes I almost forget that she isn't French by birth."

I myself had perhaps a dozen words of French, no more. "How old is she?" I asked, picturing a child of nine or ten years. If she was no older than that, we might get on well enough.

"A month or so shy of eighteen," he said cheerfully. "I want her to debut this Season, so it will be important for her to become acclimated to England before then. You'll adore her, Clara. And she can learn so much from you."

"From me? If you mean to restrict her education to sewing and housekeeping, perhaps." The words emerged tartly; I'd spoken the truth when I had told Atlas that I disliked surprises. The domestic arrangement I had begun to come to grips with in my mind was now being unsettled by a stranger—an unknown quantity. How would she affect the fragile accord that Atlas and I were building?

Seeing my discomfiture, he moved the conversation back to a less controversial channel.

"We can discuss the matter further at a later time. Just now we have our own history to decide upon. I suspect that my circle of acquaintance won't be conversant with American lineage, so let's say that you are descended from sturdy American stock on one side—moneyed, I think—and hearty British yeomanry on the other, but of sufficiently modest name that you prefer not to discuss it. You and your late husband shared a fascination with the theater that served as your introduction. Does that sound agreeable to you?"

"It does," I said, impressed that he had woven in an important element of my past that would doubtless emerge in conversation no matter how much I might try to suppress it. Having been so thoroughly immersed in the theater for the past ten years, I couldn't be certain that I would not blurt out some recollection or experience connected to that part of my life. Tact was an unexpected gift to find in this man, and I was pleased

59

to observe it. Atticus was proving to be far from the dull, gawping boy I remembered. In those days Richard had had all of the charm and quickness of tongue, whereas his brother seemed always tongue-tied.

Thinking of Richard prompted my next question. "Now, as to your own story: how much do I know of it, and of Gravesend? My impressions of you from our shared past may not be what you would have told the woman you were wooing."

"I suppose you have a point. I would definitely have made myself out to be far more dashing and accomplished." His smile was rueful. "I spent so much of my youth trying to catch up with Richard, it seems to me now. Both physically and in less tangible ways, I think. When I was a child I looked up to him so—and fell so far short of the kind of brother he could have felt a bond with." He mused for a moment, and his fingers drummed on the handle of the walking stick that was now the most visible sign of his handicap. "We were so unlike, though."

There was no doubt of that. Abruptly grief for Richard rose up in my breast like a scalding tide, choking speech off in my throat.

As if for the first time I felt the searing injustice of it, that someone so fully alive should have been struck down—and when he was so young. What might he have made of himself had he lived? Would he have had a brilliant military career, perhaps? Revived tin mining or other industries near Gravesend and built that quiet corner of Cornwall into a thriving, well-to-do community? Married and fathered a brood of many children? If he had wedded me and been disowned, his life might have been more obscure, but who was to say it would have been less happy than if he had lived to bring glory to the Blackwood line?

"I'm afraid to someone as lighthearted as Richard I must have seemed pretty joyless," Atticus said now, unaware of the direction my thoughts had taken. "When he gambled and won, he enjoyed his victory; I worried about whether those he had fleeced would be able to pay their bills. Competing with him was out of the question, but so was trying to force him to behave more responsibly. Of course, as the elder by some half an hour I was born to more responsibilities. Richard, as the younger, had no need of questioning the ramifications of his every move as I did. It was a long time before I could accept that I'd never be like him. That infectious charm and reckless energy—no, I was his opposite in every way."

Against my will I felt a grudging sympathy for him. With Richard's natural gifts, any man might have felt at a disadvantage next to him; add the misfortune of a club foot, and it must have stung far more cruelly. "What a pity that the two of you didn't have the chance to become better friends, Atlas."

His gaze returned from the far distance to find my eyes, and I felt the heat of a blush rise in my face as I realized what I had said. "I'm so sorry," I exclaimed.

"It is a long time since anyone has called me by that," he said—mildly enough, but I knew he was not pleased. "It's only natural that you should use Richard's name for me, I suppose."

"I do beg your pardon, truly."

"Of course it would come to mind. Richard always warned me against being Atlas, taking the weight of the world upon my shoulders." His tone was light enough, but there was a wry twist to his mouth. He shook his head ruefully, suddenly looking far older, as if the subject had drained his energy and resilience. "What he did not realize was that elder sons have little choice in the matter. At an estate like Gravesend, the fate of far too many people rests on the owner's shoulders, and then on those of his heir. It isn't something one takes on for enjoyment, certainly."

"Perhaps you should tell me other things about yourself," I said quickly. "Your schooling, your travels. Favorites and dislikes that I should know about when I order the menus. That kind of thing—the things that wives are supposed to know about their husbands."

This struck him as a good suggestion, and the rest of the journey passed relatively quickly as he told me of the part of his life I had not observed. He gained in interest through the telling, as I began to see him as a man whose education and travels had enhanced a native intellectual curiosity and philanthropic bent. When we arrived at the station nearest Gravesend—which I had last seen on the day that I had been sent away in ignominy—I was surprised at how quickly the time had passed.

An old-fashioned coach bearing the Blackwood coat of arms took us the last two miles of our journey. Between the season and the weather, the countryside I observed along the way was bleached of color. Drab and sere, the parkland stretched its gently rolling expanse as far as the eye could see. The afternoon sky was darkening from pearly gray to slate, and wind whistled in around the windows of the coach. The cold seeped in through my cashmere paletot, and I shut my teeth firmly so they would not chatter. I hoped that the housekeeper had had the forethought to have fires lit in our rooms before our arrival, as my mother would have.

To this point I had avoided thinking very closely about the housekeeper I would find at Gravesend. So much of the tenor of a household rested on her shoulders, and it would be crucial for me to forge a strong understanding with her, whatever she was like. Would she be a motherly, comfortable sort of woman, happy to guide the new Mrs. Blackwood through her new role? Or a stiff-necked martinet who would have no respect for me if I showed any signs of weakness? Or worst of all, a sly two-faced creature who might profess to be my bosom friend but would avidly spread tales about me below stairs? I had encountered all three specimens, and many more. She might be a nervous, dithering, ineffectual woman without the ability to keep the other servants on their tasks. She might even have expectations of some form of friendship between us, and when I tried to assert control might grow outraged and bear a grudge.

And any of these problems could be felt in a thousand tiny ways. A household whose mistress and staff were at odds could be a highly uncomfortable place. I knew, for I had committed some of the petty crimes myself, the minute forms of revenge: a bell left unanswered just long enough to put someone out of temper. Lukewarm water brought for washing. Mail "forgotten." Gowns singed by the iron . . . no, that I had never done. Surly and rebellious though I had been at times, I would not have harmed an innocent garment—not unless it had first committed the cardinal sin of being ugly.

I was distracting myself from what lay ahead by mentally creating a moral hierarchy of clothes when the carriage slowed, and the wheels crunched on gravel. "We're nearly there," said Atticus unnecessarily, and my frivolous thoughts vanished as anxiety claimed me again.

Gravesend was a bleak sight. Under the lowering sky, its white limestone was the moldy, lifeless gray of some desiccated creature in a state of decay. The flat, featureless face was as merciless as a guillotine blade. The blue panes in the leaded windows were dull in the wan light, so that there seemed to be no color at all about the scene—nothing that spoke of life. No friendly light shone from any window; the drapes must all have been drawn against the gray day. A cheerless and foreboding home for a new bride to come to.

It was not always like this, I reminded myself. I had been happy here . . . not always, perhaps not even frequently, considering how hard my work had been, but it was still the closest thing to a home that I had experienced to that point in my life. But now, faced with it again, I wondered how much of my happiness in those days had been due to Richard's presence.

"You needn't be nervous," said Atticus, and I realized he was trying to be reassuring. "There's nothing to be afraid of. Or at least"—honesty compelled this emendation—"if there *is* something to be afraid of, it isn't the house itself."

How can you be so sure? I wanted to ask, but bit the question back. Through some conflation of light, weather, occasion, and architecture, Gravesend loomed up in my path like a sheer, implacable wall, a stern obstacle whose every line and surface said *No.*

But as my mother had been wont to observe in exasperation, I am a willful person, and I was in the frame of mind to take the house's rejection as a challenge. "I have come back," I might have said to it. "You sent me running once, you took from me security and my beloved and my mother, but you have not beaten me. I intend to stay—and this time I've no weaknesses for you to exploit."

CHAPTER SIX

There was no more time for such reflection, for the coach was drawing up before the imposing staircase. As a footman was handing me out of the carriage, I glanced up and saw a man watching my descent. A servant, to judge by his rough woolen and homespun clothes; a discontented one, to judge by his glower and the fact that he did not touch his cap when he saw me looking at him. I placed him at forty or over, not disagreeable in appearance except for the surly expression and heavy brow that hooded his eyes. He was above middle height and broad across the shoulders, and as I continued to gaze at him he folded his arms across his chest and deliberately spat. Charming.

"Who is that man?" I asked Atticus as he joined me.

His jaw tightened as he saw the direction of my gaze. "A villager," he said. "He sometimes comes to work at Gravesend when we need extra staff. I'm not aware of any business that brings him here today, though. Robert"—this to one of the footmen—"has my father hired Collier for anything at present?"

"Not that I know of, sir. I'll find out and tell him to move along if he's no business here."

The man called Collier exchanged a few words with Robert, who matched him in height and build, a fact that I found reassuring. Even though the man did not show outright signs of violence, there was a tension about his stance that suggested that he might be prone to physicality. After Robert had spoken to him, he looked once more toward me and Atticus, and grudgingly touched his cap—a more reluctant gesture of deference I had never seen—and set off down the drive the way we had come, his hands clenched into fists.

"I hope this Collier isn't emblematic of the welcome I'll receive," I said. I meant it to sound light and jesting, but it didn't quite emerge that way, and Atticus took my hand and drew my arm through his as if to reassure me.

"Collier is discontented with his life, I'm sad to say. Wherever he looks he sees the happiness that he feels has been denied him. Pay no attention to him, my dear. I'm certain you'll be welcomed warmly by everyone who matters."

I did not share that certainty, having discovered through questioning him earlier that a few employees of Gravesend might have known me during my time there as a girl. They might be put out to find me placed so far above them now. Perhaps this Collier was related to one of them and had a personal reason to resent my arrival as the new mistress of Gravesend.

Of more immediate concern, however, was the staff actually resident at Gravesend. I took a breath to calm my too-rapid heartbeat, smoothed my skirts—taking some comfort in the feel of the twilled silk—and touched the tiny velvet toque riding atop my head to assure myself that it was still in place. "I'm ready," I said.

"Have no fear," said Atticus in a low voice as we proceeded to the front doors, which were thrown open for us by two of the footmen. "You're mistress here now. No one can rob you of that place."

The words and their significance echoed in my mind as I gazed down the astonishingly long line of servants assembled in the great hall to be introduced to me. I had never before entered Gravesend by the main entrance, and the effect of the great hall, with all the household assembled, was awe inspiring. The black-and-white marble floor and lofty ceiling evoked the grandeur of a cathedral. And there, in the center, her hands clasped above her chatelaine of keys, was the housekeeper.

None of the categories I had contemplated for her seemed to fit. Older than I she definitely was, but by how much I could not tell, for her face was smooth save for faint lines at her eyes. Her hair was gray, but it appeared to be prematurely so. Her figure was neither stout nor slender; her bearing was erect, which seemed to bespeak youth, but that impression was then belied by the stately dignity with which she advanced toward me. Her step was silent on the flagstones, and suddenly I pictured a cat's paws hidden by the long skirt.

"Mrs. Blackwood," she said, and her voice, like her outward appearance, defied easy categorization. She was neither icy nor effusive, but neutral . . . and perhaps just a trifle wary. No doubt she was sizing me up just as I was her, and perhaps she was having just as much difficulty in determining how to feel about me. "I am Mrs. Threll, the housekeeper. Welcome to Gravesend."

"Thank you," I said, conquering my nervous impulse to smile. Better to appear aloof than ingratiating—or, worse, gloating. Nor did I mention that this was not the first time I had called Gravesend home. "I can see that the house is in excellent hands, and I look forward to our further acquaintance."

"As do I, Mrs. Blackwood. Allow me to introduce the staff. The butler, Mr. Birch."

This was my first real test. I remembered the present dignified figure before me, now balding and double-chinned, as a young and eager footman called Terence. I nodded a greeting, pleased to see no sign of recognition in the butler's face. Birch seemed aware that dignity was a butler's stock in trade and was acting accordingly. I only hoped that he also maintained sufficient distance from the lower servants not to trade gossip with them.

However, there was nothing in his position to prevent him from discussing his new mistress with the housekeeper, and what *she* might do with revelatory information about me I had no idea.

I shook off the thought; pointless to worry about it at this moment, when it was not in my power to change. All I could do was act appropriately for my new station and try to demonstrate that, whatever my past history was, it had ended when I stepped over the threshold of Gravesend as Atticus Blackwood's bride.

I did my best to pay attention as Mrs. Threll introduced each servant in turn, but I knew it would take me time to learn all their names, especially since many of them would be largely invisible to me, their work designed to take place out of sight. If I did encounter a servant in the course of their duties, protocol demanded that they turn their face to the wall and pretend to be invisible in my presence. I remembered the humiliation of this and wondered how my husband felt about the custom. The one advantage was that it might make Lord Telford all the less likely to recognize my face now.

"You're to have the Swan Room, Mrs. Blackwood," said Mrs. Threll after all the introductions were over. "Mr. Blackwood will be in the Clock Room."

When we were shown to our rooms I found that they were separated only by a dressing room, but the doors at either side possessed locks, so I would be assured of privacy. The Swan Room must have been redecorated since my time at Gravesend, for it seemed different from my recollection of it—a discovery that came as a relief, for if I had been made to reside in a room that I had vivid memories of cleaning, I could not imagine that I would ever have been quite comfortable; I would have half expected a scolding each time I climbed into bed.

The decorations were largely in gold and black, influenced by the Japanese style, with wallpaper and a folding screen sponge painted in metallic gold with a bold, colorful design of swans and flowers. The wardrobe and bureau were lacquered in black and had elaborate inlaid designs of mother of pearl. Draperies of gold silk velvet framed windows that offered a view of the glasshouse and gardens but not the folly—and that, I reflected, was probably for the best.

The Clock Room, where Atticus would sleep, was a handsome and thoroughly masculine chamber fitted out in walnut paneling and oxblood leather, boasting on the black marble mantel the namesake clock: ornamented with an extraordinarily elaborate arrangement of allegorical figures, it dated, I learned later, from the time of Napoleon Bonaparte. Lord Telford was situated in the finest suite of rooms, of course, and that was where Atticus took me to formally introduce me to his father after we had freshened ourselves from our travels. The old gentleman was too infirm to stir from his quarters except for the exercise prescribed by his physician.

At least, that was what Atticus gave me to understand. When I came to stand before his father, however, and made my curtsey, it seemed to me that the wiry figure in the bath chair was yet hale enough to have easily endured being taken downstairs. Perhaps he had relished the idea of having us pay our call on him in his own chambers, as if he were royalty. But of course in this house he *was,* in every way that mattered.

"Clara, eh?" he said, giving me a sharp glance as he held my hand tightly in his. "A good, solid, plain name, is Clara. No nonsense about it. Yeomanly, one might say."

In other words, common. The spiteful glint in his eye told me that this man was not to be underestimated. Nor was he, even for a moment, to be trusted.

"I am glad it pleases you, my lord," I said, and was rewarded with a cackle of a laugh.

"I did not say it pleased me, daughter-in-law. Perhaps your powers of perception are limited. Would you say you come from intellectually inferior stock, girl?"

I kept my temper with little trouble. It seemed my father-in-law was going to enjoy trying to bait me. Fortunately for me, he had all the subtlety of a brickbat. Now, before I could respond to his sally, he addressed Atticus. "Don't tell me you went and married a fool, Atticus. A pretty face is well enough, but an undeveloped mind is too high a price to pay."

Atticus started to speak—to defend me, I had no doubt—but I gave him a slight shake of the head to indicate that I would answer for myself.

"My intellect is well enough, my lord. I was giving you the benefit of the doubt and assuming that you meant to pay me a compliment, as befits a gentleman addressing a lady—particularly a lady who has become a member of his family."

I saw Atticus cock a questioning eyebrow at this audacity. It was a gamble, but I was confident that I had correctly assessed Lord Telford's character. He would enjoy a pert daughter-in-law more than a conciliatory one, I suspected.

A satisfied bark of a laugh confirmed my hunch. "A spirited thing it is, then. Take care that your impudent tongue doesn't get away with you, my girl. A true lady knows when discretion is the better part of valor."

"A true lady," I rejoined, "is exactly what your son's wife is and ever will be, by virtue of her position. And a bit of eccentricity is not without precedent in the aristocracy, is it, Lord Telford?"

The glittering eyes narrowed, and he gave a grudging nod. "She'll do, Atticus," he announced. "You shall have trouble with her, I've no doubt, but she'll do."

Hunched and almost gnomelike, Lord Telford was much smaller and less imposing than I recalled from eighteen years ago. No doubt part of it was my changed relationship to him, but age and ill health had also played a hand, I knew, and I felt a twinge of pity. His pate was nearly bare except for a few straggling strands combed sideways across it, and his face was a web of wrinkles, which concentrated around his mouth to give the permanent effect of a mean little smile. His strength—judging by his continued grip on my hand—was greater than I had expected given his infirmity, but his form had dwindled. This was not the same barrel-chested man who had been so imposing to those of us under his command. His voice was no longer booming but almost reedy, as if his diminished size had robbed it of resonance, and the left side of his face seemed less animated than the right, as if some paralysis lingered from the stroke.

"A pity you're not younger," he mused. "Better see about getting an heir on her right away, Atticus. If she cannot provide one, better to know sooner than later, so you can put her out to pasture and find a woman fit for breeding."

That did test my composure. Bluntness I had expected, but not coarseness. My cheeks burned, and I was relieved when Atticus said firmly, "I'll not be setting Clara aside for any reason, Father, and you'd better accustom yourself to that fact. Now, how have you been faring during my absence? Are you taking any exercise?"

The baron's voice grew peevish. "That fool valet of mine insists on my walking every morning and afternoon. He fusses over me like an old woman."

"You know perfectly well that the doctor advised just that." Atticus's voice was calm, and I admired him for keeping his patience with his ailing, petulant father.

As they continued their conversation I took a seat on a brocade-upholstered chair and took the opportunity to acquaint myself with my surroundings. The room showed every sign of being the most magnificent one in the house. The oak wainscoting was carved in a linen fold design, and above it the walls were covered in a rich black and gold brocade. The same brocade made up the hangings of the bed that I saw through a half-open door; we were evidently in the sitting room. Glass-fronted curio cabinets dominated the furnishings, and I saw that Lord Telford must be a collector. But the most startling feature of the decor, and the one that immediately seized my eye now that the hurdle of introductions was past, was that on the wall were mounted what looked like dozens of plaster and wax life masks.

"Go on, my girl, take a look," the old man interjected, and I rose to follow his suggestion as he resumed his conversation with his son. The two voices—one shrill, the other reassuring— carried on as a backdrop to my tour through my father-in-law's collection.

I began my scrutiny with the masks nearest me. As I had suspected, these were casts of distinguished persons' faces— mostly death masks, I discovered, although occasionally an identifying label would note "life mask," with the year. The collection seemed to be roughly chronological, starting with early, famous figures, like Cromwell, proceeding through such personages as Voltaire and Robespierre, and in the present century including prominent persons both living and dead, as well as many whose names I did not recognize. Then, as I progressed to the curio cabinets where more wax masks were on display, the neatly hand-lettered labels began to bear names unfamiliar to me. "Cecile, Lady Abrams, d. 1854," read one; "Owen Black, tin miner, d. 1855," said another. Some were highborn, some apparently laborers. Were these actual acquaintances of Lord Telford? My suspicion was confirmed most disturbingly when I reached the mask labeled "Lady Telford, née Elizabeth Malvern, d. 1856." My father-in-law had a death mask of his own wife.

People mourn in different ways, I told myself. It was his way of remembering her, of keeping her present in his life. Still, my impression of my father-in-law took on a darker and more repellent quality.

The next item shook me even more. The label read, "Mr. Richard Blackwood, d. 1855." Somehow he had acquired a death mask of Richard, even though his death had taken place far away. A cold pit seemed to open in my stomach as I looked at the mask of the man I had loved. The high, broad brow; the strong, straight nose . . . all his features were as I remembered, and I had to squeeze my eyes shut against sudden tears. I forced myself to look away before I lost what remained of my composure.

The remainder of the shelf was empty except for two more labels: "Mr. Atticus Blackwood, d. _____," read one, and a chill crept up the back of my neck when on the other I saw my own name written.

"You see that I've already made a place for you, my dear," called the cracked voice.

"Indeed," I said, attempting to speak lightly. "I'd scarcely feel like one of the family had I been omitted."

That won an appreciative glance from the old gent, but I thought I saw a flash of anger cross Atticus's face. "It's a gruesome welcome," he said briefly. "Clara, I apologize for us. I ought to have made certain before our arrival that you hadn't been incorporated into my father's curio collection."

"Don't apologize for me, boy." There was venom in the old man's voice, and the jesting tone had vanished. "I'm still master here, and I'll greet my daughter-in-law in any fashion I wish."

"So long as it's within the bounds of decency," said Atticus in a voice I had not yet heard him use: clipped and icy cold. He rose from his seat and bowed stiffly. "We'll leave you now, as it's nearly time to dress for dinner. If you would like to join us for the meal, you'd be welcome."

71

"And be wheeled about by my valet like some great baby in a perambulator? I should say not." Now the old man sounded sulky, and his eyes glittered with something like malice as I made my farewell curtsey. "I shall expect you to visit me often and brighten my sickroom, daughter-in-law," he told me. "I crave amusement."

"I suspect he doesn't much lack for it," I told Atticus in a low voice when the door had closed behind us. "Your father strikes me as a gentleman who derives much entertainment from the discomfiture of others."

The look in my husband's startling eyes was enigmatic. "My father is not the easiest of men to live with," he said. "But he finds you amusing, which for him is close to affection. I'm glad you didn't let him upset you."

The label reading "Mrs. Atticus Blackwood, d. _____" had upset me, though. Perhaps I had been in the company of actors too long and had taken on some of their superstitious nature, but it gave me a sense of foreboding. And I had to force myself not to think of Richard's mask at all.

CHAPTER SEVEN

When I returned to the Swan Room to dress for dinner, I found my amethyst satin dinner dress laid out for me. With its black Mechlin lace trim and sweeping train it was probably too formal for a quiet dinner with my husband, but I could not fault the maid, since I had been unable to instruct her.

Atticus had hired for me a French lady's maid.

"She has scarcely any English at all," he had told me on the train, enthusiasm warming his eyes. "Isn't it ideal? She'll not be able to spread gossip among the other servants."

I had stared at him in consternation. "She'll not be able to understand a word I'm saying, either," I said. "How are we to communicate?"

"I'm sure you'll work something out. I have faith in your intelligence—and your powers of improvisation."

I wondered if he was laughing at me. "It's rather cruel," I said shortly. "The poor girl will be alone in a strange country with no one she can speak to." And I would be forced to resort to crude pantomime in order to converse with the one person who was most responsible for my personal needs. How was I to present an appropriate appearance if I could not indicate my desires?

"There's no need to distress yourself over her," said Atticus in some surprise. "When Genevieve arrives, the two of them can pass the time of day."

"That's not enough." The difference in their positions would mean that such pleasantries would be the only conversation they could have. He wasn't deliberately being obtuse, but perhaps he simply could not understand what it would be like for a servant to be so isolated and cut off from her peers. And in a strange country at that. Could I find someone to teach her English? I wondered. Now that she had been hired, replacing her was not an option; to be sent away so soon after her arrival, no matter how glowing my reference, would place her in a dubious light when she sought another position. Somehow I had to make a place for her in my household.

"If it troubles you so deeply," said Atticus after a time, noting my silence, "we can find another place for her. Do give her a chance, though."

"I have nothing against her," I said. "But I cannot help but see this arrangement as problematic for us both. Don't worry, I'll not dismiss her without due consideration. But . . . are there any English primers to be found at Gravesend that we could offer her?"

Henriette, my maid, turned out to be no inexperienced girl but my elder by some ten years, and her manner betrayed no uncertainty despite our inability to converse. After she had bidden me *"Bon soir, madame,"* she set about preparing me for dinner with brisk efficiency. She dressed my hair in mere minutes, deftly taming the wild locks into a stylish upsweep with long ringlets descending to lie becomingly against one shoulder. I had pointed to one of my less elaborate gowns, but she shook her head emphatically and pointed at the ring finger of her left hand, saying something I did not understand, but her conspiratorial smile suggested that her words meant I should present myself at my finest for my new husband.

Even had I the vocabulary, I could hardly argue with that; I ought to be accustoming myself to living my new role, which regardless of the sentiment (or lack thereof) motivating my marriage should include establishing myself as a Blackwood, a woman of importance and one worthy of adorning the halls of Gravesend . . . and if that meant amethyst satin and Mechlin lace, well, who was I to object?

In truth, I was delighted to be able to wear such a splendid gown. I was as enraptured with my trousseau as a child would have been with a box of colored marbles, and for much the same reason: it gave me pleasure just to look at the pretty things. But they pleased more than the eye. The sensation of soft fabrics next to my skin, the satisfying weight of substantial skirts supported by a bustle, the lightness of high-heeled slippers of satin and kid, the tickle of lace at my throat and arms . . . these sensory pleasures filled me with contentment. When I caught sight of myself in my mirror, I saw that I was holding my head high, with a touch of pride. It was impossible not to feel the effect of the grand clothes: they granted me the illusion of grandeur myself, and it was a novel—and heady—sensation.

Atticus joined me in my sitting room, which opened off my bedchamber on the opposite side from the dressing room. Usually, he said, the family used the breakfast room for meals when there were few or no visitors; but on this, our wedding night, we dined in my sitting room, where we were afforded an unusual degree of privacy. The servants vanished discreetly after they had made certain we had everything we needed.

I wondered uneasily what the conversation downstairs was: what did they think of their new mistress? Did they speculate as to the motives behind our marriage, or accept it as a matter of course? "The lady's no spring chicken," I could imagine the cook commenting, "and not as refined as some . . ."

I dismissed the thought as my new husband smiled at me across the table. In the candlelight his hair shone with the red lights that contrasted so oddly with his very light blue eyes. Those eyes dwelled with approval on my gown, I thought, but he cast a thoughtful look at the black velvet ribbon Henriette had tied around my throat. "I've been remiss," he said. "I haven't retrieved the Blackwood jewels for you to wear."

"Jewels!"

My tone made him laugh. "I've caught your interest, have I?" I took a sip of wine to gather my composure. "I'm sorry if I sounded greedy. I don't imagine for a moment that they are to be given to me, but I look forward to the chance to borrow them. I've always taken a childish delight in bright, shiny things."

"Not childish at all. You're quite the sensualist, Clara."

I wasn't entirely certain that this was an acceptable thing for me to be. "What do you mean?" I asked guardedly.

He leaned back in his chair, one hand idly turning the stem of his wine glass, and smiled. "You take such relish in things that bring pleasure to your senses. The way you stroke the fabric of your sleeve, and the look of ecstasy on your face just now when you took your first taste of the Nesselrode pudding—"

"Is that what it's called? I've never tasted anything like it!"

His laugh was too delighted to be taken as a rebuke, and I couldn't help but join in. I was grateful that he had sent the servants away for this first dinner together, so that we could speak frankly. "I suppose you're right," I said. "I never thought of myself that way. I just love being around beautiful things, and until now I didn't have a great many opportunities to do so."

That had been one of the lovely things about sewing for Miss Ingram; working with the beautiful fabrics and trimmings that she ordered was almost as satisfying as wearing the finished gown would have been. The way fine weaves felt in my hands as I pinned and cut and stitched them was a pleasure I relished after working with rough cotton and woolen goods in the factory. The rich, vivid colors were refreshing to look upon after the years of drabness, just as music or poetry recitations after the racket of a hundred sewing machines going at once brought an exquisite delight.

"Is your room satisfactory to your keen sense of aesthetics?" Atticus inquired. "I had it done over in a style that I hoped would appeal to you, but it's no trouble to have the furnishings changed again if you dislike it."

"Goodness, no, please don't think of it," I said, startled to learn that so much had been done for my benefit. "It is beautiful. Although . . ."

"Yes? What can be done to make it more pleasing to you?"

"I would like to have my sewing machine closer at hand," I said. It had been placed in the small downstairs salon that Mrs. Threll had informed me was for my use alone, for writing letters and the like. It was scarcely a convenient location. "Perhaps it could be moved to my bedchamber?"

His eyebrows rose. "Naturally, if you wish. If you don't mind my mentioning it, though, it isn't generally expected that a lady of your station will sew her own clothes."

"Oh, I have no intention of doing so," I hastened to explain. "But some of my new gowns can be improved upon. They were made in such haste that some of them would benefit from altering. I thought to make a few small adjustments."

"Ah, I see. How industrious of you." He grinned. "Or is it vanity? Take care, Mrs. Blackwood, lest you become known for being self-smitten."

"It isn't that," I exclaimed, unable to refrain from defending myself even though I was almost certain he was simply jesting. "But some of the gowns fit me rather badly, and I don't think it would be very becoming in your wife to appear in gowns that gape or pull across the—the—well, it would reflect poorly on you for me to appear in ill-fitting gowns."

"A conscientious bride indeed," he mused, but the twinkle was still present in his eyes. "I'm in your debt for attending so carefully to my reputation."

"Poke fun at me all you wish. You'll find that the women in your circle—gentry *and* servants—will lose respect for a lady who doesn't take trouble with her appearance." I remembered the gossip that had passed among us below stairs when visitors' trunks revealed surprises about their clothing: the duchess whose husband was reputed to be one of the wealthiest men in the country, but whose gowns had been made over from older garments; the foreign relation whose moral fiber we criticized after finding that she wore corsets of bright purple, red, and peacock green; the haphazardly sewn toilettes of a neighboring lady whose carelessness about fashion had led, we speculated, to the known tendency of her husband to let his eye stray to other women—women whose gowns displayed their figures to better advantage and flattered their complexions with deliberately chosen colors. I tried to explain to Atticus. "One can learn a great deal about a person from her clothes," I pointed out. "And I do not want anyone to have cause to fault the new Mrs. Blackwood on that front. Dressing well is crucial to . . ."

"To your role?" he finished. "I can see that your time in Miss Ingram's troupe has taught you a great deal about the importance of costume to a character."

I did not explain that I had begun forming my impressions of this matter years before, while at Gravesend. Instead I asked, "How do you feel about our performance so far? Are you satisfied with your father's reception of me?"

He poured me more wine—a courtesy, since I had scarcely touched it—before refilling his own glass. "I am," he said thoughtfully. "He has taken a liking to you."

"He does not seem as overjoyed as I rather expected he would from what you told me. He would have preferred a younger bride, I gather."

"Father would have found cause to be displeased had I brought home the Queen of Sheba."

"But after going to so much trouble with our story, my trousseau, everything—surely this is not the reception you had anticipated?"

He gave a philosophical shrug. "The perfect daughter-in-law, as far as he is concerned, must not be perfect in every respect, or else he'll have nothing to growl about—and growling, contrary as it seems, puts him in rather a good humor. So I congratulate you, Clara, on your success." He raised his glass to me in a toast, and I could only follow his example.

When at last we finished with our meal and our discussion of the day, Atticus bade me ring to have the table cleared and suggested we retire early. "I've no doubt you're fatigued from the journey and from the rigors of your first day as mistress of Gravesend," he said. "May I suggest that we make a habit of talking over the day here in private before retiring? We'll not have much privacy in which to talk during the course of the day, and it would be wise to take the opportunity to discuss whatever problems or perplexities may arise without the chance of being overheard."

"That sounds quite perfect, thank you." How considerate of him to realize that I might have a great deal to ask him as I became acclimated to my new role.

We were standing on the threshold of my sitting room where the door opened into the hallway, as Atticus had declined to access his own room by making his way through mine. The delicacy he showed in this, as in so much else, pleased and surprised me; I had wondered if he might be less concerned for the niceties given that I was of lower birth and more of a business partner than a wife. But he was behaving in all respects like a gentleman, and as he took my hand for a parting kiss I confess that I felt a tentative satisfaction with the bargain I had made. A few months of this, until his frail father succumbed to a merciful release, might not be so harrowing after all. If only I could come to feel secure in my role—and to look at my husband without the stab of chagrin that he was not his brother.

Even after Atticus had parted from me, I remained standing there musing instead of closing the door, and it was only for this reason that I heard the voice.

The hallway was shadowed in darkness except for the one flickering candle in a wall bracket between my bedroom and his. Beyond my sitting room, all was as black as pitch. It should not have been surprising, then, that I saw nothing. But then I heard a disembodied voice, like a whisper from beyond the material realm.

"*Clara,*" it said.

It was a long sigh, a husky exhalation of—wonder? warning? I could not even tell if the voice was a man's or a woman's.

Surely it was Atticus who had spoken. But when I turned my head, expecting to see that he had returned to my side unheard, I saw only the vanishing sliver of light from his chamber down the hall as he drew the door closed behind him.

I swallowed hard and peered into the darkness. Nothing moved, nothing disturbed the inky black well of shadow. A little shiver crept up my neck, and I did not quite dare to call out a challenge.

The old house was constructed so strangely, I told myself, that if Atticus had spoken my name, the echo might have seemed to make his voice come from the opposite direction. Neverthe-

79

less, I made a brisk retreat through the sitting room to my bed-chamber, the rustle of my skirts betraying my haste, and locked the adjoining door.

The luxurious appointments of my room helped to soothe my nervousness somewhat. In the warm glow of firelight and the oil lamp I removed the triumphant amethyst gown, sparing a moment of gratitude that it boasted the fashionable button front and did not require me to ring for Henriette to free me from it, and put on for the first time one of my fine new lace-trimmed silk nightdresses. The fabric was airy soft against my skin, and when I climbed into the magnificent bed the perfect smoothness of the sheets made me sigh in pleasure. The room was blissfully quiet, free of the sounds of street noise, and no cooking smells assaulted my nostrils, only the faint scent of dried lavender given off by the linens. A sensualist, Atticus had said. Very well, then; I was guilty as charged. But I had experienced the worst Gravesend could muster; it was only right that I enjoy some of its material comforts as well.

The memory of that ghostly whisper, though, was like a voice of reproach. I had allowed myself to become so caught up in fri-volities that I had managed to put out of my mind what a mock-ery this arrangement was compared to my girlhood dreams. As a young woman I had sometimes dared to imagine myself as mistress of Gravesend—with the crucial difference that in those fantasies I was Richard's bride, not Atlas's. In those dreams, moreover, I was not alone in my bed on my wedding night.

Suddenly cold despite the warm bedclothes that enfolded me, I grasped for the cautious optimism that had visited me such a short time ago, but it had fled. When at last I fell asleep it was with a troubled heart. And if a few childish tears happened to fall before I slept, no one but my pillow was any the wiser.

CHAPTER EIGHT

My new life proved not quite as easily donned as one of my new frocks, but at least the first day went remarkably smoothly.

As was only fitting in welcoming a new mistress to Gravesend, Mrs. Threll led me on a tour of the house. I was forced to pretend ignorance, letting her introduce me to rooms I had cleaned year after year. The house seemed no less grand and imposing to me now than it had when I had first entered it as a girl, and this surprised me; I had expected to feel, if not at ease there, at least less intimidated. But in room after room I felt a cool, aloof watchfulness, and I was intimidated by not just the size but the grandeur and age of the furnishings. As much as when I had been a girl there, I moved among the precious antiquities with unease, afraid that I might break something. The house had not accepted me—had never accepted me, either as its handmaiden or as its mistress.

This, I told myself sternly, was simply my own anxiety about exposure coloring my perceptions. I did not feel comfortable or welcomed because I was there under false pretenses, not because the house had sense or feeling to know my secrets and condemn me for them. But there was something so un-lived-in about the main reception rooms, perhaps because Lord Telford had ceased entertaining since his stroke, that they looked as if they had fallen into a kind of disuse that suited them and would be resentful if I woke them to their former service.

I shivered, and Mrs. Threll asked dutifully, "Are you cold, ma'am? I'll send one of the maids to fetch you a shawl."

"No, thank you."

Mrs. Threll was difficult to take the measure of. Her tone was always even and respectful: never animated, never showing any sign of emotion. I had resolved to preserve that mutually respectful but cool cordiality, and that seemed to suit us both. She gave no sign of either resenting me or warming to me, but she saw that my orders were carried out, unless she had practical emendations to suggest, which were always sensible. I valued her, but I could not say that I liked her . . . or even, yet, that I trusted her. Perhaps it would be possible to find a window into her character through a topic that would surely be of mutual interest. "Mrs. Threll," I said, "what can you tell me about the curse on Gravesend?"

Her face was impossible to read; I had no idea what she thought of the question. "Stories of the curse go back as far as the death of the lady who was to be the first mistress of Gravesend," she said. "They spring to life again whenever a misfortune visits the house or the family. What is it that you wish to know?"

We were standing in the banquet hall, the largest room in the house; the faint smell of beeswax rising from the floorboards reminded me of how much work it had been to clean and prepare it for use whenever the Blackwoods were having a grand party. The high windows, my own height at least, permitted the wan light of an overcast day to reach us. The long table was bare, the chairs neatly ranked against the walls, and our voices echoed in the great emptiness.

"Do you believe in the curse?" I asked, without having intended to.

Still no change came over the impassive face. Was she so skilled at disguising her feelings, or did she simply have none? "Yes, ma'am, I do," she said evenly.

This response, coupled with her neutral tone, astonished me at first. If she were so certain, surely she would have sought a position elsewhere . . . but perhaps she had. Perhaps, like my mother, she had found it the least dire choice open to her. "Do you fear it?" I asked hesitantly.

For a moment I thought that a flash of emotion passed across her eyes, but it was gone so quickly I could not be certain. "I don't fear it, ma'am, no. The curse is said to rob one of what one most treasures. And I am not a treasuring sort of person."

How very odd. Did she mean she felt no attachment to anyone or anything? Glancing at the still, erect figure in her plain black gown, I could not imagine Mrs. Threll showing affection or attachment. But was this a hard-won place of resignation, or a lack of natural sympathies?

It was hardly my place to ask. The housekeeper deserved her secrets, and I had pried enough.

Before I could suggest we proceed to the next room, she asked unexpectedly, "Do you not fear the curse, ma'am, that you accepted Mr. Blackwood and came here to live?"

I had prepared myself for this question, fortunately. I smiled in a way that I hoped made me look like a smitten bride. "I believe it would have been a far worse fate never to have married Mr. Blackwood than to risk whatever dangers Gravesend may bring," I said.

She did not seem moved by this profession of wifely devotion. "Perhaps," she said. "But you may live to regret that decision."

"Perhaps," I echoed, startled by the dire words. "But no one is safe from regret at any point in life. One may regret ordering lamb for dinner instead of mutton. All of life is a succession of risks, and each of us must judge for ourselves which risks are worth the taking."

Hoping to close the conversation, I started for the nearest door, but Mrs. Threll's voice followed me. "Ma'am, I think you'll find the entrance to the larger parlor this way."

Her words, and their faintly condescending tone, brought me up short. Out of old habit I had been proceeding toward one of the servants' doors. "Of course," I said, feeling rebuked. "Please lead the way, Mrs. Threll."

One place that I explored without Mrs. Threll's assistance (or, indeed, her knowledge) was the corridor onto which my sitting room opened. I needed to know whether it offered any concealment to someone who might have been lurking there and whispering my name on my first night in the house as Mrs. Blackwood.

My sitting room was the last room on its side of the corridor. Across from it, as I discovered when I tried the doorknob and found it unlocked, was a spare bedroom. It was furnished but not in immediate readiness for a tenant. I stood looking at the purple-and-buff brocade hangings and mused. Someone could have hidden behind the door easily enough, but who—and why? And why take such a risk, when I might so easily have taken three steps across the corridor and peered around the door, exposing the prankster? With no means of escape, he would have been bottled up.

Frowning, I shut the door behind me and examined the wall near the window at the end of the hall. It was just possible that there might be a hidden door here; I did not remember one from my earlier tenancy at Gravesend, but then I had not had a great deal of leisure for exploring in those days, between my duties and, in the final year or so, my rendezvous with Richard. I ran my fingers lightly along the floral wallpaper, seeking an interruption in the smooth surface, but had not yet found anything when the grandfather clock down the hall tolled the time, and I had to join Lord Telford for tea.

At his express request, we met without my husband; Lord Telford wanted, he had said, for us to be able to speak without constraint so that we might become properly acquainted, as befit new family, and although it was odd, I found it a reasonable enough request. An uncomfortable one, though, since if the conversation led into dangerous waters I alone would have to steer it into a safer course, without any ally.

But I felt it incumbent upon me to entertain my father-in-law when he was so inclined; it was no more than what my contract required, and for what Atticus was providing me, it was little enough to ask in return. And I was certainly equal to an elderly, ailing man. I felt only the smallest flicker of apprehension as I knocked at the door to his sitting room, and when his voice bade me enter I did so with, I think, every appearance of being collected.

"Daughter-in-law, how lovely you look. Forgive my not rising." He seemed to be in an amiable mood, judging from his expression, and he was neatly dressed, in a slightly old-fashioned collar and cravat. Today his lap rug was a cheerful red. "No, no, don't curtsey as if we did not know each other. Come and kiss me."

I stooped to touch my lips to his dry, papery cheek, and he chuckled. "Very nice. Now pour, if you will be so good—two lumps and a touch of milk for me—and tell me all about yourself."

Concentrating on filling his cup and adding the requested sugar and milk gave me a little time to gather my thoughts and remember the story that Atticus and I had decided upon. I related briefly my background as we had concocted it, hoping to move quickly to the present.

"And why did my son not bring you here to be married from Gravesend, pray?" my father-in-law wanted to know. "Did you wheedle him into a London wedding?"

"I did, I'm afraid," I said promptly. Atticus and I had prepared an explanation for this also. "Being well past the age of most brides, and a widow what's more, I confess that I feel the passage of time quite keenly. I asked if we could dispense with the usual long preparations and obtain a special license, and Atlas was good enough to humor my wish."

"Good? Nonsense. He probably felt just as impatient as you. I should have, in his place."

I was trying to decide if he had meant this to sound as suggestive as it had when his next question shocked me out of my train of thought.

"I am curious as to how you learned my son's childhood nickname," he said, pleasantly enough, but with his eyes slightly narrowed as he watched me. "I can't imagine that he would have brought it up, disliking it as he did."

My stomach gave a little flutter of dread. All my efforts to school myself out of thinking of him by his old name had not worked. "Did others call him Atlas?" I asked. "He never said so."

"His brother, Richard, used to tease him with it. Surely he did not mention that."

I reached for the teapot to warm his cup, then mine. "He did not, no."

"What a remarkable coincidence, then, for you to concoct such a pet name for him."

The thin, insinuating voice was fretting my nerves, and I allowed him to see that I was a bit flustered. I set my teacup down with a clink of porcelain and reached for the sugar without meeting his eyes. "I really would rather not say," I said. "I'm afraid you'll think me a very silly woman."

"Come, now! Give me more credit than that." His curiosity was piqued even more.

I took a breath and let it out. "It's just—well, I know I sound like a lovesick girl, but one of the first things that struck me about Atticus when I met him was how broad his shoulders are. Nearly broad enough to shoulder the world, was my fancy. And with his name but a step away . . ." I gave a little shrug of assumed embarrassment. "The pet name just came to mind."

"Hmm." I could not tell from his expression whether Lord Telford believed me, so after a quick peek at his face I dropped my eyes as if in shyness at my revelation. Presently he said, "And my son has not indicated that he dislikes this particular endearment?"

This was trickier. "He seemed surprised when I first used it," I said. "But I do not recall that he objected to it."

"How interesting. Perhaps, coming from such lips as yours, the name has lost its power to hurt." He stretched out a thin, unsteady hand for his tea. "He certainly protested it vigorously in his childhood. He and Richard came to blows over it more than once."

It would have been courteous to thank him for the compliment, but I was more interested in pursuing this unexpected insight into the past. "He and Richard fought? I knew there was some, well, fraternal rivalry—"

The old man's face split in a grin. "That is a most lady-like way of putting it. Richard loved to bait Atticus. There was nothing to stop him for many years, until Atticus finally showed some spirit and began to defend himself. Even then he took many a beating."

"I'm certain you are exaggerating. If there had been violence between them you would have intervened."

He waved that away. "It was their quarrel, not mine. Boys have to be let alone to learn how to settle these things. It took a few black eyes and bloody noses—and a broken bone or two—but they finally came to a kind of armed truce."

This was so unlike what I remembered, and what Atticus had told me, that I did not know whether to believe it or not. "But Atticus admired his brother so."

He shifted in his chair, and his valet stepped forward to rearrange the lap rug as it threatened to slip to the floor. The conversation seemed to be making Lord Telford testy. "My dear, if your husband has a fault, it is that his view of the world and humankind is too upright and unyielding. Were the matter left to him, no one would ever transgress in the slightest way. What harm is it when a young man sows some wild oats, plays at dice once in a while, and the like? Atticus expected his brother to stay on the pedestal on which he'd placed him, but Richard—my Richard was too bold to be bound by such conventions." His voice dropped into a gruff note that must have been sorrow. "If he had a few less than pristine episodes in his youth, what matter? At least it showed he had spirit. Let the milquetoasts of the world stick to the strait and narrow if they are so fearful of the consequences of living life to its fullest." Abruptly he flung his napkin onto the table, and I had the strong certainty that if he had still had the full use of his legs he would have leapt from his chair and walked away.

The picture forming in my mind was disturbing, and I had the gravest doubts about its veracity. He was implying that Richard had been a libertine, a gambler, and a seducer—and that Atticus had been a poor-spirited creature who resented and condemned his brother for these failings. "But Richard was not like that," I exclaimed, and instantly wished I could call the words back again, for Lord Telford cocked an eyebrow and turned his sharp eyes back toward me.

"How certain you are," he observed. "Is it possible that you knew my younger son? Did you cross paths with him before his all too premature passing?"

"Indeed, no," I said, casting about with my mind for some reason for my outburst. "It's only . . . it's only that Atticus speaks of him with genuine affection and regard, and I cannot reconcile the man he has described to me with the one you are painting."

"Ha! Has Atticus whitewashed his brother so, then? He must have decided the truth would be too distressing for your woman's ears." There was a contemptuous twist to his mouth—for me or for Atticus, I was not sure. "I wonder if the words lodge in his throat when he has to perjure his pure samite soul so."

The contempt was for Atticus, then. "Lord Telford," I said, "I must ask you not to speak so of my husband. He is a man of honor, yes, and I rejoice to say so. I will not listen to him being criticized in such terms, and if you continue to do so I must draw this visit to a close."

That earned me raised eyebrows and an exaggerated moue. He made a point of looking over at his valet as if to demand whether he had heard the same unbelievable speech. But it seemed to have amused him rather than affronting him. "My goodness, such a queenly air! I'd not expected to be so roundly put in my place by my daughter-in-law."

My face was burning, but I did not capitulate. "If my manner of expressing myself was insolent, I ask your pardon. But I stand by my words. Even from his own father, my husband should not be subjected to—"

"Yes, yes, I understand. Quite right of you to be so loyal to him . . . surprising to me that he could inspire such loyalty, especially in a woman of spirit, but I am impressed."

He was not alone in his surprise. I had not imagined myself so attached to my nominal husband that I would become so angered at hearing him slandered. Perhaps being unable to stand up for Richard as I would have liked left me full of unspent indignation that had sought an outlet. But in any case, Atticus did not deserve to be dismissed so. He was no joyless prude, but a kind and humorous man. And it must have taken considerable courage to have stood up to Richard despite his own physical disadvantage.

But Lord Telford was waiting for my reply. "I did not speak with any intention of impressing you," I said, but more calmly. "I simply felt that as his wife—"

"Quite correct, of course. Let's not discuss it further. One is naturally pleased to have one's children praised, but I don't need you to parade your husband's virtues to me."

"I had no intention of parading anything."

"And there she is again, the queenly one! 'O, what a deal of scorn looks beautiful in the contempt and anger of her lip!' How Richard would have appreciated you." Then his eyes narrowed, and an unpleasant smile tugged at the corners of his lips. "Indeed," he said more thoughtfully, "I wonder if that is the secret of your attraction to my older son? It must give him no little satisfaction to wed a woman whom Richard would have wooed were he still living. With Richard dead, the playing field is level for Atlas."

That jarred me. Lord Telford could not have recognized me as Richard's old sweetheart, or he certainly would have said so— but had he stumbled on part of the truth? I told myself firmly that Atticus did not see me as a prize he had claimed over the dead body of his brother, but the doubt had been planted. Was this what Atticus gained in marrying me, the motive he had not disclosed? Did he take satisfaction in winning some one-sided competition in his mind?

This would not do; I could not let my father-in-law see how troubled were my thoughts. I cast about for another topic of conversation, and my eyes fell on the masks adorning the walls.

"Lord Telford, I'm curious about your collection," I said. "What moved you to collect something as out of the ordinary as death masks?"

His eyes narrowed ever so slightly as if he scented a diversion, but he tolerated the change of subject. "I find their honesty fascinating," he said. "Death lays all secrets bare, you know. These masks capture the real person after all the artifice and pretense have been stripped away. Observe this one of my father, for example." He jerked his head in a summons to his valet, who obediently stepped forward to wheel his chair over to one of the curio cases. "Come, have a look."

I rose and joined him, albeit without enthusiasm. The wax casting he was indicating with one clawlike hand showed a masculine face, not a young one, drawn in lines of pain and suffering. "Poor man," I exclaimed. "Was it an illness?"

"Why, it was the curse, child. That husband of yours told you of the Gravesend curse, I hope? Surely he would not have led his bride here all unknowing." His voice dripped mock concern.

"I know of the curse," I said shortly, hoping he would drop the subject. But my wish was not granted.

"Take heed, then, daughter-in-law." His eyes glittered in malicious pleasure. "When I was still a child, the waltz took the fashionable world by storm. My father was newly wedded to his second wife—my stepmother—and found no greater joy than in waltzing with her. But the curse seizes on what we most love. One night on their way to a ball their coach was in a terrible collision. My stepmother was killed instantly. My father survived, but both his legs were crushed; they had to be taken off at the knee." My exclamation of horror seemed, if anything, to please him. With a thin smile, he concluded, "He never waltzed again, needless to say."

"And his secret?" I inquired, not certain I wanted to know the answer.

The old man's smile became a sneer. "For the rest of his short life, he put on an absurd pretense that he was contented with what remained to him. In my few recollections, he was like the two Cheeryble brothers in one body. A brave front, he probably thought it. Sickening hypocrisy, to my way of thinking." His eyes showed no affection as they rested upon the pitiful likeness of his father. "But now it is plain to be seen how much suffering the curse caused him."

Reflecting that I would probably have preferred his father's company to his own, I said, "It is dreadful that he suffered a double tragedy. But I hope that his pretense, as you call it, was more than that. Perhaps he truly did treasure what was left to him after having lost so much."

Impatiently he beckoned for Brutus to wheel him away from the curio case. "Wait until the curse strikes you, child," he snapped. "We shall see what fortitude you are able to summon up in the face of calamity."

If only he knew. I strove to keep my voice pleasant when I said, "This has been a most illuminating afternoon, my lord. I don't wish to tire you, though, so I had best draw my visit to a close."

He gave a wheezing laugh. "Had enough of my company, eh? Run along then, child. You'll have tea with me again tomorrow, of course."

It was not a question, but I would not be ordered about by him. "I shall ask Atticus if we have any prior engagements," I said, unable to resist a final dig. "As a bride, you know, I must place my husband's wishes first."

A raised eyebrow registered appreciation of this riposte. "Such a spirited lass," he mused as I made my curtsey. "What a pity the curse makes no exceptions for charm." His eyes followed me all the way to the door, and even after it closed behind me I thought I could still feel that amused, malicious gaze.

CHAPTER NINE

After the unpleasant thoughts that Lord Telford had planted in my mind I found myself wishing for the calming reassurance of Atticus's company, so as soon as I left his father's rooms I descended to the main floor in search of him. Arriving at the library I interrupted a discussion between him and a visitor, a young man who looked up from their work at the large desk and made me a deep bow.

"Bertram, meet my wife," said Atticus, looking, to my relief, not at all put out at my interruption. "Clara, George Bertram is my agent and my chief consultant on one of my pet interests."

I approached to offer Mr. Bertram my hand, making the appropriate pleasantries, and then asked Atticus, "And what interest is that?"

"A rather innovative system of philanthropic institutions," Mr. Bertram said, answering for him. He was a broad-chested man of less than thirty, with a wild bush of brown hair in want of cutting and an amiable, open face that surely had never known malice or calculation. His enthusiasm made his voice robust enough to fill the room. "Your husband, Mrs. Blackwood, is not only a compassionate man but a visionary."

"Bertram, you needn't work so hard to convince my wife of my virtues," said Atticus mildly. "Clara has already married me, after all." His eyes were bright with interest as they returned to the papers on the desk, which I saw now seemed to be building plans.

Mr. Bertram waved away the demurral so vigorously that for a moment I feared he would knock the nearby globe from its stand. "You know my admiration for this venture, Blackwood. I'm certain your wife will share it once its features are made known to her. Or have you already taken Mrs. Blackwood into your confidence?"

"I know nothing of this," I said, "but I'm eager to learn what animates you and my husband with such enthusiasm." For Atticus did seem to be full of a vitality that I found as appealing as I did mysterious; one hand made notations in pencil on the sketches, and the other drummed in an excess of energy. His cravat was askew and his hair slightly rumpled, as if he had been dragging his fingers through it.

It probably would have been a wifely gesture to restore some order to his appearance, so I approached with the thought of straightening his cravat. I lost courage at the last minute, however; it seemed too intimate a contact. Atticus proved himself a better actor than I when he took my hand and held it to his lips for a long moment, gazing into my eyes. For a moment I lost my breath. It was like being with Richard again, stealing a few minutes together on a long-ago day when my future seemed full of possibilities, and all of them including him.

"Now, fond marrieds, remember you're not alone," said Bertram cheerfully, and I returned to the present with a little sinking of my heart. "There'll be time enough for all your billing and cooing when I've gone."

"Spoken like a true bachelor," said Atticus lightly, tucking my hand into the crook of his arm. "Once you marry—assuming you can find a bride who'll have you—you'll be forgetting your-self in company too."

He was so relaxed in the way he spoke about us, the way he behaved, that it was a bit unnerving. "What are these institutions you spoke of, Mr. Bertram?" I asked, to cover my confusion.

"You truly know nothing of them? I'm astonished that your husband hasn't told you of his grand scheme!"

Now Atticus did not look so relaxed. He coughed into his hand. "I thought it better to seek an appropriate time for pre-senting Clara with the plan."

Bertram burst into laughter. "And I've spoiled your careful strategy. Well, out with it, Blackwood. You've no choice now."

Releasing me, Atticus stepped over to the desk to pick up one of the building plans. "This is the first one," he said. "It should be ready for habitation by the end of the summer. The others will be built along similar lines, with changes as made necessary by the location and so on."

The drawing told me little; it seemed to contain sizable dor-mitories, which made me think of a workhouse, but that was not a scheme that could be called visionary, nor one that I could imagine evoking such enthusiasm. "I'm afraid you'll have to say it in so many words," I said. "Who is to live here?" And why had he thought he needed to break it to me in any special way?

He said carefully, "The unfortunates generally called fallen women."

This did surprise me. "The Anglican sisterhood already offers shelters for these women, does it not?"

"Yes, but these will be different. Here the women will be permitted to keep their children by them, instead of being sep-arated." He was watching me closely to gauge my reaction. "I've long thought it an unconscionable cruelty to separate mother and child, no matter how unfortunate the circumstances of the child's birth."

"That's very good of you," I said. "Were you expecting me to be shocked or distressed that my husband is exerting him-self in this cause? I am surprised, but my sensibilities are not offended." In fact, to my surprise, I found myself feeling some-thing akin to admiration. I could not imagine any of the other men I had known—gently born or not—looking with so compassionate an eye on the population of ruined women. "What put the idea into your mind?" I asked.

He looked at me for a moment, and I thought it a searching look. "I was slightly acquainted with one such case," he said at last, his voice pitched so low that I doubted Bertram could hear. "The young woman's child was sent away to be raised by strangers. I have never forgotten the injustice of it."

"But surely the child is in some cases an unpleasant reminder of the girl's ruin," I suggested. "It's distressing for us to think about, to be sure, but I know there are cases where the child is made to feel his mother's resentment."

"Truly?" Atticus looked shocked, and I was sorry to be the one to disillusion him. But if he embarked on this venture as fully as he seemed determined to, he would soon learn that his pretty ideas about the sacred bond of mother and child did not always hold true.

"I am sad to say it, but sometimes the child is better off with those who don't view him as a reproach or an unwanted responsibility. Especially when the mother struggles to find a means of feeding herself alone, the obligation to feed another can sometimes drive these poor creatures to extremes that would horrify you."

My words seemed to remind Atticus that I had had a very different experience of the world from his. Indeed, I had met several women of the kind deemed fallen, even apart from poor Martha, and while some took a bittersweet pleasure from their children, there were others the memory of whom made me suppress a shiver.

"I see," he said, subdued. "Yes, you make an excellent point. A distressing one, but an excellent one nonetheless."

"We would certainly not force the mother to keep the child, in a case such as that," offered Bertram. "Would we, Blackwood? I should think we might be able to help both mother and child by seeking out a better situation for the child."

"Perhaps we could even offer a school," said Atticus thoughtfully, rubbing his jaw. "Train the youngsters up so that they'll have a trade, like their mothers. That's another of my hopes," he told me. "Some of these unfortunate women were driven into their present circumstances by having no means by which to earn a living . . . no wholesome means, I should say. The Anglican homes have offered the solution of training their residents as laundresses, which I think a very sound scheme."

Now it was my turn to be thoughtful. "It is a valuable trade, to be sure. But some will surely have natural abilities suited to more skilled tasks. Sewing, for example. Most machine-made garments are still finished by hand; it is—" I only just stopped before saying that this had been my particular skill. Quickly I amended, "It is easy enough to determine whether a woman has an inclination to such work. Deft hands that might be ruined by laundry work may find occupation in fine sewing and finishing."

"A capital idea," Bertram announced. "Isn't it, Blackwood? I say, Mrs. B, that's some first-rate thinking."

Atticus slipped his arm around my waist and drew me closer. I had to avert my eyes from his; after that momentary glimpse of Richard in him a few minutes before, seeing him look at me with such a convincing imitation of the adoration in Richard's eyes made my heart constrict painfully. "My bride has a first-rate head on her shoulders," he told his friend. "Her beauty and her compassionate nature are equaled only by her intelligence."

This excess of admiration would only awaken suspicion, I feared; he was playing his role with a reckless degree of exaggeration. "Please don't overpraise me so," I said, and to soften the words added, "you'll make me blush before your friend."

"And that would become you just as much as the praise. However, I know how uncomfortable you are being the subject under discussion, so I'll find an innocuous topic on which to discourse. Has Father given you the guest list?"

"Guest list?" I replied, a feeling of dread beginning to form in me.

"Why, for the house party beginning next week. Did he not tell you? All our friends from the surrounding counties will be coming to Gravesend to meet you and celebrate our wedding."

This froze me with horror. So many people, so many high-born people, all of them here to examine me and question me and make note of everything that I said or did that rang false with my professed identity—my panic must have been obvious, for Atticus patted my hand in what was meant to be a reassuring gesture.

"My dear," he said, "they'll love you. You've nothing to fear."

I was not at all certain of that. And if they found me out, what then would happen to Atticus? He would be a laughing-stock—or a pariah. "You must tell me all about your friends," I said, as lightly as I could manage. "I'd like to know how best to make their stay here a pleasant one."

That night when we met in my sitting room for our nightly consultation, I was rather more free with my words. "How could you invite all these people here? They'll recognize at once that I'm not their kind. It isn't just of myself I'm thinking, Atticus—it will do your standing no good to be seen to have made such a match."

"Clara," he said firmly, from his seat by the fire. "Stop your pacing and sit down." He would not speak again until I complied, so I did so—unwillingly, for I was restless with worry. I picked at a slub in my taffeta overskirt until he reached out and placed his hand over mine, stilling my fidgeting.

I stared down at his fingers. Richard's fingers, they were. Entwined in my hair . . . unfastening the button at my throat . . .

"Please listen to me," came his voice—and that, too, was Richard's, making me bite my lip. "It would look far stranger for me *not* to invite my friends to celebrate my wedding. Yes, they will be curious about you, but you are not a notorious criminal mastermind liable to be exposed and hounded. Are you?"

A reluctant smile touched my lips. "I can safely say I am not."

"Very well, then." His hand gave mine a reassuring squeeze and then, to my relief, withdrew. "We have our story, and it is a good story. Any minor eccentricities or lapses will be easily chalked up to your many years among the uncivilized Americans. There shall be few enough lapses, in any case, as you bear yourself with great dignity and poise."

The compliment was kindly meant, but it was scarcely reassuring.

"Moreover," he continued, "I've observed that when you are ill at ease your speech and manner tend to become more composed and formal. Such dignified reserve is a most suitable default."

Rising to part, he reached for my hand to kiss, and I reluctantly surrendered it to him. "I'll do all in my power to put you at your ease," he promised. "Please believe that I'd not put you to such a test if I didn't believe you are more than equal to it."

Even though I knew the coming days would most likely be taxing ones, after Atticus left me I was too restless to think of sleep. Instead, I prowled around the sitting room, picking up books and setting them down again, going over in my mind all the things that I would need to remember. I finally realized I needed to find some way of soothing my nerves or I would not sleep at all, so I set about making alterations in one of my new gowns, whose imprecise fit betrayed its hasty creation.

Ripping out the seams was quiet work, and even when I moved to the sewing machine, which had been placed in my bedroom as requested, I thought that the noise would not carry far enough to be heard. However, in an interval when I had finished a seam and took my foot from the treadle, I heard a knock at the dressing-room door. "Clara?" came Atticus's muffled voice. "May I come in?"

"Just a moment," I called, starting from behind the machine to fetch a peignoir, but the door opened at once, and I hastily sat back down, hoping the machine would screen me from his view. "Did the noise of the machine wake you?" I asked. "I didn't mean to disturb your rest."

"Don't distress yourself; I hadn't retired yet." Sure enough, he was still dressed except for his suit coat. He came to within a few yards of where I sat, and leaned against the bedpost with his hands in his trouser pockets. "When I heard your machine I was merely concerned for you. I hadn't realized just how much I was demanding of you, and at such short notice. I didn't know if you were trying to run up new hangings for the parlor."

"I knew I wouldn't be able to sleep," I confessed. "I keep thinking about all the preparations still to be seen to, and all the new faces and names I'll need to learn, and then I remembered that the bodice of my violet day dress doesn't sit correctly, and I determined that *that,* at least, was one problem I could solve." I was talking too much, and I tried to halt my nervous prattle. "Anyway," I finished, "sewing soothes me."

"That's fortunate. A much more respectable panacea than, say, brandy."

"Are you teasing me?"

"A little, perhaps." He was silent for a moment, and then in the most deferential of voices he asked, "Is it customary, may one ask, to sew in one's underclothes?"

So much for my foolish hope that he might overlook my state of undress. "Not customary, as far as I know," I said, my face aflame. I fixed my eyes on my work so that I would not have to meet his gaze. "It simply makes fitting so much easier."

"Ah, I think I see. You aren't forced to dress and undress each time you wish to try the thing on."

"Exactly." Thank heaven he was being so accepting of it instead of making me feel even more self-conscious.

"A bit chilly, though, surely?"

Perhaps I had rejoiced too soon. "Sewing can be warm work," I said. Working in a state of undress had never been a problem before because I had always locked the door when I sewed at the theater, but I had been perfectly capable of locking this door as well, had I remembered to. To this point, though, Atticus had never used that means of passing between our rooms, so I had not formed a habit of locking the connecting doors.

I had reached the point of needing to mark the new placement of the darts. I slipped my arms into the sleeves of the bodice and caught up the pincushion as I left the machine and walked over to the full-length mirror. Insufficiently clad as I was, every step I took under his eye was burdened with self-consciousness, but I was determined not to show embarrassment. At least when I was busy pinning the bodice closed I did not have to look at his expression.

"I don't pretend to any expertise in women's fashions, but it seems rather an odd-looking dress," he said. "Why does it have all those raw edges?"

"It's inside out," I said, turning to stare at him, only to find him trying to hide a smile. Ridiculous man. I couldn't help laughing. "I ought to have told you that inside-out gowns are the latest trend," I said, tugging the bodice smooth. "Would you fetch me that piece of chalk?"

He brought the chalk to me but remained there at my side, watching my activities in the mirror. "You could start a new fashion. In fact, I dare you to." His grin was mischievous. "Go waltzing in to dinner next week wearing a dress that's all over raveled edges and loose threads."

"Oh, I surely will." With the chalk I began to mark where I would take in the darts. "While I'm about it, perhaps I'll raise hemlines. All the more convenient for dancing."

"An excellent thought. You'll make fancy stockings all the rage. And I think you should add big fringed epaulets, here." He stepped behind me and placed his hands on my shoulders in imitation of epaulets that looked poised for flight. I found that I was smiling. "And a great cheesecloth sash about your waist—good lord, what a small waist you have. I could practically span it with my two hands." His hands settled snugly around my waist, testing his theory, and in the mirror I saw him purse his lips in a silent whistle. "Never mind the cheesecloth. You can wear one of my collars as a belt."

"Such flattery," I scoffed, but with him standing so close behind me, clasping my waist in his hands, I felt warmed by his laughter and high spirits—a more than physical warmth, a buoyancy and euphoria I had not felt in years. When he caught my eye in the mirror, his roguish grin and the devilry in his blue eyes were Richard's—and then memory returned, and I gave a painful gasp as the illusion vanished. It was only Atticus that I bantered with, and Richard was stolen from me once again.

At my gasp and the sudden change in my face, I saw his expression go from laughter to something almost desolate, and his hands tightened convulsively around my waist. "Don't see him," he rasped in a voice I scarcely recognized. "See *me*."

Tearing his hands from around my waist, I plunged across the room to belatedly snatch up a dressing gown and wrap it around myself so that I would not feel so naked. "Why are you determined to blot him out of my memory?" I demanded, and it shamed me that my voice was not quite steady.

"Clara, that's unfair." His voice was still raw, and I averted my eyes so that I would not have to look again on the desolation in his face. My own face probably mirrored that expression. "I only ask that you see me for myself, not as the constant reminder of your broken heart. It hurts me that you've been through such pain, but what Richard did I am blameless of."

"What Richard did? What are you talking about? You know he bore none of the fault." It was all Gravesend—and the Blackwoods.

His voice was gaining strength and energy. "He wasn't worthy of you. You didn't know him as I did—"

"And you did not know him as I did. You have no idea how loving and tender he could . . ." I shut my eyes and took a deep breath, trying to quell the fierce regret that rushed so chokingly to my throat. I spoke again only when I could summon a calmer voice. "Atticus, perhaps this is a good time to tell you that I think we're a great deal more demonstrative than necessary. I'd be more at ease if we could decrease our—our displays of physical affection."

"Oh?" he said shortly. "Why is that?"

"They make me uncomfortable. I know we are striving for verisimilitude, but most married couples in your class comport themselves with more restraint, don't they? I don't think we need engage in quite so much . . . well . . . touching and the like."

His brows were no longer drawn down quite so far with anger, but I could tell that my words were not welcome. "Hm," he said. "I've seen a number of married couples who are a great deal more demonstrative than we are—especially those but newly married."

"You know better than I, of course, but it does not strike me as implausible for a new bride to be shy." Shyness was not at all what I felt, but the outward appearance would be much the same—and outward appearance was all that I had contracted to provide.

"As for being plausible," he continued in an even voice, "I am an affectionate man, and it comes naturally for me to engage in such displays, as you call them."

Especially, I thought, if in his eyes I represented his victory over Richard. If I stood for all that Richard had had that Atlas had not, it was perhaps natural for him to be inclined to gloat a bit over his prize, over having defeated his dead brother by claiming me. But his possessive gestures made me feel as if I had lost Richard all over again—or, worse, as if I were being faithless to him.

"Your face has changed," he said, and his voice was gentler. "Clara, I didn't mean to frighten or distress you. I assure you I won't violate the terms of our agreement. I'll not try to seduce you."

This was so far from my thoughts that I must have stared at him as if he had begun speaking Chinese. And this, too, he misinterpreted.

"I realize it may be difficult to believe that, considering my behavior just now . . . but the last thing I wish is to make you regret our arrangement. It's true that I got a bit carried away, and I'll guard against that in the future." He seemed to have difficulty framing the next words. "In our special circumstances, I believe honesty between us is vital. So it's only fair to tell you that I find you a beautiful and stimulating companion. But I promise I won't let that—"

"Please stop," I commanded, withdrawing to the far door. "I—I think that knowing of your brother's feelings for me may be swaying your judgment," I added desperately, as he moved toward me with one hand extended in conciliation.

That stopped him as abruptly as if he had walked into a wall. "You believe," he said at length, "that I only hold you of value because Richard did?"

"I oughtn't to have said anything." It had been a mistake to broach this topic, at least in the present circumstances. Desperate now for him to leave, I pleaded, "Take no notice of what I said; our arrangement is perfectly fine."

"Clearly it isn't," he said, his eyes going to the agitated clenching of my hands. "I can only apologize, Clara. I have too much respect for you to look upon you as some fortress that must be conquered because—" He stopped and turned abruptly away, and for a moment the only sound in the room was the snapping of the fire on the hearth. He braced an arm on the mantelpiece and seemed to be staring into the flames. At last, without turning his head, he said in a different voice, "Does it make you think of him when I touch you?"

"Yes," I whispered. My mouth was too dry for me to speak more clearly. "You remind me so much of him sometimes, and . . . it's very painful."

The words were so feeble compared to what I felt, but he seemed to recognize the emotion behind them. He straightened and moved toward me once again, and I swallowed hard to try to keep my composure. I would not let him see tears.

"I'm very sorry," he said, his eyes dwelling on mine with so much understanding that I believed him. "I can't, of course, refrain entirely from touching you during the course of our time together. It would look strange indeed for a husband never to offer his arm to his wife or take her hand. But I'll try to be more respectful of your degree of comfort." A faint smile did not quite reach his eyes. "I shall have to convey my high regard for you in a less corporeal fashion."

His regard for me? "Atticus, no. Please don't think of me as anything more than a—a partner in a business arrangement. It would be disastrous to feel anything more. You know what happened to your brother. The curse would—"

Abruptly he wheeled away from me and aimed a kick at the corner of the sewing table that came near to upsetting it. "That damned curse," he swore softly. Then he seemed to regain his composure. The face he turned to me was white, and his eyes were full of sadness, but he was calm once more.

"You're right," he said. "Neither of us can afford to learn to care for each other. I don't want to fall in love with you, any more than I want you to fall in love with me. Because we both know that if that happens, Gravesend will find some way to destroy us."

Before I could reply—even had I known what to say—he strode out the way he had come, shutting the dressing-room door with a resounding bang. I heard the other door similarly emphatically shut, and then all was silent.

CHAPTER TEN

The following days were a bewildering blur of activity. Mrs. Threll was in charge, of course, and I quickly became grateful for her expertise and efficiency as she directed the disposition of the guests to their different rooms. Most of the guests were known to her and the rest of the household from previous stays, so their likes and dislikes, their peculiarities and aversions, were already planned for: everything from the two extra hot-water bottles for Sir Faneran to the arrangement of tea roses and violets from the hothouse in Lady Stanley's room. I suspected that it was the lady of the house's role to learn these individual quirks and provide for them, and I was relieved to have this responsibility lifted from my shoulders. If I was going to be the mistress of Gravesend in more than name—and for more than the immediate future—I would have my work cut out for me. Fortunately for me, if not for Lord Telford, my role would surely be short-lived.

The old baron and I developed an interestingly barbed friendliness. He seemed to like it when I challenged him, and from time to time he acted almost fond of me. At these times, especially when I saw his frustration at his own physical weakness, I found myself saddened by the recollection that his prognosis was so poor. But at other times there was something disturbing about him: he would speak with relish about the deaths of those whose masks ornamented his room, seeming to delight in distressing me. I would glance over at the curio cabinet awaiting my own mask and repress a shudder, and when the visit was over I would emerge from his room with a rush of gladness at being released.

Whenever the Gravesend masquerade wore on me—whenever Mrs. Threll's dry tones made me flush in embarrassment, or the baron made a stinging reference to my social aspirations, or the intimidating grandeur of the rooms reminded me how unworthy an upstart I was—I let myself daydream about the place where I would lead my independent life after my bargain was fulfilled. It would be nice to get away from the city, I decided, but village life would bring too much scrutiny and gossip. Perhaps a smaller city than London, though; perhaps I would indeed settle in America, where there would be so many people of different origins that no one would question my past or my means. The glimpses of American cities I had caught during Sybil Ingram's tour there had been comparatively rough and short in creature comforts, but society seemed more fluid, more accepting. I might find some occupation there, some charitable work, even. The comforting knowledge that I would not have to worry about money ever again was a refuge I sought when my present strange existence fretted my nerves or plagued me with uncertainties.

When the house party arrived, however, life at Gravesend instantly became so busy that I had no time for such retreats into fantasy.

There were twenty of us to dinner on the first night, which was my first social event as Gravesend's new mistress. Lord Telford was of course not well enough to attend, so Atticus took his seat at the foot of the table, and I was at the head . . . uncomfortably far away, I felt, for I would not be able to confer with him in moments of uncertainty. I had walked the length of the table that afternoon, reading the place cards, as Mrs. Threll went through the motions of conferring with me about the seating—in actuality schooling me on the different guests and the principles of arranging them. I wondered how long it had taken the late Lady Telford to learn these matters; but then, she had been born into this world, had probably grown up being trained in the ways of social etiquette at her mother's knee. She would have known by instinct that the notorious rakehell should not be seated next to the restless young wife of a much older man, that the reckless baronet with a poor head for business should not be seated opposite the feckless dreamer replete with dubious schemes in need of "investors." I attended her closely, but my head was soon swimming in unfamiliar names and scraps of gossip, and I despaired of being able to find my way through this labyrinth without making mistakes.

But if my internal self was fraught by nerves and uncertainty, at least my external one would not bring embarrassment to my husband and his family. My claret-red velvet evening toilette would make its first appearance this evening, and although I was alert for any imperfection as Henriette dressed me, I could find in the mirror nothing to cause me concern. The reception bodice had the fashionable square neckline and tight three-quarter sleeves, and was trimmed in ruched satin bands of the same claret color as the velvet. A velvet apron-style swag, trimmed with a pleated satin flounce, surmounted the satin skirt and attached to a poufed overskirt, caught up with satin rosettes, that extended into a long train behind. The tiny garnets inset in the front buttons winked in the light, and I drew on white kid gloves as Henriette dressed my hair in an elaborate upswept arrangement with descending sausage curls that nestled on one shoulder. As I was giving my toilette a last examination before the mirror, a knock sounded on the dressing-room door.

"Come in," I called, and Atticus stepped into the room, wearing his black evening suit with white tie. His auburn hair was smooth and gleaming, his impeccably tailored tailcoat set off his fine broad-shouldered form admirably, and altogether he was so handsome that I felt a dart of uncertainty that I would look suitable next to him. "Will I do?" I asked.

He took a moment before answering, giving me a long look that took me in from the toes of my evening slippers to the small feathered ornament Henriette had pinned in my hair. When he smiled, I felt my shoulders relax, releasing some of my tension.

"You're magnificent," he proclaimed, and even though Henriette must not have understood the words, she seemed to understand the tone and gave a self-satisfied nod of acknowledgment, stepping back with her hands folded in front of her, like an artist receiving the critics' accolades. Atticus held out a black velvet-covered box to me. "As promised," he said. "There are many more, of course, and you must come with me another time to choose those you'd like to wear in the future, but tonight I'd like you to wear these."

My sumptuous skirts rustled as I crossed to take the jewel box from him. "Oh, Atticus," I gasped when I saw what the case contained.

"The stones are pigeon's-blood rubies," he said, as I stared. "They've been in the family for generations."

"And I'm to wear them?" The necklace was a heavy collar of pearls and rubies set in gold, with a pair of dangling earrings to match. Each stone was as big as my thumbnail, and in the light of the lamp they glowed with a splendid fire against the black velvet interior of the box. I had never been so close to anything this valuable in my life, and it occurred to me that I would be taking on a great responsibility by wearing something so precious.

"By tradition, these are worn by every Blackwood bride on the night when she makes her first social appearance after her marriage."

I had extended one tentative finger toward the jewels, to assure myself that they had actual substance and were not some gorgeous mirage, but at these words I drew my hand back and met his eyes in consternation. Even though I was almost certain that Henriette would not understand me, I lowered my voice to a whisper. "Are you certain it's right for me to wear these? I'm not a Blackwood bride in the true sense."

"But you are as far as the world knows," he said easily, unruf-fled by my protest. "Those familiar with the tradition of the jewels—and you may be certain that some of our older guests are aware of it—will find it strange if you don't wear them. They are part of your persona."

Although I ought to have been reassured, I found that my uncertainty about wearing the jewels had merely changed rather than vanishing. If he was correct, although none of the guests might raise an eyebrow at my wearing the jewels, I still somehow felt that I was transgressing against their real mean-ing. But if Atticus felt that it was right for me to wear them, I had no grounds for protesting.

Still, as Henriette fastened the heavy jeweled collar around my throat, while I carefully held my ringlets out of the way, I felt some sadness settle onto my frame with the weight of the necklace. It seemed a pity for something so beautiful to adorn a woman who was only pretending to the position they were meant to ornament. Surely they—and Atticus—deserved a proper Blackwood bride, someone who really would make her home with this family, would devote herself to her husband's happiness . . . and find happiness of her own in him.

But, I reflected as I screwed the earrings onto my earlobes, it was not as if I were usurping the place of such a bride. Had Atti-cus found such a woman, he would have married her. I was not preventing him from marrying his ideal bride; I was just filling the space that would otherwise have remained unfilled.

And there had probably been previous Blackwood brides who had filled that role with less than complete devotion and enthusiasm. Arranged marriages would have set this collar around the throats of women who had no greater claim on the Blackwood name than I. I found this thought strangely sadden-ing, and sighed.

Atticus, misinterpreting, said in satisfaction, "I am delighted that you are so pleased with them. Come, we must show our-selves to Father in all our finery before we descend to our guests."

"We must?"

"Of course! He'll want to see the jewels on his daughter-in-law." He offered me his arm, and I took it, telling Henriette *"Merci, bonne nuit"* as we passed from the room.

I had never before seen Lord Telford's sitting room by night, and when we reached it I found that, curiously, it was sparingly lit with only a few isolated candles instead of the branched candelabra or oil lamps. It created an unsettling effect: in the dim, flickering light the death masks on the walls seemed to move and become animated, making grotesque expressions, and I averted my eyes from them.

"Too much light is tiring for my old eyes," Lord Telford explained. He was in a soft-front shirt and smoking jacket, and clearly was not planning to join the company or receive guests. His red lap robe was the most festive part of his appearance— that and his eyes, which held a glitter that might have been either enthusiasm or mischief. Or perhaps both. "When you're as old as I am, you appreciate the tact of dim lighting," he added. "But Clara will understand, I'm sure. Women always know what flatters them best. In this dimness you look almost young."

The barb did not sting, however. "Thank you," I said with a straight face. "I am happy to know that the darkness softens my defects."

"Ha. Defects of appearance, maybe. Not so with those of character."

"Don't the rubies look beautiful on Clara?" Atticus interposed, before we could become embroiled in the sparring session his father seemed to wish to launch.

"Hmph." The old man may have been put out by this blocking tactic, or perhaps he was vexed that he could not join the festivities that would be taking place. At any rate, it did not sound like a compliment when he said, "I never thought to see the Blackwood collar gracing a neck such as yours, daughter-in-law."

"Your surprise can hardly exceed mine," I said gravely.

He shook his head. "Ah, clever Clara. So quick with an answer to a feeble old man. You'll find the wits among your guests tonight more difficult to keep up with, I'll warrant. But no doubt you feel yourself more than equal to the task of entertaining all of the most important people from three counties. Or perhaps you expect them to be so dazzled by your appearance that they'll disregard your conversational limitations." He chuckled at my discomfiture. "Ah, she blushes—and now the picture is complete. Red gown, red jewels, red cheeks."

"Father, I'm afraid you'll have to continue teasing my wife another time," said Atticus lightly. "We are expected downstairs, and despite your attempts to frighten her, Clara is going to be a marvelous hostess."

"As if you cared. As long as it took you to snare a bride, I daresay a broom in a ball gown would make you happy."

"If that's the case, then you can imagine what a lovely surprise Clara will be to our guests," Atticus returned. He seemed to have no difficulty remaining calm during his father's baiting; years of practice must have inured him to this treatment, and I felt a stab of sympathy for the young Atticus, who had been subjected to such barbs from both his brother and his father. Now he merely said, taking my arm, "We must go down to dinner now."

"One moment, one moment." The old man's grin was grotesque as the firelight glistened wetly on his teeth. "Our Clara's pretty blush reminds me: I have not seen you kiss your fair bride, Atticus."

"I hardly think—"

"Humor a sentimental old man. The happiness of the young—well, shall we say, the *almost* young—is a beautiful thing. I should like to witness a loving conjugal embrace once more."

The prospect was uncomfortable in so many ways I hardly knew how to reply. "Lord Telford," I began, "I'm sure you'll understand that to request to see such an intimate exchange—"

"Good God, woman, I've not asked you to strip naked. A kiss is nothing. Why, you kissed *me* on only the second time we met." That had been at his command, which he did not acknowledge. "If you refuse to grant your own father-in-law so minor a request—"

"Please don't agitate yourself, Father, you know it isn't good for you." Atticus sought my eyes with his, and there was a mute appeal in them. He would have saved me this embarrassment had circumstances been different, I knew, but if his father worked himself into a state of rage, it could damage his already fragile health still further.

It isn't such a great thing to ask, I told myself, and managed to smile assent. How long had it been since I had been kissed?

There had been a time or two since Richard . . . some of the men in the theatrical troupe had possessed more audacity than discretion, and during opening-night festivities occasional liberties were taken. But the real, true lovers' kisses had all been Richard . . . and it was of him I thought when Atticus drew me to him and bent his head to kiss my lips.

I started at the intimacy of that touch, but in the next moment I was back again on that last afternoon with Richard in the folly, feeling the warmth of the sun on my skin and the different, more tantalizing warmth of Richard's lips on mine. Grassy ground was beneath my back, or else I might have fallen ceaselessly, so gloriously adrift my body felt. I felt his hands alight on my shoulders, so gently that they might have been birds, and to assure myself of his nearness I rested my hands on his chest, feeling his heartbeat there, vital and alive. Alive.

My eyes opened of their own accord, and the kiss was over. I found myself staring into ice-blue eyes that I knew as well as my own, yet for a moment I was not certain to whom they belonged. *Richard . . .*

I blinked as if it would clear my head, and Atticus must have seen that I needed to compose myself. "I hope that sufficed, Father," he said with a heartiness that I knew was false.

"Very pretty," was the reply, and Lord Telford's voice could not be read. "Go on with you, now. Don't keep your guests waiting."

"Always happy to see you as well, Father." Atticus squeezed the frail shoulder in parting, and then we had made our escape.

"I'm sorry about that," he said presently, after we had walked some distance in silence. "Father gets these strange whims, and the doctors say it's dangerous to thwart him. I wouldn't have subjected you to that otherwise, knowing your feelings."

"You needn't apologize," I said, in a voice so composed that I scarcely believed it my own. "It wasn't of your doing, and anyway . . ."

"Yes?" Interest seemed to sharpen his voice, and I tried to shrug the subject away.

"It's nothing. I was reminded of a time in my girlhood, that's all." *And for just one lovely moment, I was with Richard again.*

CHAPTER ELEVEN

Dinner, I think I may say without exaggeration, was a success.

The guests seemed so delighted to be there that my inevitable social gaffes were brushed off as of no consequence. I did forget the name of one gentleman, but he laughed it off without seeming to take offense. Atticus was an affable host, quick to turn the conversation to topics that allowed our guests to speak a great deal of themselves, and as a consequence they seemed to find my husband the most clever of conversationalists. I tried to follow his lead and found that drawing out our guests was interesting for its own sake. The more I listened and observed, the more I realized that Atticus was well liked among his peers, and they kindly extended that feeling to me.

I remembered of old the place settings—hadn't I polished those very oyster forks and asparagus knives myself all those years ago?—so I was confident at least that I would not commit the gaucherie of using the wrong implement for a particular course. As a girl I had secretly watched the family and guests on grand occasions such as these, and it was a novelty to be seated at the table, to be offered each exquisitely presented course from the gloved hands of a footman, to be gazing at my tablemates across a beautiful vista of cut crystal goblets and elaborate flower arrangements, whose perfume mingled with the savory scent of each course and the cologne water worn by those around me to create a unique and festive fragrance.

Only one discordant note did I observe during dinner. While amiable old Lord Cavendish was regaling us all with the story of how his best saddle ended up at the bottom of the trout pond, I noticed Birch, the butler, gliding silently up to my husband's chair at the foot of the table. He stooped to speak into Atticus's ear, even holding up one gloved hand to prevent being overheard.

Atticus's face grew still, and then into a frown, as he listened. He looked not disappointed or distressed, but startled. But as I watched, his brows lowered, and his lips compressed just slightly. Whatever Birch was telling him was making him angrier than I had yet seen him.

When Birch had said his tale, Atticus spoke to him in a low voice, but from my place at the head of the table I could not make out the words. Then he noticed me watching him and flashed me a quick smile meant to be reassuring. I raised my eyebrows in a question, but he shook his head as if to say, *It is of no consequence.* So, like the good wife I was trying to imitate, I turned my attention back to my guests.

Conversation was livelier after dinner when I had led the female portion of the party into the parlor so that the men might enjoy their brandy and cigars. Freed of the constraints of mixed company, the women regaled each other with tastier morsels of conversation than had been possible at table.

"I hear that Lord Finney's mistress has a fine new carriage," one matron disclosed. "Specially painted to match her favorite dog's coat, if you please!"

"I hope her dog isn't a Dalmatian," murmured a stout widow, and received a titter of appreciation. "It seems to me, though, that we may not wish to disillusion our dear hostess when she is so newly married."

"Mrs. Blackwood will learn all too quickly what common clay men are formed from," said the first matron.

"Indeed, I know they are not angels," I said. "But no more am I." They seemed to expect me to continue, so I improvised, "I like to think that my husband and I are very well situated for a happy marriage, both of us being past our first youth and, I hope, possessed of a bit more wisdom than most newly wedded couples."

"A very sensible attitude," the widow said approvingly. "I'm certain you'll be equally sensible about the new addition to your household."

It took me a moment to recollect. "Oh, my husband's ward? I know very little about her, I'm afraid."

A speaking look passed between some of my guests, and the elegant wife of a marquess said, "I'm not surprised to hear that. Sometimes men have a difficult time explaining the presence of their . . . wards."

The pause was evidently intended to be fraught with meaning, but that meaning was lost on me. "I'm afraid I don't understand what you mean," I said. "Is there something about"—I flailed for a moment before the name came to me—"about Miss Rowe that Atticus isn't telling me?"

"Oh, dear, what a ghastly blunder I've made. I should never have said a thing." She didn't look at all perturbed, however, and continued to move her fan lazily in the air near her face.

"What Lady Renfrew is reluctant to tell you," interposed the widow, Lady Stanley, "is that sometimes gentlemen hide their natural children in plain sight, calling them wards. It is not uncommon."

For a moment I must have looked completely foolish, gaping at her. All other conversation in the room had ceased, and I was painfully aware that every single woman in the room was watching me intently, waiting for my reaction.

"My husband," I said carefully, "is a man of principle."

"None of us has suggested otherwise," said Lady Stanley. "In its way, it *is* principled for a gentleman to take responsibility for the fruits of his wild oats." She stopped and frowned. "I daresay that's a mixed metaphor, but you take my meaning."

My husband was being accused of siring an illegitimate child, and she was trifling over grammar? Before I could take her up, the young Mrs. Morse interposed. "Helene, I'd scarcely call it honorable of a man to force his lawful wife to accept his by-blow into the household and countenance her presence! No wife deserves such humiliation."

I set my teacup aside. It was past time to put a stop to this. "Ladies, as much as I appreciate your concern, I'm certain that my husband would never introduce anyone into our home under false pretenses. He and I have no secrets from each other." It sounded well, but the truth of this pretty sentiment I could not pause to scrutinize. "Whatever Miss Rowe's origin, my husband would never bring her to Gravesend if he did not think it best for all of us."

There was a strained silence. Then, fortunately for my rapidly crumbling composure, at that moment the door was opened and the gentlemen swarmed in. A cheerful hubbub filled the room, and the awkward, silent watchfulness was swept away in inconsequential chatter.

Atticus detached himself from the throng and joined me. "You look a trifle strained," he said in a low voice. "Is everything well?"

"Well enough. There is a great deal of curiosity about your ward."

No start of guilt greeted these words. Rather, the beginning of a smile tugged at his lips. "I shouldn't wonder," he said. "A beautiful young woman of mysterious origins and no visible attachments is a bit of a curiosity in any setting, but especially when she carries the taint of that most disreputable race—the French." He widened his eyes in mock horror, and I could not help laughing. The ladies' insinuations had almost made me doubt Atticus, but speaking to him made those doubts dissolve like sugar in hot tea.

"Perhaps that is the source of their fascination," I said. "I've no doubt that if she arrives with a trunk full of the newest dresses, they shall find it remarkably easy to overcome their suspicions and visit us at every opportunity . . . in company with their modistes."

That was the last wrinkle in the evening. By the time the guests had at last dispersed to their rooms, except for a small party of gentlemen who had sequestered themselves in the billiard room with a decanter of the best brandy, the tiny spots of awkwardness seemed to have been subsumed into "a marvelously successful dinner," as Atticus said when we stood at my door.

"I am glad you're pleased." I was almost dropping with weariness, so high a degree of concentration the evening had demanded, but I found enough energy to smile at him. Then I remembered that strange interruption in dinner. "What was that business with Birch? Was something amiss?"

He hesitated a moment. "Nothing that need concern you. Birch took care of him—of it, I should say."

I folded my arms and gave him a narrow look. "Your concerns are my concerns, Atticus. Is there anything wrong?"

"Oh, it was just that fellow again, Collier. He somehow got himself hired on as extra staff for tonight and used that as a means of getting inside the house." Seeing my expression, he added quickly, "I'm sure his intentions weren't violent. But he had found his way to the upper floors before he was discovered and seized."

"What did he want?"

He shrugged, but the gesture was not as offhand as he had intended it; there was a remnant of tension in his posture. "I suspect he got wind of the news that Genevieve will be arriving soon. He's determined to insert himself into her life again."

"Again?" I repeated, at a loss.

"I must not have mentioned it. Collier and his wife fostered Genevieve until I took her into my care."

It perplexed me that he had omitted to mention something so significant until now. "So why does he resort to such subterfuge, when for all he knows she may be delighted to see him?"

Again the hesitation. "I'm afraid he has a kind of monomania where Genevieve is concerned. He has found the means to send letters to her at her school, and he's managed to frighten her. I don't think she's eager to be reunited with him."

"Then what does he believe such a reunion will achieve?"

He rubbed his hand along his jaw, and I realized that he must be as weary as I—wearier, for I saw that he was putting his weight on his cane—and my conscience smote me. "Never mind," I said before he could speak. "This can wait. As long as the house is secure from Collier from now on . . . ?" At his nod of confirmation, I said firmly, "We can discuss the matter tomorrow and decide then whether we need to take any more stringent measures to protect our guests from further incursions from the man."

He smiled down at me, and the candlelight from the wall bracket found endearing little crinkles at the corners of his eyes. "Spoken like a born Blackwood," he said. "Clara, I hope you don't mind if I say that I'm proud of you. You were splendid tonight—you've been splendid from the moment you arrived here. You've dealt gracefully with my father's caprices and malice, you've taken upon yourself the running of an entire household, you've triumphantly hosted your first massive social event, and you've kept your temper with me, despite all my shortcomings. I admire you for it, and I thank you."

Flustered, I groped for words. "As to the dinner, you're too generous—the gown and jewels did my work for me. You dressed me like an empress; all I had to do was avoid scratching myself or picking up my plate to lick it clean, and I'd have looked the part."

"Looked the part, perhaps," he said gently. "But not inhabited the person of my wife."

My wife. By now I was accustomed to his calling me that . . . or at least I had thought I was. Somehow, said just now, while I stood with Atticus in this still silent hallway with the rest of the household fast asleep or many rooms distant, the intimacy of it made my breath catch. My mind flew back to his father's sitting room a few hours ago, where we had embraced at Lord Telford's command. It seemed to me that although the gesture was born of duress, it had nonetheless brought us closer together. And the thought came to me that if Atticus had been a different sort of man, at this moment he would have kissed me again.

But I had asked him not to touch me, so touch me he did not. Instead, driven by a sudden urge I did not stop to question, I took a step toward him and brushed my lips against his cheek, feeling the faint rasp of the whiskers there and inhaling the scent of sandalwood and cedar that clung to his skin. "It was my privilege," I said.

When I closed the door behind myself, he was still standing in the hall. Perhaps he wanted to see me safely inside, an impulse possibly born from Collier's invasion; or perhaps I had startled him so severely that he had momentarily lost the power of movement.

I had startled myself nearly as much. I was not prone to these displays of affection, certainly not with Atticus. It was the impulse born of a triumphant evening, I decided, as I removed the pearl and ruby collar from my throat and laid it on the black-lacquered dressing table; it was Atticus's generous words to me that had brought a little burst of gratitude and even camaraderie.

More than that, perhaps, was the deeply embarrassing revelation that our enforced intimacy earlier in the evening had brought me. I had discovered that I liked kissing Atticus. My stupid senses had not been able to tell the difference between him and Richard, so my treacherous body had responded to Atticus as to the man I had loved. The man I still loved. And Atticus was not unattractive. He was warm, honorable, humorous . . . even lovable in his own way, if I were forced to examine him in those terms. It was no wonder that after all the emotion of the evening I had been moved to be demonstrative with him.

But as I unbuttoned my velvet bodice and stepped out of my high-heeled shoes, smothering a sigh of ecstasy as my toes were freed, a sobering reflection came to me. I *thought* Atticus was honorable, that he was honest with me. What if the ladies' insinuations had truth to them, though? Was Genevieve Rowe actually his illegitimate daughter?

It's no business of yours, I told myself. I was not going to be part of the Gravesend household for very long. Whatever Genevieve's real relationship to Atticus, it could scarcely have an impact on me once I had settled in my new home, far away from England. I tried to envision the cozy little house I would have in Boston, or New York, or Philadelphia; I had not made up my mind on the precise location. But it would be Gravesend's opposite: no army of servants working to keep it running; no Sphinx-eyed Mrs. Threll to observe every detail of my behavior; no mischievous invalid to fashion humiliations for me; and most of all, no more being a wife.

I would be able to do entirely as I pleased. No exerting myself to entertain and deceive a bewildering succession of distinguished (yet indistinguishable) visitors. No enduring the endless crimping, braiding, and pinning of my wild hair to tame it into fashionable styles; no more struggling to communicate with Henriette—who would, no doubt, be equally exhilarated to be freed from her frustrating and lonely service to me! No more tactical evening meetings with Atticus as we took tea together and discussed all the endless, endless details of our lives here under the guise of man and wife. No more sharing clandestine laughter at some near mishap or unanticipated awkwardness. No more comradely glances from the ice-blue eyes across the breakfast table . . .

I had been brushing my hair after having removed the feather ornament and all the pins, but now I set the brush down gently on the vanity and took a long look at the opal ring on my left hand. In just a short time my hand had become used to the weight of it; and when I drew it from my finger, the shape of the band was impressed into my skin, a visible reminder that lingered even after the object itself had been removed. The ring, whether I wished it or not, was becoming part of me.

A sigh escaped me, and I reached for the velvet case to put away the jeweled collar. When I sprang the catch and the lid raised, however, I found that it was not empty. A scrap of paper, evidently torn from a larger sheet, rested in the place where the necklace would lie. A few words were scrawled on it in pencil in an uneven hand.

You have no right to the name of Mrs. Blackwood. You are no true mistress of Gravesend.

CHAPTER TWELVE

After a triumphant first evening, perhaps a letdown was inevitable. Breakfast the next morning was sparsely attended; many of my guests were breaking their fast in their own rooms, and those who had gathered seemed to be coming to life slowly. My wits were dulled from a late night followed by hours of sleeplessness when my thoughts were in too great turmoil from the nasty little note. It had to have been Collier, of course. In his fixation on his foster daughter, he must wish to see her installed as the mistress of Gravesend in my place. It made no sense, since there was no blood connection to the Blackwoods . . .

Unless he had wished her to become Atticus's wife.

Of course. My hand froze with my teacup raised halfway to my mouth, and the desultory conversation of my guests rose and ebbed around me as my thoughts pursued their unhappy path. Atticus had said he had been unable to find a suitable match to marry, and Genevieve, of uncertain parentage, would have certainly fallen into the unsuitable category. But if she was as beautiful and charming as report would have it, Atticus's abiding interest in her fortunes and his determination to bring her to Cornwall were explained. He might not have been able to marry his young French beauty, but he could take her as his mistress.

I stole a glance at my husband where he sat conversing with one of the men about getting up a hunting party. I could scarcely reconcile the idea of a mistress with the man I thought I knew. His whole being, from his broad and lofty brow to the keen sympathy in his gaze, spoke of integrity. He had acted with decency—no, more, with compassion—in all his dealings with me, when he might so easily have forgotten my existence entirely after my dismissal from Gravesend.

But there again was the little sore spot that I winced away from probing too thoroughly: the very real likelihood that I was the rope in a game of tug-of-war with his dead brother. And, too, wouldn't a wife—any wife—be a great convenience if a gentleman in his situation wanted to carry on with a mistress? My presence would help to disguise the true nature of his relationship with his ward and would make it possible for them to live under the same roof without the appearance of impropriety.

The thought of being used this way, and by a man I had come to trust, turned my stomach. I pushed my chair back from the table, with the assistance of a footman who quickly stepped up to take my chair, and dropped my napkin on it.

"My dear?" Atticus had noted my abrupt motion. "Are you quite well?"

I did not know for certain that my gloomy suspicions were true. The last thing I ought to do was to reveal that I harbored them, especially before others. "My head is pounding so," I said, "I thought to take the air. Perhaps those ladies who have finished breaking their fast would like to join me; we could stroll through the grounds and visit the glasshouse."

"I should like that a great deal," announced Lady Stanley, rising also. "I fear I overindulged in your splendid dinner last night, Mrs. Blackwood, and some mild exercise would do me a world of good." None of the other ladies chose to join us, and when she tucked her hand companionably through my arm, I saw the conspiratorial look in her eye and realized, with a sinking heart, that far from subduing my ugly suspicions I had merely saddled myself with a companion eager to add to them.

Sure enough, her first words were about the painful topic. "I have been thinking about the subject of our conversation last night," she said in a low voice as we strolled across the entrance hall toward the front door. "I do hope I haven't distressed you. But I think it is best to know as much as possible about one's husband. Without a full knowledge of one's situation, one may easily be manipulated."

"I cannot believe my husband would manipulate me, as you call it." But my tone might have been firmer, and she seemed to note my lack of conviction, with a little comforting pat on my arm.

"My dear, you may be twice a bride, but I fear you are as innocent as a green girl. Marriage is in its way as much a form of strategy as chess—or war. One hopes, of course, to be on the same side as one's husband, but in any event a knowledge of the larger game is vital to securing your happiness. Have you asked Mr. Blackwood about young Miss Rowe?"

I had been too busy congratulating him, and myself, about the success of our dinner. Heat rose to my face as I recalled laughing with him, kissing his cheek. No, suspicion had not been foremost in my mind last night. "We have both been so busy—and she is not to arrive for another week—"

"Pray don't feel you have to defend yourself, my dear. It is a difficult subject to broach." A footman opened the door for us, and we emerged into the wan sunlight just as a coach drew up before the broad front stairs. Birch must have heard what I had been too preoccupied to make note of—the sound of wheels on the gravel of the drive—for he was already directing more footmen to hold the horses' heads, to place a step before the coach door—and to hand down the Titian-haired, beaming young woman who emerged from the interior in an airy agglomeration of white muslin printed with yellow butterflies.

Her eyes were blue, with long curling lashes, and her mouth was as pink as any rose. Her bright ringlets were surmounted with an absurdly tiny hat of coral faille trimmed with white ostrich feathers, and the coral grosgrain ribbon that served as her sash encircled a waist so small that my husband's collar might in fact have fastened around it, as he had once said in jest of mine.

"At last!" she cried as she picked up her gauzy, abundant skirts and darted up the stairs. "You must be my darling Uncle Atticus's bride, Clara!" Before I could respond she had seized my hands in hers and placed a kiss on each of my cheeks. There was a waft of heliotrope scent, and my dulled wits belatedly realized that her words had been tinged with the most piquant of French accents. "I should have known you anywhere," she continued, beaming at me. "He has spoken so much of you in his letters. I beg your pardon, madame," she added to Lady Stanley, and dipped into a graceful curtsey. "I forget my manners. But I have come to think of Clara—Mrs. Blackwood—as an aunt almost, and I am so delighted to meet her at last!"

Lady Stanley's eyes were as round as the very carriage wheels. Birch and the footmen could not take their eyes from the girl. I forced a smile to my lips. "My lady," I said to my companion, "allow me to introduce you to Miss Genevieve Rowe—my husband's ward."

And who knew what else besides?

It was not as if I had any grounds to be offended. If she was in fact Atticus's mistress—well, our marriage had not been a matter of affections, so Genevieve could scarcely have been said to have alienated them. Without a wife in more than name, a man as warm-hearted as Atticus would naturally seek some form of attachment. I had no grounds for objection, as long as his arrangement—if such it was—posed no danger to my future after I left Gravesend.

Why, then, did I feel the painful tightness in my breast when Atticus emerged from the breakfast room, drawn by the commotion, and opened his arms to Genevieve with such delight?

"We didn't expect you for another week," I said, trying, not entirely successfully, not to sound disapproving.

AMANDA DEWEES

"You're welcome, Vivi, of course," Atticus added, "but your room's not yet ready." This was in a muffled voice, for she was hugging him around the neck.

The girl (for so I could not help thinking of her, even if she was more properly called a young woman) kissed him on both cheeks before releasing him. "I could not bear to wait any longer. You are not angry with me?"

"As if anyone could be angry with you for long, Vivi." He took her in from the foolish little hat to the tiny slippers showing beneath the hem of her dress. "This is a fancy rig-out you're wearing. Is it new?"

"But of course! How silly of you. I told you I needed a new frock." She cast a glance at me from beneath her lashes. "After you told me that your Clara had such an eye for *les modes,* I could not appear before her in my old things."

"It's perfectly sweet," I said. "A trifle crumpled from the journey, but that can't be helped . . . let's find a room for you, and your maid can help you get settled."

"Oh, I have no maid," she announced airily.

"Clara's maid can see to you, I'm sure," said Atticus at once, and my opinion of his intelligence took a sharp drop. Perhaps he didn't realize how much effort Henriette put into my coiffures and the maintenance of my elaborate gowns. "It's perfect, really," he continued, "because Henriette will at last have someone to speak French with."

"Henriette will have twice as much work to do," I pointed out, "and more, since she will be forced to go back and forth between our rooms."

"Hmm, that's right. And I know you two will be longing to spend more time together, getting to know one another." He turned to the housekeeper, who had obligingly appeared at his elbow. "Mrs. Threll, I believe the room across from my wife's sitting room is available, isn't it?"

He was *not* going to give that room to the little—to this girl. "I'm afraid we couldn't possibly put Miss Rowe into such a poky, drab little room," I said firmly.

"Oh, I am certain it is delightful," Genevieve interposed, but I shook my head.

124

"No, it's far too small and old-fashioned. We must have something better suited, Mrs. Threll. In the east wing, perhaps?" She understood my intended meaning. "I believe the Blue Room would be quite suitable, ma'am, and it isn't in use at present."

The Blue Room was at the other end of the house from mine. "Excellent. Please have it made up. Oh, and can any of the maids be spared to look after Miss Rowe? She has brought no abigail."

Mrs. Threll left just enough of a pause to register disapproval. "I shall see to it at once, ma'am."

Our pretty guest's face was falling more each second. "I am truly sorry if I am causing you inconvenience," she said, and so injured were the wide blue eyes that my heart might have softened toward her if I had let it. But Atticus was quick to cushion the blow, I observed.

"Nonsense, Vivi, we're just a bit at sixes and sevens this morning. We're delighted to have you with us. Aren't we, Clara?"

I smiled with as much grace as I could muster. "Delighted," I said, and to my shock the girl flew at me and kissed my cheek again.

"I knew you would not scold me," she confided. "Uncle Atticus has told me all about you, Aunt Clara—may I call you that? He told me that you have such dignity, such grace even when all about you is in turmoil. He said he knew that we should love each other. And I know already that we shall be inseparable!"

I turned my head to look at Atticus, and my expression must have been terrible indeed, for his face reddened slightly and he cleared his throat.

"Genevieve, why don't you and I go for a stroll while Mrs. Threll has your room readied. I believe that being cooped up in that coach has made you a bit restless."

She found the suggestion delightful, of course. Her "Uncle Atticus" could no doubt have suggested that her Titian ringlets be singed off with burning pincers and she would have thought it the most adorable idea ever conceived by mortal man.

"A charming young woman," came a murmur in my ear, and I found that Lady Stanley was at my elbow once more. She was watching Atticus and Genevieve proceed to the front door,

Genevieve half dancing in excitement and casting eager looks all about her, exclaiming Frenchly to Atticus about how *merveilleuse* Gravesend was. "Very vivacious," she added.

"A delightful creature," I said. "I can see why my husband is so fond of her."

"As can I," she said under her breath.

As soon as I could, I excused myself and retreated to my rooms. I was determined to remain there until such time as I could look upon the adorable Miss Rowe without desiring to shake her until her teeth rattled. And if that time was years off? In my present mood, that suited me quite well.

It was not jealousy, of course. There was certainly some *envy*, if only for the girl's extreme youth and beauty, and the security of having a protector like Atticus Blackwood to smooth her way in the world, to make her feel loved and wanted. Obscure parentage notwithstanding, Genevieve looked as if she would never know want or loneliness, and Atticus was to be commended for that. How different her life might have been without his generosity and compassion—the same impulses that lay behind his sanctuaries for castoff women and their children. He was acting as defender to those who had none other, and I ought to have been moved, even proud to the extent that I, as his wife in the world's eyes, was connected to such a person.

Instead I was out of sorts, and disgusted with myself for being so, which merely worsened the feeling. It was absurd for me to feel displaced, for my place was entirely ornamental. It was fruitless to feel overshadowed, for I had no delusions of beauty or social brilliance to be set into stark contrast by this youngling's charm and loveliness. On the contrary, I should have welcomed the relief her presence would bring from the guests' scrutiny of me. The more absorbed they were in Genevieve, the less notice they would take of my mistakes and awkward moments. I ought to have been grateful to her, and to Atticus for introducing her into the household.

That was the sticking point, I decided. We had been well on our way to establishing a kind of family, settling into a comfortable habit with regard to each other as I began to feel that I had a role to play at Gravesend, and the girl's arrival had upset the tentative harmony of that arrangement. I no longer knew where

I stood in Atticus's plan. Was I to be a kind of stepmother? Or if the girl truly was his mistress, was I to stand to one side because my own place gave me no right to object? The uncertainty made me snappish, and I pleaded my supposed headache at noontime so that I would not inflict my mood on my guests at the midday meal . . . although I was certain that my pretext deceived none of them. They would no doubt have a satisfying gossip while I temporarily abandoned my duties as hostess.

But I was not the only one to resist the new domestic arrangement, as I learned later. Having returned from their walk, Atticus and his ward had discovered that Lord Telford refused to meet Genevieve.

"He says he's not equal to the strain of visitors at the moment," Atticus told me crisply as we made our way to the drawing room to await the dinner gong that evening. "It's ridiculous. Vivi isn't a visitor—she's family."

"They have not met before, then?" I asked, to hide my shock at hearing the girl thus described.

"No, Father always refused to join me when I went to visit her at school." Atticus's expressive eyes were troubled, and I wondered with a pang whether he would have worried thus if I had been the one his father refused to welcome. "I don't know how to break this to her," he said. "I won't have her feelings hurt."

"Your father's fragile state of health is not in doubt," I observed. "*You* may see his refusal to meet her as a deliberate snub, but on the surface it's perfectly plausible. Are you so certain he's avoiding her?"

His lips tightened, and he gave a single sharp nod. "He's never approved of my taking her into my care, even though she is so . . . closely connected to the household."

"Connected in what way?" is what I wanted to ask, but I wasn't certain I would like the answer. If the girl was indeed Atticus's illegitimate daughter, his father might well be angry at the idea of accepting her into the household. As would I, for that matter. To have my husband's child by another woman so close at hand would be a constant reminder that I was not the only woman in his life—indeed, it would be as good as an announcement to those around us.

The girl herself appeared then, darting out of the drawing room in a robin's-egg blue dinner gown whose tulle overskirt was caught up with garlands of pink silk roses. It was an absurdly extravagant dress for a girl who was not yet out. In contrast, I felt very elderly indeed in my midnight blue cashmere trimmed in cerise passementerie, which just minutes before had made me feel quite elegant and grand.

"I thought I heard your voices!" she exclaimed, and danced up to link her arm through her guardian's free one. "Now you have a belle on each arm," she informed him, and instantly began chattering to him in French. I realized to my discomfiture that Atticus must understand her. Of course he would speak French; he probably spoke several languages. They could converse on any number of subjects and I would be none the wiser.

Atticus's appreciative chuckle caught my attention. He was watching the girl with an indulgent smile. I could not recall whether he had ever looked at me with such an expression.

But why should he? I was no soul mate to him, nor had he ever promised that I would be. Somehow it had not stung as much before, though. It seemed to me now as if his primary object had been to bring Genevieve to Gravesend and I was merely a necessary part of that plan, even though I didn't wholly understand what part that was.

I was absorbed in these and similarly cheering thoughts. Atticus and Genevieve were absorbed in what, to judge by their faces, was the most fascinating conversation since Dr. Johnson's day. And so the three of us proceeded into the drawing room: the handsome heir, the beautiful young ward, and the convenient fiction.

CHAPTER THIRTEEN

"How long will Genevieve be with us?" I asked Atticus that night when we met for our nightly council meeting. "You mentioned bringing her out this Season."

A questioning lift of one eyebrow accompanied his response. "Genevieve's home is with us," he said, "until she marries."

I stared into my teacup, hoping my face didn't reveal my dismay. "If this was your plan from the beginning, I wish you'd told me of it when you made your proposal to me."

"I didn't think it would be such an upheaval for you," he said, and though I did not look at him, I could picture his serious expression, the penetrating look in his vivid eyes, perhaps even a look of concern—for he was, after all, a considerate man. "Genevieve has never known her mother, and I knew that your own natural impulse to nurture would find an outlet where—if you'll pardon my mentioning it—it had none before."

I stirred my tea and tried to frame my response. "It isn't as if she were my own child. And Genevieve is practically grown; I don't think she needs a mother." Even if I had known how to be one, which I did not.

He did not answer at once. When I finally looked up, I met his eyes and wondered why there should be a kind of perplexed sadness there. Slowly he said, "I ought to have discussed it with you before she arrived, I see that now. But since she *is* here, and is out of her element, it would be a kindness in you to befriend her." He seemed to be choosing his words with care when he said, "And even if the two of you don't share a family name, I think you'll find that you are related in a sense."

I smiled, a little wryly. We were only related in the sense that this surprising man had taken an interest in us, out of whatever motive or motives, and had chosen to offer his protection. Beyond that, I suspected his ward and I had precious little in common.

"As to not needing a mother," he was saying, "I must disagree. Especially when the Season begins, she'll need someone she can look to for feminine wisdom and guidance."

Which I was scarcely in a position to provide. Navigating the complexities of life in society would be every bit as new to me as it would to her. "I'm not certain I have much to offer her," I said.

"Of course you do. You only feel this way because she took you by surprise. When you come to know Vivi better I know you'll adore her. I'm happy to say she is kind, intelligent, charming—in many ways she reminds me of you, in fact."

I could not repress a laugh that was as much startled as it was amused. "Of me!" Kindness and charm were not prominent in my makeup, I knew. Intelligence, too, I sometimes doubted.

"Very much so," he said, still regarding me with that peculiarly intense gaze. "I see the two of you as kindred spirits. I'm certain that when you've spent more time with her you'll come to see it yourself. Why, she could even teach you French, so that you may converse more freely with your maid."

"No doubt," I said, my pride struggling with the realization that it would be a great relief to be able to carry on a conversation with Henriette that did not leave us both frustrated at the gulf of understanding between us. I risked another glance at Atticus. His enthusiasm was touching. If he saw kindness in me, I thought, it was because he himself possessed it in such abundance. I owed it to him to make an effort, at least. Whatever his reasons for attaching her to the household, Genevieve herself had shown no signs of wishing to usurp me. I ought to give her the benefit of the doubt for as long as I could.

I rose to signal the end of our meeting. "I shall endeavor to make Genevieve welcome," I said. That was as far as I would commit myself tonight.

It seemed to be enough for Atticus, at least. He started to reach for my hand, then checked himself, no doubt remembering my fiat against contact. But such a prohibition seemed foolish now that I myself had broken it, and when I put my hand out he took it at once.

"Thank you, Clara," he said softly. "It means more than I can say that you and Genevieve become friends."

I had no answer for that. Questions I did have, but not the courage to ask them—not yet.

The next day I was still so troubled in mind that I finally made a pilgrimage I had been putting off for too long: a visit to the folly. It was, I felt, the one place where I might find a haven from the strain of the present, but I was almost afraid to put it to the test.

The wood at its back had grown up much closer to it in the time since I had last been here with Richard, but from the direction of the gardens the path was easy. When I gained the little hillock where the ruin was situated, I looked back the way I had come. From here Gravesend Hall looked so much smaller and less imposing—almost like a doll's house, and I smiled at the fancy; if only the house and its residents were as easily managed as a child's toys, and then when Lord Telford's innuendos and Mrs. Threll's watchfulness grew too much for me I could simply toss them into a box and put them away.

I was dwelling on the view because I was reluctant to let my mind dwell here, within the two fragmentary walls of the folly. Today there were no violets, and the grass was dead and leached of color; the stones of the broken walls and tower were stained with moss and lichen. The top of the tower looked uneven, as if some of the stones that made it up had loosened and fallen. The passage of time was lending the folly verisimilitude, taking it closer to the ruin it had been designed to mimic.

I could scarcely picture Richard and my younger self there. In my memory the folly had been a treasured secret haven, a little corner of paradise; now it was nothing more than a picturesque assemblage of stone and mortar. Nothing of Richard remained here. If his ghost did walk, I reflected, perhaps after all it would not be here, where he and I had been happy together; it would be on that far-away battlefield, more likely, where his life had been cut short . . . and in what circumstances of pain and anguish I could only guess. There was nothing for me here except my memories.

I looked once more across the grounds to Gravesend, the white stone walls gleaming like snow under the rare sunshine. If I was to find even a temporary place there, it behooved me to stop dwelling on the past. Atticus deserved a convincing bride, and I owed it to him to put my best effort into my masquerade. Indeed, the thought of being exposed as a fraud still held great dread for me, so for my own sake as well I ought to live in the present entirely.

What, though, was I to think when the very house itself, or some remnant of the past that had been imprinted upon it, spoke my name in Richard's voice? It had not happened since that first night, but each night after I parted from Atticus I found myself lingering on the threshold of my sitting room, half longing, half fearing to hear it again. If only I had been able to tell what it meant—whether it had spoken in yearning, or pleasure, or warning—

Enough. I could not continue thus, hoping for a sign that a dead love lived on in some fashion. I would drive myself mad that way. Much later, perhaps, when this charade was over and I was comfortably settled in my new life as an independent woman—then I could indulge in memories of Richard and dwell in them to my heart's content. But not until then.

It might not have been Richard's voice I had heard, at that. If a ghost from my past were here, might it not be my mother's? Perhaps she had spoken from beyond to remind me to be strong. *A curse is no match for women of independent spirit,* she had told me on that long-ago day. Now, with her words lending determination to my steps, I left the folly behind and strode back across the grounds toward the house where I was now mistress.

Over the next week or so I strove to keep my word to Atticus. I found that his assessment of Genevieve's character seemed to hold true: she did seem to be kind, without malice or calculation, and was charming in her enthusiasm for other people—which, strangely, extended to me. If her piquant beauty and youth and power to attract made me painfully aware of my own shortcomings, it was not her fault. When male eyes followed the girl with admiration and eagerness, she was stealing nothing from me, I reminded myself. But something—whether insecurity or consciousness of my own shortcomings, or perhaps simple envy—prevented me from opening my heart to her in any real sense.

In return for my somewhat guarded overtures, Genevieve attached herself to me as if we were already sworn friends. She seemed eager for my approval and my liking, even seemed, bafflingly, to admire me—although it did occur to me that Atticus, for what purpose I did not know, might have told her to use her charm on me. Perhaps he wished her to have another defender besides himself, for Lord Telford continued to keep to himself in his rooms and did not send to meet her.

Genevieve and I took to meeting each afternoon for a French lesson, and I had to admit that she was a patient instructor. My tardy beginning she herself explained away. "You had more important things to do than to learn another tongue," she said generously, although I did not inquire what she thought these things might have been. I had no idea what she knew of my background and did not invite discussion of it. But even though she was tactful about my ignorance, my pride smarted that I had to be taught that *"la robe"* meant "the dress" and *"le visage"* meant "the face." I think I might have warmed to Genevieve more quickly if this, too, had not been a sphere in which she was demonstrably my superior.

One afternoon when I arrived at her room for our lesson I found her quite downcast. "I am very much afraid my favorite dinner dress is ruined," she lamented. "Uncle Atticus says that you have a gentlewoman's skill with a needle, though—perhaps you can tell me if it can be rescued?"

I said I would give her my expert opinion, and she produced the sumptuous light blue dress with silk roses, which I had not seen since her first night at Gravesend. The skirt had a long tear near one seam and had been clumsily sewn together, with dark thread bunching the fabric.

"It is a nasty tear," I said. "It would have been better to have given it to your maid to mend."

"Oh, I did! This is Letty's handiwork, not mine."

That startled me, for I had never seen such poor stitching. Any of the Gravesend maids ought to have been capable of better work. "How did it come to tear?"

She puffed out a sigh. "Letty again, *hélas*. She had just finished helping me dress, and I was leaving the room when she trod upon the train. I declare she must have put her full weight upon it!"

The rip was more than a foot long. It was astonishing that such damage could have been done accidentally, particularly since Letty was a slight creature. "Is she satisfactory in other respects?"

"Oh, quite well."

Her voice left room for doubt. "What else has she done?"

"Nothing at all, truly. Only . . ."

"What is it?"

"I was not going to say anything, but the other maid, the girl who lays the fire every morning . . . I have asked her if she could possibly come earlier, for often Letty has finished dressing me before the fire has been lit."

That meant Genevieve was waking and dressing in a frigid room, when the fire ought to have been laid before she rose. "Has she begun coming earlier since you spoke to her about it?"

"No, but it is my fault. She cannot understand my accent, I think."

That was preposterous. "I'll speak to Mrs. Threll," I said. "If nothing else, she can have your dress mended more ably."

The blue eyes brightened. "Oh, that is so kind of you, Aunt Clara! I did not think of asking Mrs. Threll—I confess she frightens me a little."

I just managed to refrain from confessing that I, too, was not entirely comfortable with the housekeeper. But I held my tongue.

The damage to the dress might have been an accident, made worse by a maid who was clumsy at sewing and hesitant to reveal that shortcoming by asking for help. The fire was another matter and suggested poor scheduling on Mrs. Threll's part. But it was strange all the same. Now that I took a closer look at Genevieve's room, I could see signs of neglect. The flowers in the vase on the bureau were not fresh, and there was a faint film of dust visible on some of the elaborate picture frames.

That night at dinner, I observed other ways in which the staff seemed to be singling out Genevieve for poor treatment. At table, the footmen offering her dishes gave her insufficient time to serve herself before moving to the next person, so that her plate was sparsely filled, and one footman even managed to spill gravy on her.

I could have chalked the footmen's behavior up to carelessness. But taken with the other incidents, the little snubs formed a larger pattern. When I added them all up and recollected how poorly Genevieve's room was being kept, I knew that the staff were purposely showing her disrespect.

The next morning I summoned the housekeeper to the small salon that was my private domain. When she joined me, I bade her close the door. "Is something amiss, ma'am?" she asked in that neutral voice that gave me no window into her thoughts or feelings.

"I'm afraid so," I said. "It seems that Miss Rowe is being made to feel unwelcome at Gravesend. She does not understand that these slights are deliberate, but I believe that's exactly what they are."

Mrs. Threll continued to listen with her hands folded in front of her, the picture of patient acquiescence, but I thought her eyes had sharpened. "To what slights do you refer, ma'am?"

"I've observed the condition of Miss Rowe's room and the gown that Letty damaged and nearly ruined with her mending.

I've also seen the slapdash way she is served at dinner. I'd like you to personally see that these incidents come to an end."

Mrs. Threll inclined her head. "The footmen come under Mr. Birch's purview, ma'am. As for Letty, I grant that she is still green in some ways, but she's learning."

"Is she? I would have hoped that she would have completed her learning before being given the responsibility of seeing to Miss Rowe's needs. If Letty is unable to discharge her duties without incident, perhaps her training was inadequate. Is that the case, Mrs. Threll?"

The housekeeper's lips thinned. I had touched her pride. Still, all she said was, "I've had no other complaints about the girl, ma'am."

It seemed I would have to be firmer. "It reflects poorly on the staff as a whole that they are so discommoded by the addition of one young woman to the household," I said. "Such inefficiency will almost certainly come to be noticed by our guests. I'm certain Lord Telford would not wish to become known to his neighbors as a man whose staff is so lax." By this point Mrs. Threll's lips had compressed almost to the point of vanishing, and I hesitated. I did not want to make an enemy of her, and I knew that my own lack of warmth toward the girl might have encouraged the staff to be careless in their duties toward her.

"I fear I may bear some responsibility in this," I admitted. "My own welcome to Miss Rowe was not as warm as it should have been for my husband's ward. Her early arrival took me by surprise, and I let my displeasure show. It may well be that I set a poor example to the staff in doing so. But I intend to make that up to her. Anyone whom my husband has taken to his bosom should be made to feel at home." A sudden mental image of Atticus literally clasping Genevieve to said bosom swam into my mind, and I quelled it firmly. "Miss Rowe is just out of the schoolroom—a child, practically—and in a strange country, and I ought to have made certain that she felt welcome from the moment she arrived at Gravesend."

Mrs. Threll's face, not for the first time, was unreadable. "Lord Telford has expressed no dissatisfaction with the quality of the staff's service, ma'am."

"Ah. I see." So the malicious old man was setting the tone for Genevieve's reception. I tried to keep the disgust out of my voice and find a line of reason that the housekeeper would respect. "I would have hoped that my husband's wishes mattered as well—as his father's heir and the future baron, if nothing else. The staff's treatment of Miss Rowe is a sign of their respect for Mr. Blackwood, since it was he who brought her here." I could not tell whether my appeal to her loyalty and pragmatism was having any effect, but I felt I had made my best effort. "If Lord Telford is at all discommoded, I'll be happy to address the matter with him. In the meantime, if you could see that Miss Rowe's needs are more fully met, I would be much obliged."

"Very good, ma'am." The words were rote, but the housekeeper's eyes rested thoughtfully on me. She was reevaluating Genevieve based on my words. I was surprised that my opinion counted for so much with her, but grateful for the girl's sake.

Or perhaps it was not Genevieve who was the object of Mrs. Threll's consideration. I wondered suddenly if Lady Telford had ever admitted fault to her housekeeper. Perhaps I had won some credit by admitting a failing and, in a sense, meeting her halfway. "I almost forgot," I added. "I've been meaning to speak to you about the rule dictating that servants turn their faces to the wall in the presence of the family. I should like you to inform the staff that it's no longer in force."

"Ma'am?" For once I had awakened a visible emotion on the housekeeper's face—surprise.

"You heard me aright. It's a degrading custom, and I see no reason to preserve it. If Lord Telford objects, you may refer him to me."

She mastered her surprise quickly enough. "As you think best, ma'am. And I'll have a word with Letty and Jane about taking better care of Miss Rowe."

"Excellent. Thank you, Mrs. Threll."

After that conversation I was pleased to notice that Genevieve's smile was once more in evidence, and there were no upsetting incidents at dinner. I had some qualms that I might hear from Lord Telford that he resented my interference, but the only acknowledgment he granted was a summons to his chambers one day—for Genevieve.

"I am more than a little nervous," Genevieve confessed to me as we neared the baron's rooms. Atticus and I were accompanying her, since Lord Telford had not specifically commanded her to come alone. She was somewhat pale. "You are so calm and composed, you make me feel stronger."

I was neither of these things, or at least not internally, but my heart (or at least my vanity) was touched. I gave her hand a squeeze. "He shall adore you," I said. "Just as my husband does."

Indeed, I must admit that I had begun to feel some grudging fondness for the girl as well. She was so guileless and affectionate that it felt churlish to dislike her; and her oft-expressed admiration for me could not help but make me warm to her.

There was another reason as well, one that renewed itself when Atticus knocked at his father's door and Lord Telford's voice testily bade us enter. If my father-in-law had hardened his heart against the girl, my own had correspondingly softened. A quixotic impulse to champion the girl he had snubbed made me feel closer to Genevieve. We were kin in a sense . . . as my husband had said.

Now Atticus gave the girl a warm smile to reassure her. "Just be yourself, Vivi," he said, and then the valet opened the door for us.

"So you're my son's latest charitable case," was Lord Telford's less than gracious greeting. He sat hunched in his chair with a petulant twist to his lips, a dark blanket, as always, over his legs. "Another stray lamb to be added to the fold."

"My lord," said the girl, with a deep and graceful curtsey. "I am delighted to have been—"

"Yes, I'm certain you are. You've landed on your feet and no mistake. Fine gowns and fine food, mixing with the county— you're doing quite well for yourself."

Atticus spoke firmly. "Genevieve is part of our family, Father. This isn't an instance of charity. Her place is here at Gravesend."

The old man fixed a baleful eye on his son. "You're very high-handed about telling me about *my* family, my boy. Next you'll say the knives-and-boots boy is a cousin and must be given a place at table. Still trying to rescue every soul with a sad story, make yourself responsible for everyone's happiness—Atlas."

Genevieve cocked her head at the name. "Is that your nickname, uncle? I like it."

The old lord gave a sly smile, which turned into a wheezing laugh as Atticus hesitated, unable to respond at once. "He doesn't like it," the baron told her.

"It's a foolish name," I said. "A wife's endearments for her husband should never be made public, for they cause nothing but embarrassment." I tucked my hand through Atticus's arm and gave him what I hoped looked like an apologetic smile. "I am so sorry, dear, but it slipped out once when I was speaking to your father."

Lord Telford gave one of his death's-head grins. "Oh, now it's your turn to cast yourself on the sacrificial altar, is it, Clara? It won't work, you know. My son was Atlas long before you became his bride."

"I think it suits you, uncle," said Genevieve, either not noticing the tension or else deciding to ignore it. "The mythological Atlas was a figure of strength."

"The mythological Atlas was none too bright," said Atticus lightly, but I thought his smile did not reach his eyes. "He had a chance to be relieved of the weight of the whole world, and he lost it through foolishly trusting the wrong person."

"Ah, but that will never happen to you, my son," said Lord Telford, his bright little eyes fixed on Atticus. "You'd have no purpose if you let anyone take on their own burdens."

I tightened my arm to draw Atticus closer. "It's a noble quality in Atticus that he always seeks to help others. In any case, we mustn't tire you, Lord Telford. Genevieve can pay you a longer visit tomorrow, when you are more rested."

"Don't be preposterous, woman. I've scarcely said two words to the girl. So, tell me," he barked suddenly to Genevieve, "what are your plans?"

"Plans?" she stammered, caught off guard.

"Yes, plans," he repeated irritably. "I'm certain you didn't come all this way merely to amuse yourself. You Frenchwomen are all so damnably practical. You must intend to use my name to secure marriage to some rich dolt who'll turn a blind eye while you amuse yourself."

"I beg your pardon, but I am not French," said Genevieve, who had never sounded more so. She stood quite straight and still, her hands folded quietly, but her chin was raised at an angle that suggested that she was not prepared to quietly suffer the old man's gibes. I liked her more at that moment than at any time since meeting her. "My parents, rest their souls, were English."

"Oh they were, were they? And just what do you know about them? Were they married? To each other?"

"Father," said Atticus warningly. "There's no need to drag Genevieve into a sordid discussion. She knows only what she has been told, after all, and the subject may be painful to her."

"It is not painful, uncle. I know very little about my parents, so I cannot take offense at stories about them—however unkind those stories may be." She tossed her bright ringlets and fixed the old baron with a challenging look. "I know only that Uncle Atticus felt that I should be happy as part of *his* family with his beautiful wife Clara. We have yet to discuss any future beyond that. Does that answer satisfy you?"

The old man's face was reddening. "Impertinent baggage!" he spat. "Atticus, take your so-called ward out of my sight, and don't let her come near me again until she can keep a civil tongue in her head. If you're wise you'll give her a whipping, but then you're too soft-hearted to raise your hand to anyone, woman or not." He raised a tremulous hand to point to the door. "Brutus, show them out."

Atticus did not move at once, even as the valet briskly stepped over to throw the door open for us. I felt the muscles of his arm tighten against mine, and I remembered then that he had been trained in bare-knuckle fighting. He was not afraid to raise his hand against a bully, despite his father's taunts.

But the baron was old and frail, and in any case his father. Atticus made him the most civil of bows and, with no word of farewell, led me to the door. Genevieve, head held high, was hard on our heels, and no sooner had she stepped into the hall-way than Brutus shut the door with a swiftness that made her jump.

"I am sorry, uncle," she said contritely. "I was rude. Your father is elderly, perhaps wandering in his wits, and I ought not to have taken offense at his words."

A smile almost too fierce to deserve the name came and went on my husband's face. "Father would be most disappointed had you *not* taken offense; his chief delight nowadays is in sticking pins in people to see what makes them flinch. You'll apologize to him, but not until he's had a night to enjoy nursing his offended pride."

"Very well," sang Genevieve, her penitence vanishing as quickly as winter sunshine, and hummed a little tune as we left Lord Telford and his spite behind us.

CHAPTER FOURTEEN

U nfortunately, over the days since Genevieve's arrival I had been unable to find the right moment to tell Atticus about Collier's note. Our nighttime meetings were consumed by discussion of our guests and what it was incumbent on me to do or not do in order not to disgrace myself (or my husband) before them, and when my thoughts did return to the note it was never a convenient time to detain Atticus alone.

It was the same the following day. He and the male guests were out with the guns all day, and they returned with barely enough time to dress for dinner. I gritted my teeth and made pleasant conversation with the women in the parlor, where I kept one eye on the doorway, waiting for Atticus to appear. Birch would sound the dinner gong soon, and then I'd have no chance to speak privately with him until hours later when we met for our usual late-night conference.

The decorous murmur of feminine conversation was shattered by the irruption of the men into the drawing room. Energized from their day outdoors, they seemed to fill every corner of the room, both physically and with their boisterous voices. Mr. Bertram was the only exception. Looking comfortingly unassuming with his wild hair and two-seasons-old dinner coat, he was speaking to my husband in a voice I could not hear over the bragging of Lord Veridian about how many grouse he had bagged. But Bertram's next words caught his attention.

"If we are concerned about the local men haranguing the girls on their way to church, as has happened with some of the Anglican institutions, we can consider building a chapel wing onto the facility itself."

"I should think the exercise and fresh air would do the residents good," mused Atticus. "To be bottled up in one place day and in and day out would make it seem a prison. But you're right, we don't want the young women to suffer unwanted attention. I wonder if perhaps—"

"What's this?" boomed Lord Veridian. "What young women are these? Are you starting a harem, Blackwood?"

"Cecil, please," murmured his wife.

Atticus hesitated, clearly unwilling to elucidate for an almost certainly unsympathetic party, but Bertram helpfully provided the answer. "Quite the opposite," he said brightly. "Young women who have come to grief will find a refuge for themselves and their children in the institutions that Mr. Blackwood is planning."

I nearly groaned aloud. Even I knew that this was not a suitable topic for the time and place. Anything likely to create controversy was anathema to a gathering like this one, and most especially in mixed company.

Sure enough, I saw shocked glances pass between some of the women. "I scarcely think," one matron said reprovingly, "that discussion of such depraved creatures is appropriate."

Her husband laughed too loudly. "And yet *I* find it a fascinating topic! Tell us, Blackwood, how do you propose to locate the despoiled lasses to populate these homes? If you need scouts, you have a willing volunteer here. I'll happily search the neighborhood for undiscovered wantons."

A rumble of appreciative laughter from some of the gentlemen greeted this sally. It was time I took command, like a proper hostess. "I'm certain that my husband will explain the entire scheme to all of the gentlemen after dinner," I said, raising my voice to be heard over the sniggering, "when you won't be constrained by the presence of ladies."

"Exactly so," said Atticus firmly. "The topic is ill suited to the present company. Not because I find anything salacious in the unfortunate circumstances that make such a scheme necessary, but the presence of my young ward—"

"I've got it," Lord Veridian interrupted. "These are all of your brother Richard's castoffs, eh, Blackwood? With all of the wild oats he sowed, you're probably talking several acres' worth of crops."

"How dare you." I had not meant to speak, but the words flew from my lips. "How dare you speak so of Ri—of a member of my family."

His lips spread in an oily smile, and he treated me to the honor of a long scrutiny of my entire person. I felt as if his gaze were leaving a film on me. "Pardon me if I give offense, dear lady, but I'm only repeating common knowledge about young Blackwood. You never had the opportunity to know him, but if you had—" A nasty grin. "Let us say that he might have left you a sadder but wiser woman."

"How brave of you," I said witheringly. "Casting aspersions on a dead man. If he were here to defend himself, you'd not be so free with your vile claims."

Suddenly Atticus was beside me, and although he did not actually put his arm around me or in any physical way offer support, I suddenly felt less vulnerable. "Clara, my love, it is like you to spring to my family's defense. But I assure you"—he directed a look at Lord Veridian that was so cold in its fury that the man's head retracted as if he had been struck—"you'll not have to listen to such filth any longer. Veridian, you are no longer welcome at Gravesend."

I did not see him make a gesture, but instantly Birch and two of the strongest-looking footmen were there, positioned around the slanderous peer as if creating a barrier between him and the rest of the company.

"Escort Lord Veridian out of the house," Atticus ordered. His words were clipped, and I had never seen such icy anger in his eyes. To the man in question he said, "Your belongings will be sent after you."

There was an instant's silence, while Lord Veridian, whose face was slowly crimsoning, stood swaying as if from a blow or from too much wine. Those nearest him had fallen back, as if he might contaminate them—all except for Lord Cavendish, whose kind face was perplexed.

"Blackwood, is this not a bit rash?" he said gently. "Surely so drastic a measure is unnecessary. Veridian, apologize to our host, and let's put this unpleasantness behind us."

But this seemed only to rouse the man. "I've no intention of apologizing to this madman," he barked. "You can't just throw me out like rubbish, Blackwood. For God's sake, I'm the Viscount Veridian!"

"You're a disgrace to the peerage," Atticus informed him. "Birch, get him out of my house." One of his hands had descended to rest gently on my shoulder, and I found the touch reassuring. My hands were shaking, and I clasped them in my lap to still them.

Shocked murmurs arose as the footmen hauled Lord Veridian from the room. They met with little resistance; either he was too stupefied at the turn of events to put up a fight, or he had some belated impulse to recall the dignity of his position—an impulse that had not been present earlier, or it might have prevented him from saying any of the repellent things that still echoed horribly in my mind.

"How could he?" I whispered. What was the point of inventing such disgusting lies?

"My love, don't distress yourself." Atticus's voice was so low that I could scarcely hear it over the avid buzz of conversation that was already filling the room. I realized that the scene had provided my guests with an even tastier morsel of scandal to gossip over than Genevieve's obscure origins. "Don't pay any mind to what he said," he urged.

How could I not? But he gave me no chance to reply. "I'll just see that he's giving the men no trouble," he told me, and made his way out of the room.

"What a disgusting man," announced Genevieve distinctly, and there was some laughter—but also mutterings of disapproval. Bertram gave her a smile.

"Miss Rowe, you have just witnessed something that may be nearly unique among the English peerage," he said. "A viscount doing a job of work." His voice was so cheerful that I was first astonished and then, belatedly, grateful.

Genevieve shook her red-gold ringlets in pretty puzzlement. "And what work is that?"

"Why, digging his own grave."

She wrinkled her forehead at him. "Is that clever, Mr. Bertram? I cannot tell."

He laughed rather than taking offense. "No more can I, Miss Rowe. Now, I have heard that you are a delightful singer. If I accompany you on the piano, would you be so kind as to favor us with a few songs? I think some sweet tunes are just what we need after that ass's braying."

There was a silken rustle from across the room as Lady Veridian rose, and the murmur of conversation halted at once. "If this is the kind of hospitality you offer, Mrs. Blackwood," she said quietly, "I think you'll find your acquaintance shrinking rapidly."

I had momentarily forgotten the viscount's wife, and I must have looked like a half-wit, gaping at her as she continued, poised and calm.

"The only charitable assumption one can make in the face of such a preposterous gesture is that your husband has lost his wits."

"No more than your husband has," I snapped before I could control myself, and the ripple of shocked laughter told me, too late, how inappropriate the remark was.

Lady Veridian's stare might have been the coldest thing I had ever seen, and yet it made my face burn. She said distinctly, "I hold you personally responsible for this scene, Mrs. Blackwood."

"Ladies, I beg of you," Lord Cavendish began, but she silenced him with a look.

"You may not know it," she continued, biting each word off with angry precision, "but my husband's family is one of the oldest and most distinguished in this country. Perhaps you consider yourself an American and have little respect for the noble tradition of the peerage, but I assure you that if you were a man, my husband would have had every right to call you out for the things you said."

The entire room was awaiting my response. Even if Atticus had been there, I knew he could not save me this time. If I did not meet this confrontation head on, I would lose face before every person present, and it would never be forgotten. A clammy dread clutched my stomach, and I rose so that I faced my accuser eye to eye.

"Lady Veridian," I said, willing my voice not to quaver, "I'm sorry if I have insulted you. But the Blackwoods, I understand, are also an old and venerated family and worthy of respect. Perhaps I do have a bit of the Puritan in my makeup, but I would think that in any country it is unacceptable to slander someone who is unable to defend himself. If my husband's brother were alive, *he* would have had every right to call Lord Veridian out." My mouth was so dry it was a marvel that I could speak at all, but she showed no signs of thawing yet. "You are welcome to stay on at Gravesend without your husband," I offered, and instantly knew it had been the wrong thing to say. If I had been on the way to gaining her respect, I lost it then.

She inclined her head and regarded me with a contempt that was almost palpable. "Mrs. Blackwood, you clearly have much to learn about English society. Among civilized people, a wife and her husband are considered one person. You cannot extend or revoke an invitation to only one—nor can you insult one without insulting the other." She snapped her fan open so suddenly that I jumped. "Pray excuse me," she said icily. "I must have my maid pack my things. I won't discommode you by remaining a moment longer than I must."

Her sweeping exit from the room left a profound silence in her wake.

I bit my lips and tried desperately to think of what to say to smooth this discordance over. Apologize to my guests? The scene had been none of my doing, but the revolting viscount's. But the terrible quiet only grew more agonizing by the second. I sought Genevieve's eyes and saw a similar helplessness in them. Strangely, that brought me a measure of calm.

"Genevieve," I said, "I believe you were going to sing for us. Perhaps, after this memorable conversation between me and Lady Veridian, you and Mr. Bertram might favor us with something in a similar vein—say, Rossini's Cat Duet?"

It could have been a devastating misstep. For a second it hung in the balance whether the company would condemn me as irredeemably flippant and impudent.

But then Lady Stanley gave her distinctive chuckle. "Clearly American bloodlines are infused with steel as well as brass," she said. "Yes, let us have the 'Duet for Two Cats'—or shall we consider it an encore?"

That seemed to turn the scale. First one, then another of my guests permitted themselves a smile or titter, and my shoulders sagged in relief. Genevieve and Bertram quickly took their places at the piano, and as their spirited meows sent the guests into more laughter, I resumed my seat and felt the panicked beat of my heart subside into something closer to normality.

"I wouldn't have had that happen for worlds," said Atticus. "Clara, I can only say again how sorry I am. Lord Veridian shall not enter this house again."

I drew off my gloves and sank into a wing chair with a little sigh of gratitude. It was a relief to close the door of my sitting room and be freed from the eyes of both guests and servants— to be offstage, in a sense. Especially after my close brush with social disaster, I was blissfully relieved that now I could finally relax.

If Atticus felt the same way, one would not have known it to look at him. He was pacing before the fire with as much restless energy as if he had just sprung from a cage. His pale blue eyes were bright with fury.

"Lord Veridian is not worth your anger, Atticus," I told him. "As disgusting as he was, his words can't hurt Richard now. I'm sure that everyone knows the truth and will dismiss his foul lies accordingly."

He halted in mid-stride and turned astonished eyes to me. "Clara," he said in a different voice. "That isn't what enrages me. I know how much it must have hurt you to have him speak so coarsely about women in that unfortunate situation."

I wasn't certain whether to laugh or take his words in earnest. "I have known several of these unfortunates," I said slowly, "and I do feel compassion for them, but I'm not certain why you should think that the subject is one that I take personally. Certainly it isn't well suited to drawing-room conversation, but I was not offended on my own behalf."

To my bewilderment, he actually went on one knee beside my chair and took one of my hands in his. "You're so brave, Clara, but you mustn't feel that you have to hide your feelings from me," he said gently. "I know how wounded you must have been by those coarse references to light women."

An explanation for his solicitousness was finally dawning on me. "Is this to do with Genevieve?" I asked. At his solemn nod—I cannot deny it—my heart sank. My voice was dull when I asked, "Is she your mistress?"

He stared at me. "My *mistress?*" he repeated, in a voice of such consternation that I had to believe it sincere. "Good God, Clara, of course not!"

But that left only one other explanation. "Your daughter, then," I said. Even, it seemed, as honorable and decent a man as Atticus was not a stranger to dalliance. With no wife for so many years, what other course was open to a man of normal passions? So he had taken a lover, who had borne him a daughter. It spoke well of him that he was taking responsibility for her, paying for her education and upkeep, even introducing her into his own circle. It was more than decent; it was generous.

Still, it gave me a little twinge to imagine how happy he must have been with this woman to have embraced her illegitimate child so completely. Would he still be with the woman of his heart if his position, and hers, had permitted it?

As I pondered these depressing thoughts, Atticus drew back as if to take the full measure of me and make certain I was the same person he thought he knew. "Clara, there's no need to keep up the pretence," he said, in so bewildered a tone that I felt churlish for having evoked it. "You don't have to hide the truth any longer. I know the sad secret that you've had to conceal."

"What secret?" I demanded. "Atticus, what is it that you think I've been concealing?"

Such compassion in his eyes. "Why," he said softly, "that Genevieve is your daughter."

Chapter Fifteen

"**M**y *daughter?*" My voice was an incredulous squeak. He bowed his head. "Don't think for a moment that I am sitting in judgment on you, Clara. I know how much you loved Richard—it shone in your face like something holy whenever you looked at him. You were young, passionate . . . without a father to guide you . . ." A wry smile flicked over his face and was gone in an instant. "And Richard could have charmed the virgin goddess Diana herself into his arms. It would have been impossible for any young woman in your position to have withstood him. I don't condemn you, Clara."

I had been silent during this generous speech only because I was too stupefied to speak. Now anger was overcoming shock, and I found that I had no lack of things to say. I rose abruptly to my feet, and the motion stopped the words on his lips.

"Are you saying," I demanded, "that you think I was your brother's *doxy?*"

He was on his feet again, but my words made him recoil. "I would never use that word, Clara."

"But you thought it of me just the same. I cannot believe your presumption. Just because I was a servant, without the moral compass of highborn, enlightened people like yourself, you concluded that I was a loose woman? That I had no sense of propriety, of how to conduct myself? That I—" I whirled away from him, unable to look at him any longer, and hugged my arms tightly around myself so that I would not reach out for the closest objects at hand and hurl them at the wall—or his head. "Do I look that debauched, or that foolish? It seems that according to you I must be one or the other."

"Clara, I . . . I don't know what to say. Am I to believe that you aren't . . . ?"

"I am neither Genevieve's mother nor anyone's mother. I never lay with your brother or with any man. But I can't expect you to believe me, no, not a harlot from below stairs. You can't trust me to give you anything but falsehoods." No wonder he had reacted so strongly to Lord Veridian's remarks about impure women—he had assumed that I was among them.

His hands clasped me firmly by the shoulders. I gave in grudgingly to the pressure, and he turned me around so that we stood facing each other. I must have looked ferocious indeed, and I certainly felt so. I could feel the heat of humiliation in my face, and my heart was flailing in my chest.

"Clara, I am truly sorry to have insulted you," he exclaimed, his eyes anxious as they sought mine. "I beg your pardon, sincerely."

His voice had never been more gentle and warm, but my pride was still smarting. "You might have asked me," I snapped. "Rather than assuming that I'd fallen into Richard's bed—even had he tried to lure me there, which he did not. He never—"

My words came to an abrupt halt as I remembered the many times Richard's wayward hands had tested my resolve; remembered the persuasive words he had murmured to me so often, telling me of the sweetness of love's pleasures stolen furtively; and I fell silent. What I had thought was a game might have been quite in earnest, and Richard had not been entirely above reproach. But he, too, had been young—nearly as young as I—

and if in his love for me he had sometimes trespassed against respectability and convention, I could scarcely condemn him for it.

My silence must have been revealing, for Atticus heaved a great sigh and drew me, astonishingly, into an embrace. "I'm so sorry," he said, his voice muffled by my hair as he held me against him. "You're right, I shouldn't have assumed it was you. For me to have blurted it out unthinkingly . . . I can only imagine how grievous a shock it must be to find out this way."

My arms struggled up between us so that I could push myself away from his chest. "What are you saying? That Richard was unfaithful to me? That's a lie as vile as any of Lord Veridian's preposterous claims."

"Clara, it pains me to say it as much as it must pain you to hear it, but Genevieve is Richard's daughter, though you aren't her mother."

"Impossible."

"Inarguable." How could a man's voice be so tender yet so relentless? "You've only to look at her, Clara! Her hair is a few shades lighter than Richard's, her eyes a bit darker, but she's his blood."

"It's absurd even to suggest such a thing!" Even her age gave the lie—Richard had been in love with me, had spent with me those last months before he was to leave for the Continent. *I* was his sweetheart. "This is the cause of your devotion to her, then?" I demanded. "You truly thought she was your niece?"

"I think it still," he said gravely. "Please try to look past your wounded pride and see it, my dear. I suppose Richard must have been trifling with Mrs. Collier. If that is so and she was actually Genevieve's mother, it's no wonder Collier thought the girl was his! I went to their cottage on a hint from one of Richard's letters, and when I found out when the child had been born I . . . well, I remembered how much time he was spending with you all those months before, and how suddenly you'd been sent away. I'd heard the rumor that you carried his child." He reached for my hand, and even though I snatched it away, his voice remained as tender as before. "I loved her for your sake, Clara. I knew that someday you'd want to be with her again, even though circumstances had forced you to give her up. From what Richard said in his letter I thought he must have told you to place her with the Colliers. They seemed happy enough for me to take her into my care and give her all the advantages they couldn't offer . . . and you know the rest."

I knew that I had never before heard of anything so monstrously presumptuous. "No wonder Mr. Collier is so angry at the Blackwoods," I exclaimed. "You took his child away, claiming she was another man's, and sent her to another country, where he would never even be able to see her. The poor man must have been half mad with grief." It would explain his resentment of me: if his child was to be brought into the grandeur of the Blackwoods' orbit, he would have wanted her decently wedded and accorded the full status of her position. A wife, not a ward.

"Collier is not her father," he said, with a firmness that made my hands clench into fists. "His wits may be too turned for him to see it, but Genevieve is a Blackwood."

"As for his wits," I said shortly, "madman or grieving father, he seems to have no difficulty in finding a way into Gravesend when it suits him. He left this note for me on my bureau the night that he made his way into the house. Evidently Birch and the others did not discover him until he had been inside for some while. I've no idea if he may turn violent if he is continually thwarted in his wish to see Genevieve, but it would probably be wise to set extra watch on the house."

I had kept the note with me ever since the night it had appeared, and now I thrust the torn fragment of paper at him so that he could read the words scrawled in the unsteady handwriting. "And now, if you don't mind, I'd prefer that you take your nasty assumptions out of my sitting room."

He didn't respond at once, so absorbed was he in staring at the note. "Collier left this? You're certain?"

"I believe one can fairly rule out Mrs. Threll," I said sarcastically. "I found it after I retired that night. It rather unnerved me to know that he had been among my things."

He looked up at me, his eyes narrowing. "Among your things, you say. Where exactly?"

"In the jewel case. I found it when I went to put the ruby collar away." As I spoke, it occurred to me for the first time that this was a curious place for Collier to have left the note; why not place it in plain sight, where I would see it at once? What meaning could the jewel case have had for him? Then I shook the questions off. A man as troubled as Collier probably did not even understand his own actions.

Atticus was staring at the note again now, and I thought I saw his jaw tighten as if in anger. "You needn't worry about being disturbed like this again," he said grimly. "I'll see to it that this isn't repeated."

"I'm sure you will. Now, if you would be so good as to remove yourself from my room?"

He seemed on the point of protesting, but a glance at me, standing stiffly by the open door awaiting his departure, seemed to change his mind. Thrusting the note into a pocket, he strode to me, looked searchingly into my eyes for a moment, then bowed and departed.

I shut the door firmly behind him, turned the key, and snatched up a cheap china vase painted with roses. My hand fairly twitched with the urge to hurl it against the wall. Such a satisfying crash it would make.

But it would make extra work for the maid whose duty it was to keep my sitting room tidy. After a moment's fevered thought, I fetched a paisley shawl from my bedroom wardrobe, spread it on the floor beneath the wall, and flung the vase with all my might.

The crash was, indeed, satisfying. Triumphant, I gathered up the shawl with its litter of china fragments, opened the window, and flung the pieces out into the darkness. Then, a fraction calmer, I retired to my bedroom.

It could scarcely have been a quarter of an hour later, if that long, when I heard running footsteps approach my door. There was a fusillade of knocking. My first thought was Atticus, but what would bring him on the run like this to rap so furiously on my door? Then a voice called, "Madame! Aunt Clara!" and I realized my mistake.

"Genevieve?" I opened the door a crack and found her standing, flushed and breathing hard, at the threshold. "What's wrong?"

"You must come," she blurted. "Uncle Atticus and his father—a terrible argument. I am frightened."

Fortunately I had progressed no further in undressing for bed than taking my hair down; I had been too occupied in continuing my discussion with Atticus in my head, adding many brilliant points and incisive observations that would have reduced him to humble capitulation. Genevieve grabbed my hand and led me at a half-run down the hall, around the corner, and through the gallery that separated my rooms from Lord Telford's.

She told me in an urgent half whisper that she had gone to Lord Telford's rooms to leave a note and a posy of flowers, since he had shown no signs of forgiving her impertinence. It was when she came to deliver these that she heard the two men in argument. "They are so furious with each other," she whispered. "I heard Lord Telford saying dreadful things. That you were not worthy to bear the Blackwood name—I am sorry, Aunt Clara—and that I was a disgrace to his house. Uncle Atticus, he spoke more quietly, but so calmly—so calmly that I knew he was quite, quite angry—and he asked, 'By what right do you have anonymous notes placed in my wife's chamber? It was a cowardly thing to do. If you had a grievance to air with her and me, you should have spoken out to our faces!' I give you what they call the gist, you understand—"

"I understand. What else? Tell me quickly."

"At that, Lord Telford begins to laugh, a dreadful laugh, and he says that he will do just that, he will tell everyone to their faces that you are—that you—I did not recognize the word he used."

I suspected from the deepening flush in her cheeks that she had understood only too well what Lord Telford had called me, but I did not press her.

"And Lord Telford, he then said that he would have you thrown out of the house to return to your proper place, and he said that I should be sent with you, as a brand of shame. I did not quite understand that."

Thank heaven, it appeared that Atticus had not shared his theory about Genevieve's parentage with the girl herself. I could not imagine how hurtful it would have been for her to have expected me to give her a mother's welcome, only to find none awaiting her. At least she had been spared that crushing disappointment.

Now that we were nearing Lord Telford's chambers I tugged at her hand to slow her steps. Cautiously and quietly, we approached the door.

It might have been wide open for all the good it did in preventing the argument inside from reaching our ears. Lord Telford's reedy voice was raised in anger. "I had my suspicions about that woman from the first. All these years you've shown no inclination toward marriage, neglected your responsibility to sire an heir, and then suddenly you marry this wealthy, mysterious widow you produced from thin air? A preposterous story. It was the night that you gave her the ruby collar that I found out—that is, I finally recognized her. A servant! You put a servant in the highest place at Gravesend under me, a strumpet no better than she should be, who departed here in disgrace—"

"I must ask you not to speak so of Clara." Atticus's voice, in contrast with his father's shrill ranting, was coldly controlled, but just the sound of that even, clipped sentence gave me the image of him: standing firm, indomitable, unmoved, his eyes glacial with anger and stubbornness, as the storm of his father's rantings broke over him. "My wife has been forced to earn her living, yes, but that is scarcely a sin. The charges you make against her virtue are entirely unfounded. And even if they had any basis in fact, Clara's life before our marriage is no one's affair but hers and mine."

A strange wheezing exclamation came. I realized it was Lord Telford laughing. "Pretty words don't expunge dirty deeds," he sneered. "Her filth will corrupt the Blackwood name, along with that illegitimate brat. Do you mean to set the child up as a courtesan? She has the brazenness for it, as well as the extravagant wardrobe—paid for with Blackwood money, I've no doubt."

"This has gone quite far enough." Atticus raised his voice to cut across his father's tirade. "I came only to tell you that you're not to do anything further to hurt or frighten Clara. No more sending your valet to plant nasty little notes in her room. No spreading stories about her past to prevent her being received. If you cannot treat her with the respect she deserves—"

"Then what?" was the triumphant rejoinder. "What is in your power to do to me, my boy? You cannot prevent me from talking."

Nor from writing, evidently. So it was my father-in-law who had written the note, and the shaky lettering that I had attributed to a working man with little practice in writing was due to age and illness having made the old man's hand unsteady. Had his words just now not been bad enough, the idea of his taking the time to deliberately write the note, and then having it delivered to my room to be planted there, made my stomach turn.

Atticus was still trying to minimize the damage his father could do. "You're ill," he said. "Too ill to receive visitors. With no one to tell them to, your ugly sentiments can go no further."

"You cannot imprison me, Atticus. Brutus will carry me wherever company is assembled. I'll spread word far and wide—"

"What could it possibly gain you? Why do you take such satisfaction in—"

The words ended in a crash that made me jump, and Genevieve darted me a frantic look. What had happened? "Atticus?" I cried, without thinking, and started back as the door was flung open.

A wild-eyed Atticus stared back at me. "He's collapsed," he said hoarsely. "We need the doctor."

"I'll find Mrs. Threll," said Genevieve instantly, and darted off before I could speak, let alone move.

"Where is Brutus?" I asked.

"I've rung for him. Can you help me?"

"I'll try."

The crashing sound, I saw as soon as I stepped into the sitting room, had been Lord Telford's chair. It lay on its side, and the bent, thin shape had fallen with it. The old man's eyes were closed and his jaw was slack, and he appeared to be unconscious; but he was twitching slightly, which I seized on gratefully as a sign of life.

"He's had a seizure," said Atticus. His face was white and strained, his voice urgent, but his hands were gentle as he slid them under his father's shoulders. "If you can move the chair when I lift him, I'll get him disentangled. I'd like to move him to his bed."

"Of course."

Once the old man was free of the chair, it was the work of moments for Atticus to carry him to the other room. Indeed, the baron looked so slight that I suspected I could have supported his weight. He wore a dressing gown over nightclothes, and his slippers had fallen off his feet. I fetched them and, when Atticus did not stop me, placed them on the fragile-looking, veined feet. He had not regained consciousness. How weak he looked in this state. If I had not known better, I would never have imagined so frail a form able to carry on so fierce and venomous an argument. Standing over the bed, Atticus looked so strong, so healthy.

"Was his first seizure like this?" I asked. I spoke nearly in a whisper. I wasn't sure whether I was afraid of waking him or whether some superstitious impulse made me afraid of being irreverent. A more cynical inner voice suggested that we could not be certain he was not mimicking unconsciousness and listening to all we said.

"I don't know. I wasn't with him when it happened." He dragged his fingers through his hair in a despairing gesture. He was still fully dressed in his evening clothes and had evidently gone straight to his father's rooms to upbraid him after I sent him away. "How much did you hear?" he asked.

"Enough to know that your father is the one who wrote the note." He must have directed the valet to place it in the jewel case as an indication that the jewels were not by rights mine to wear.

His eyes shut briefly as if his strength was unequal to this latest revelation. "I'm so sorry, Clara. I never dreamed that by bringing you here I'd be subjecting you to his revolting assumptions."

No, I thought, *only your own.* The old man had only said aloud what Atticus had thought of me. "I wouldn't have heard if Genevieve had not happened by and been frightened. She went to fetch me . . . although I'm not certain what she thought I could do."

"She heard as well?" he exclaimed. "Good lord, the poor child."

"I don't think she believed what she heard. As far as she is concerned, they must have seemed like the insane ravings of an ill old man who has lost his wits." The words were harsh, but I was in no frame of mind to be generous.

Anything Atticus might have said to that was forestalled when Brutus entered the room. The valet was younger than Atticus or I, with close-cropped hair that gave him a disreputable look and the sturdy musculature of a bull. Presumably he had been selected for his ability to easily carry his master when necessary, but now that Lord Telford was more wasted, the valet's strength was not as vital. Since the baron did not seem the type to patiently endure discomfort of any kind, he must have been pleased with Brutus enough to keep him in that office. Evidently the man was loyal enough—and discreet enough—to perform such unconventional duties as secreting hateful anonymous letters in the rooms of those his master disliked.

The valet entered discreetly enough, as one responding to a ring, but as soon as he glimpsed the tableau by the bedside, he crossed the room in two strides, staring. "Is he—"

"Alive, but unconscious. He has had a seizure. A doctor has been sent for."

The valet stepped over to the washstand, poured water into the bowl, and moistened a towel with it. He wrung it out carefully and returned with it to the bedside, where he placed it almost tenderly on the old man's forehead. I thought I saw the crepey eyelids flicker, and his head moved.

"Ma'am, if I may speak plainly—" the valet began.

I realized that if he needed to loosen or change Lord Telford's clothes I would be an unwelcome presence, as indeed perhaps I already was, depending on how much Brutus shared his master's view of me. "I'll leave you now," I said. "Atticus, let me know if I can help in any way."

"You might look after Genevieve," he said.

"I had already planned to do so. Good night, and I hope the doctor has good news."

If he had intended to say more or detain me, I did not give him the chance but walked quickly from the room. Genevieve was just nearing as I emerged.

"One of the footmen has gone to fetch the doctor," she said breathlessly. "Is Lord Telford—?"

"Still unconscious, but resting, and we mustn't get in the way. I'm sure they will send for us if we are needed." I tried to reassure her with a smile. "It's time you were in bed and getting some rest. We don't know what may happen tomorrow."

A little crease appeared between her brows, but she nodded dutifully and let me walk her to her room and see her inside.

My own steps slowed as I returned to my rooms. Until now the realization had escaped me that if this latest attack proved fatal, I would soon be free of my arrangement with Atticus. I would be able to leave this house where I was seen as an inferior and a strumpet, and could begin anew on my own terms, in a new home . . . in a new identity. I did not even have to be Clara anymore unless I chose to. At that moment, I felt that it would be a great relief to be someone else . . . someone whose past was untroubled by scandal or grief or loss.

When I reached my door, a movement caught my eye where the shadows clustered most thickly at the end of the hallway. I froze with one hand in the act of taking hold of the doorknob, but the movement was not repeated. Out of the corner of my eye I had thought I saw a form that put me in mind of Richard, but as soon as I turned my head the impression was gone. The hallway was empty save for myself.

It could not have been Atticus, for he was standing vigil at his father's bedside until the arrival of the doctor; he was not here, waiting for me, eager to explain or soothe or cajole. I must have imagined him simply because my emotions were in such upheaval that he was foremost in my thoughts. Unless my heart had conjured up Richard himself . . . the Richard I remembered, not the tarnished figure evoked by Lord Veridian and Atticus.

Suddenly I remembered my first night at Gravesend, when I had thought I heard my own name whispered, and realized I had never completed my inspection of the hallway for hidden rooms or passageways. But in that moment I was grateful for the omission. I would far rather imagine that the disturbance had been caused by a servant on his way to a tryst in a secret chamber than that there was no such chamber where a person could hide.

With new resolve I turned the doorknob and stepped into my room. It was not truly a shelter from all the ills that took place at Gravesend, but at that moment it felt like one.

CHAPTER SIXTEEN

After that strange moment in the dark hallway, it was perhaps not surprising that I dreamed of Richard and of our
last meeting, when, warmed by sunlight and kisses, I lay
dreamily enfolded in the assurance of his love. Even the scent
of the violet he had placed in my bosom returned to me, sweetly
lingering over the dream. When I opened my eyes in the morning
I saw why: on my pillow, next to my head, a single violet lay.

I sat bolt upright, my eyes darting to the doors as if I would
find the deliverer of the flower just exiting, but all was still. In
any case, who would have thought to place it here? No one but
Richard and I knew the meaning that a single violet held for us.

A cold shiver raced up my backbone to tighten my scalp, and
I extended one finger to touch the flower. It seemed real enough.

My mind returned to that uncanny instant last night when
I thought I had glimpsed Richard. Perhaps, I thought, staring
at the tiny flower, which was still as plump and fresh as if it had
just been plucked from a dewy plot, perhaps I had been letting

Atticus take on too much importance in my mind. I had not been loyal to Richard. If my own mind had been responsible for what I thought I had seen, then my conscience had clearly been upbraiding me. Richard had been and always would be the most important man in my life.

Or perhaps there was a sweeter explanation. If the things I had heard and seen were signs that the house was haunted after all, perhaps Richard's soul had found a way to lift the curtain between our worlds and leave me a token of his undying love. At that still, quiet hour of early morning, after a disturbed night and dreams of love, it did not seem so farfetched an explanation.

Whether Richard had been a spirit or a memory, the violet was real. When Henriette arrived to dress and coif me, I tried to ask her if she knew where it had come from. *"Cette fleur . . . d'ou?"* was the best I could do, and Henriette replied with a stream of French I did not understand. Finally she gave a shrug and spread her hands, but I was not certain whether she was saying she did not know where the flower had come from or simply did not understand what I was trying to ask her.

I laid the violet on my bureau, and after Henriette had departed, I unbuttoned my bodice far enough to slip the flower beneath my chemise and between my breasts. As a reminder.

The news that morning was sobering, but not dire: Lord Telford had been weakened by this latest seizure and was keeping to his bed on the doctor's advice, but he was conscious and able to converse for short periods, and he seemed to have all his faculties. The guests expressed their concern and asked if they should leave, but Atticus assured them that they were welcome and that the ball planned for the evening would proceed as planned. Then he disappeared once more to his father's chambers. His haggard face and the bruised color under his eyes suggested that he had not slept, and if I had not been so angry with him I would have felt the stirrings of sympathy. His limp was troubling him, another sign that he was exhausting himself.

But that is no concern of yours, I told myself. My concern, and it was one that occupied the greater part of my concentration, was to keep my guests contented and entertained. It was a dismal, dripping day, a poor prospect for out-of-doors excursions, and I was grateful to Genevieve when she showed a natural flair for leading some of the more restless guests into playing tableaus while the more placid ones were content with piquet. The day was much shortened, fortunately, since everyone needed to array themselves for the ball, and many of the ladies withdrew even earlier to have a brief nap to refresh them for the late night.

I was too restless to do the same. When I sent for news of my father-in-law's condition, the word came that there was little change; I thought of offering to stand vigil by his bedside long enough for Atticus to have a little sleep, but hardened my heart and reasoned that Dr. Brandt would send him away if he thought my husband's own health needed attending to. The doctor, whom I had seen in passing, was a crisp-voiced, level-eyed man of middle age who was not given to softening harsh truths, and I knew that he would have no hesitation in ordering Atticus away if he deemed it necessary.

For the ball I was wearing the skirt of my claret-red reception gown with its evening bodice. This bodice was so brief it might have been made with the scraps of fabric left over from fashioning the other: it exposed nearly all of my arms and a great deal of my bosom, but although daring it was the very apex of fashion, and the mirror's reflection told me that all of that bare skin made an effective background for the ruby-and-pearl collar.

The revealing cut did give me a qualm. *If he did not already think you a harlot, he would now,* came the unwelcome thought. But I stared my reflection down as Henriette fussed with my hair. This was how proper ladies dressed, ladies of Atticus's class. As a servant I had never worn any dress half as revealing. The key was not to act self-conscious but to parade my bare shoulders and half-bare bosom as if they were no less magnificent than the Blackwood jewels. He would have no reason to be ashamed of me tonight . . .

. . . unless Lord Telford made his knowledge about me public.

I shifted uneasily on the slipper chair as Henriette pinned red roses from the glasshouse into my hair. He was in no condition to do that, surely. And if he was, could I truly be harmed by it? Humiliating his son might give the old man a mean satisfaction, but I would not be touched by it; indeed, I would simply be released all the more quickly from my term as Atticus's bride, no doubt dispatched with great haste, the better to permit everyone to forget about the entire shameful incident. The shame would touch Lord Telford too, though. Or would it? Did he feel himself close enough to death that he didn't care if scandal encompassed him as well as the son he despised? Altogether this train of thought was making me feel entirely too much sympathy for Atticus. As I buttoned my gloves and Henriette fastened my bracelets for me, I reminded myself how furious I was with him for making such coarse assumptions about my character and Richard's. It astonished me that he had been able to hide them during all our time together. Never once had he betrayed that he thought me a fallen woman. He had treated me with respect, even affection. *So that he might claim the prize Richard had lost,* I reminded myself, but that Atticus had even considered me a prize was a marvel.

Shrugging off the thoughts, I gave my reflection a final scrutiny in the looking glass, and Henriette, likewise surveying me, gave a nod of approval. *"Trés belle,"* she said.

"It is a beautiful gown," I agreed. And the elaborate hairstyle with its crowning flowers and long, seductive curls was a marvel. No, I would not embarrass the Blackwoods tonight. I pressed her hand and said a clumsy but sincere *"merci"* before I rustled my sumptuous way out of the room and down the stairs to the banquet hall.

Under Mrs. Threll's supervision, the staff had done a magnificent job of decorating it. It was clear that so much work had been necessary that I was glad I had told her to hire on temporary help from the village, even though that had been the means of introducing the unhappy Collier into our midst before. Swags of fabric in gold and black, the Blackwood colors, draped the stone walls, and garlands of hothouse roses in white and red shed their lush sweetness on the air. On the sideboards, which were covered in white linen cloths and lighted with shining silver candelabra, reposed serving dishes filled with all manner of delicacies. The pleasant beeswax-and-turpentine scent of the highly polished floor met my nostrils, and for a moment I felt the tug of aching muscles between my shoulder blades at the memory of polishing it years before.

I would ask Atticus to provide all the servants with a bonus for their efforts, I decided, as well as a holiday in which to recover from their exertions. Tonight Gravesend did not feel hostile to me. On this, the night when I might be exposed as unworthy to be its mistress, it chose to reveal its festive and welcoming side.

Genevieve soon popped up at my side, brimming over with excitement. Her ball gown of pale green mull with gold ribbon stripes had one of the new Worth fan trains and a bodice slightly less revealing than mine; but then, at my age, I had a bit more bust to fill it out—one of the few advantages my age held over hers.

"Gravesend is so beautiful," she sighed, looking about her at the festive scene. "It is more than that, though. It is . . . what is the word the English like for their homes? It is *stately*. Like you, dear Aunt Clara."

"Genevieve, you needn't butter me up," I said, wondering if she was familiar with the idiom. "I suppose Atticus told you to heap me with compliments."

"Indeed, no; why should he do that? He told me that he knew I should love you as if you were my own mother."

My lips tightened. The poor girl's own mother, I had learned through carefully indirect questioning of Mrs. Threll, had been dead some seven years, without having been reunited with Genevieve. I wondered if it had been wrenching for her to part with her child—or was it a relief, knowing she never need fear her husband's recognizing something suspicious about the girl's looks or manner? Perhaps she had even been grateful that her child would live a life of comparative luxury, far beyond what her real parents could provide.

But that did not make it right for Atticus to have thrust Genevieve and me together on the assumption that we would adore each other. Even though he had thought he was doing us both a kindness, it had been rash. Extraordinarily generous to have turned his own life over to the building of a family of three relative strangers, yes—but decidedly rash.

Remembering last night's disastrous reckoning, I wondered if he was regretting that decision now. Genevieve, for her part, seemed to have largely recovered. "You have not asked me about what Lord Telford said of me," I said in a low voice. "About my having been a servant."

She cocked her head with a perplexed air. "I did not think it mattered," she said simply.

Atticus joined us then, his evening clothes flawless but his face pale. Though his expression was bleak, his eyes seemed to widen with appreciation at the sight of me. "By heaven, Clara, you take my breath away," he said in a voice that made the words a vow. He did not even seem to notice that Genevieve was present.

My only reply was to incline my head, and when he offered his arm I rested my fingertips on his sleeve in the smallest amount of contact consistent with the appearance of normality. We entered the banquet hall in silence and walked the length of it toward the dais—a distance that was longer that night than it had ever been before, lined as it was with so many watching eyes. After the drama we had provided on the previous night, our guests might well be anticipating entertainment far beyond the music and dancing.

Finally I broke the silence. "You've not slept, have you?" I asked. It sounded more accusatory than I had intended.

"I don't recall," he said. "Clara, I must tell you again how very sorry—"

"Your father, is he much the same?"

"Much the same, yes. He took a little broth. But—"

"I'm glad to hear it." I was neither glad nor sorry, but I took a mean pleasure in preventing him from speaking, knowing that he would not risk drawing attention by pressing the point. I had won the last word, for now that we had reached the dais at the far end of the room, it was time for him to address the guests and officially begin the evening.

If I had not been so angry at him, if the sight of him had not made me seethe with indignation, I would have thought him at his best then. Bone weary he most certainly was, worried and sick at heart, but he stood tall and strong, even appearing at his ease, though his knuckles were white on the hand that grasped his walking stick and my eyes detected a slight tremor in his bad leg. His smile was genuine as he surveyed the guests in all their finery. Their numbers were swelled by neighbors not staying at the house, so this was the first time that I had laid eyes on many of the company, and they me. Nearby was Genevieve, most gorgeously arrayed of them all, who stood beaming in the center of a crowd of admiring young men.

"Friends," he said, and I had forgotten the full effect of that warm, slightly husky voice until I heard it raised and amplified by the vaulted ceiling of the banquet hall, "I am delighted to welcome you to Gravesend to celebrate my marriage."

How little there is to celebrate, I thought, but I did my best to summon a smile the equal of his own.

"Thank you for coming to meet my beautiful wife, Clara, and the other wonderful addition to the Blackwood family—my ward, Genevieve." She curtseyed gracefully, and I wondered if I ought to have done the same. But it was too late now. There was polite applause—or perhaps more than polite where directed toward Genevieve, who seemed to have the capacity to make people fall in love with her almost on sight. Atticus continued, "Traditionally, I would ask you to join me in a toast to these two ladies. But, as you know, my father's health has suffered a setback, so I would ask that you raise your glasses to him and drink a health to Lord Telford."

"To Lord Telford," echoed the company, and the sound echoed until it was as loud as thunder. Then the musicians struck up Sir Roger de Coverley, and I wondered with a sudden dart of anxiety how on earth Atticus expected to lead the dance, as exhausted as he was.

Evidently I was not the only person to feel concern about this, for Genevieve darted up to us, towing Mr. Bertram by the hand. "Uncle, may Mr. Bertram and I lead the first dance?" she begged. "Just this one night, as a special favor for my first ball at Gravesend? Do be an angel and say yes."

Of course it would have been churlish to refuse so pretty a petition, so the two of them were soon gaily leading the guests through the boisterous figures. The sight of the bright Titian hair and the unkempt mop bobbing through the throng together inexplicably raised my spirits.

Soon, however, my attention was diverted to the many guests who came to be introduced to me and to greet my husband. So many hands to clasp, so many titles to remember . . .

if I had a prayer of remembering any of them, which I doubted. I smiled until my face ached, exchanged pleasantries on the weather, the musicians, the dancers, and the felicities of married life. Fortunately these discussions were too superficial to permit any deeper inquiries into my origins and how I had met Atticus.

After what felt like weeks but had probably been no more than half an hour, Genevieve attached herself to my elbow. "You need refreshment," she informed me. "Come, take some punch with me and help me decide how many more waltzes to give Mr. Bertram. He declares that he wants them all, and of course that will not do."

I waited until we had passed out of earshot of those nearest us and said in a low voice, "Is this a pretext of some sort?"

She smiled sunnily. "I merely wished to speak to you a moment. One cannot help observing that you are not best pleased with my uncle."

So Atticus was contriving to mollify me with the help of his ward. "One cannot help observing," I said tartly, echoing her words, "that married couples do sometimes quarrel—and it is not in a husband's best interests to send a messenger to plead for him."

"Oh, you mistake me! Uncle Atticus did not send me."

I searched her face, but the candid blue eyes gave no sign of deception. I restrained a sigh. "Go on, then, and have it out," I said in resignation, and to my surprise she gave a laugh.

"You make my little speech sound like a bad tooth, Aunt Clara. Probably I am intruding where I ought not, but it distresses me to see you so stiff and cold with my uncle. He loves you dearly, you know."

This was awkward. If she idealized him—or both him and me—to the extent that she thought ours a love match, I did not want to upset her by telling her otherwise. There was a polite fiction to uphold. All the same, Genevieve was certainly old enough to know that marriages were often based on any number of considerations other than personal attachment—or had she romanticized the institution so much that she did not accept that? I finally said, "It's dear of you to concern yourself, but we are very well."

The look she gave me then would have done justice to the most iron-willed major general ever to quell an uprising. "I beg your pardon, but you are *not* very well. If the three of us are to be a family, you must not tell me lies."

"Genevieve!"

"I am sorry to be impertinent, but I shall not stand by and watch the two of you wound each other. You have only to look at him to see how deeply he loves you. Why, in his letters to me he told me of your beauty, your courage, your strength—he spoke of you as his heart's darling."

Unexpectedly I found myself wondering if he had used that very phrase—such a sweet, quaint expression—or if Genevieve was giving me "the gist." But I said nothing, and she continued.

"Now, I can see that you are thinking, 'Vivi, you are telling a story,' but I swear to you it is not so. You must have seen it in his face and heard it in his voice when you are with him."

She was so persuasive, with her pretty accent and appealing eyes, that I could almost believe her. "Even if that is so," I said, gathering the armor of my pride around me, "he has behaved appallingly toward . . . toward someone very close to me. He has maligned this lady's character and made unwarranted assumptions about her virtue." And then had defended her against just such assumptions when his father had uttered them, came the unwilling rejoinder.

A little furrow inserted itself into Genevieve's smooth forehead. "Appallingly? He has exposed her shame in public, do you mean? Or made her husband throw her out of her home?"

"Well—neither."

"Did he set her family and friends against her?"

"Not exactly." No, he had opened his home to me, given me his name, shown me respect and kindness and even affection. He had sought and courted and married me, believing all the time that I was fallen, without once hinting that he found anything in me to condemn or criticize. He had—I realized with a jolt—been so moved by what he thought was my plight and my "child's" that he had taken it upon himself to found a charitable institution to help other women in that sad predicament. As unflattering as his assumption had been to me, it would end up benefitting countless women and children.

And no matter how much I told myself otherwise, this was not a man who had gathered me up to score a point against the brother with whom he once competed. If that had been the case, he would not have shown so much interest in my welfare—or my company.

"Vivi," I said slowly, "what has Atticus told you of your own family?"

The change of subject did not faze her. "I was a child of love," she said promptly. "My parents were devoted to one another, but they were not able to marry and could not keep me. So they placed me where Uncle Atticus would find me and take me away to be well looked after. I would not tell everyone this," she added, "for I know that many people would refuse to receive a girl of unknown heritage. But not my uncle. No one can help their parents, he said to me, or the lack of them."

She told the tale simply, trustingly, with every evidence that she knew I wouldn't shrink from her. Her so-called uncle had accepted her despite what he believed her origin to have been. I had moved among theatrical folk, many of whom had had checkered pasts, shadowy origins, or scarlet careers, and even they had not been without prejudice. Nothing had prepared me for a man who truly accepted and honored women whom most of his class would reject on principle.

At that moment Mr. Bertram joined us. "I think the next waltz is mine?" he said to Genevieve, and his honest young face brightened when she nodded.

"Let us fetch an ice before it begins," she told him. "I believe Aunt Clara would like some time in which to collect her thoughts before the next dance, yes?"

"Genevieve," I said, "I owe my husband a great apology."

She beamed at me and shook her head, setting her gold earrings dancing. "Ah, you know little of marriage still if you think that a wife must apologize! Even I know that a clever wife merely permits her husband to wheedle her into a forgiving humor." She stood on tiptoe to add, whispering into my ear, "Preferably with the gift of a few jewels."

"You have much to teach me," I said dryly, which sent her into gales of laughter. As she led Bertram away, she turned back briefly to blow me a kiss.

CHAPTER SEVENTEEN

When I looked around for Atticus, he was easily found. Even in a crowd of this size he drew the eye. It was partly his build and bearing, nature's gifts, but there was something else. He did not shoulder his way around as some men did, so eager to assert their stature that they ended in diminishing it. Nor did he stand diffidently as if hoping to disappear. He simply *was*. Without insistence or apology, making his presence felt precisely because he felt no need to do so. And this man's many kindnesses I had thrown back in his teeth.

Were he any other man, I might have been wise to do so, for he would no doubt have expected recompense of the form that a fallen woman might be assumed to provide. But Atticus had asked so little in return, and none of it offensive to me.

With brief excuses to the guests I brushed aside in passing, I made my way toward where he stood conversing with one of the male guests. It was one of the younger peers of the house party, and I paused so that I could try to dredge up his name before joining them. And perhaps, to be honest, so that I might have a few more moments in which to find the courage to say what must be said.

"There seems to be a fair bit of frost down your way just now," the young man was saying to Atticus, with a smirk that I did not understand.

Atticus, too, must have been confused, for the weather had been damp. "Frost?" he repeated.

The young man grinned. "The missus, Blackwood. So early in the honeymoon and the chill has set in already?"

I could not see Atticus's face, but his voice was quiet. "The fault is mine. As new to marriage as I am, I fear sometimes I am prone to missteps."

"Well, you know, old chap," said the other, with a wink, "with that rum leg of yours you're bound to put a foot wrong now and then."

Indignation at this monstrous lack of tact flushed hotly through my veins, but after the slightest of pauses Atticus said only, "You're quite right. For my wife's sake I hope I learn to conduct myself with more grace."

If that isn't grace, what is? I was at his side almost before he finished speaking, slipping my arm through his. He started in surprise, but I held fast. "Every husband may be forgiven an occasional stumble," I said, addressing them both. "And if mine does occasionally make a misstep, at least he knows enough to keep his foot out of his mouth. My lord."

I would not have been surprised if he had been offended by my rudeness, but Lord Montague, whose identity I had finally remembered, was generous enough merely to sketch me a bow and say, "Brava, dear lady. Well put."

But it was Atticus whose response mattered more than anything else. I gazed into his face, trying to read beyond the exhaustion and what I feared was actual pain, and those remarkable eyes looked back into mine as if he, too, were searching. "I wronged you," I said softly, for his ears alone. "I am heartily sorry for it—and I hope you can forgive me."

To my annoyance, it was Lord Montague who spoke. "A pretty speech, Blackwood. The least you can do now is to take your lady for a turn on the floor."

I knew, even as the opening strains of a waltz began to play, that in his present state of weariness dancing would probably tax Atticus too much, and I opened my mouth to protest. But his arm was already slipping about my waist, and he smiled at me. "Will you do me the honor?"

Startled, I let him lead me away from Lord Montague, and then I realized that dancing would give us more privacy than we would have had otherwise. "Lean on me if you wish," I said quietly. "I know you must be weary."

"Not any longer," he said, but this was gallantry, for I could feel the unsteadiness of his gait as he swept me along to the music. "I don't know how I was restored to your good graces, Clara, but I'm more happy than I can say. The last thing I ever wished to do was insult you."

"Let's not speak of it." I had not danced in such a long time, and the excitement was heightened by the happiness I felt at being once more in accord with Atticus. This was so different from galloping around the servants' dining hall with another maid for my partner, shrieking with laughter to the accompaniment of a footman's squeeze-box. All around me were the gleam of fine jewels and satins, the fragrance of perfume and flowers, the joyous accompaniment of the musicians. And holding me in his arms was the handsomest of partners, whose clear eyes held a mixture of wonder and delight that I was here with him.

No, there was something else. Something that brought a chill to my skin and a sickening lurch of my heart. He was starting to care for me—and that would lead only to grief. And if I began to care for him as well . . .

Without warning there sprang into my mind the old baron's horrifying tale of his father and stepmother. I could hear his reedy voice saying with relish, *"He found no greater joy than in waltzing with her."* How could I have let myself put the Gravesend curse out of my thoughts for so long?

Abruptly I felt Atticus stumble, his weaker leg nearly going out from under him. In an instant he had righted himself, with little more than a sudden tightening of his hold on my hand to betray him, but I knew that his stumble must have been seen.

175

Instantly I swayed slightly, putting a hand to my forehead, and drew him to a stop. His moment of difficulty must be attributed to me.

"Clara? What is it?"

I could not tell if he realized that I was feigning when I blinked in confusion. "I'm so sorry, Atticus, but I feel a bit faint. This crush of people . . ."

"Let's get you out of this crowd," he said at once, and escorted me from the floor. I hoped that my ploy had worked, but even if Atticus's stumble had been noted, I realized that now our guests had a much more interesting morsel to contemplate. Without having intended to, I might have just complicated our arrangement most inconveniently.

"Are you unwell?" he asked, as he led me to a chair and stood over me while I sat and fanned myself. "I'll have the doctor fetched from Father's room."

"No, no, I'm quite all right. Only I fear I will have given all your friends a suspicion that may be unwelcome."

"What do you mean?"

"There is only one reason for a bride to feel faint," I said. "In the eyes of other women, at least." Holding my fan up to screen the words from others, I said, "I fear everyone will now believe I'm carrying your child, Atticus." I raised my eyes apprehensively to his. "I'm so sorry—I didn't think."

The expression on his face was contemplative, however, not angry. "That's nothing for you to worry about. In any case, time will prove the gossip wrong." More softly he added, leaning toward me, "I would have been honored for it to have been true, Clara."

I could feel myself blushing and looked away, plying my fan more swiftly to cool my cheeks.

He must have seen how flustered I was, for he straightened, and his eyes swept over the room. "I asked Brutus to make certain I was kept informed," he explained, his voice now matter-of-fact. "If there is any change in Father's condition . . ."

"I'm certain he'll send for you if that should happen." I patted the chair beside mine. "Come, rest for a bit. You ought to conserve your strength."

The evening passed quickly. The music, the loud babble of happy conversation, the brilliant light of the chandeliers seemed to blur time. I danced from time to time with Mr. Bertram and other guests, with my husband's blessing, but I was always aware of where he was. Twice a footman approached Atticus, and both times the quick tensing of his shoulders told me what he dreaded to hear; but each time, I learned, the footman merely reported that there was no change in his father's condition. On a third occasion the doctor himself appeared and drew Atticus aside for a brief conversation, then set out briskly, and I saw that he carried his bag.

"He is leaving," Atticus confirmed when I joined him, and the relief was plain in his eyes. "He says that Father's condition is stable enough that he feels confident in leaving us for the night."

"I'm so glad," I said, even if it was only for Atticus's sake. Then he smiled at me, and I realized my words might be taken another way. As long as Lord Telford lived, I would stay at Gravesend.

That was a minor enough consideration compared to a man's life. But the thought persisted, and I wondered uneasily if Atticus and I had already carried on this masquerade too long, and too assiduously. Once we had learned that his father knew my real identity—and since Atticus now knew that I was not Genevieve's mother—there was surely no point in continuing the charade.

But there was the considerable matter of Atticus's good name and his standing. These would be tarnished if I were to suddenly disappear. There would have to be a judicious tapering off, perhaps, of our apparent attachment to one another. Of our appearing in public together. Then the separation would not be sudden and shocking.

"Clara, you look so sad," came his voice, breaking into my thoughts. "What is troubling you?"

I shook off my ruminations on our future and found that I did not have to look far for another reason to be troubled. "Your father is a rather horrid man," I said. "I can only imagine how painful it must be that he is so ungrateful for your care of him— that he doesn't even respect you for it. I know that you are too kind and dutiful a son to do otherwise—"

His laugh, loud and abrupt, cut me off. Instantly he subsided, but the eye he fixed on me had a wry expression. "Kind and dutiful, am I? I confess that when he was infesting the air with venom and spite about you and Genevieve, I felt I could have easily done violence to him." He fell silent for a moment, and when he spoke again, his voice was almost calm. "We've never been kindred in any real sense, Clara. You probably realized that Richard was his favorite, and he encouraged my brother in his contempt of me. Richard was, I sometimes think, the only person on earth to have my father's approval."

"Then why devote yourself to his care to the point of risking your own health?"

He gave a long sigh. "I won't be able to respect myself if I don't take every care of Father. It would give him great satisfaction if I acted like the petulant weakling he thinks me, and for that reason as well as my own peace of mind I won't stoop to the level that he expects of me." Then he added more slowly, "There have been times in the last year or two that I thought we were finally coming to an accord, that he had learned to see me for what I've become and even, perhaps . . . but no. He'll carry his low opinion of me—and the world—to the grave, and no matter how badly he and I chafe each other, it's my duty to put off that destination as long as possible."

I said nothing, but the unwilling thought was clear in my mind: *It will not be easy not to learn to care for this man.*

This warning was still echoing in my thoughts by the time, hours later, that Atticus and I parted at my door. He bowed, with as formal a show of respect as if we were still among our guests, and raised my gloved hand to his lips. "Good night, Clara," he said, and I had to look away from the expression in his eyes, so greatly did it please me—and alarm me. "Thank you for being the most elegant hostess Gravesend has ever seen."

I managed to laugh at that. "Pray don't perjure yourself so, Atticus. The ghosts of all your ancestresses will rise up as a body to harry me out of the house if they think you serious." I made to draw my hand from his grasp and open the door, but his hand tightened on mine, stopping me.

"Earlier this evening, I fear I distressed you in saying what I did. If I was clumsy, I apologize . . . but I meant what I said."

His eyes were so tender that I had to bite my lip and look away. The idea of having a child with him, absurd though it was, held an aching loveliness that momentarily transfixed me. But even to think of such a thing just compounded the danger that threatened us, and both of us ought to be on our guard.

"It wasn't that, exactly," I said. "I think I've let myself become careless about the risk we're taking. As you said, it's dangerous to tempt the curse."

"When did I . . . ?"

"When I was sewing," I said uncomfortably. "You remember that evening."

"Oh, I see. That was my temper speaking, I'm afraid, not reasoned judgment." His eyebrows drew together quizzically. "In any case, I thought you felt that you had nothing more to fear from Gravesend, or you wouldn't have married me."

"That was when I'd lost everything, or thought I had. Now . . . now I know I have something to lose." I hoped he would not ask me just what this was.

There was a silence while perhaps he contemplated what I might have meant. Finally he said, "Curse or no curse, everyone takes a risk when they open their heart. I for one don't intend to wall my soul round with stone and iron so that I never cherish anyone again. That would be a living death—at least, it would be for me, and I think for someone like you as well."

"What do you mean, someone like me?"

The pensive quality that seemed never to be far from his eyes had returned. With a faint smile he said, "You're a passionate woman, Clara. It's part of your beauty."

This was not helping matters. With something like desperation I said, "Good night, and do let me know if I may be of use should your father's condition require it." Before he could answer I had drawn my hand from his, slipped inside my bedroom, and shut the door firmly behind me.

Safe. Another moment and I might have fallen headlong into the tenderness in his eyes, the caressing warmth of his voice. The unwanted thought came to me that gentleness, coupled with such a face and form, could be most seductive. I had been right to put some distance between us.

By morning the danger would be past, I told myself: whatever luster we had gained in each other's eyes tonight from the excitement of the ball and the pleasure of reconciliation would have died away, and we would be able to greet each other as friends, without any quickening of the pulse or too-fervent rush of pleasure at the sight of one another. Yes, friendship we could safely permit. Anything more would be too great a complication—and too great a risk.

Suddenly my own words came back to me. *All of life is a succession of risks, and each of us must judge for ourselves which risks are worth the taking.* Atticus was right: I did not want to wall up my heart. Indeed, I feared it was already too late for that. But for that very reason he and I needed to find our way back to safer footing.

If the night had ended there, the risk might have been averted. *Might* have, I say, but the truth is that we were probably already too far gone . . . and the consequences would be beyond my imagining. For Gravesend was no place for a Blackwood—by blood or marriage—to seek happiness.

CHAPTER EIGHTEEN

I tried to push Atticus out of my mind as I placed my jewelry back in its case and began undressing. My body was weary, and I looked forward with relief to the prospect of soon nestling into my soft bed. Off with the claret-red evening slippers, and I gave a glad sigh. Off with the magnificent but heavy skirt and overskirt, with their elaborate trimmings; off with the bustle petticoat with its spring-steel frame, the architecture of support for the gorgeous skirt. Off with the bodice—

Ah. Now I had a problem.

Unlike most of my other bodices, which followed the fashion of buttoning up the front, this one laced up the back. And try as I might, with my upper arms pinioned by the small off-the-shoulder sleeves, I could not reach around behind myself and get a purchase on the lacings. I was trapped.

I could have rung for Henriette, but the hour was much later than that at which I usually retired; it would have meant waking her from her sleep and forcing her to rise, dress, and come to my aid after a long and busy day. I had not the heart to do that to her. Genevieve? She was probably abed herself; she had been yawning during the last two dances, although like everything else she did this so adorably that not only Mr. Bertram but many of the young blades had been watching her with yearning eyes. And her room, thanks to my own jealousy, was not close to mine; I would have to don the rest of my ensemble again for that journey.

There was a solution close at hand, however. And though I hovered indecisively at the dressing-room door for long minutes, I knew that if I was going to ask him, I ought to do it before he, too, undressed and retired.

The prospect of this, which would be mutually embarrassing, propelled me abruptly through the dressing room and up to Atticus's door. I knocked briskly before I could change my mind. "Atticus? May I trouble you for a moment?" I called.

There was a pause that might have been puzzlement. Then came the polite reply, "It's no trouble," and I heard his footsteps approach and then the key turn in the lock.

Fortunately he was still dressed save for his coat, waistcoat, and tie. His eyebrows rose at the sight of me, and I knew what a peculiar sight I must be: from the waist up, still attired and coiffed for the ball; from the waist down, in under-petticoat and stocking feet. "It's my bodice," I said hastily. "I'm afraid I can't unlace it myself, and it's so late—"

"Of course," he said, as readily as if the request were perfectly normal. "There's no need to disturb your maid at this hour. Come nearer the light, and I'll see what I can do."

"Thank you." He stepped back to allow me to enter the room, but the way he favored his bad leg reminded me that it was troubling him, and I should not keep him standing. "Would you mind if I sat down?" I asked. "My feet are so sore from dancing."

"As you wish," he said, and with a gesture indicated the divan near the fire; but his bed was closer, and I did not wish to make him walk more than necessary. I perched on the edge of the mattress, where the coverlet had already been turned back, half turning so that he could reach the lacing more easily, and fixed my eyes resolutely on the bedpost. This would not take long, and then we could both retire—and Atticus, in particular, needed the rest.

I thought he hesitated for a moment, but then I felt the mattress sink as he sat next to me. "Would you mind moving your hair out of the way?" he asked, the words startlingly close to my ear, and I gathered up the long ringlets and held them against my head as he set about finding where the end of the lace was tucked in at the top of my bodice and drawing it out.

He worked gently, and in silence; I was aware of the faint feathering of his breath against my neck, and there was no sound but the sibilance of the cord being drawn through one eyelet and then the next. Gradually I could feel the bodice easing open. Somehow my breathing seemed to have become strained, at least to my own ears; it was the only other sound I could hear besides cord against fabric, and I cast about for something to talk about that would prevent Atticus from becoming aware of it. There should have been a hundred pleasantries at hand, a thousand observations about the ball. Yet not a one came to mind.

"You may let your hair down now," he said presently, and I did so, realizing that he was almost finished. Perhaps it was my imagination, but I thought that he was working more slowly.

"Thank you for doing this," I said lamely. "And thank you for the gown as well. It's quite beautiful."

"You're quite beautiful in it. And out of it as well."

I was still trying to decide whether he was teasing when I felt the last constraint of the bodice give way, and realized that he was done. Then, even through the sturdy coutil of my stays, I could feel his hands poise at either side of my waist. His voice sounded slightly breathless when he asked, "Do you need me to unlace your corset as well?"

"No, there's no need. It hooks in the front." My own voice was strangely husky, and I cleared my throat. "Thank you again. It was most kind of you."

This time he said nothing. I waited for my body to rise, walk to the door, and return to my room. I continued to wait, but it did no such thing. Why was I not going? But when I did move, his hands tightened ever so slightly on my waist.

"*Clara,*" he said. It was a hoarse whisper.

I could not read that one word; I must see his face and know what was in his mind—or his heart. Slowly I turned my head and found myself gazing into his eyes. His eyes had always been the most soulful I had ever seen, and now as he gazed at me there was something in them that made me raise my hand and place it against his cheek—and then draw his face down toward mine. That first kiss was like wine after years of thirst, even more so for being a thirst I had not known was in me. Then he was kissing me with soft, slow kisses that melted my bones and woke shivers all over the surface of my skin, deep luscious kisses that coaxed my lips apart and made me feel faint, but deliciously so. I was vividly conscious of every sensation, every thudding heartbeat, every soft exhalation of his breath mingling with mine, the heat of his mouth and the strength of his arms holding me.

Then he raised his head, and the clear blue of his eyes had never been so breathtaking. He said softly, "Clara, be with me tonight. As my wife."

For a long moment I made no answer, and there was no sound but our breathing. At last I nodded, and instantly overcome with shyness, bowed my head.

But his hand cupped my chin and raised it so that he could look into my eyes again. Stroking my hair back from my face with his other hand, he whispered, "I need to hear you say it."

I swallowed. I waited for my brain to awaken, to present a reason I should not do this. It was silent. I looked into his face—into my husband's face—and knew only that I felt closer to him than to anyone on earth, and wanted to be closer still, to comfort him and bring him delight . . . and be comforted and delighted in my turn.

"I will stay with you," I said, in a voice that was very low so that it would be steady. "As your wife."

After a silent moment he took my left hand, the one wearing his ring, from where it rested against his cheek. With a curious solemnity he brought it to his lips. Then, gently but inexorably, he bore me back onto the bed.

I do not know how much time passed, or how many kisses—first light teasing ones that made me strain toward him and curl my hand around his neck to draw him closer; then soft nuzzling kisses as if he were tasting my lips, growing deeper and

184

still deeper, searching and masterful, until the heat of languor was drugging me. But at the same time my skin was sensitized, so much so that when his hand stroked my bare arm and shoulder I shuddered at the loveliness of it; never had anything, no silk or satin or velvet, felt as sweet against my skin as did his touch. When his lips left mine to trail down my throat, a feeling of beautiful rightness descended on me, a golden certainty that this was unfolding as it was destined to.

Then he drew the bodice of my gown away and laid it aside. There came a gentle tug at the front of my chemise as he took one end of the ribbon tie and drew it toward him, untying the bow that fastened the drawstring. The ribbon loosened, and his fingertips touched my skin.

Abruptly memory crashed in on me, and I gasped. My hand flew to cover what he had laid bare, but it was too late. He had drawn the violet from its hiding place and now gazed at it wonderingly.

It was as if Richard had appeared and laid a sword between us. Suddenly we two were not alone in the bed, and I was shamed and furious at myself for having been the one to bring the ghost of this intruder upon us. Even though Atticus could not know what the flower meant, I felt as guilty as if I had struck him.

But it *did* mean something to him, I saw. Something blazed into his eyes—something that was not anger.

"You remembered," he said softly.

My mind was still hazy from the spell of his touch, and I did not understand at once. "Of course I remember," I said foolishly. "But how could you know of it? He wouldn't have told you . . ."

Only then did comprehension break upon me. The delicious languor of moments ago evaporated, and a cold shock surged through my veins.

"It was you," I whispered. Queasiness roiled my stomach, and I scrambled off the bed and backed away. "You had the violet put on my pillow. It was *you,* that day in the folly. Not Richard."

Now it was his turn for confusion. "I thought you knew," he said. "I was certain you'd realized it was me and not him. When my father made me kiss you the other evening, you said . . ."

185

There was an imploring note in his voice but also what sounded like pity, and I rejected it. I had backed away until my body was against a wall, and I shut my eyes to escape the sight of him. "How could you do such a thing to me? You made me think I could trust you, and all the time you hid this. Was it a prank, something to laugh over—the time you fooled Richard's stupid sweetheart into your arms?"

"It was no prank." His voice was stronger, and even with my eyes shut I could tell from the sound that he was rising from the bed and coming closer. "I only meant to keep you from being hurt. Richard told me he wouldn't be meeting you that day, that he was keeping an appointment with another woman."

"I don't believe you."

"Listen to me, my love." His words were rapid, urgent, but I turned my face away, trying not to hear. "Richard was deceiving you. I knew you'd be heartbroken if you learned that you were only . . . that you weren't his only sweetheart. So yes, I pretended to be him."

"You kissed me. You . . ." The memory of him unbuttoning my dress as my younger self lay there, innocent and trusting, sent another chill through me. "You took advantage of my trust."

"Clara, I'm sorry. It wasn't calculated." His voice sounded so sincere, but I would never be able to trust his sincerity again. "Partly I was trying to convince you I was Richard, and—"

"Partly? So you were only *partly* betraying my trust."

"Please listen." His hands closed on my bare shoulders, and I shoved him violently away.

"Don't touch me!"

His bad leg buckled under him, and he almost fell. But he regained his footing and approached me again, more cautiously this time. He came so close that, although he did not touch me, meeting his gaze gave me an almost physical jolt, and I averted my eyes. "Clara," he whispered. "I was in love with you."

"You were no such thing. You just wanted to take something from Richard. To feel that you'd won something that was his." Hot tears were starting down my cheeks, and that added humiliation was more than I felt I could bear. I darted away from him and looked wildly around for the discarded bodice of my red gown, swiping at the traitorous tears.

"That isn't true," he exclaimed. "Or if it is, it's only a part of the truth. It killed me to see how little he valued your love."

I snatched up my bodice from the bed and plunged toward the door, but I could not escape the horrible words. His voice went on, steady and relentless.

"He was a libertine, and no matter how much it hurts you to hear it, it's time you knew the truth. He had other women."

"*Stop it!*"

My shout startled us both into immobility, and we stood facing each other for a moment. In that tense and jagged silence the only sound was our breathing, which was as labored as if we had been trading physical blows. And then came the sound of running feet.

We've awakened one of the guests, I thought numbly, but the pounding at the door was too urgent to be from that source.

"Mr. Blackwood!" came a muffled voice, and I recognized the voice as Brutus's.

Atticus did not move at once. He was still staring at me, awaiting a response. Only when Brutus renewed his tattoo on the door and shouted again did he rap out in reply, "What is it?"

"Lord Telford is worse, sir. I think we should send for the doctor."

The words woke Atticus from his trance. He strode to the door and opened it—a crack merely, so that I would not be seen in my state of undress. "Saddle one of the horses and go fetch him here," he directed the valet. "I'll watch over Father in the meantime."

"I ought to stay with him," came the protest.

"My God, man, do you want to stand here quibbling while my father may be dying? You're already awake and dressed, which puts you that much closer to the doctor than any of the other servants are. I told you, I'll stay with my father. I can do as much as you can to make him comfortable."

"Very good, sir." The reply was grudging, but the footsteps receded with alacrity.

I came to myself. Before Atticus had time to close the door and turn back to me, I had darted through the dressing room and back into my own bedchamber. I slammed the connecting door and turned the key in the lock just as I heard his footsteps in pursuit.

"Clara—"

"Go away," I said childishly. "Your father needs you."

A moment's silence. Then, heavily, "We'll talk later, when he's out of danger."

I made no reply. After a second more, his footsteps slowly retreated. In another few moments I heard the door that led from his chamber to the hallway close, and I went limp in sudden reaction, sliding down the wall to sit on the floor.

My mind could scarcely hold the realization that Atlas had betrayed me all those years ago. I had trusted him—with my body as well as my heart—and he had let me believe it was Richard I was trusting, that it was Richard whose love for me held his desire in check. That single perfect afternoon, my talisman for all my life after, my absolute proof that no matter how others might slander him, Richard was a true and tender and honorable lover . . . shattered, stolen from me.

Now the beliefs that I had cherished for so many years were thrown into uncertainty. Had Richard truly loved me as I had him? That afternoon in the folly I had felt so enfolded by his love, lifted and buoyed on it as by the ocean, yet that love had been a charade. The house had already stolen Richard from me; now Atlas, with his devastating confession, had stolen my certainty of Richard's love. I'd thought I had nothing left to give Gravesend, but the curse, greedy for more of my suffering, had found something that remained to rob me of.

Could Atticus have spoken the truth about Richard having deserted me that day for another woman? I winced away from the thought, but it wouldn't stop eating at me. It would have been preferable to believe that Atticus had lied, that he had invented the whole story to exorcise his brother from my mind and heart . . . and if Genevieve had spoken truly and Atticus had come to care for me, this might have been a way of freeing me from Richard's hold on my heart so that I might be able to love Atticus. But that was calculating in a way that I had never seen in him—and foolish, too, if he had expected the story to make me think more fondly of him. And Atticus, whatever else he might be, was not a fool.

If only I had someone to talk to, a confidant, but Atticus—fittingly—was the only person who truly knew me and my secrets. I needed a friend who could listen and give me comfort, even guidance . . .

There was only one possible person, though she was scarcely a neutral party. But I quickly dressed in one of my day dresses—something simple enough that I needed no other pair of hands to assist me—and slipped from my room.

My route took me past Lord Telford's chambers, and I could see light at the bottom of the door. I thought I heard male voices, but I walked all the faster to put the room and its occupants behind me.

When I reached my destination I had to knock a few times before a response came. Then there came a drowsy *"Qui est-ce?"* and Genevieve opened the door, sleepily pulling a dressing gown on over her lacy nightdress.

Her appearance struck me as if for the first time, and I stood frozen, staring dumbly at her. The reddish tint of her hair . . . the blue eyes and high forehead . . . the wide mouth, mobile and expressive . . . all so familiar.

Atticus had not lied. She was Richard's daughter.

"Aunt Clara," she exclaimed. "Is something wrong?"

"Yes," I said through dry lips.

"What is it? Come in, tell me how I may help."

This girl might have been my daughter. If I had been less vigilant, or Richard more persuasive . . . or perhaps even that was a pretty lie I was telling myself, and maybe I had never held for him the attraction of the woman who became Genevieve's mother. I stared at her with hot eyes, and the girl, concerned, touched my arm.

That shook me out of my stupor. "Lord Telford has taken a turn for the worse," I said flatly. "The doctor has been sent for."

"Oh, I am so sorry. What can I do?"

"There's nothing. I just . . ." With her guileless blue eyes gazing at me with such concern I couldn't think of a plausible explanation for my presence. "Has anyone told you Gravesend is cursed?" I asked abruptly.

"Cursed?" She was perplexed, the poor innocent. "No, I do not believe so."

"A curse was laid on it that anyone who lives here will lose what they most treasure. And it's true. It has stolen what was most precious to me—and it stole him twice."

"Why, Aunt Clara, you're crying." She reached out to take my hand, but I backed away.

"You should run," I said. My voice was almost unrecognizable as my own. "Leave Gravesend. Go back to France, marry, do what you must but get away from here—before the house ruins your life as well."

Questions were hovering on her lips, but I could not bear to be with her any longer, this living reminder that Richard had been untrue, that the vile things Lord Veridian had said were more real than my own memories. I turned and almost ran back to my own room.

I huddled sleepless in a chair until Henriette arrived sometime after dawn to prepare me for another day at Gravesend . . . another day as Mrs. Blackwood.

CHAPTER NINETEEN

I had scarcely finished dressing, with Henriette's help, when there was a knock at the door. To my surprise it was Mrs. Threll who entered at my invitation. Her face was marked by its usual impassivity, so I was unprepared for the news she had come to divulge.

"Lord Telford has passed away," she told me. "The doctor arrived too late."

My first thought was of Atticus. Later I would wonder why my mind had not flown at once to the fact that I was now free, that this sham marriage needed to be continued no longer than strictly necessary for form's sake. But in that first moment I thought only of how difficult this would be for him. Despite the conflict and lack of real kinship that existed between him and his father, this loss would no doubt awaken sadness and regret in him.

My mind was so occupied with him that it took me a moment to register what Mrs. Threll had said next. "If you could let Mr.

Blackwood know when you see him, the doctor would like to speak to him in private."

"When *I* see him? He was with his father all night, surely. As soon as he sent Brutus for the doctor, he went to his father's room." A tiny change seemed to take place in the careful neutrality of her face, but I could not pinpoint what it was. "Brutus tells me that when he returned with the doctor, no one was with Lord Telford. He doesn't know where Mr. Atticus was."

"No more do I," I said, a bit shortly. It was exasperating to be assumed to be in my husband's full confidence when in fact he seemed quite adept at keeping vital information from me. "If I see him before you do, I'll tell him to go talk to the doctor."

"Very good, ma'am. I shall direct the servants to begin setting the house to rights."

It had been a very long time since I had been in a house where a death had taken place, but at a house as grand as Gravesend, and with the deceased so prominent in society, there would no doubt be elaborate measures—crape over the mirrors, the drapes drawn, a wreath on the front door, stopped clocks . . . "I'll ask my husband to speak to you if he has particular preferences as far as that goes," I said. "I'll need to have some of my dresses dyed black, if any of the maids can be spared for the task."

"Of course, ma'am."

The guests would almost certainly depart without my having to ask them; it was a pity for their sakes that their visit would be shortened, but it could not be helped. The house would no doubt be in upheaval all day. The very thought made me weary, after my distressing and unrestful night.

For my father-in-law—although it was still difficult to think of Lord Telford in that capacity—I did not feel the need for sorrow. His poor health had so obviously been a frustration and a burden to him that I could not imagine that he was anything but relieved to have been plucked from the terrestrial sphere. To be reunited with his beloved Richard was probably the happiest fate he could have desired . . . and, sadly, I suspected that his absence would not be an occasion of grief to many.

There had been a time, I recalled, when I had been so distraught over Richard's death that I had wished I might join him. I flinched now to think of it. That I had been so devastated by the loss of a man who had not been true to me, had not, perhaps, even loved me, woke the humiliation to burn anew in my heart. And facing Atticus again, knowing that he was fully aware of my ignorance and had known of it all these years—had heard me insist upon Richard's goodness when he knew I had been fooled—would have smarted even worse, had there not been the serious matter of his father's death at the forefront of our minds.

I elected to break my fast in my sitting room, knowing that the guests were probably too busy with preparations for departure to assemble for what would have been an uncomfortable meal together. News like this, as I knew of old, spread like wildfire in even the most distinguished of houses: the servants' network would be passing word to every corner, and the guests' valets and ladies' maids would be telling their masters and mistresses. Soon enough I could descend to the morning room in case any guests wished or needed to see me. But it would be Atticus they would wish to convey their condolences to, and I wondered how I would go about finding him. Where could he have gone that none of the servants had been able to tell Mrs. Threll?

There came a knock at the door, and when I called out a welcome, it was the man himself. But so changed. He was still in his evening clothes from the night before, which startled me, and he was unshaven, but the real change was in his manner. He moved like a man under water, as if at every step he were fighting against a force that tried to immobilize him. Every gesture seemed hard won, and the weariness in the slope of his shoulders and the heaviness of his eyelids squeezed at my heart despite my conflicted emotions about him. His hair was disheveled, his tie undone. Most shocking of all, though, were his eyes. Always they had held a tendency toward the contemplative, even toward sadness, but now they were the eyes of a man who had been dealt a shock that rattled him down to his soul. *Do my eyes look like that?* I wondered. *After he told me about his deception and Richard's faithlessness, was this what he saw in my face?*

It was but a passing thought. One look at Atticus thrust my own grief and shock to the back of my mind. I had not imagined that this loss would jar him so severely. He had stopped by the fire as if uncertain what to do; I rose and gently steered him to a chair, then rang for a maid. She could bring him breakfast, more tea, whatever he needed. In the meantime I brought him my own teacup, since it was the only one at hand. "Drink this," I said, and he did. I wished I had brandy or some other stimulant at hand. "You've heard, then?" I asked, as gently as I could.

"Heard?" His voice seemed to come from far away. "Heard what?"

My eyes widened. What could have left him looking so shattered except the news of his father's death? "I'm afraid it's your father," I said hesitantly. "I'm sorry to tell you this, but he has passed away, Atticus."

He was still for a long moment. Then he gave a long sigh as if his own life were leaving his body. "When?" he said dully, without looking at me.

"Before Dr. Brandt arrived. You—you weren't there, Mrs. Threll said."

"My father told me things that . . ." He shook his head. "I had to get away. He was still conscious when I left." His voice rasped as if he had been talking a great deal, or shouting. Or perhaps his throat was parched. I refilled the cup and brought it back to him.

"You need rest," I said. "That's the first thing. Later your valet can shave you and make you tidy."

He shook his head again. Not once had he looked me in the face. "There are arrangements to be made, too many things to attend to."

"Let Birch and Mrs. Threll and me see to all that. You must take care of yourself."

With a suddenness that made me start, he bounded up from the chair and began to pace. He buried his hands in his hair, and at once I realized why it looked so unkempt. He must have made that despairing gesture more than once in the night that had just ended. Now the strange paralyzed weariness was gone, replaced with a restless energy that had him prowling the room. The hitch in his gait told me that his bad leg was paining him still . . . or that he was in too much mental distress to control it.

"The things he told me," he said. "Clara, my God, the burden he laid on me . . ."

"Is there a way I can help?"

"I can't tell you what it is. He made me swear." His hand was actually shaking when he curled it into a fist. "He knew I couldn't break an oath I made to my dying father. He counted on it."

"There's no need for you to break your oath," I said to soothe him. "It's right that your father would entrust you with his final wishes. I'm sure everything will be all right."

For some reason those words caught his attention, and he halted in his restless circuit of the room and turned his haggard face toward me. "Clara," he said, as if newly conscious of my presence. "You're still speaking to me."

I could not prevent a tired smile from rising to my lips. "So it would seem."

"I'm sorry about that day in the folly. How different things might have been if . . ."

"Please don't let's begin tormenting ourselves with what-ifs. The past is done, and there is no good to be had from dwelling on it." I needed to believe it at least as much as he.

He regarded me with so much sorrow that doubt crept into my mind. Nor was it merely sorrow, but something else as well—compassion? "You have no idea," he said in a voice that was scarcely above a whisper. "But how could you? He kept his secret well."

"You needn't speak of your father if it distresses you so." Going to him, I took one of the clenched fists in my hands and gently coaxed the curled fingers open until I could hold his hand in mine. "Just tell me, does this change things for us?"

"Not at all," he said slowly, laying his free hand against my face. "Nothing can change what's between you and me—I'm determined on that."

I realized that he must have misconstrued my words, or perhaps the fact that we were on speaking terms made him think that we were again united in that sweet intimacy we had experienced so briefly the night before. But that, too, was in the past, and not to be recaptured.

This was not the moment to make that plain, however. Not with him reeling already. "Well, then," I said, keeping my voice calm and matter-of-fact, "what is there to worry about?"

His hand dropped, and he turned away. "Perhaps nothing. Perhaps everything."

My words had brought him no comfort. I realized that he was drunk—not on spirits, but on exhaustion and sadness and confusion. He had little idea what he was saying, and in this state he might let slip something he would later regret having said. If he blurted out his dead father's secrets to me, I didn't want either of us to have to live with the bitter regret that would ensue.

I wondered what the old man had told Atticus that could have devastated him so. A secret child, perhaps—a rival heir, even? Some underhanded business dealings that might place Atticus's legacy in jeopardy? Either of these might have come as a terrible shock to his son, especially if they meant financial ruin. If that disaster fell, the servants would be dismissed, all of Atticus's dependents—like me and Genevieve—would be forced to fend for themselves, and perhaps Atticus himself would even be compelled to find an occupation. But from the little he had said, despite its incoherence, that did not seem to be the case. He had said the secret changed nothing, so my imaginings must have been wide of the mark.

Now was not the time, however, for such speculation. "You've had a terrible blow, and you are worn to a thread," I said gently. "Everything looks darker when viewed through the lens of exhaustion. Rest, eat, and then see how you feel. Rest won't conquer sorrow, but it can make it a tiny bit easier to bear up under it."

I think he was about to accede when a peremptory knock sounded and Dr. Brandt entered the room without waiting to be invited. Perhaps he felt that his position made him immune to usual courtesies, and no doubt he was accustomed to having business too urgent to permit any delay. "Mrs. Blackwood, how do you do," he said crisply. "A very sad business, this."

"Indeed, Dr. Brandt. Thank you for all your efforts." I saw that the maid Jane had entered the room silently behind him and stood awaiting her orders. "I imagine you're in need of refreshment after your long night—"

To my astonishment, he cut me off. "I haven't time for such inessentials. There is something of the utmost gravity I must discuss with your husband. Blackwood, where can we speak in private?"

"Here," said Atticus shortly. "I have no secrets from Clara. That is to say," he amended, no doubt realizing that this was not the strict truth, "you may speak freely before my wife. What concerns me concerns her also."

"Very well," said the doctor. "Pray dismiss your servant, Mrs. Blackwood, so that we may talk in confidence."

I was not particularly pleased at being ordered about in my own sitting room, but I asked Jane to bring a fresh tea tray and leave it outside the door. When she had closed the door behind her I locked it, more to reassure the doctor than out of any real fear of being intruded upon.

"That other door," he said, jerking his head toward it. "Where does it lead?"

"To my bedchamber. I'll lock it if you wish, although no one would have cause to use it except perhaps Henriette, my maid."

"French, is she? Yes, do lock it. Are there any other places where someone might eavesdrop?"

"None," said Atticus. A certain amount of nervous energy had returned to him with the doctor's appearance, and although I took a seat on a divan and indicated the place next to me, he remained standing. "What is it you have to divulge that is so deadly secret, Dr. Brandt?"

The doctor gave a short bark of a laugh. He was a stocky man with a round balding head and eyes notable more for their intelligent expression than their beauty. His suit was of serviceable brown wool, and his waistcoat plain. Clearly he did not care greatly about his appearance, but that gave me more confidence in his priorities.

"Deadly it is indeed," he said. "I am sorry to tell you this, Mr. Blackwood, but there is something very sinister about the manner of your father's passing."

"Sinister?" Atticus repeated. "What do you mean?"

"The late Lord Telford did not die a natural death," said the doctor grimly. "He may have been at death's door, but it was some other party who pushed him over the threshold."

CHAPTER TWENTY

"Y"ou mean to say that someone *killed* him?" I exclaimed.
"That appears to be the case, yes."
In my agitation, the question of *why* was not upper-
most in my mind. "But someone was with him almost all night,
were they not?" I asked. "Atticus, you went to him as soon as
Brutus went for the doctor . . ."

"I did, yes, but that means there was an interval when no
one was with Father. Just as when I left, although I don't know
how much time elapsed between my leaving and Dr. Brandt's
arrival with Brutus." His face had gone gray, and as I went to
his side, worried, he again raked a hand through his hair. "This
is beyond all belief. Nothing of the sort has ever happened at
Gravesend. You're quite certain, Brandt? There isn't a chance
that you could be misinterpreting something?"

"I am not in the habit of crying murder where there's room
for doubt," said the doctor acidly. I liked him less every moment.
"Marks on Lord Telford's body indicate to me that someone

placed a hand over his nose and mouth to stop his breathing. If you would care to examine him yourself—"

"Yes, I would," Atticus said. "Not that I don't trust you, but I would like to see exactly what you're describing." He shut his eyes briefly in reaction. "I suppose I'll have to question Brutus myself. What his motives might have been I have no idea. If Father promised him a legacy . . ."

"Why are you assuming it was Brutus?" I asked. "When he left, your father was still alive, and when he returned, it was in the company of the doctor. Someone else must have slipped in between the time that you left and Brutus and Dr. Brandt arrived."

A weary smile crossed my husband's face. "My love," he said, "do you realize how unlikely that is? The fact is that, as you've just pointed out, I'm the last person known to have seen my father alive. From that perspective, I'm the most likely suspect."

"That's absurd! You had no reason to do such a thing." I stopped short. In fact, Atticus had plenty of reasons that might look like motives to an outsider. The long-standing discord between them; the threats his father had made to expose my origins, and Genevieve's; even the estate itself, depending on how his father had disposed of his money and property.

My consternation must have shown on my face, for the doctor gave a grim nod. "You see how it is, Mrs. Blackwood? The authorities must be called in. There's too much room for suspicion to attach to your husband."

"And to me," I said, for the realization was breaking upon me that, to an outsider, I had reason to murder my father-in-law. His threat to expose me as a fraud might look to a jury like a powerful inducement to murder. Not that anyone but Atticus and Genevieve knew of those threats, but . . .

"No one could suspect you, Clara," said Atticus, with renewed authority. I could not tell him in the doctor's presence that what he meant as reassurance sounded dangerously like naïveté. "And as for me, I don't care what the gossips may say; that sort of thing dies down on its own. But whoever did this terrible thing can't be allowed to go free. We must contact the authorities. Scotland Yard, I think; they have experts who surpass the abilities of our local constabulary."

"Very good." Dr. Brandt clasped his hands behind his back and nodded. "I imagine they'll make short work of the case, Blackwood. I wouldn't be at all surprised if it turned out to be a servant."

"And why is that, doctor?" I snapped. "Criminal tendencies are scarcely unique to the working class."

"I had no such thing in mind, Mrs. Blackwood, but servants are best situated to go in and out of places without being questioned—without, even, being observed closely. This Brutus may have had a confederate. It could have been a matter of a legacy, as your husband suggested. Or perhaps one of them had been caught stealing—I beg your pardon, Mrs. Blackwood, but despite your egalitarian principles theft *does* occur from time to time among the less privileged—or was on the verge of being dismissed and sought to prevent it in this way."

I shuddered. "What a monstrous thing to do." But I could not dismiss such a motive. I had landed on my feet, comparatively speaking, when I had been dismissed from my post here. I had had my mother's connections and knowledge to help me. Another servant might not be that lucky; dismissal, and all that it implied about the fitness of the employee, could be the beginning of a short journey to poverty, infamy, even death.

Atticus's hand descended to my shoulder, and when I looked up, he gave me a reassuring smile, tired but so tender that it brought a twinge to my heart. "Never fear, Clara. Whatever the investigation turns up, we'll not condemn anyone without clear proof."

"It won't be up to you," said the doctor briefly. "Once the investigation begins, it's out of your hands. If you suspect any of your servants will make a run for it once the word gets out that the baron was murdered, I advise you to take measures now to prevent that. Now, I recommend that you contact the Yard at once. They'll wish to examine the body, and that shouldn't be postponed."

"Thank you, doctor," I said, grudgingly, and went to unlock the door for him. Jane was just cresting the staircase with the heavy tea tray, and Dr. Brandt gave her a hard look, as if he suspected her of having been listening despite the physical impossibility of this.

Abruptly I remembered the voice I had heard the first night. If it had come from some hidden room or passage, then it stood to reason that the same hiding place could be used to eavesdrop. But how much would such a thing matter? All too quickly the news would spread of Lord Telford's shocking cause of death, and any of the servants could have observed the coolness—alternating with heated words—between Atticus and his father. They would have learned nothing new by eavesdropping.

Still, the thought made me uneasy. Especially I did not like the idea of suspicions forming around Atticus.

The doctor gave a nod of farewell to us both. "Send quickly," he said again. "I'll be waiting for word to return and give my own account."

Atticus took the heavy tea tray from Jane and sent her on her way. "An investigation," he said quietly, when the door had once again closed and left us in privacy. He set the tray down with so abstracted an air that it was sheer luck that it landed on a table. "I wonder what they'll find. Clearly there was more going on in my father's life than I knew."

"I'm certain the Yard will get to the bottom of things," I said, feeling ill equipped to offer comfort in this startling situation. "Then you'll be left in peace and can mourn your father properly."

He sank into a chair, knitted his fingers together almost as if in prayer, and rested his chin on his linked hands. "I suppose so," he said, and the weariness was even stronger than before in his voice. "Once I determine what 'properly,' in the case of a man like my father, actually is."

I was uncertain how to respond. Mourning my mother had been complicated because of the gulf that had opened up between us when I was dismissed from Gravesend. I had never quite forgiven her for not standing with me, even though I understood her reasons. But my mother had not slighted me in preference for a sibling; nor had she laid any heavy charge upon me as apparently Lord Telford had done to Atticus. Certainly her death had not been murder, so I had no idea how Atticus must be feeling now.

I leaned over from my seat on the divan and touched his linked hands. "I am so sorry," I said.

He took my hand in both of his before I could withdraw it. "I'm glad you are here with me, Clara."

My answering smile was uncertain. He would not think so for long if it should prove that my presence at Gravesend was in some fashion connected to his father's death. "Are you going to speak to the staff? Stories are no doubt already circulating and may be creating unease about their positions here."

"You're quite right." He straightened his shoulders, and I thought again how suited his nickname was, although not in the mocking fashion in which Richard had used it; he always seemed to have a burden to shoulder, yes, but he was always equal to the task, and his taking on that burden meant that others did not have as great a weight to bear. He would have made an excellent father, I realized—with some sorrow, since it seemed that he would never have the chance to become one. If I went away . . .

If I went away? Why was it a matter of doubt? That had always been the arrangement.

Even as I reminded myself of this, however, I realized that that was not the case. Atticus had told me, certainly, that once my duty was discharged I would gain my independence. But by bringing me and Genevieve together he had hoped to create a family that I would not want to leave—that would be my permanent place.

Even now, knowing that Genevieve was not in fact my child, he seemed to be cherishing a hope that our unconventional little family arrangement might continue. At least, that was what I supposed had been in his mind last night when he had asked me to stay with him. If I had become a true wife to him, it would have been for more than just one night; a man like Atticus would not take me to his bed unless he meant us to be truly wedded.

And I? What had been in my mind? Not a great deal, it seemed to me in the cold light of this grim morning. Whatever mental faculties I possessed had seemed to dissolve in the sweetness of his touch.

No, that was not strictly true. I, too, had recognized that taking that irrevocable step would mean changing the terms of my future. "I will stay with you as your wife," I had told him—and I had meant it. Not just for the night, but for all time. The dream I had cherished, the goal that had brought me back to Gravesend—an independent life somewhere new, a fresh start on my own terms—had been replaced by a new dream of living on at Gravesend with Atticus.

But that was before I had learned of his deception. Gazing at him now, at the lofty brow and clear, pensive eyes, I had a difficult time believing him to be anything but completely honest. He had deceived me, though, all those years ago—and might be deceiving me again now.

Atticus insisted on addressing the servants before seeing to his own rest. I had lost count of how many hours now he had gone without sleep. He had Birch and Mrs. Threll gather the household in the banquet hall, which still bore all the remnants of the ball: the melted stumps of candles, the tablecloths showing spills, the wilted flowers dropping their browned petals. All the usual activity of putting things to rights had been postponed while making the house into a fit place for mourning.

"By now I'm sure you have all heard the news," Atticus said. He was addressing them from the dais, standing just where he had opened the ball the night before. "Many of you have been at Gravesend for years—a few of you, even, since before my birth— and I know that my father's death, while not unexpected, will be deeply felt." An elegant sidestep, that seemed to me. "I am afraid I do have news that will be a shock, however," he continued. "The doctor has told me that my father did not die a natural death. He is certain that someone else had a hand in it."

A murmur rose among the gathered servants, and I saw Birch's mouth tighten—whether with disapproval at the response or at the news itself I could not have said. It would not have surprised me to learn that he and many of the other servants felt that murder was a breach of taste and cast their home in a poor light. Indeed, it was strange to have to adjust my picture of Gravesend to include this sensational new bit of history. It was like turning the pages of a volume of poetry only to find a lurid illustration from a penny dreadful.

Atticus raised his hand to acknowledge and quell the rumble of conversation. "An inspector from Scotland Yard will be coming here to determine the truth of this theory and, if it is indeed a case of murder, to pinpoint the guilty party. But that is the *only* matter that will be under investigation. Have no fear that your privacy will be invaded or the security of your position cast into doubt. The only person who need have any apprehension is whoever is responsible for my father's death."

I hoped it would be possible for him to keep his word about the staff's privacy. I remembered all too well that as a maid none of my few possessions had been sacrosanct, nor was the room I shared with another girl: at any time, if there was any suspicion of theft or of any of us possessing inappropriate goods (such as the aforementioned penny dreadfuls), my mother or the butler could march in and command us to present all of our belongings for their inspection. I wondered if conditions had changed during Mrs. Threll's tenure or if Atticus simply did not realize how little privacy servants were given as a matter of course.

One of the footmen said something into Birch's ear, and the butler gave a deferential cough. Atticus indicated with a nod that he might speak. "Lord Telford, sir," he said, and I think I was not the only one who was startled to hear the title given to Atticus for the first time, "is there any danger to anyone else in the household? If the guilty party has not yet been found, should we be on our guard?"

Atticus hesitated, torn, I could tell, between wanting to reassure but not wanting to divulge too much. "This does not seem to have been a random crime," he said at last. "I believe my father was targeted for a specific reason. But it might be a good idea nonetheless to exercise vigilance. Birch, Mrs. Threll, perhaps you can rearrange everyone's duties for the time being so that no one need be alone. I'll also contact the local constabulary to ask for a police presence here in the house."

I hid a wry smile and shook my head. He could not realize it, of course, but "rearranging" every servant's duties so that each was always accompanied by a partner would be a tall order—and would probably cause a fair amount of upheaval in the running of the household. I resolved to speak with Mrs. Threll to discuss how best these changes might be made and what housekeeping chores could be dispensed with for the time being to make this peculiar arrangement practical. With luck, though, their employer's reassurance would prevent any from leaving their positions—whether through guilty consciences or fear of being sent after the old baron.

After he had dismissed the staff and spoken privately to Birch, and I to Mrs. Threll, I laid hold of him by the arm and told him, "Mrs. Threll is going to have your valet bring hot water for washing to your room. And then he is going to force you to sleep for at least five hours."

His smile was a ghost of its former self. "Force me?"

"Indeed he will. And if you don't cooperate, I'll help him. I will hold you down if necessary."

His eyebrows rose, and I realized too late the mental picture that my words might evoke. Hastily I continued, "You need to be rested by the time the man from the Yard arrives. He must find you clearheaded and with all your wits about you."

"You think I'm so likely a suspect that such elaborate precautions are necessary?"

The question was posed gravely, and I answered in kind. "No, *I* don't. But as your wife I may be biased."

"Sweet Clara," he said, and that phantom smile came and went again in the space of a heartbeat.

I had grown accustomed to his dropping "my love" into his speech as part of our masquerade, but for some reason this new endearment made me stumble over my next words. "It isn't so much a matter of your being a suspect," I said. "But the inspector will be far better able to form a theory about the culprit if you present all that you know clearly and completely. The more information he has, the better able he'll be to perform his duty." And I ought to get some rest as well, I realized, for the same reason: I needed to be in full possession of my faculties to be of use to the investigation.

"Genevieve," he said suddenly, halting halfway up the stair. "Has she been told? The poor child, she'll be terrified."

"I'll go to her," I said, keeping firm hold of his arm to make him resume his progress. "She may not have awakened yet, considering the late night." The interruption to her sleep that I had caused might also delay her waking. Perhaps my intrusion would turn out to have been a blessing, though; if she was still sleeping and had not yet heard the news, I might be able to break it to her more gently than another.

At last we stood before his door, so nearly where we had stood less than twelve hours before—and how much had taken place in that time, I could not help reflecting. At that parting I had worried about the curse, about what might transpire if Atticus and I grew too dear to one another. Such disaster had struck the household since then that I could almost think that we were somehow to blame, except that I knew neither of us had dealt the killing blow to his father. His death could not be laid at our doorstep.

Or so I then believed.

CHAPTER TWENTY-ONE

Genevieve, when I awakened her from rosy, picturesque sleep, was shocked and distressed, as Atticus had predicted. She had many questions, and I few enough answers, and I resolved to try to find some occupation to keep her busy so that she would not have much opportunity to dwell on these unfortunate events.

I was surprised not to be called in to speak to the inspector upon his arrival, but evidently he was in no hurry to question me. It was not for hours that I was summoned to the library, which Atticus had turned over to him for the duration of the inquiries. This Birch told me when he came to escort me to the library for my own turn. He said that my husband and Brutus the valet had already been interviewed at length by the Yard man. I was on the point of asking him if he himself had been questioned when we arrived at the library and he announced me.

Inspector Strack was a man of just over middle age, with iron-grey hair and a drooping moustache. He had a strange habit of squinting, which made me wonder if perhaps he needed spectacles but did not wear them. This did not bode well for his powers of observation, I felt. His suit was plainly made and of some years' wear, to judge by the lapels and sleeves; he was either thrifty or not generously paid, or both.

"Inspector," I said, offering him my hand, and he shook it briefly without bowing. Evidently the inspector did not believe in obsequiousness to the landed class. I hoped this reflected an egalitarian approach to investigating rather than class resentment that might lead him to look for his perpetrator among those of the sphere I had married into.

"Lady Telford," he said. It was odd hearing my title from him, but he spoke it in as matter-of-fact a way as if it had not been a title at all. "Thank you for agreeing to speak to me. This should not take much of your time."

"I'm glad to hear it." That suggested to me that he was already well on his way to determining the guilty party.

But he evidently took my response in another spirit. "Indeed, I know you have many crucial domestic duties to attend to, and I'd hate to cause any disruption to your dinner menu and social calendar for so minor a reason." His accent was not as harsh as some I had become accustomed to in London, although the sarcasm was certainly not unheard of in that region.

"As you say," I returned, taking a seat in the straight-backed chair he had placed before the great desk, which he seemed to have appropriated. "I have a crowded schedule of beating housemaids and squandering my husband's money, so it's best we wrap up the trifling matter of my father-in-law's murder as quickly as possible."

That won me a grudging smile. "My apologies, Lady Telford. Murder cases do not find me in the best of humors."

"Most understandable. How may I help you?"

He seated himself in the worn leather-upholstered chair behind the desk, and I wondered suddenly how many years Lord Telford had conducted his business from that very spot— all of the day-to-day matters that came with being a landowner. How indignant he would have been to have his chair borrowed by a mere inspector.

But Strack was speaking, and I gathered my wandering attention.

"I'd like your account of the day and night leading up to the discovery of your father-in-law's death," he said. "I'm looking for corroboration of certain facts that have been disclosed by other witnesses—"

"Witnesses?" I exclaimed.

"Not to the death itself," he explained. "No, we haven't been fortunate enough to locate any such creature yet, although that would be ideal! I meant only witnesses to some of what seem to be key events leading up to the crime."

"Such as the argument between my husband and his father," I said, suspecting that this unfortunate episode would have been made known to him already. Atticus was too forthright not to have disclosed the distasteful event.

Sure enough, the inspector gave a curt nod. "I'd like to hear your version of that, if you please."

"I only overheard part of it; not as much as Genevieve, my husband's ward. Unfortunately what we heard convinced us that we two were . . . less than welcome in Lord Telford's eyes."

"Be plain, please. What exactly did you hear him say about you?"

Of course it was pointless to engage in polite euphemism. "He indicated that he knew of my true origins," I said, "and had the gravest suspicions about Vivi's."

"And what are your origins, my lady?" He leaned back in the chair, lacing his fingers across his waistcoat, and regarded me steadily.

"Irrelevant to your investigation," I said crisply. "Have you any other questions for me?"

For a moment I thought he would pursue the point, but then he seemed to change his mind. "Quite a few, yes," he said. "I've been informed that earlier on the night of that argument your husband was involved in another violent confrontation. He forcibly ejected a guest from the house, I understand."

"You make it sound as if he engaged in a brawl," I protested. "It wasn't like that. My husband is a civilized man."

"So these explosive rages are rare events?"

"Of course! That is, there was nothing explosive about it."
I must be more careful; the man clearly had no compunction
about twisting my words. "I do not know who you've spoken to,
but if they gave the impression that my husband was violent in
any way, they misled you."

"Ah. So your husband has never engaged in any physical
confrontations that you know of?"

I chose my words carefully. "I have never once seen him
raise his hand against anyone. He is not a violent man—it takes
a great deal to anger him."

"And yet twice in twenty-four hours he was observed in an
angry conflict. What am I supposed to believe, Lady Telford,
when your husband's behavior changes so markedly? Has he
taken leave of his senses?" He leaned forward over the desk,
his eyes fixed on me as if he could catch me in a lie. "Or has his
marriage to you created some change in him?"

"He has not changed," I protested. "Only . . ."

"Only what?"

The words emerged in a rush. "When my husband had Lord
Veridian thrown out, he believed he was defending my honor."

The inspector pulled a face of such withering skepticism
that I could feel myself shrink. "Pardon my plainness, my lady,
but that makes no sense. From what I hear, the only parties
maligned by the viscount were your late brother-in-law and the
women with whom he consorted."

I opened my mouth but found I had no words.

Now the inspector's chilly eyes, as gray as his hair, fixed
on me even more closely. "If you have anything to say that
may remove suspicion from your husband," said Strack, weight-
ing the words with significance, "you owe it to him to speak.
If you have anything to say, however embarrassing, that could
keep his neck out of the hangman's noose, now is the time to
say it."

With part of my mind I knew that this man was using
manipulation to make me speak. But with word already having reached him of the altercation with Lord Veridian as well
as the argument with the old baron, he certainly had good
reason to view Atticus with suspicion. I could remove some of
that suspicion by telling him of my past and Atticus's mistaken

assumptions about me . . . by revealing my social credentials and my marriage as the lies they were.

For an instant I felt a terrible doubt. What if being forthright with this man brought infamy upon me—and, what was more important, on Atticus? What would the inspector do when armed with the whole truth about me?

I knew that if Atticus had been with me he would have told me not to concern myself with the consequences for him, and yet it was for his sake that I dreaded letting the truth be known. But this was a matter of his innocence—and moreover, until he was ruled out as a suspect, the real killer would walk free. I had to believe that telling the truth was the right thing to do, no matter how much havoc it might cause when word escaped Gravesend . . . as it was bound to do. I took a deep breath, folded my hands in my lap, and looked squarely at the inspector.

"The truth is this," I said. "As a girl, I was a servant here at Gravesend. My mother was housekeeper. When I was seventeen I was dismissed and sent away when it was discovered that I had been meeting with Atticus's brother, Richard." This was more difficult than I had anticipated. I sat up straighter as if it would lend strength to my will. "It . . . it was assumed at the time that I was carrying Richard's child. A false assumption."

His expression had not changed, so either I had not shocked him or he was adept at disguising shock. "So Richard left no children behind when he died at Eupatoria."

He had been doing research, it seemed. "As to that," I said slowly, "I cannot say for certain. I only know that there was no child of my body."

A quick nod seemed to indicate that he approved of my precision, but, to my great relief, he did not press for more details. "After you were dismissed, what happened?"

I sketched in how I had passed the years that followed and how Atticus had emerged once more into my life with his peculiar proposition. "At first I think his father was deceived into thinking me a proper match, and he accepted me, more or less. I don't think he would have respected any bride Atticus brought to Gravesend, but he seemed to find amusement in my conversation. If he had suspicions, he did not bait me with them—and I'm certain he would have done so, had he the opportunity."

"So how did he discover the truth about you?"

"From what I heard him say to Atticus, he must have remembered me and belatedly made the connection that I was the maid who was dismissed."

"Did this strike you as peculiar, this belated realization?"

I shook my head. "Unlike some masters, Lord Telford did not take great notice of the female servants—of any of the servants. I think we were largely faceless to him. Literally so, in fact, for it was the rule then for us to turn our faces to the wall if he came upon us about the house. I think that would have made it difficult for him to recognize me. But not impossible, especially given the notoriety of my dismissal." I tried to recall what else I had overheard and what might be useful to the inspector. "He seemed to think that Atticus had done something shameful in bringing me here as his wife; he took it as a personal slight."

"You must admit that he had some right to feel that way," observed the inspector. "For a man of his standing to discover that his son has foisted an impostor onto him and has presented him with a chambermaid for a daughter-in-law . . . well, many men would be incensed at such a thing. I'm putting it as he might have seen it, you understand."

"Of course," I said, quelling the indignant flare of anger that had tried to rise in me. Perhaps he was trying to evoke just such a response from me, perhaps even . . . a new thought made my eyes widen. "I did not kill him, if that's what you mean," I said sharply. "My pride was not stung to the degree that I would have murdered an old man merely for saying some unflattering things about me."

He spread his hands in a conciliating gesture, but my outburst had not visibly startled him. "I have not made any such accusation, Lady Telford."

"It would be in your mind, though; naturally it would. From your perspective it may seem that I had a great deal to lose should Lord Telford spread word of my true history."

"So you had not, in fact, a great deal to lose?"

"Of course not. My husband was fully aware of my past when he proposed our arrangement, so he wouldn't have abandoned me had it become common knowledge. The worst conse-

quences would have been our being cut by all his acquaintance."
My voice slowed, and the inspector leaned forward, seizing on
my sudden doubt.

"Indulge me for a moment, my lady. If we were to make a
hypothetical case for your murdering your father-in-law, you
might have killed him if it would have saved your husband
from becoming a pariah, mightn't you? Think of the shame that
would have followed. He would have been dropped from his
clubs, snubbed by all his neighbors, derided until the two of you
were forced to—what? Leave Gravesend? Sell the property, take
up a trade? A living death for a peer . . . and for his luxury-loving
wife, who feared poverty to the extent that you did."

"That's quite enough," I snapped. "I'm aware of this possibility—indeed, it still exists. Silencing my father-in-law would
only have been a temporary stopgap. Once he said the words,
they were out in the world; there was no calling them back."

That surprised him, perhaps the first thing I had said that
did. "Are the walls of Gravesend so easily permeated that one
word of gossip can spread through the air of the entire country?" he inquired, only half facetiously.

"Deride it if you wish, but a house as big as this one always
has listening ears. For a start, a good valet is never quite out of
earshot of his master if he can prevent it; he needs to be close
enough to respond quickly whenever his presence is desired,
to the point that he seems to anticipate his master's wishes if
possible. And servants speak to each other about their masters;
anything that affects those above stairs affects those below,
sometimes to a far greater extent." My voice had taken on a lec-
turing quality, and I stopped to gather my thoughts and make
certain I was not letting Strack lure me in a direction that I
might regret. "What I mean is," I said, "no matter how much I
may dread a future in which my husband and I are cast out of
Gravesend, there would have been no advantage, and every disadvantage, to trying to silence Lord Telford in that way. Indeed,
I think that if he still lived he would greatly enjoy keeping the
secret, precisely so he could hold it over our heads and torment
us with it." Belatedly I realized that this was not strengthening
my case, and I fell silent, vexed with myself.

"Hmm." He made a few notes in pencil on a sheet of Gravesend stationery. "How would you describe the state of your marriage, Lady Telford?"

"I assume you have good reason to ask something so intimate."

"I do. Are you and your husband generally in accord?" I hesitated. There flashed into my mind the memory of lying in Atticus's embrace as he kissed me half out of my wits . . . and then fleeing from him in anger and wounded pride. "Like every married couple, we have occasional differences; but for the most part, yes, we are on good terms."

"Yet not on good enough terms that you can vouch for his whereabouts on the night that his father died."

This was so clumsy an attempt to shake me that I almost laughed. "Inspector, my husband's father was seriously ill—enough to warrant sending a servant out in the middle of the night to fetch the doctor. If you think that in those circumstances a reasonable man would calmly compose himself for sleep at his wife's side . . . well, you either underrate the bond of filial loyalty or greatly overrate my charms."

He did not find my riposte amusing, however. "This kinship you speak of," he said intently. "Were your husband and his father close, then?"

I knew he would catch me out if I overstated the degree of warmth between Atticus and his father. Feeling my way with caution, I said, "I'm sure you know by now, having spoken to my husband, that he and his father argued from time to time, that they have—*had*—incompatible personalities."

"I've heard something to that effect, yes."

"The truth is that Lord Telford loved Richard better than Atticus. And perhaps in the years since Richard's death his father, in his grief, exaggerated Richard's virtues and turned him into a paragon." My voice slowed as I realized I might have been describing my own mental processes. "He viewed Atticus's normal human weaknesses with a more jaundiced and resentful eye, contrasting him always with the son he had loved and lost, whom he had come to look on as impossibly superior."

As had I, not so long ago now. Unlike Lord Telford, however, I had come to appreciate the man Atticus had become . . . so much so that the idea that he might be prosecuted for murder struck a terrible cold into my heart. The thought of losing him filled me with something akin to panic.

Strack was watching me closely, and I wondered what my face had revealed to him. Mentally I gave myself a shake. "My husband is the kind of man who feels the obligations of honor and loyalty very deeply," I said. "He and his father would have had to have been seriously alienated for him not to have had Lord Telford's welfare uppermost in his mind. Whether he liked his father I cannot say, but he would have died himself it if could have prevented this terrible thing from happening."

"So even though your husband had gone so far as to throw a peer of the realm out of his house for having indirectly insulted you, he would not have raised his hand against his father for making specific, personal aspersions about your character."

I knew how weak my argument seemed, but that only made me more desperate—and more stubborn. "He would never have struck his father," I stated. "Lord Veridian was different; he would have been able to defend himself if there had been any question of a physical altercation."

"What you are telling me, then," said the inspector, "is that your husband had neither the motive nor the temperament to kill his father."

"Exactly," I said in relief.

"Whereas you, on the other hand, did."

"But I've told you, it was too late—"

He silenced me with a curt gesture. "Even if I grant that it was too late to stop word of your true origins from spreading, that in itself could be powerful motive for murder. Your father-in-law was doing his best to poison your marriage and your place in this house, Lady Telford. It might have been too late to undo the damage he had done, but it would not have been too late for revenge."

After what I had said, I could not now pretend to be indifferent. Certainly the old baron's berating of Atticus had roused a primal rage in me. Perhaps I had a streak of the Furies in my character. But if that were so . . . "Inspector Strack," I said, "you seem a good judge of character. If I had wanted to avenge myself on my father-in-law, do you think I would have chosen so peaceful a means of dispatching him as smothering?"

Feminine voices rose in the hallway, and Strack's eyes flicked toward the door, behind me. He must have instructed Birch not to enter without permission, for a knock sounded. I had to repress my now-instinctive response and let Strack answer. It was strange to realize how proprietary I had become after so short a time as Gravesend's mistress.

It was indeed Birch who opened the door, but it was Genevieve who fairly flew into the room, towing a reluctant-looking Henriette by the hand.

"Inspector Strack?" she demanded. "We must speak with you at once. Henriette has evidence that is vital to your investigation."

CHAPTER TWENTY-TWO

Her attempt to sound serious was undermined by her charming accent and the pretty sight she made even in her mourning dress of sober black. Her blue eyes were bright with determination, her cheeks flushed, and I was not surprised to see an answering flush darken Strack's cheeks. Without seeming to be aware of it, he smoothed down his moustache with one knuckle, first one side, then the other, all without removing his eyes from the girl. He had risen upon her entrance, and seemed now to be trying to stand up even taller. Poor man—he little guessed how signally he was failing to impress her. But the flash of sympathy I felt for him suddenly made him feel less like an intruder.

"Miss Genevieve Rowe, I believe?" he said deferentially. "I had intended to speak to you confidentially. If perhaps we could meet alone after Mrs. Blackwood and I are done—"

"I won't hear of it," I said sweetly. "Without a chaperone? It would be unseemly. Why not carry out your questioning now?"

Strack shifted his weight from one foot to the other and coughed. "It isn't how I prefer to conduct an investigation—"

"Listen to me, if you please." Genevieve's imperious tone should have been comical, coupled with her frivolous appearance, but she had a trick of tipping her head back and narrowing her eyes that seemed to be quelling the inspector most effectively. I reflected that I should learn how to use the technique myself. "I have come to tell you what Henriette saw. Henriette is my Aunt Clara's maid, and she is most concerned that she witnessed something important."

"Why does she not say so herself?"

"Henriette speaks very little English," I explained. "Of all the household, Genevieve is most fluent in French, so it's natural that Henriette would go to her with information." Despite my calm words, I was troubled by this unexpected intrusion. I did not like having no advance warning of what the maid was about to tell Strack.

Strack, too, was troubled, but for a different reason. "I don't speak French. How can I trust that you're translating her testimony accurately?"

In response, Genevieve offered up a performance that would have made Sybil Ingram proud. Her lower lip quivered ever so slightly, and her eyes went huge and wounded for an instant before she squeezed them shut and turned her face away as if fighting tears. "I am no liar, Mr. Strack," she whispered pitifully. "It is true that I want to clear my foster father's name, but to suggest that I would deliberately tell a falsehood . . . !" She broke off as if words had failed her, and I rose from my chair to put my arms around her.

"Inspector, you must see that Vivi is incapable of such a thing," I chided, as she buried her head in my shoulder and gave a long injured sniff. "The sweet girl has been very sheltered, and to accuse her so—!"

"Pray don't distress yourself so, miss," he exclaimed, rounding the desk to offer her his handkerchief. "I am a blunt man, and I spoke too roundly. I merely wish to make sure that—"

"That I do not deceive you with false information, like a—a common criminal!" She sniffed again and uttered some broken French phrase. I patted her back and did my best not to smile.

"Not at all, miss, not at all. Nothing could be further from my mind. Please, be seated, and be good enough to forget my words. Lady Telford, do you think we might have some tea brought for the young lady? Or perhaps some spirits of ammonia? Dear me, I never meant . . ."

"I shall be quite well," Vivi announced tragically, seating herself in the offered chair and crossing her ankles with a martyred air, "once you have heard Henriette's testimony. Then we shall trouble you no more."

Henriette herself had been observing these goings-on with a faint crease between her eyebrows that suggested perplexity, but in all other regards she was so composed as she stood quietly by with her hands folded that I wondered whether Genevieve had prepared her for her theatrics. I had to trust that Genevieve knew what she was doing . . . and that Henriette's testimony would not prove dangerous. It was impossible to read anything from her calm demeanor.

"Henriette happened to be crossing the long gallery just after dawn this morning," Genevieve announced. "As you must know, the late Lord Telford's chambers are located at the east end of the gallery."

"Why was she in that vicinity?" asked Strack, seating himself again behind the desk, but with a far less confident air than that with which he had questioned me.

"I shall ask her." Genevieve directed a question at the maid, and Henriette replied in a calm stream of the same language. "Henriette was on her way to Aunt Clara's rooms to ready her for the day," Genevieve told us when Henriette had fallen silent. "She took that route because she knew that I had dropped a glove yesterday and thought that it might have been when Mr. Bertram and I visited the gallery to look at a painting of the first Lady Telford."

Bertram again, was it? If Genevieve intended to accept him as a suitor, I must begin acting as chaperone. Now was scarcely the time to be distracted by a side issue, however.

"What did she observe when she passed?"

Again Henriette gave her answer and Vivi translated it. "All was quiet. Then the door opened and a man emerged, walking quickly. He did not notice Henriette, for she carried no light,

219

and he quickly crossed the gallery and made for the small servants' door just before the entrance to the main stair."

"So he knew his way about the house," mused Strack. "Can Henriette describe this man?"

For the first time Vivi looked genuinely troubled. She glanced at me and then dropped her eyes to the floor. "Yes," she said slowly. "She says it was my Uncle Atticus."

From the sudden alert tension of the inspector's posture, I knew that this must be a damning statement. "What time did my husband say he left his father's rooms?" I asked. The words forced themselves out of me.

Strack gave me an even look. "At least a half hour before that," he said, and let that sink in before continuing to Genevieve: "She had no doubt it was Mr. Blackwood—I should say, Lord Telford?"

Genevieve put the question to Henriette, who shook her head decidedly. "Mr. Blackwood," she said in heavily accented tones.

"She is positive," said Genevieve sadly.

"Even without a light? In conditions so dark that he did not even see her?" I objected. "I don't mean to suggest that Henriette is deliberately misleading us, but I would hate for Mr. Strack to be misled by testimony that isn't entirely certain."

Genevieve, to my embarrassment, repeated this in French to the maid, who shook her head again, this time even more stubbornly, as she answered. "She says she is certain," Genevieve told us.

"This changes matters," said Mr. Strack, and suddenly he was brisk and almost jaunty as he scribbled notes. "Changes them materially. I believe I've detained you ladies long enough, and I'll need to speak to Lord Telford again."

"A moment," I said suddenly. "Was the man carrying anything?"

Genevieve translated the question, and Henriette shook her head with emphasis. That meant the man had used no walking stick. My heart beat just a bit faster as hope swelled in me.

"Henriette said that the man she saw walked *quickly* as he crossed to the door." I wasn't certain how to phrase my question without putting the answer in her mouth, and I knew that

Strack would be quick to discount the response if I seemed to lead Henriette to it in any way. "Was there anything else that struck her about his—his manner of progress across the hall?" I asked carefully.

After the usual back-and-forth, Genevieve said, "She says no." Then her eyes widened as if she realized the purpose behind my question, and a smile began to curve her mouth. "I shall ask her to show us, *non?* To give us a demonstration?"

"What is this in aid of?" Strack wanted to know, but I said, "Indulge us just a minute more, and we'll tell you."

Henriette gave Genevieve a baffled look when the girl conveyed our request, but then she seemed to reconcile herself to it; this was, after all, probably not the first eccentricity she had encountered during her years in service. After a moment's thought, she set off across the room to the door with a long, easy, rapid stride. When she reached the door she turned, said, *"Voilà!"* and spread her hands as if to ask if that had satisfied us.

Indeed it had. Vivi and I clutched each other's hands in delight, and I almost laughed with relief. "Mr. Strack," I told him, as he stood giving us a long-suffering look, "my husband was born with a club foot. He received treatment for it as a boy, but it still troubles him sometimes. That means that he generally walks with a stick, and a slight limp is still evident under certain circumstances—"

"Such as when he is weary from an evening of dancing followed by attending his deathly ill father all night," Vivi chimed in. She darted over to Henriette and kissed her on both cheeks. "It was not Uncle Atticus that Henriette saw after all!"

The inspector was not easily convinced, however.

"She said she recognized him," he pointed out. "I find it difficult to believe that this house contains another man who could be mistaken for someone she is so familiar with."

"Well, the house *was* full of guests and their servants," I said, "a great many of them men. They have all departed by now, so it's impossible for us to ask them to assemble where Henriette can examine the features of all of the men. It's possible that one of them bears a resemblance to my husband—enough to pass for him in a dim gallery, seen not at all at close quarters, when my husband is the man that Henriette might have reasonably expected to be emerging from his father's room." The look Strack gave me was not at all friendly, but I was too happy and relieved to care. He might glare at me from then until doomsday if it suited him; I knew only that Vivi and Henriette and I had to some degree lessened the suspicion that had hovered over Atticus. "In other words," he said tonelessly, "you think that one of your house guests murdered his host? Or a servant did so? What possible benefit could such an act be to them?"

I could not keep from smiling. "That's for you to determine, isn't it, inspector? A man as ill-tempered and eccentric as my father-in-law may well have made enemies among his neighbors and tenants. I'll be only too happy to make up a list of all of our guests with their addresses so that you may go interview them all."

"You are too kind." The sarcasm fairly dripped from the words, but in my giddiness I let it pass without rebuke.

As much (I suspected) for the sake of appearances as from any real hope of turning up additional evidence, the inspector remained for another few hours, questioning other servants. Brutus he had already spoken to, but he brought him in to examine further. By the time Atticus and I stood arm in arm by the front entrance to see the inspector on his way—Strack having declined rather rudely our offer of hospitality for the night—he looked to be in an ill humor.

My own high spirits had ebbed, if truth be told. Now that I felt Atticus was safe, the knowledge that some unknown person had invaded our home and brutally killed a member of my family finally seemed to be sinking in. I squeezed Atticus's arm more tightly, and after a swift glance at my face he placed his hand over mine.

"It's a horrible business," he said quietly.

I nodded, unable to speak for a moment.

"Don't worry. He strikes me as a tenacious man, and a just one. He'll find whoever did it."

"I hope so," I whispered.

"You and Vivi should stay together tonight," he continued. "I'll tell her to have her maid gather whatever things she needs and take them to your room. And I'll sleep on a cot in the dressing room so as to be close at hand should anyone try to disturb the two of you. If that won't be an intrusion," he added.

I made myself smile. "It seems a very sensible arrangement." More sensible, probably, than my sharing his room and his bed . . . as bewitching a prospect as that seemed for the instant before I firmly shut my mind against the idea.

Less than twenty-four hours earlier, I would have been horrified at entertaining such a thought, as betrayed as I had felt. But the irruption of far graver matters had made that long-ago breach of trust seem like a relatively minor transgression, and one that I found I could forgive in view of the countless ways Atticus had shown consideration for me.

Indeed, perhaps it was more than consideration. From what I had overheard his father say during that last argument, it seemed that Atticus might have deliberately misled me with his tale of being rejected as a suitor by all the marriageable women in his circle. If he had truly not sought anyone as a bride in earnest until he approached me, that led me to consider the possibility that he had held me in his heart during all the years after I had left Gravesend. It was a thought of poignant beauty—a thought that humbled me.

Thinking about the cause of our parting, however, reminded me of a more pressing matter. "I must warn you," I said to him, "that I told Strack all of my history, and all about our agreement. I suspect that word will spread—may already have begun to, in fact. I felt that in so serious a matter I ought to be completely honest, and for my own part I'm not ashamed . . . but I do hope that you won't be made to pay a price for my low origins."

He seemed lost in thought, and I wondered with sinking heart if I had done the wrong thing. The last thing I wanted was for him to suffer because of me.

After a moment he seemed to come to himself. "I'm sorry, Clara, my mind was somewhere else. What were you saying? No, of course you should not regret having been forthright. Whatever comes, we shall weather it."

We would weather it. In spite of all of the tension and worry casting a cloud over us, I felt my heart lift at the implied promise that he and I would face the future together.

Because of the excitement of the day, Genevieve was in a talkative mood and did not want to let either of us sleep. When she climbed into bed beside me, looking in her nightdress like the princess before encountering the pea, she was chattering away and showed no signs of stopping until Atticus's voice, muffled but plaintive, came from behind the dressing-room door: "Vivi. Have some mercy, for God's sake."

That quieted but did not silence her. "He is probably cross at giving up his place to me tonight," she told me in a whisper, and smothered a giggle behind her hand.

"Genevieve! You should not be thinking about such things."

"You need not sound so shocked, Aunt Clara. But if it embarrasses you I shall not speak of it further."

"Good."

"Though why you should be embarrassed I cannot imagine. You are married, after all, with a baby coming! And what a beautiful baby it shall be, with the two of you as parents. I shall love to have a little cousin to play with."

"I'm far too old to be thinking about having a child," I objected.

She waved that away with a grand unconcern. "I have known ladies older than you who had babies. *Plenty* of babies."

The discussion was threatening to get out of hand, and in any case a question had been nagging at me ever since our session with the inspector. "Genevieve," I whispered, "when you brought Henriette to see Inspector Strack, did you already know that the man she'd seen walked without a limp?"

She was silent for a moment, then: "I did not *know*. But I was nearly certain. Henriette is sharp eyed; she would have told me of such a thing at once if it had been so. Just as she would have said if he had carried a walking stick."

"So you brought her in while I was with the inspector so that I might raise the possibility."

"*Exactement!* It was more convincing coming from you."

Good heavens. Such a gift for strategy seemed wasted on a debutante; Genevieve should have been ruling nations alongside Queen Victoria herself.

I was still not entirely convinced, though, that it was suggestibility that had led Henriette to believe she had seen Atticus, and that troubled me. There had been that time when I, too, had thought I had glimpsed him where he was not . . . . "Genevieve," I said softly, "do you believe in ghosts?"

At any other time I might not have asked the question. But huddled together like children in the darkness, which woke strange fears and invited the sharing of secrets, it did not seem so foolish to ask.

Genevieve, too, seemed to be more susceptible to talk of spirits in this setting. "I do not know," she answered, and her whisper was very thoughtful. "I do not *think* I do . . . but I should die if I ever met one. I do hope that, if there are any about, they leave us be tonight." She surprised me by kissing my cheek and then sank her head deep into the pillow beside mine. "Good night, Aunt Clara."

"Good night, Vivi," I said, touched. Was this what it was like really to have a niece—or a daughter? I had never thought to find myself in that position, but I had grown quite fond of Genevieve now that I was no longer—I forced myself to admit it—jealous of the place she held in Atticus's heart. He had a big heart, after all, quite large enough to hold the both of us in it.

A sigh escaped me as I gazed across the darkened room toward the dressing-room door. There had been no sign of life from that quarter after his plea to Genevieve for quiet. Was he sleeping? I hoped so, for his own sake. The thought crossed my mind that, no matter how companionable it was to share my bed with Genevieve, how much more secure and protected I would have felt nestled up against my husband with his arms around me.

The idea was impractical, but when I tried to chase it away, the thoughts that took its place were far more unsettling. A murderer was still on the loose, after all, and the inspector still harbored suspicions about Atticus. When at last I fell into a troubled sleep, I dreamed that the ghost of old Lord Telford was leering out from behind every death mask on his sitting-room walls, laughing silently at me and Atticus.

CHAPTER TWENTY-THREE

The next day Inspector Strack resumed his questioning, having departed no farther the night before than to a nearby inn. When I passed the library door, I could hear his level voice alternating with the higher, nervous tones of one of the maids.

I was at a bit of a loose end unless he decided to question me again. Atticus had been gone when I had rather hesitantly knocked at the dressing-room door that morning, and I had not seen him at breakfast or about the house. As I passed the drawing room a big, familiar laugh rang out, and I found Mr. Bertram and Genevieve within, sitting close together on a settee with a large volume of watercolors spread over their laps. Both looked up quickly when I entered, and I thought there was a little dimming of the smiles on their faces when they saw me. I was intruding on their wooing, evidently.

"Mr. Bertram," I said calmly, crossing toward him, and he hastily set the book aside and rose to clasp my outstretched hand. "I'm glad to see you, and I know Vivi must be as well."

226

"My dear Mrs.—I mean, my dear Lady Telford," he said contritely, "I am so sorry that you find me in such unbecoming mirth. I came to express my condolences to you and your husband, but I was waylaid by this impertinent miss as soon as I had said hello and goodbye to Blackwood. Please accept my sympathies for the loss of your father-in-law."

"It was most kind of you to come, and I'm grateful to you for bringing a smile to Genevieve's face. I'm afraid we have been keeping company with no little anxiety and horror here, and a friendly face is most welcome. But you say my husband has gone?"

"To the building site, yes. I had planned to ride out with him, but he begged me to excuse him so that he might have some time in solitude." He rubbed the back of his neck in a boyish gesture of unease. "I hope I did right, Lady Telford. I didn't feel I ought to insist upon accompanying him."

"You did quite right," Genevieve announced before I could reply. "My uncle no doubt needed some time alone after all of the commotion. I was telling Mr. Bertram about it all—the doctor's findings, the investigation, Uncle Atlas being treated like a suspect! It is little wonder if he wishes to escape it all for a time and have some peace and quiet."

"*Atlas,* is it?" Bertram inquired. "Has Blackwood set himself up as a god, now? I shall have to chaff him about that."

Genevieve gave an indignant squeal. "You shall do no such thing! Uncle Atlas is a lamb, and he must not be teased, unless it is by me or Aunt Clara."

"Did my husband indicate when he might return?" I asked, cutting across the badinage, and Bertram's face sobered once more.

"I'm afraid not, Lady Telford, but I do know that he decided to go on foot instead of riding. So he'll be a few hours at least—more, if the weather turns bad."

Something about this abrupt absence disquieted me. It might well have been the truth that Atticus desired time alone to sort through the recent events and regain a measure of calm. But I wished he had taken Bertram with him. "He didn't go to speak to the foreman, I take it?" I asked, and the young man shook his head.

"He sent word yesterday to call off all work on the building until the investigation into his father's death is closed. I'm not certain whether it's a financial difficulty that won't be resolved until the estate is—but here, I'm speaking coldly of money when you are mourning a member of your family. I heartily beg your pardon."

I reassured him that we had not taken offense, and then sat back in a wing chair and left him and Genevieve to their conversation. It was cheering to listen to their exchange and to see how taken they were with each other; with the resilience of the young, they had pushed the sobering matter of the old baron's death to the back of their minds and were happily absorbed in other, gayer concerns. It was fortunate that I had happened by, for Genevieve clearly had not concerned herself with the need for a chaperone, and even though I had a high opinion of Mr. Bertram I would not have wanted Atticus to have felt me remiss in my duties as de facto aunt.

Atticus himself did not return until shortly before the evening meal, which was to be taken in the breakfast room now that our guests had departed. I scarcely had time for any words with him before we joined Genevieve and Mr. Bertram, who had easily been persuaded to stay until Atticus's return. "I cannot be at ease until that madman is caught," Vivi had said plaintively, and although I suspected that her liking for the young man's presence had more to do with him than with the killer, I myself was just as pleased to have him near. There was something comforting about his cheerful, straightforward manner.

Atticus, in contrast, still looked drawn and weary, with his ice-blue eyes sunken deep and his gaze far away. When I asked how he was, he said briefly, "Well enough," and changed the subject. This was far from reassuring. At table, Genevieve and Bertram conversed valiantly to fill the silence, and I contributed what I could, but Atticus's silence was conspicuous and cast a damper on a meal that was already lacking in vivacity.

It was during one of the uncomfortable silences that the sound of footsteps came to us from the hallway, and Birch's voice saying, "If you would be so good as to wait while I announce you—"

"Never mind announcing me. They'll be pleased enough to see me when they hear my news." With a fretful Birch at his heels, Strack appeared on the threshold, but a Strack I had not seen before: jubilant, satisfied, brimming with barely suppressed excitement. "Lord Telford," he said before any of us could speak. "I bring news."

"Pray join us and refresh yourself while you tell us." Atticus gave Birch a nod, and he sent one of the footmen away, presumably to procure a new place setting. Another footman silently retrieved another chair and held it for Strack, who flipped the skirt of his frock coat out of his way almost cheerfully as he took a seat. "Do you have news of my father's killer?" Atticus asked.

"I do indeed, my lord. I do indeed." He sat back while footmen placed plate, goblet, silver, and so on before him, but the instant that they had withdrawn, he leaned forward avidly. "I went to see this man Collier who had been acting so strangely. Took a constable out to his home—run-down kind of place, I must say. Evidently he'd let it rather go to seed since his wife's death."

Atticus sat listening intently, his hands steepled before him, dinner forgotten. Genevieve, Bertram, and I were no less absorbed.

"When we approached we weren't truly expecting to learn anything vital, you understand. It was more in the nature of being thorough and not leaving any leads unexplored. So when we found the front door open a crack and saw through it that Collier was hanging from the ceiling with a noose around his neck—"

Genevieve gasped, and I think I may have as well. Bertram choked on his food and reached for his wine glass. And Atticus's eyes shut briefly, as if in pain.

"I do beg your pardon for being so blunt," said Strack, who did not look at all repentant. He was almost grinning, so satisfied was he that he had sprung this explosive information on us all unexpected.

"I say, you might have a care for the ladies," Bertram said rebukingly. "And at the dinner table, yet. You may skip over the details. This Collier, he'd done away with himself?"

Slightly deflated, Strack gave a grudging jerk of his head in confirmation. "He had indeed, sir. Guilty conscience always gets them. He even left a note. It seems he had never brought himself to believe that he wasn't the father of Miss Rowe here . . ."

"Oh, *le pauvre*," whispered Genevieve. Her eyes had filled with tears. "That poor, unhappy man."

"That poor man, as you call him, murdered the baron," Strack returned. "It must have been him that your maid saw, Lady Telford. In a low light, they were of similar enough build and coloring."

"So when Henriette thought she saw my uncle, it was really Collier stealing out of Lord Telford's rooms after . . ." Genevieve shuddered.

"Exactly. He must have acquainted himself with the geography of the house when he was hired on as an extra footman during your house party."

"But why?" asked Atticus, and his voice, quiet and calm, was like a current of cool water in the emotional exchange. "What did he have to gain?"

Strack speared a piece of roast beef on his fork and permitted himself a slight smirk. "You're assuming Collier was in his right mind, Lord Telford. Apparently seeing Miss Rowe return after all these years upset the balance of his mind. He clung to two beliefs, contradictory though they seem: that she was his daughter, and that she was the rightful heir after your lordship. When your lordship brought Lady Telford to Gravesend as your bride, with Miss Rowe a mere ward, Collier appears to have become unhinged and taken out his fury on the head of the family that, as he saw it, had cheated his daughter of her rightful place."

"Convoluted thinking indeed," said Atticus quietly. "How do we know that Collier believed these things?"

"The note he left was quite clear." Strack chewed a morsel of food as we watched in anticipation, then swallowed and added, "It's of little comfort, I'm sure, but he did express remorse for having killed the late Lord Telford. It was that belated flash of conscience that must have driven him to put the rope about his own neck."

Atticus leaned toward him. "Might one be granted a look at this note?"

"I'm afraid not, my lord. It's been taken into evidence."

"All for me." Genevieve shook her head in stunned disbelief, and the tears in her eyes overflowed onto her cheeks. "I never asked for what he wanted for me, but I feel partly responsible nonetheless."

Bertram took her hand in his. "Nonsense, Vivi," he said, using her pet name for the first time in my hearing. "Collier was a dangerous lunatic, and his obsession with you doesn't mean that any of the blame is yours."

"Bertram is quite right," Atticus told her. "Don't distress yourself for a moment, my dear." More quietly he added, "I bear the blame here. I ought to have taken his measure when I removed you from his and his wife's care and sent you so far away. And when he began acting in such a peculiar manner I should have insisted on more stringent security measures. I was thoughtless—and lax. Damnably lax." He crumpled his napkin and flung it on the table as he rose, pushing his chair back so suddenly that he lost his balance briefly and clutched at the table to keep from falling. I rose as well, in concern, but he gave me a shake of the head. "Excuse me, won't you all? I need a bit of air."

Reluctantly I resumed my seat as he caught up his walking stick and left the room. I felt sick at the thought of him being consumed with guilt over this crime. Perhaps a brief time alone would help him think through all that had passed and realize that the blame was not his, but all Collier's. If not, perhaps he would listen to me. I could not bear it if he were to let his conscience torment him for something that was not of his doing and that he could not have prevented. A madman would not be daunted by measures that would deter a sane man, I knew. Once Collier had formed his deadly intent, the old baron would never have been safe.

Strack continued to regale us with information about the crime and its aftermath, but I scarcely attended him. "I'm sure you and your husband must be greatly relieved, Lady Telford," he said at one point.

I spread my hands. "Relief is not my primary emotion after the death of two men, Inspector Strack."

"I commend the tenderness of your woman's heart, my lady. But Collier's death, along with the note he left, removes all suspicion from your husband. What a weight off your mind, eh?"

"Oh. I see. Yes, I'm quite glad of that—and that there shall be no more deaths."

"You could never have thought for an instant that my uncle was a killer," Genevieve told Strack hotly.

"Oh no, mademoiselle? He had the strongest motive of all: money. But making such a case against a baron would have been difficult to say the least, so as far as I'm concerned this whole business has concluded in a most satisfactory way." Dabbing at his moustache with his napkin, he rose. "I'll be on my way, then, Lady Telford. Thank you for your hospitality."

"Not at all," I said automatically. "Thank you for putting us out of our suspense. I know my husband would wish for me to thank you on his behalf as well."

Now the household would have a chance to recover and proceed with the usual comforting rituals of mourning. Lord Telford could be laid to rest, neighbors could leave their cards—secure now in the knowledge that they would not be condoling with a murderer—and Atticus could proceed with the building of the refuges for the fallen women. And, in due time, Genevieve and Mr. Bertram would no doubt be married.

As for me, in my relatively short time at Gravesend I had come to feel that I had a place here—that is, not in the house itself, but with Atticus. I was no longer making my way in the world alone. I even felt that I could make a good wife to Atticus . . . if he wanted me to. But what if he didn't wish me to stay? On the night of the ball I had convinced myself that he had wanted me to stay with him for more than just that one night, but could I be certain that he truly wanted me for longer than that?

It would not be an easy question to bring myself to ask him, and Atticus did not make it any easier; he made himself so scarce that a suspicious woman might have thought he was avoiding her. He neglected to come to my sitting room for our usual discussion of the day's events, and when I gathered the courage to knock at his door, it was his valet, Sterry, who opened it. Atticus had not yet returned from wherever he had disappeared to after the evening meal. I retired without having seen any sign of him since then.

He was absent from breakfast the next morning, as well; Birch told me that he had again gone to visit the construction site, and this was echoed by Genevieve and Mrs. Threll.

Evidently Atticus had broadcast his plans widely, and I was the last to learn of them. I wondered at this sudden, consuming interest in the building; was it merely a pretext for time by himself to come to terms with all that had lately passed? Or, perhaps, did he wish to put some distance between us? The thought of waiting who knew how many hours for his return chafed me, and I returned to my room and quickly changed my dress for one better suited to walking.

Genevieve scented my purpose and determined to join me. Mrs. Threll was able to give us directions to the building site, which was but a few miles distant, and furnished us with stout walking sticks. We set out in good spirits, for the day was fair and mild; a light breeze cooled our cheeks when we became warm from our exertions, and in the sunlight even the winter-bleached landscape took on some beauty. The gently rolling parkland and copses of wintry trees were a welcome sight, and it felt good to be out of doors and breathe in fresh air. After all of the recent rains I had feared that the walking might be difficult, but the ground had dried enough that our progress was fairly rapid.

"How are you faring?" I asked presently, after we had made our way in silence some half a mile.

"Oh, I am quite well; I am fit to walk many miles yet."

"I didn't mean that," I said, trying to find a way to phrase the question delicately, but she caught my meaning then.

"I am well enough, Aunt Clara, although it is kind of you to ask. At first it was rather dreadful, feeling that I was the cause of so many terrible things."

"But you weren't," I objected, and she nodded.

"When I thought a little longer, I realized that," she said. "This Collier, he had a mono—what is your word?"

"Monomania?"

"That, yes. And I do not think it had much to do with *me*, exactly. I think it had much more to do with *him*. In the end, the choices were all his."

This was so mature an insight that I found myself wondering what extraordinary school it was that had brought her up to think with such clarity. Or perhaps it was all Genevieve herself. She was a Blackwood, after all, and I had not met a single dull-witted member of that clan. I wondered about her mother, the late Mrs. Collier. Perhaps she had been a woman of intelligence; perhaps that had even been part of what had attracted Richard to her.

It still hurt, the knowledge that I had shared Richard's affections with another woman—or more than one—but the pain was already far less than it had been. Now it was not Richard but his brother who was foremost in my thoughts. Where once I had looked upon Atticus as simply the least objectionable of my options, he had now become more precious to me than Richard had ever been. When I remembered that idyllic day in the folly and that conviction of being enfolded by love, it had not been an illusion; only it had been Atticus's love, not Richard's, that cast that day in such radiance for me. I realized now that all those times in our youth when I had seen him, as I thought, tagging along after Richard, it must have been me that he truly wanted to be close to. And I wondered not for the first time whether my own love for Atticus was endangering him—and if the curse would bereave me once again.

Even as my thoughts took this direction, a figure came into view over the next rise that I knew must be Atticus. But something about the sight of him struck me with inexplicable urgency. The dazzling sunlight and the mist it was lifting from the meadow obscured him to an extent, but I knew suddenly that all was not well with him. "Something is wrong," I exclaimed, quickening my pace; I could not have explained how I knew, only that the motion of his progress struck disquiet into my heart.

"Why, so it is," said Genevieve, likewise walking more rapidly, until she was almost trotting to keep up with my longer strides. "Uncle!" she called, waving her arm over her head, and after a moment an answering wave came—but more slowly, and with an odd constraint, as if . . . as if it pained him to move. I picked up my skirts in both hands and broke into a run.

When I caught up with him, Atticus did not at first glance seem to be the worse for wear. But his gait was less than regular because his left hand was the one wielding his walking stick, instead of his right, and there was a stiffness to the way he held his right arm that I noted with anxiety. His brow was furrowed as if in concentration or endurance, but when we came within hailing distance he said, lightly enough, "You organized a rescue party. That was most prescient of you, my dear."

I didn't know which of us the endearment was meant for, nor did I ask. "What's wrong?" I demanded instead. "Are you unwell?"

"An accident at the construction site. Nothing serious, no bones broken . . . only I think I pulled some muscles in my shoulder. If you would permit me to lean on you, Clara, I think you would be a better help than my stick."

"What kind of accident?" pressed Genevieve, taking his stick from him to free up that arm to pass about my shoulders. "Was it a sinkhole? Mrs. Threll was telling me how dangerous the ground can be after as much rain as we have had. With so many old mines, she said, one must be very careful indeed."

His wan attempt at a smile betrayed how much pain he must have been feeling. "I had the same thought, which is why I went to inspect the site. No, fortunately the ground is all intact. But while I was there, I thought to go up into the scaffolding to examine the progress on the upper floor."

"You *climbed* up?"

"There's a kind of moving platform with a hoist and pulley device. It's awkward for one man alone to operate, but not impossible. But I slipped—some loose boards shifted—and I managed to snare myself in the ropes." He turned his head and gingerly held his collar away from his throat, and with a gasp of horror I saw a raw red weal like the mark of a noose on one side of his neck. Then Genevieve snatched at his hand and, ignoring his hiss of pain, pried his fingers open to reveal a similar raw mark across the palm.

"Atticus," I breathed. "You could have been killed."

"Now, don't alarm yourself. If the rope hadn't snared me I quite possibly might have been, but as it happened, it saved my neck." His laugh was slightly forced. "It just left it a little the worse for wear."

"I am going ahead," Genevieve announced. "I shall send a servant for the doctor and have warm water and unguents and bandages prepared."

"Thank you, Genevieve." I watched her set off at a run back toward Gravesend, her sausage curls bouncing wildly and her skirts billowing out in her wake, and then looked long and deeply into my husband's face. "Was that the truth?" I asked softly.

His eyes met mine briefly before drifting away. "It was an accident, Clara. Please don't try to make it into anything more significant than an instance of clumsiness and carelessness."

He made as if to resume our progress, but I held him still and reached down to grasp the hem of my topmost petticoat. "What are you doing?" he asked, startled, but when I ripped a strip of the fabric away, he held out his injured hand to be bound without having to be asked.

"This will be sufficient for the journey home," I said, as I wrapped the cloth gently around the wound and tied it in a knot. "The doctor can clean the wound properly and bind it better."

"It isn't worth troubling the doctor for," he said. "I should have called Genevieve back. If only she hadn't gone haring away so fast . . ."

A little cold shadow that had started to form over my heart grew colder. If the doctor thought Atticus's injuries looked like an attempt at doing away with himself, he would be forced to report it to the authorities—as my husband must know quite well.

It only *looked* suspicious, I told myself. It was nothing more than a mishap, as he said. Still, as we resumed our walk, he with one arm about my shoulders, I holding him tightly around the waist, I tried to find a way to tease out what he was not saying.

"No one was at the site to come to your assistance?" I asked.

A shake of the head. "No, I've not yet given the foreman orders to resume work. I wanted to examine the site, as I said, and make certain it was safe."

"Which it clearly wasn't," I commented. "I consider the foreman to have been very much at fault. You should have the incident investigated."

He turned his head to glare at me. It was an expression I had not yet seen from him, and the heat in his pale blue eyes made me recoil. "For God's sake, Clara, I've told you," he snapped. "I took a foolish chance on a hoist meant for two men, I lost my footing on an insecure surface, and if I got a bit banged up, it's hardly worth mentioning. I'll thank you to let the matter drop."

My injured pride closed around me like armor. "As you wish," I said coolly, looking straight ahead, and neither of us spoke again for the remainder of our halting progress to Gravesend.

Atticus must have assuaged any suspicions the doctor might have had about his wounds, for they parted on good enough terms—as best I could tell from my vantage point, overlooking the entrance hall from the stair landing above. Atticus had made it plain that he did not want my company; nor did he give me any opportunity to speak with him alone, shutting himself in the library all afternoon with Bertram, who was visiting once again, and who perhaps had expected to be closeted with Genevieve rather than her guardian. I had hoped to speak to Atticus at dinner, but he asked Birch to make his excuses and send in some sandwiches to him and Bertram in the library. Nor did he come to my sitting room as the hour for retiring drew near.

It was not until I at last retired to my bedroom for the night that I found myself at close quarters with my elusive husband. Through the closed doors of the dressing room I could hear the rise and fall of his voice, rapid and forceful; not quite loud enough to distinguish words, but I gathered that he was instructing his valet in something important.

Then the answering voice came, and my hands froze in the motion of unfastening an earring. Though low and rushed, and more difficult to hear, the second voice was his own. Atticus was carrying on a conversation with himself.

It would not have chilled me as much had it not sounded so passionate. He seemed to be arguing some important point, something urgent and yet furtive. What had unsettled him to this degree? Hesitating only briefly, I unlocked the dressing-room door as quietly as I could and crept into the little room.

When I pressed my ear against the opposite door I could hear his voice—or his voices—slightly better, but still only enough to capture a word here and there.

. . . knew I would be there . . .

. . . only an accident . . .

. . . Collier . . .

. . . his neck or mine . . .

Terrible thoughts tumbled through my mind. Had Atticus's so-called accident been some deliberate attempt to do himself harm? Did he bear some responsibility for Collier's death, or feel that he did, and was that guilt driving him? Listening to the rise and fall of his monologue, the tone alternating between entreating and placating, anger and dismissal, made my heart hurt as if it were being closed in a giant stone fist.

This agony of mind . . . the peculiar injuries he had sustained, almost an echo of how Collier had done away with himself. His sudden secrecy, the taste for solitude, distancing himself from me—as if he were trying to hide something. What if Atticus was no longer in control of his own actions? Could he truly have become two people, two personalities in one body? I knew that such a premise had been employed in sensation fiction, but never had I considered that it might happen in reality, and the idea made my heart thud in dread.

What torment was he in that could make his own soul so divide itself? Did he feel guilt over his father's death or Collier's? Had he—I forced myself to contemplate it—actually played a part in one or both? Such a thing might drive him to injure himself. His determination to take his full measure of responsibility was one of his noblest features, but it might be one of his most dangerous now. Or perhaps it was the secret with which his father had entrusted—or afflicted—him. Whatever that confidence had been, I would never forget how it had devastated Atticus even before he learned of the old man's death. Could that mysterious legacy that he was pledged to protect still be tormenting him, and to the point that he might harm himself?

The only consolation at hand was the reflection that, had Atticus truly posed a danger to himself, Dr. Brandt would surely have noticed and taken the matter in hand. Brandt was not so easily fooled, and too tenacious to have let Atticus put him off with a slim pretext. If there had been more to his accident than met the eye, I reasoned, Brandt would have insisted upon speaking to me about watching my husband—would have assigned someone to watch over him, or removed him to a private clinic or the like.

Listening to his voice arguing with itself in the next room, I shivered, overwhelmed with horror and pity. I resolved to stay by him as much as I could, to make certain that he had all the aid I could offer—whether he liked it or not.

Chapter Twenty-Four

My plan was dealt an immediate blow. At breakfast the next morning, Atticus raised thoughtful eyes to mine across the table and announced, "I'm opening the house in London for you and Genevieve. It should be habitable within the week."

I put down my teacup abruptly. "For me and Genevieve?" I repeated. "You're to join us, I hope?"

He took a moment to answer, and the response when it came was unconvincing. "I'll try."

"Oh, but you must come with us," Genevieve exclaimed. "I cannot imagine making my debut without you!"

The smile he summoned for her benefit was so ghastly that it struck dread into my breast. "I'll see what I can manage," he said.

"Genevieve, would you mind giving us some privacy?" I asked. Blessedly, she made no protest, perhaps knowing that I would be arguing for us both, and made a swift departure, shutting the door behind her.

"Atticus, what do you mean by this?" I asked.

His eyes were now on the newspaper that rested beside his plate, but I was almost certain he was not absorbing anything printed there. "Just what I say. You and Genevieve are to move to London as soon as the house is ready and stay there through the Season—or for as long as it takes for Genevieve to become engaged, which shouldn't be long. Once she's married, you'll move to your own home."

"My—what?"

His voice remained steady, neutral, as if he were reading to me from the financial pages. "Bertram can help you with your preparations. Once you decide where you wish to live, he'll assist you in finding a house, furnishing it if necessary, all of that. It's what we agreed on, after all."

"But that was before." This entire conversation felt unreal; I could not be certain it wasn't a strange dream I was having, so little did it resemble the reality I had been living. I looked down at my left hand, which still bore the ring he had given me; I looked at my right, with the fingers clasping the delicate china handle of the teacup; and it seemed to me that these objects were the only things I could be certain of, with everything else in my world shifting so drastically that I could no longer rely on the very ground beneath my feet. "I thought . . . well, even though Genevieve isn't my daughter, I thought that you rather wished for me to stay with you. For the three of us to be a real family." I took my courage in both hands and said clearly, "That is what I want."

There was a silence so profound that I could hear, very distantly through the closed windows, the song of a curlew. Atticus did not look at me when he said, "The situation has changed."

"Changed how?" I burst out, and reached out to touch his bandaged right hand. "Please, Atticus, look at me. Speak to me. What has changed?"

For one moment I thought he would tell me. In that instant his eyes were naked as they looked into mine—and haunted.

Then he looked away again, withdrawing his hand from my touch. "Please just accept what I say, Clara. Gravesend is no place for you anymore."

"Are you angry with me still for what I said about your accident?" I had searched my memory, and that was the only time I could recall his being seriously out of temper with me.

"No, I'm not angry," he said. His voice, indeed, was empty of that or any other discernible emotion. "I'm sorry I spoke harshly to you, but it has no bearing on the matter. You must leave Gravesend."

There seemed no arguing with that. If he had had a change of heart regarding me, nothing I might say could alter it.

But that was not the case, I felt. Something was weighing on him, something he felt he could not—or should not—share with me. All I could do was try my utmost to determine what it was . . . and find some way to set things right.

There was a knock on the door, and when Atticus answered, Mrs. Threll appeared. "I thought we might discuss arrangements for the funeral, Lord Telford," she said.

He rose from the table. "I'd be obliged if you and Lady Telford planned the service and so on. I'll instruct the stonemason regarding his part, but everything else is in your purview, Mrs. Threll."

With that he was out the door. I rose, on the verge of calling after him, when my eye fell on the figure of the housekeeper and I held back the words. I would not embarrass Mrs. Threll by becoming emotional before her.

Even so, she seemed to have picked up on my state of mind. "Bereavement takes some gentlemen very hard, my lady," she said to me. Her voice was as expressionless as ever, but I felt that she was trying to be of comfort.

I only wished that what was troubling Atticus were as straightforward as grief. I did my best to smooth out my expression and find a modicum of calm, saying, "How right you are, Mrs. Threll. Perhaps you and I can save my husband some distress by taking care of all the planning that lies in our power."

Despite my effort to appear calm, my voice caught when I said *my husband*. How much longer would we be even nominally husband and wife?

If only I could find out the source of his trouble of mind, I knew I could break through this terrible barrier between us and help him. Remembering his haunted eyes and distraught manner on the morning of his father's death, I wondered if old Lord Telford had entrusted him with a secret so devastating that it was endangering his sanity.

As if it had been only yesterday, I suddenly heard again the old baron's words: *Death lays all secrets bare.* The death masks, he had insisted, revealed the truths that their models, in life, had hidden. Were there hidden revelations to be found in one of the baron's masks—perhaps that of someone Atticus had known, someone whose life had touched his? Maybe his father had confided some terrible revelation about Lady Telford's death . . . or about Richard's. And perhaps I could unearth it without any need for Atticus to break his pledge of silence.

As soon as I could, I ended my discussion with Mrs. Threll and set out for the old baron's rooms. If there was anything to be learned from the masks, I was determined to find it out.

What I had not anticipated was that the staff had already begun to clear the rooms. When I opened the door of my late father-in-law's sitting room, I was startled to find the walls nearly bare. Many of the furnishings were gone, and what pieces remained were shrouded in sheets. Wooden packing crates crowded the floor, from which the rugs had been removed. Lifting the corner of the sheet that covered one of the curio cabinets, I found the shelves empty of masks or labels.

My heart sank. The masks must all have been packed in the crates. I could tell with a glance that the lids had not been nailed down, so I would not need to ring for assistance in order to begin my search, but I wished that my task had not been complicated thus.

Stifling a sigh of impatience, I knelt down by the nearest crate and lifted the lid. A layer of cotton-wool wadding met my eyes, and when I drew it back I found the plaster mask of Voltaire lying beneath. Fortunately, as I learned when I delved deeper into the crate, the masks had been packed in roughly the same order in which they had been displayed—that is, more or less chronologically. When I had peered into five crates I found one whose topmost mask bore the features of the hapless miner whose death had taken place almost twenty years before, so I concentrated my efforts there. After some minutes I was rewarded, and I lifted the mask of Lady Telford from the crate.

It was a strange sensation, holding in my hand the visage of the woman who had evicted me from Gravesend all those years ago. Naturally the casting had not captured her eyes, whose relentless coldness I could still call up in my memory. But the resemblance between her features and those of her sons was clear. The strong, straight nose that was handsome on Atticus was a bit too pronounced for beauty in a woman, but its assertiveness certainly accorded with my recollection of her personality.

Beyond these observations, however, I learned nothing. Had I known what to look for—whether her illness, for example, would have left some physical imprint on her face that the mask would have preserved—it is possible that the thing would have enlightened me. Instead I felt more baffled than ever, and frustrated at my helplessness. I set the mask aside and lifted the next layer of cotton wadding to find the cast of Richard's face.

My heart was beating just a bit more rapidly than before with anticipation mixed with dread. Might I find the answer here to my husband's transformation? I picked up the mask and rose to my feet, thinking to carry it to the window for better light.

But I had not taken a single step when suddenly, from close behind me, came a cough. Startled, I jumped, and the mask flew from my hands. Before I could move to try to catch it, it had shattered on the floor.

"No!" I gasped. The mask lay in countless fragments, so many and so minute that even if they could have been put together again I knew I could never learn anything from them.

"My lady, I am most dreadfully sorry." It was Birch who had, unobserved, come up behind me and frightened me.

It was a moment before I found enough composure to respond. "It cannot be helped, Birch," I said dully.

"I shall see about having repairs made, my lady."

"Don't go to the trouble; it is past saving." I tried to swallow my bitter disappointment, but with little success. "Why have the masks all been packed up? And why are the baron's rooms being cleared?"

"Lord Telford ordered it, my lady," he informed me. His normal dignity seemed undiminished by recent events. "He indicated that the rooms should be closed and his father's collection shipped to the British Museum. It was the late baron's wish that the masks be donated to the museum upon his demise."

Was it indeed—or was this a pretext by which Atticus intended to hide whatever revelations the masks might have contained? It hardly mattered now, thanks to my clumsiness. What might have been my best chance at unfolding the mystery of my husband's torment of mind was now shattered into a thousand pieces. "I'll leave you, then," I said, "unless there is anything requiring my attention."

"Thank you, my lady. I am merely selecting appropriate attire for the late Lord Telford's viewing and interment."

Now I could see, when I looked past the butler to the door of the adjoining room, that there were articles of clothing laid out neatly on the old man's bed.

"Very good," I said. "If you think Brutus will have any knowledge of my father-in-law's particular desires, you may wish to consult him."

"I have already done so, my lady."

I hesitated. There was nothing in the butler's face or demeanor to indicate that he had heard anything of the personal history I had disclosed to Strack, but as I myself had told the inspector, there were few secrets in a house of this size. It was, I felt, far better to make a clean breast of it than to pretend ignorance as word passed through the household. Besides, secrets could be poisonous, as I was learning.

"Birch," I said, "there may be a story circulating about my past—that I was not an American widow, that in fact I used to be a chambermaid here at Gravesend and was dismissed under scandalous circumstances."

"I try not to attend to low gossip," he said gravely.

He had not said there *was* no gossip, I noticed. So the story had most likely leaked out. "Those things are true," I said. "You may even remember me from that time. But I was not guilty of all that was suspected of—"

"Pray don't feel you must defend yourself, my lady," he interrupted. He must have been deeply distressed to forget propriety so much as to cut me off. "I'm certain you were innocent of wrongdoing."

A pink tinge was creeping over his domed head, and I knew I could not risk embarrassing him by specifying the exact

AmandaDeWees

degree of my impropriety or lack thereof. I settled for saying, "My husband shares that certainty. He married me in part to make amends for the injustice of my dismissal. He wanted me to be able to leave that unhappy part of my past behind me, but I think it is important for all of you in Gravesend to understand that although I have nothing to be ashamed of, I would hate for any rumors about me to lessen anyone's regard for my husband. He is a fine man, as you know, and I'm determined not to bring shame upon him or give him cause to regret having made me his wife."

Birch's face was a study as he registered these words and their implications, and I felt myself holding my breath. I hoped that his respect for my husband would move him to discourage further discussion of my deception among the servants . . . or outside the household. "My lady," he said at length, and I was not certain if it was my own nervous imagination that lent the words such weight, "I think I may speak for all of us in the servants' hall when I say that we are loyal to a man—and woman—to Lord Telford. Anything that is in our power to do to save him unhappiness, it is our honor to do."

"That is exactly what I feel on my part," I said, daring to hope I understood correctly.

The butler permitted himself a brief smile. It was a paternal expression, but in it I glimpsed something almost conspiratorial. "Then we are of the same mind, my lady," he said.

My relief and gratitude were so great that it took me a moment to find my voice. "Thank you, Birch," I said. "And if I should have to leave . . ." I paused to compose myself.

"Leave Gravesend?" The shock in his voice told me, if his words had not, that in his eyes I had truly become part of the family. If decorum had not so strictly urged against it, I might have kissed him at that moment.

"Naturally I would not do so willingly," I said, "but if I were forced to leave, you would continue to make my husband's welfare your first concern?"

"We would indeed, my lady. But permit me to say that I hope it will not come to that."

I summoned a smile. "Again you and I are of one mind, Birch."

246

When I turned to go I caught sight of Lady Telford's plaster visage where I had left it atop one of the crates. *You've not won yet,* I thought. *You or your curse.*

The funeral arrangements kept me busy for the next few days, far busier than I was comfortable with. I didn't at all like being kept away from Atticus. George Bertram was conspicuously present, however. Etiquette declared that he should have been giving us a wide berth, since we were a house of mourning, but evidently Atticus had set aside the conventions and asked Bertram to be close at hand . . . although whether in his capacity of agent, friend, or suitor to Genevieve I did not know. I managed at one point to draw Bertram aside and ask him to stay with my husband as much as was in his power, but I knew I could not expect the younger man to carry the full weight of responsibility for his employer's safety . . . not least because the prospect of time with Genevieve would be forever tempting him away from Atticus.

Genevieve, not surprisingly, was full of questions, and I had none but the most perfunctory answers for her. I knew that she had tried speaking to her uncle and had made no progress; her face wore an unhappy pout for days on end. I could sympathize, but I could not help her. "I am delighted to be going to London," she told me at one point, "but I cannot imagine why Uncle Atticus would wish to be separated from us—especially you, Aunt Clara."

Her candor might once have made me smile, but now it merely awoke all the questions and fears that lay just beneath the surface of my own mind. Why was Atticus isolating himself so?

The funeral itself was almost as elaborate an affair as the ball, but of course in an entirely more somber vein. Atticus's father was laid to rest in the family's private burial grounds on the estate. The day was fine, so there were many at the graveside. I observed my husband's still, remote expression, his eyes clouded by who knew what dark thoughts, and reflected on how much had changed for me. When first he had approached me with his proposition, and for the earliest days of our marriage, his resemblance to Richard had caused my heart to lift every time I caught sight of him—then to plummet again when recognition came. Then, for a time, that sinking of the heart vanished, leaving only the instinctive response of pleasure at seeing him. Perhaps for a time I had ascribed this to his mere physical attractiveness, but I now knew that it was because my feelings for him had changed.

But now the circle was complete: my unthinking reflex of joy at the sight of him was now succeeded by that terrible cold dread—the baffled sorrow and fear at being shut out, of wondering what was in his heart and fearing I had lost him.

With so much violence around us, so many disquieting events, it was not surprising that he had been affected, but I was heartsore to see this transformation . . . and not a little frightened. If he had indeed tried to follow the path the wretched Collier had taken, I needed to convince him that he had every reason to live. But how could I, when he seemed unwilling to speak to me at all?

After the graveside service there was what seemed like an endless stream of guests who came to offer condolences and partake of the huge collation set out in the banquet hall. I greeted neighbors and listened to condolences and murmured thanks and all the time kept an eye on my husband, hoping for some crack in the facade, some sign that he would be receptive to me again. It never came. Once I did catch a glimpse of Dr. Brandt and tried to make my way over to speak to him, but evidently he was there in his professional capacity: he disappeared with Atticus for a short while, and by the time I saw my husband again the doctor seemed to have departed.

Nervous strain made the rest of the day exhausting, and I retired early. There was no convivial sitting-room meeting with Atticus; that custom had died with his father, it seemed. I sat listlessly brushing my hair at my dressing table, wondering how many more days I would be at Gravesend. How many more chances would there be for me to try to break through my husband's reserve?

And then, from Atticus's room, as on that horrifying previous occasion, I heard the whispered tones of my husband in a furious argument . . . with himself. My door to the dressing room was ajar, and when I concentrated hard enough, I could occasionally distinguish words.

. . . just like Collier . . .

The whisper was fierce with emotion, but just what that emotion was I could not tell. I set the hairbrush silently aside.

. . . only of yourself . . .

. . . safe for anyone . . .

I couldn't stand by this time and witness his disintegration without taking action. Swiftly I crossed the room and passed through the dressing room. When I rapped at his door, for a second there was silence.

"Who's there?" he demanded, and the touch of panic in his voice killed the last shred of hesitancy in me.

"It's Clara. Are you all right?" I grasped the doorknob and turned, but the door was locked. "Please let me in, Atticus. I need to see you."

Silence still, and a vague impression of some kind of movement. Was he hiding something? His footsteps were slow as they approached the door, and he seemed to fumble with the key for long moments . . . but then, I remembered, his abraded right hand was still healing and might be clumsy. After what seemed like an eternity he opened the door to me.

His face was almost as pale as his white shirt, the pallor so marked that the faint gingery beginnings of beard were etched clearly on his jaw. His handsome face looked as if it had aged a decade, and his eyes were fixed and staring. What had the doctor done to him? Had he bled him, or forced him to take an opiate or a stimulant of some sort?

"What do you want?" he asked.

Never were there less welcoming words from husband to wife, but I stepped toward him before he could change his mind and shut the door on me.

"Atticus, I'm worried about you. I heard your voice and—"

"How much did you hear?" The question was quick and sharp.

"Not a great deal. I couldn't make out many words. But you sounded so wretched, and I wondered if there is anything I can do to help you."

"Help me!" The words were somewhere between a laugh and a groan. He turned and made his way wearily to the fire, favoring his bad leg; leaning with one arm braced against the marble mantelpiece, he stared into the fire. "There's no help you can give me, Clara. Just . . . leave me in peace."

"But you aren't in peace." I moved to his side and took hold of his shoulders to make him face me again. He offered no resistance, but this lack of will frightened me as much as anything else I had seen and heard tonight. I searched his face for the source of his unrest. "I did hear you mention Mr. Collier," I said slowly. "Are you not satisfied with Inspector Strack's findings?"

"It doesn't matter," he said shortly. "My father is dead, and so is Collier. We'd be fools to interfere any further in matters that the inspector has solved to his satisfaction."

I reached toward his face, and he actually flinched. Though wounded by this, I didn't draw back but put my hand to his high forehead to smooth back his disordered hair. "You don't seem yourself tonight," I said.

His lips drew back in a grimace so humorless that it made my heart seem to falter in my breast. "Who else could I possibly be?" he demanded bitterly, and my hand froze against his hair.

Had he somehow intuited my fear that his very personality was unraveling, separating into fragments? I swallowed, realizing my mouth had gone dry. How could I know that this was even the same man I had married, the man of integrity and compassion I used to know? If his mind had become unsettled, he might be anyone . . . might be capable of anything.

My silence had become conspicuous, and Atticus turned his head away from me, shaking off my hand. "If you have said all you came to say, it's best that you leave," he said. "I'm damned poor company tonight, anyway."

Again his manner held almost nothing of the Atticus I knew. It was too terrible a thought to be borne, yet at the same time I could not seem to put it out of my mind.

"I want to help you," I said softly. "Won't you please share your troubles with me? You have shouldered so much on your own."

His eyes shut briefly as if in weariness. "Some things are far better borne by me than put on others' shoulders."

Such refusal to let others help him might, I feared, prove dangerous. Drawing closer, I laid my hand on his arm. "Even the Atlas of myth sometimes had assistance," I said. "He sought help from Hercules, you know. I am no Hercules, but please, Atticus, let me take on some of your burden."

"I don't want you involved." The words were short, clipped.

"I already am involved. I'm your wife."

"Only in the contractual sense, and that is how I intend to keep it."

That stung, but I persisted. "I don't believe that. I think we have become closer than contractual partners or even friends, and I want our marriage to be a true one." I slipped my arms about his neck, careful to avoid the place where his skin was still healing, and looked into his eyes. "I want to be a real wife to you," I whispered. "Please don't keep shutting me out. I love you, Atticus—let me in."

I had no experience in seduction, but I kissed him with all the tenderness and longing in my heart, refusing to release him until I felt his lips respond to mine. For a brief, beautiful instant his arms went around me and clasped me tightly, so tightly that I could hardly breathe, but I gloried in that fierce embrace. He kissed me with more than eagerness—with a kind of desperate hunger. And then, so abruptly that my head reeled, he broke my hold on him and pushed me away.

"Our business arrangement is fulfilled, and our marriage is at an end," he told me. His voice was ragged, and his eyes were a stranger's. "You'll leave for London tomorrow. Have Henriette pack your things." He strode to the dressing-room door and held it open for me.

"I don't want to leave you," I said numbly. I was too stunned to move, almost too much to speak.

"I'm afraid that changes nothing." He would not even look at me.

"But—tomorrow? The house won't be ready," I stammered.

He rubbed his knuckles against his brow as if kneading out tormenting thoughts. "Bertram will find a respectable hotel for you and Genevieve. Gravesend is no place for you anymore. Now please leave me so that I may retire." I stood unmoving, almost stupefied, and that seemed to demolish his last reserve of strength. Harshly he demanded, "Will you go now, woman, or must I remove you bodily?" It was very nearly a shout.

The violence of his words brought me to life. Painfully I made my way to the door, each step feeling like a mile under the hostile, icy blue gaze. When I had reached the threshold I thought I might make one final appeal, one last attempt to break through the wall he had built between us, but when I opened my mouth to speak I was silenced by the expression on his face. For one second, so quickly I might have imagined it, I saw a terrible anguish in his eyes, as if he were being torn apart. Not Atlas but Prometheus, chained to a rock as his liver was devoured. It struck me dumb.

As I stood frozen to the spot he pushed the door to, and I had to step back or risk being struck by it as it shut. The sound came to me of the key being turned in the lock.

I made no move, and an answering silence came from the other side. It seemed each of us was determined to wait the other out.

This was no way to win my way into his confidence. I slowly made my way into my bedchamber, but when I shut the dressing-room door on my side I stood for long painful moments as I tried to decide whether I should lock it or not. Secure the door, and I might prevent Atticus from reaching me if he later decided to confide in me and seek my help. Leave it unlocked, though, and I risked the intrusion of that unpredictable, even frightening stranger who had looked out at me through my husband's eyes.

God help me, I thought, as I hesitated with my hand on the key in the knowledge that one small room's distance away stood a man who might now be a stranger to me.

CHAPTER TWENTY-FIVE

S ometime in the night I must have slept, for I opened my
eyes to find light creeping into the room around the edges
of the curtains. I lay in bed, exhausted and unrefreshed,
my mind endlessly replaying the events of the night before.

They were so bizarre I could hardly believe them to be real
in the light of morning. But the fears that rushed in at my heart
were real. If Atticus meant to do away with himself as Collier
had, I must make certain he would not succeed.

There was, however, another possible explanation for the
mental anguish I had seen in him. The thought was abhorrent
to me and struck a painful guilt into my heart, but I had to hold
it in my mind long enough to consider whether there could be
any truth to it. Could my husband have killed Collier?

Preposterous it probably was, but remembering those terrible, urgent arguments I had overheard, demonstrating so
clearly that Atticus was a man whose soul was divided against

itself, I knew that this possibility—as much as it horrified me to contemplate it—could not be dismissed altogether. Perhaps some buried part of Atticus had risen up when his father was killed to exact vengeance upon the killer.

It was true that the kind, loving man I knew could never have killed anyone in cold blood . . . but it was possible there was another side to Atticus, a dangerous one capable of such an act. "I felt I could have easily done violence to him," he had said once of his own father. If somehow an impulse to violence had mastered him, then the honorable and just Atticus must surely be in an agony of guilt and remorse. The harrowing thought came to me that the very sense of honor and justice that had convinced me of his innocence in his father's death might have led him to seek reparation for it. And if Atticus had killed Collier, his better self could well be bitterly regretting the deed now. Such a conflict of wills and thoughts might well drive a man mad.

Could it possibly be true that he had Collier's death on his conscience? I resisted the thought with all my being, and felt miserably that I must be the most disloyal wife who ever lived even to conceive of such a horrible idea, but it would haunt me until I could blot it out with certain facts. Until he told me what lay behind this terrible torment, I could not wholly believe in him as I used to.

And if he did not in fact have blood on his hands, he needed me all the more to stand by him and help him find his way back to peace of mind in whatever way I could. Abruptly I realized how thoroughly my dread of the Gravesend curse had been pushed out of my thoughts . . . yet the dreadful turn things had taken suggested that it might have been unwise not to reckon with that eerie possibility. That, too, could be tormenting Atticus. Perhaps he feared losing what he loved—and if that was me, then the very fear itself might have given him reason to push me away.

I flung the bedclothes back and darted to the dressing-room door. If he had harmed himself during the night, I would never forgive myself. I rushed through the first door and reached for the knob of the second, but I rattled it in vain; it was still locked.

"Atticus?" I called, knocking urgently. "Are you awake?"

There was the sound of footsteps, then the key turning in the lock. Relief washed over me, then turned to embarrassment when the door opened and I found myself facing Sterry, my husband's valet.

"My lady," he said, just managing to keep the phrase from turning into a question.

"I beg your pardon," I said, with as much dignity as I could muster given that I was in a nightdress with my hair in a tangle down my back. "I was looking for my husband."

"Lord Telford rose early, madam, and is probably either in the breakfast room or in the library with Mr. Bertram."

I thanked him briefly and withdrew to my own room. Henriette had appeared in that brief sliver of time in which I had been in the dressing room, and she took note of my impatience, helping me dress quickly and making no attempt to remonstrate with me when I fumbled my hair into a quick chignon instead of submitting myself to her hands for a more elaborate coiffure. Every instant that I spent apart from Atticus I would be in great unease.

In my haste I was taking little care to look where I was going, and so perhaps I bore part of the fault for what happened next.

I moved swiftly down the hall toward the stair and had taken the first couple of steps quickly—perhaps too quickly—when the ground seemed to slip out from under me. There was a sickening sensation of falling, a sharp and agonizing pain at the back of my head, and then my body was hurtling into nothingness.

Voices surrounded me.

The feminine one speaking rapidly and tearfully in a language I did not understand: that must be Genevieve.

Another, lower feminine one saying urgently, "Until the doctor arrives, what should we do, sir?"—that had to be Mrs. Threll.

My head was lifted gently, and fingers probed beneath my chignon. "Her hair seems to have cushioned the blow. I think it's safe to move her." Mr. Bertram.

"I can walk," I heard myself say, and opened my eyes to be greeted by a circle of anxious faces. When I spoke, there were exclamations of relief, and Genevieve bent to kiss me on both cheeks.

"Don't crowd her, now," admonished Mr. Bertram, and she retreated.

"Aunt Clara, you frightened us so! For a moment I almost thought . . ." She gulped and fumbled for a handkerchief, which she touched to her eyes. "I do not know what we would have told my uncle."

I struggled to sit up, but my head gave a horrible throb, and I subsided. "As to walking," said Bertram, observing me, "I think that's a bit much to ask just yet. With your permission, Lady Telford, I'll carry you."

Nodding only made my head register a strenuous complaint, so I settled for saying, "As you think best."

"Do not drop her, George," implored Genevieve, as Bertram drew one of my arms around his shoulders and got his arms beneath me.

"I don't plan to, Vivi. Is there a divan close at hand?"

"In here," said Mrs. Threll, leading the way into a darkened room that I supposed to be the parlor. All of the rooms were dim, with windows and draperies shut in accordance with mourning tradition. She opened the curtains to let in some light as she continued, "I'll have some tea brought—or brandy, do you think?"

I was groggy enough already without brandy to make me more so; I requested tea, and the housekeeper bustled away, evidently relieved to have something to do. Bertram and Genevieve hovered over me.

"How do you feel now, Lady Telford?" Bertram asked. "Did you—have you—can you tell—"

"What, for heaven's sake?" The fall had not improved my temper.

He chewed his lip in indecision, then leaned over to whisper in my ear. "Will the baby be all right?" he asked almost inaudibly.

That made me laugh, albeit shakily. "Do not credit every rumor you hear, Mr. Bertram. That story never had a grain of truth in it . . . did you see what happened?"

Genevieve shook her head, making her bright curls fly. "By the time we realized what was happening, you were already falling. I did not see what caused it. Did you trip on something?"

"I don't think so. It was more as if the carpet slipped out from under me."

"I'll go take a look at it," announced Bertram, and departed the room. As soon as he was well away I looked at Genevieve with as much severity as I could muster.

"'George'?" I asked.

She blushed, but a smile curved her mouth. "He is going to speak to my uncle as soon as he thinks a decent interval has passed."

Slightly disquieted, I did not reply at once.

"You disapprove, Aunt Clara?" she asked, more subdued.

"Not exactly, only you've known each other so short a time . . . and I've not been acquainted with him for much longer, at that." I did not speak aloud the more serious reason for my unease. Perhaps the blow to my head had stirred some new ideas, for I had realized in a flash of insight that if someone other than Atticus had had a hand in recent events, Bertram was well placed to do so . . . and if he felt sure enough of Genevieve's attachment to him, he might have taken measures to ensure that she would inherit the Blackwood wealth. Atticus's suspicious accident might indeed have been deliberate—but brought about by another party, someone who did not want him to inherit his father's estate.

And if Atticus's wife were to either die or suffer an accident that would cause her to miscarry the baby she was widely believed to be carrying, that would leave the way clear for Atticus to name Genevieve as his heir.

Such thoughts were shocking, of course . . . but after being shaken to my very bones by the realization that Atticus seemed to have a secret self whose existence I had never even guessed, playing devil's advocate about my friends seemed a comparatively minor infraction.

Indeed, Genevieve herself might have desired to ensure her place as heiress to Gravesend. I realized now that my words to her the night that she had shared my bed had been capable of misinterpretation, and she might still believe I was carrying a child. If she did, or even thought that the possibility existed, she might have good reason to do away with me.

But this was foolishness—worse than foolishness; it was a terrible injustice to the girl. She was so obviously in distress at my accident, as was Bertram. If either of them had truly wished for me to come to grief, they were doing a magnificent job of disguising their feelings.

And Genevieve was now looking wounded at my lack of enthusiasm about her planned betrothal. She sat twining one of her Titian ringlets around her index finger, looking at the toes of the black silk slippers that peeped from beneath the hem of her mourning dress. "What do you know about him, Vivi?" I asked.

She met my eyes and spoke with a dignity that was unusual in her. "I know that Uncle Atlas respects and trusts him," she said. "I know that he is kind and clever and that when he gives his word it may always be relied upon. I know that he is financially well placed to take a wife."

Her gravity was so different from her usual manner that it was beginning to tickle my sense of humor. "These are impressive credentials," I said solemnly. "Clearly you have weighed all of the significant factors and determined that this would be a most practical matrimonial alliance."

Her eyes narrowed, and in a moment a returning smile began to tug at the corners of her mouth. "Aunt Clara, you are baiting me."

"Tsk, such an idea. Do you mean to tell me that a rational young woman like yourself would let her decision be swayed by any other considerations?"

She gave an exuberant bounce on the hassock where she sat. "Oh, indeed yes. There is the consideration that he dances beautifully and that he pays compliments divinely. There is the fact that his kisses are more divine even than his compliments." She leaned closer, her eyes dancing, and confided, "There also is the fact that his mother has gone to be with the angels, and I shall have no mama-in-law to contend with." Straightening, she beamed at me and made a flourish. "*Voilà!* He is perfect."

"Very well," I said, relenting. "If Atticus needs any persuading, I shall see what I can accomplish on your behalf." It had not escaped me that if Genevieve married, she would not need a London Season—and Atticus would have no pretext for sending us away.

"Oh, Aunt Clara!" She was about to launch herself at me to kiss me again, but I wished not to be jostled and held up a restraining hand.

"Save that for George," I pleaded, and she subsided, all smiles and blushes, as Bertram returned.

"I think I found the problem," he announced, oblivious to what we had been discussing. "One of the stair rods toward the top of the staircase seems to have come loose. It looks as though the carpet slipped and caused you to lose your footing."

"But that's impossible, sir," said Mrs. Threll when she arrived with the tea and learned of this theory. "No one has had cause to clean the stair carpet today or, indeed, for the last few days. There's no reason at all for anyone to have touched the stair rods."

She could have merely been protecting the staff, but I was inclined to believe her. They had been thoroughly occupied with preparing the house for the old baron's funeral, and their efforts were concentrated on the ground floor. It would have been conspicuous if one of the maids had instead chosen to clean that portion of the carpet.

"If the stair rod was tampered with, it must have been after I retired last night," I reasoned.

"But Atticus didn't fall," Bertram pointed out. "Which would suggest a very narrow window of time indeed—between his coming downstairs and your following after."

Mrs. Threll's mouth had tightened in disapproval. "I do not see that any *tampering* need have taken place. And perhaps the rod has been loosening for some time now."

Our theorizing had only succeeded in putting her on the defensive. With this in mind, and because the throbbing in my head was growing so painful it discouraged further conversation, I dismissed her.

The doctor, when he arrived, examined the back of my head minutely and announced that rest and sleep would be my best healers. I chafed at this mandated inactivity, but with my head aching so dreadfully I was not fit for much at present in any case. I retired to my room and slept—and I am not certain whether it was my injury that made my dreams so troubled and violent.

At one point I woke to see someone sitting on the edge of the bed, indistinct in the gloom. With the drapes closed, the room was sunk in a twilight dimness. "Atticus?" I ventured drowsily.

"Hush, my love." I felt his lips brush my forehead. "Rest."

But I had little talent for being silent. "Did Bertram tell you—"

"He did." I heard the steely sinew of anger in his voice. "I would never have forgiven myself if you . . ." He seemed unable to complete the thought.

"Why should you feel responsible?"

A brief silence. He took my hand, which lay atop the counterpane, and held it in his. In a different voice he asked, "Do you wish Richard were the one you had married?"

"What?" I said, startled.

"You loved him very deeply, didn't you?"

"That was years ago." I freed my hand and pushed myself up into a sitting position. "Light the candle—I want to see your face. What on earth are you talking about?"

He made no motion to strike a light. "I simply wondered if you'd be happier if you had married Richard."

"Of course not. In any case, what is the purpose even of thinking about it? He's dead, so the question is moot."

I thought I could hear a wry smile in his next words. "Very reassuring for me."

"Atticus, don't." I touched his face, wishing I could read his eyes. "I'm the one who wanted to make our marriage a true one, aren't I? You could have had your reassurance in spades last night if you hadn't sent me away."

"Reassurance," he repeated, and this time I was certain of the smile. "Not a very romantic word for it, surely?"

At least in the darkness he could not see me blush. "If you are trying to embarrass me—"

"Never think it, my Clara." His hands cradled my face, and then he drew me to him for a kiss that was strangely anonymous in that darkened room, but also touched with an urgency that I had not heard in his words or voice. He kissed me so long and so fervently that, even as my blood quickened and warmed with answering passion, the strange idea came to me that it was as if this were the last time, as if he knew there would be no more chances.

"Atticus, what is wrong?" I asked breathlessly when at last he released me.

A heavy silence, then: "A great deal is wrong. I am going to try to put right what I can." His hands still framed my face, and with his thumb he traced my lips. "I love you, Clara," he said.

He had never said this to me before, though he had indicated it in ways large and small. Why say the words now? More than ever I wished he would light a lamp or open the drapes. "You sound so *final*," I said, hearing the thin note of panic in my voice. "Please tell me what is in your mind."

"It doesn't matter." Suddenly his voice was brisk, and he rose briefly to return holding something. When he placed it in my hands, I realized it was a wine glass. "I almost forgot—Dr. Brandt left a sleeping draught for you. He wants you to rest as much as possible."

"I'll drink it," I said, "if you will tell me what you are about." His portentous manner had filled me with unease.

"Very well, it's a bargain."

Satisfied, I drained the goblet. The sleeping draught had been mixed with red wine, and the taste was sweet. I handed the empty glass to him. "Now, tell me," I ordered.

"I lied," he said softly. "I'm sorry, but I'll not have you involved in this any more than you already are."

"You *tricked* me?" I was almost too astonished for anger.

"I'll explain everything tomorrow, if—" He hesitated for a fraction of a moment. "I'll explain tomorrow."

"Don't you dare leave," I gasped as he rose to do just that. "You have to . . . you must . . ." Suddenly my tongue was thick, and the room seemed to slide sideways before my eyes. I felt my eyelids drooping, felt myself sinking toward the bed. The part of my mind that had not yet been claimed by the drug wondered if the doctor had indeed sent the sleeping draught or if it had been Atticus's own idea—to prevent me from pursuing him to get to the bottom of these mysterious hints and implications.

It was my last coherent thought as the opiate effect of the drug filled my head with velvet sleep. I could not be certain whether the voice I heard saying *goodbye* was my husband's—or my imagination. There came the sound of a door closing, very soft and far away, and then unconsciousness claimed me.

CHAPTER TWENTY-SIX

I woke to the sound of rain and thunder. *Construction will be halted again,* I thought drowsily. Then memory began to return, and I dragged my heavy eyelids open and looked around.

The room was even darker than before, but a flash of lightning briefly showed through a narrow opening in the drapes, and I saw that I was alone. I pushed back the bedclothes, noticing that it took a greater effort than usual; evidently the effects of the substance Atticus had given me had not yet completely worn off.

I felt my way over to my bureau and struck a light. My head still ached from my fall, and other parts of me had begun to ache as well. Picturing the length of that flight of stairs, I could not repress a slight shudder. I had been extremely fortunate not to have been more severely injured.

I drew a simple wool frock from my wardrobe and began to dress myself. My movements became faster as my mind cleared.

I must find where Atticus had gone and what he had intended to do. Without a doubt he was putting himself in danger, but I could not imagine how . . . unless he intended to give himself up to the authorities for something. For Collier's death, perhaps.

It makes no sense, I fumed as I drew on my walking boots. *Atticus is no killer.* All those signs of guilt had to signify something else, for I could not in my heart of hearts think him capable of murder . . . could I? Perhaps the man I knew and loved was not, but there was that other self, the one who had spoken with such biting anger and coldness. That unknown Atticus might be capable of anything.

Which made it all the more crucial that I find him and forestall any plan he might be embarking upon. I strode to the dressing-room door, steadier with every passing moment, and found it unlocked. The second door, likewise, was unlocked, and I emerged into Atticus's bedchamber, where a fire was burning but no one was present.

The room should have looked peaceful, normal. Nothing stood out at first as unusual, yet my mind twinged with a faint unease. Atticus's evening clothes were laid out on the bed, the patent-leather shoes placed neatly on the floor beneath. A glance at the elaborate timepiece on the mantel told me it was nearly eight o'clock. He should have been dressing for dinner, or have already finished doing so.

The door to the corridor was ajar, and perhaps that was what had awakened that stirring of unease. I crossed the room and opened the door wide: the hallway was empty. From the far end past my sitting room, I could hear rain flinging itself against the window, and intermittent flashes of lightning showed around the edges of the drapes.

It was there, at that end of the corridor, that I had thought I saw Richard one night—and from that direction I had thought I heard my name spoken on my first night as a bride at Gravesend. I had never resumed my scrutiny of that portion of the corridor for anything unusual, and with a decisiveness I could not entirely explain I strode down the hall in the direction of those mysterious manifestations.

The wainscoting was almost shoulder height, and above it the wall was papered in a dark, elaborate pattern of flowers and acanthus leaves. It confused the eye, so I decided to use my other senses instead. With my eyes shut, I walked slowly toward the window, trailing one hand lightly along the edge of the wainscoting. For the distance of several paces I detected nothing unusual.

Then I felt it: the faint cold breath of air emanating from a place where there was no aperture. When I opened my eyes and looked closely, I could see the tiniest fissure in the paneling—a break that was suspiciously straight and symmetrical. Like the edge of a door. I traced it down to a small knot in the wood and pressed it. It gave easily—so easily that it must have been designed for the purpose—and a door in the wainscoting opened gently inward into darkness.

My scalp tightened. Without any evidence to the contrary, this seemed the most likely place for Atticus to have gone. But which Atticus—and why?

After returning briefly to my room for a candle and matches, I set out to explore what lay beyond the hidden door. I had to duck my head to pass through it, and when I did I found a small empty chamber with stone walls and floor. Perhaps "chamber" was giving it more than its due: there was scarcely much to it beyond a stairwell with stone steps leading downward. Its size must have been determined by what space there was at this corner of the house between the windows on the two perpendicular walls.

When I examined the door, I found that the latch on the inside was controlled by a button similar to that on the wainscoting side. I made certain it worked from this side before I shut it behind me. I had no desire to be trapped in the little room—or wherever it led.

From the stairwell I felt again that chilly current of air. Was the other end of this passage open to the outdoors? I could only find out by making the journey.

That journey was the strangest of my life. Not only was I venturing into uncharted, even unguessed territory, but I did so with a combination of urgency and reluctance. My instincts told me that I must stop Atticus from doing whatever his dark hints had referred to, whatever—I inferred—was putting his future, or ours, in danger; but the prospect of what might lie ahead struck me with an almost paralyzing dread. Whether it was some dark side of Atticus himself or some unknown party, I knew this was not an adversary I would find it easy to confront. I had begun to evolve a theory about the hidden player in this gruesome ongoing drama of Gravesend, and I wasn't certain which outcome would be more horrifying: to be right or to be wrong.

The steps led down past a similar small landing or chamber at the next floor, and then another at what would have been the bottom floor with the kitchen, scullery, pantry, wine cellar, and the like; but it descended again before feeding into a stone-lined passage through which the cold breeze came, more strongly now, stinging my cheeks. I hesitated at the mouth of it. The candle's flame illuminated a long stretch of tunnel narrowing into a wall of darkness. I could not tell how long the passage was, where it led, or whether anyone was guarding it. All I knew was that I did not want to give anyone a hint of my coming.

I extinguished the candle and placed it on the bottom step against the wall where, I hoped, I would be able to retrieve it later. The matches I kept in my pocket. I unlaced my boots and set them aside as well; otherwise the sound of my footsteps would reveal my presence just as readily as would the light of the candle. Thank heaven I had not dressed in taffeta or any such rustling fabric.

The passage was so narrow that it would have been impossible to walk two abreast. As I progressed I felt along the left-hand wall with one hand, with the other extended before me in case I encountered an obstacle. The stone walls of the passage were rougher than those in the stairwell through which I had come; evidently this was not a route intended for much traffic, although this I had already gleaned. I thought of what Richard—no, Atticus—had told me about the Blackwoods' smuggling days, and I knew this must be a remnant of those times. That meant that this tunnel probably led to a bay of some kind where ships could have unloaded the contraband goods.

I could not tell how long I felt my way along the passage. Hours, it seemed. The passage sloped downward, but so gently that I could not say how far beneath the earth it descended. It turned occasionally, sometimes so sharply that only the hand extended before me prevented me from walking into the opposite wall. Soon I had lost all sense of what direction I was going in. Occasionally one stockinged foot would come down on a pebble—or dislodge one, and each time I caught my breath, listening to the echo of it skittering against the walls, and hoped that no other ears had caught the sound. The darkness became oppressive, my hands and feet grew colder and colder, and I had to suppress panicked thoughts about never finding my way out again. All I knew for certain was that I was moving farther away from Gravesend with every step . . . and closer, I devoutly hoped, to Atticus.

At one point the faint echoes of my own progress vanished, and the wall on my right seemed to fall away. When after listening hard I caught no sign of any presence other than my own, I drew a match from my pocket and struck it against the rough stone wall.

The light that sputtered into being was drowned in a great dark space, but when I moved the match I could see that I was in a large, rough-hewn chamber. A few old wooden barrels were stacked along the far wall, along with a newer packing crate. On the crate rested a candle in a holder, matches, half a loaf of brown bread, a bottle that must once have held wine, and a pewter mug. Someone had been here recently, for the bread was neither moldy nor bitten by vermin. Before the match sputtered out I also saw a straw pallet, a stack of folded blankets, and an upended crate with a broken mirror upon it. Had someone been living down here? And if so, for how long? There was no answer to be gleaned from the scant objects I saw, so I struck another match, located the arched opening where the passage continued, and resumed my journey.

It grew colder. The breeze strengthened all the time, and at last it brought something with it besides the numbing chill and what I was beginning to think was the briny tang of the sea. It brought the sound of voices.

Or was it merely one voice—Atticus, again, in a terrible dialogue with himself? More swiftly I crept along, but taking pains to be ever more stealthy. If the last incident was to be taken as precedent, my intrusion would bring the discussion to an end. I must overhear without being noticed. Fortunately the sound of thunder had ceased, so I did not have to strain to hear over it.

When the voices—or voice—came again, closer, my footsteps slowed and I clung more closely to the wall.

"I refuse to believe you've no conscience." That was certainly Atticus.

But the answering laughter was also Atticus's. "A conscience is a heavy burden," came the drawled response. "I've traveled lighter without one."

There was an exclamation of . . . disbelief? disgust? "How can you say such a thing? You cannot claim your soul is at peace with itself after you murdered two men in cold blood."

My involuntary gasp was drowned out by an impatient sigh. "A sick old man with one foot in the grave, and a dangerous lunatic? Some might say I did them a service. Besides, Collier's death was crucial. Without that admission of guilt, you'd still be on the hook for Father's death."

There was a silence. I could hear, faintly, the sound of surf or rain; I could not be certain which. "I know you have some scruples left," the first voice said. "Show it: be a man, and turn yourself in to the authorities."

"So you aim to school *me* in being a man?" scoffed the second voice. "You with that pistol you're afraid to use, and your comely bride a virgin still? I was more of a man than you when we were still in short pants."

I bit my lip. Still I could not be certain whether this was Atticus alone. I crept forward a few more steps until I neared a corner, beyond which I could see light glowing faintly on the rough stone. Candlelight, perhaps—or a lamp, since its illumination was steady. *Illumination,* I thought desperately, *is sorely in need here.*

"I'm not afraid to use it," came the voice of Atticus—*my* Atticus—quiet and grave. "I'm simply hoping it won't be necessary and your better nature will prevail. Despite our differences, and despite the terrible things you have done, I would still prefer not to have to shoot my own brother."

My hands flew to my mouth to hold back a gasp. So it was true. It had seemed so farfetched an idea . . . but the more I had considered it during that long, strange progress in the dark, the more logical it had become. All except for the central mystery: *how?*

I edged closer to the light and very, very slowly moved my head to peer around the corner.

Atticus and his twin stood confronting each other in a shallow cave formed where the passage opened out. From where I stood, a narrow set of roughly hewn stone steps led down to the sandy ground on which they stood. Beyond, although I could not see it in the darkness of night, must be a cove, and I knew I had been right to suppose that the passage and the underground chamber had been constructed with smuggling in view.

A lamp placed on a flat rock lit up the two figures as if they were on a stage. But the pistol in Atticus's bandaged hand was no prop, and this confrontation, as fantastical as it seemed, was no playwright's creation.

Atticus held the gun trained on his brother. There was no wavering in his grip or in the sober gravity of his eyes, but a telltale tremor fluttered in his bad leg. I wondered suddenly how long the two men had been wrangling here, how long Atticus had been on his guard, so focused and so intent. How much longer could he maintain his watchful stance before his concentration broke and his brother made a move to disarm him—or worse?

Richard, in contrast, seemed as relaxed as if he were at a garden party. As I watched, he lit a Turkish cigarette from the lamp, then replaced the glass chimney and propped one foot on the rock as he regarded his brother.

The years had wrought some changes, but they had not been unkind to him. His clothes were rough, but his movements as easy and powerful as ever. He sported several days' worth of ginger whiskers, and his hair wanted washing, but the lean rangy lines of his body were not blurred, nor was the speculative gleam in his ice-blue eyes. The half smile that curved his mouth was so familiar that it clenched my stomach with dread and a kind of superstitious fear. He did not fear his brother—no, nor did he even take him seriously. Atticus was not going to win the day by appealing to Richard's better nature.

And Atticus knew it.

He knew that a man ruthless enough to kill his own father and a relative stranger would not be motivated now by contrition or a sense of justice. But, being a man of honor himself, Atticus could not give up trying to evoke those long-buried impulses in his brother. *After all,* he must be thinking, *in spite of everything, we are twins. We are branches of the same root.* But Richard had traveled far since their common origin, and I despaired of his retaining all but the faintest glimmer of kinship with my husband. Even as I watched, his eyes flicked over Atticus, taking in, I was certain, the slight spasm in his bad leg. His walking stick was nowhere to be seen. No—there it was, broken in half and lying on the sand. I noticed now how churned up the sand was. Had they struggled here before Atticus drew the pistol? It seemed likely. Surely he would have saved it for a last resort.

My heart swelled suddenly with a fierce, hot rush of love for him that was actually painful, and tears squeezed from my eyes. My brave, foolish, steadfast husband was going to confront this matter according to his own sense of fair play, whatever the risk to himself. And the risk was so terribly great. For an instant I sagged against the wall, overwhelmed by the crushing weight of what seemed an inevitability.

Then I straightened, wiped my eyes with my sleeve, and set myself with renewed determination to watching, listening, and waiting for the moment to make a move. He had an ally, and Richard did not know it. Somehow I would help tip the scales in Atticus's favor. *You are not in this fight alone,* I silently vowed.

Richard lounged casually where he stood, one elbow propped on his bent leg, flicking ash from his cigarette. "You're looking a bit seedy, old fellow," he said. "Tired, are we? Why don't you stop this charade? We both know you would never kill your own brother."

My husband's smile belied the tension in his stance. "Perhaps not, but I might wound you severely. Enough to incapacitate you until the authorities arrive." A pause, as if he were weighing choices. "In the thigh, say. It might not kill you, but it would slow you down well enough. And it would be damned painful." His eyes always on Richard, he carefully switched the pistol to his other hand, and I remembered with a jolt the injuries to his shoulder and hand—more weaknesses Richard might know to exploit, especially if he had been the cause of his brother's so-called accident. "That's a bad place to be wounded," he continued, as calmly as if he felt no fear. "Through no intention of mine, you might even bleed to death before assistance arrived. Are you willing to chance it?"

This did not ruffle his brother. "I'm a pretty tough specimen, and far more ruthless than you. If you injure me but don't finish the job, you can be certain I'll not stop until I have made an end with you." He drew on the cigarette again, and observed, "It isn't that I bear you any ill will, you understand. But you must go somewhere if I'm to step into your shoes, and I can tell you are too stubborn to vanish as I did. No, if I'm to become the new baron—"

It was then that I slipped.

I had been inching closer to the two of them in my stocking feet, when I stepped on a pebble that abruptly rolled under my foot and nearly threw me off balance. I caught myself in time, but there must have been some sound—the rattle of the dislodged stone, some rustle or gasp or simply the rush of my body through the air—and both faces turned in my direction.

It all happened in an instant. Atticus's shock was the greater, and his attention rested on me just a moment too long. Richard, recovering more quickly, lunged across the distance that separated them and, even as the warning cry hovered on my lips, brought something down on Atticus's head that made him crumple to the ground. He lay there unmoving.

"Thank you for your help, Clara," said Richard almost gaily, as dread churned in my stomach. Atticus could not be dead, surely? Richard nudged the pistol away from him with one foot, and when Atticus neither moved nor protested, he bent swiftly to retrieve it.

"What did you hit him with?" The question forced itself from me.

"A blackjack," he said, and flourished it. It was a small thing, so small that—I realized now—he must have had it concealed in his sleeve all this while, just waiting for a moment when his brother's focus wavered . . . the moment I had blunderingly created.

"Aren't you glad to see me?" he continued, still in high spirits. "This isn't the greeting I expected from a former sweetheart. For that matter, how did you end up married to the martyred Atticus here?"

"I thought you were dead," I said. I did not mean it as an answer to his question; it was simply the only thing that came to me to say. A kind of numbness seemed to have descended upon me, and I sounded quite calm. "We all did."

He chuckled. "I did quite a thorough job of dying, didn't I? Not even Father guessed. Although I didn't expect him to have a stroke when I returned. That was a bit more of a reaction than I had anticipated. But let's have a look at you! Come closer, pet."

There was a thread of command in the words, and although he was not pointing the pistol at me, we were both aware that this could change at any moment. Slowly I descended the stone steps into the cavern. Atticus still had not moved, and I needed to get closer to him so that I could see if he still breathed. On that everything else hinged.

Richard had pocketed the blackjack, and now the hand not holding the pistol caught my hand. "My soul upon it, but the years have been kind to you, Clara. Come, give us a kiss."

Gazing on Richard's face again after so long was unsettling, in more ways than one. Seen up close, however, he did not look as untouched by time as he had seemed at a distance. There were traceries of red blood vessels showing in his cheeks and nose, and together with a puffiness about his eyes they suggested that he had grown immoderate in his habits. The end of a scar showed just above his collar beneath his left ear.

"Were you wounded in the Crimea?" I asked, indicating it. An irrelevant point, but I was still trying to collect my wits. And I did not wish to kiss him.

"Wounded—? Oh, the scar. No, that I received one fine dawn from an outraged husband." He laughed at my expression. "My dear girl, I do not claim to be a saint, or anything like it. I have always enjoyed feminine company, and when one has to move about rather unexpectedly, as I have, married women are so much less of an encumbrance." He smiled as he held me at arm's length and surveyed me again with evident pleasure. "It was most considerate of Atlas to provide me with a bride along with the other perquisites of the barony. Come, Clara, you've not even said that you missed me."

"Missed you!" But his self-certainty would work to my advantage if I could but shore it up sufficiently for him to assume me an ally. "My life ended when yours did," I said, and the remembered grief and agony of those years came back in a rush. I saw my younger self from a remove, with the pity of one who now knew that the man I had lost had not been worth shedding tears over. "Why did you let everyone believe you had died?"

His shrug was magnificently unconcerned. "Oh, life as myself had become damnably complicated. Some rather highly placed chappie was after me for bilking him of a good sum of money at cards. And then at Eupatoria another officer accused me of interfering with his wife, and suddenly death seemed quite convenient."

I was nearly certain then that there had been a faint movement from Atticus. The more time I could buy for him, the better situated we would be to overpower Richard. I could only steal quick glances at him, or else I would arouse Richard's suspicion—especially since, as I recalled, Richard preferred to be one's entire focus of attention.

"The death mask was a clever touch," I said, and his chuckle was richly self-satisfied.

"I fancied so. It was unpleasant enough being cast, but having the sawbones send it along with the news of my death seemed like the perfect way to convince my father that I was truly gone."

He narrowed his eyes at me speculatively. "I had not expected to find you wedded to my brother, even if it is merely for show."

During his boasting I had had time to think of an explanation. "When Atlas proposed, I thought it might be like having you back in some ways," I said. "Being here at Gravesend, with all its memories of you, seemed worth enduring him for."

"How fortunate that you overcame your revulsion to him and accepted him. Now you shall have me back *and* remain the lady of Gravesend."

I forced myself to smile. "Fortunate indeed! But how did you know that our marriage is no more than show?"

His smile was more of a smirk this time. "I was there last night, pet, lurking in the wardrobe—an audience of one while you played your romantic scene. By the gods, I have never despised Atlas more than I did then—or admired you more! *You weren't going to let him fob you off with some stingy settlement; no, my magnificent Clara was prepared to go to any length to secure the marriage and the position of Lady Telford, even if it meant seducing my plaster saint of a brother. Don't shut me out, Atticus. Let me shoulder your burden.* I wanted to cheer for you."

Nausea rose in me at the knowledge that he had been a witness to that wrenching confrontation. No wonder Atticus had ordered me away: whether he had wanted me or not, he would never have subjected me to his brother's spying eyes and ears for longer than he must.

And even in my horror at the knowledge of all that Richard had done and planned to do, I must confess that there was a part of me that rejoiced: Atticus was not mad, nor was he a killer—nor was he as uninterested in marriage with me as it had lately seemed. I was almost certain now when I risked a glimpse at his prone form that he still breathed. Surely that had been a faint motion of his fingers. Bright, jolting energy sang through my veins. I could save him, save *us,* if I could only think how.

"How frustrated you must have been when he came under suspicion for your father's death," I said. "If he had gone to prison or the gallows, you'd not have been able to take his place."

"Exactly. When that fool maid tattled about seeing me, I was half desperate. And it needn't have come to this, either." Roughly he nudged his brother's prone form with a booted toe, and I bit back a protest. "I *tried* to persuade him to leave. He would have had some difficulty in making his way alone, for he never had the stomach for thieving. But it would have been a life, even under some other name and far away . . . and, I must admit, with a few unsavory types after his blood. Not our Atlas, though." His self-satisfaction had waned, and his expression had gone sour. "Such a joyless creature, my brother. He couldn't see it as an adventure; no, he had *duties* here to see to."

I wanted to slap his face. Atticus knew more of joy, the kind that came from caring for those who relied on him, than any man I had ever known. I remembered his bringing Genevieve into our lives, remembered his excitement as he discussed his plans with Bertram, remembered dancing with him and his saying *I would have been honored.* "Atticus takes his responsibilities seriously," I said, and had to strive to keep the censure from my voice. "I expect you'll be a very different baron now that your day has come."

That won a grin from him. "Very different indeed, pet." Before I knew what he was about, he had drawn me closer and kissed me lingeringly on the lips. It was like kissing a stranger . . . indeed, that is exactly what it was, for I had never known this Richard, or had never allowed myself to know him. In the hard, demanding pressure of his mouth I caught the not unpleasant taste of tobacco and brandy, but it was nothing like the way Atticus kissed me. I was scarcely able to pretend a response, so struck was I by the difference and by the injustice of being embraced by the wrong man, the wrongest of men.

Apparently it was satisfactory to him, however, for he released me and tweaked my nose. "We'll have a fine time, pet. I should have known better than to—I should have known you would cleave to me after all."

"Did you think I would betray you?" Memories of that fall down the stairs gave me a shiver I tried to suppress. He must have been the one to remove the stair rod.

He winked at me. Throughout, he had been of such high spirits that it baffled me. Engaged in this most deadly of enterprises, he approached it as if it were—what was the word he had used?—an adventure. It held a certain perverse charm, and I did not wonder that I had been so in love with him in my girlhood. Charm and enthusiasm could make even the most sordid things seem exciting, especially to a naive girl. "I wasn't certain," he admitted. "At first I thought it would be better to be safe than sorry. But having you by my side will allay any possible suspicions that may arise. If the dour, joyless Atticus Blackwood suddenly seems to be possessed of more *joie de vivre,* it can be credited to his recent marriage."

"And what do you intend to do with him?" I nodded in my husband's direction. He lay still, as before, but something in me whispered that he was doing so deliberately, listening, even as I had listened, for a moment when he might gain the advantage. "If he is still alive, you would be wise to keep him that way for a few days or weeks, until you have learned everything from him that you'll need to know to assume his identity. You must learn to copy his signature, for a start."

"Such a clever Clara! But that is where you're mistaken. I can learn that easily enough from studying his papers." His eyes were less amiable now, and my heart gave a thud of apprehension. "So you want him alive, do you?"

He faced me, and behind him I saw, for a certainty, Atticus's hand move slowly across the sand, toward the broken fragments of his walking stick. I took a deep breath and said a brief, silent prayer.

"Alive or dead, he is a better man than you," I said. "I will never be your wife, Richard. Every time I looked at you, it's my real husband's face I would see."

I think he actually forgot about the pistol. It was his other hand he raised, as if he were going to box my ears. I ducked, reaching out with both hands to seize the pistol, and at the same time he gave a horrible rasping cry, and I saw that Atticus, without rising, had driven the jagged edge of his broken cane into Richard's ankle.

It threw Richard off his balance, and I wasn't quick enough to avoid his falling body; he bore me down with him, landing on top of me and knocking the breath from my body. Then we were struggling for the pistol, and there was the loathsome uneven sound of his breathing in hot pants against my ear, and I heard my own breath coming in gulps that were almost sobs as I clawed at his fingers, trying to pry them from the pistol.

Then I realized I did not need to hold the gun, just to aim it. I shifted my grip to the barrel, but Richard must have realized what I was about, and to my horror I felt it press against my bodice. We were still struggling when the loud report came, and after a moment that seemed to stretch on forever, Richard's body went slack.

With an exclamation of horror I pushed him off me and rolled away. When I looked at him I thought I saw his eyes follow me, but he made no other motion; a scarlet stain was blooming on his waistcoat. Within moments a film seemed to form over his eyes, and I knew that he was dead. The bullet must have pierced his heart. Lying there still, he looked so like Atticus that I gave a superstitious shudder. I scrambled over to my husband, who was slowly raising himself to a sitting position against a spur of rock, and threw my arms around him.

"Are you all right?" he asked. His voice was subdued, even a bit dazed, and I peered anxiously into his face. Yes, his beautiful blue eyes were focused; he knew me, and himself. The blow to his head had not robbed him of his wits. I kissed him long and thoroughly.

"I think that answers my question," he said presently, when at last I freed his lips for speech.

"I was so frightened you were dead." I mumbled the words into his neck, and felt his hand come to rest on my hair.

"I did not have a fashionable chignon to cushion the blow as you did," he said. "I shall have a goose egg that outshines your hen's egg, but I think that's the worst of it."

I sat up, surreptitiously drying my eyes, and summoned the courage to look again at Richard. He was a curiously pathetic form sprawled on the sand. "The night your father died—was it Richard's being here that he forced you to keep secret?"

He nodded, then flinched at the motion. "At first all I could think of was you. How unfair it was to you . . . and then when Father died and I was nearly certain Richard had killed him, it was agony. Even now, when I think that if I had spoken up, Collier might not have died—"

I put my fingers to his lips. "The blame for that isn't yours. You had no way of knowing Richard would go after him." It was shocking to think that this one man had sown so much tragedy. "Did he cause your accident at the building site?"

This time his nod was more cautious. "He pretended it was an accident, but he meant it to persuade me to trade places with him. That was his goal until he realized he would have to kill me to make me leave you and Gravesend to him."

Those tense whispered arguments in his room now took on perfect clarity to me.

"I still feel as if he couldn't possibly be here," I said. "But then, none of us could have guessed that he had staged his own death."

"Pretending to be dead let him become someone else, unfettered by expectations or responsibilities. It gave him freedom—

277

even more than he already enjoyed as a younger son." He shook his head grimly, and this time he did not wince. "Up until he decided that the comforts of Gravesend and the Blackwood fortune—and my name—warranted coming back to life."

"So you were sending me away to keep me safe from him."

"How can you doubt it?" He stroked my hair back from my face, and the expression in his eyes made warmth flood my heart. "Only the gravest need would have forced me to part from you."

I could not let myself fully enjoy those welcome words, not with the gruesome, tragic figure lying a few yards away. "What do we do about him now?" I asked, glancing again at the prone form and hastily averting my eyes.

His hand moved to my waist, and he drew me closer. "It won't be pleasant, telling Strack that his comfortable theory was wrong and revealing the ugly truth. We may be in for a great deal of questioning. But we owe it to any relatives of Collier to clear his name." He fell silent for a moment. "I suspect it will be terribly hard for Genevieve—learning who her father was and what he did. Can you help her to bear up?"

I wrapped my arms around his neck. "You made me your wife, and your wife I remain," I promised. "We shall help her together."

He smiled into my eyes.

"Yes," he said. "We'll do it together."

EPILOGUE

On a day in the middle of September the Bertrams joined us for afternoon tea in the garden. Genevieve had begun to curtail her social appearances now that her pregnancy was visible, but she never hesitated to accept an invitation to Gravesend; we were, after all, family.

Atticus had given his blessing for their wedding to take place even before the uproar over the disclosure of Richard's return— and his violent deeds—had died down; best, he thought, to have something happy to think about in the midst of the distress, and I agreed. Now, at this remove, I was more glad than ever that Genevieve and George had married soon after her eighteenth birthday; her husband had helped Genevieve weather the distress of learning who her father was, as had the discovery soon after that she was expecting a child. Together they gave her all the reason she had needed to concentrate on the future of her family, not the past.

The wedding had also given Atticus and me something positive to dwell on instead of the unpleasantness of the investigation. When that had concluded, Atticus was also able to bring his thoughts once again to bear on the completion and opening of the first of the Blackwood Homes for unattached women and their children. The success of this venture filled me with pride, as did watching my old friend Martha instruct the residents in sewing; and when I found opportunities to offer advice, comfort, or simply a listening ear I felt no small satisfaction of my own in being a part of such a worthy cause. The second of the Blackwood Homes was already well into construction.

The sunlight was slanting toward evening, but the four of us lingered on in the gardens, enjoying the fine weather and each other's company. Seeing my husband's excitement as he discussed the coming baby made me smile secretly to myself. I had a strong suspicion that soon I would have news of a similar nature to disclose to him. He would be a wonderful father—and quite unlike his own. I knew that if our son was born with a club foot or any other disadvantage Atticus would love him no less and be no less proud of him as long as he grew to be a man of integrity. But if we had a daughter—heaven help us, how spoiled she would be!

"I should like to see the monument," said Genevieve into a brief silence, and although both Atticus and George gave her questioning looks, she rose with all the imperiousness of a queen and waited expectantly until we gave in and accompanied her.

The family burial grounds were partially screened from the gardens by a stand of beech trees, and the rustling of the leaves joined with the distant sound of the surf on this sun-warmed afternoon to create an atmosphere of peace. Peace was a strange legacy indeed, I reflected, and hard won. Then we came in view of the new monument. To the side of the tomb where the old baron had been laid to rest stood a new obelisk, its granite still glittering white in its newness, inscribed RICHARD BLACK-WOOD / b. 1835 / SON, BROTHER, FATHER.

"I wasn't certain what date to put for his death," said Atticus quietly. "In many ways he did die when he went to the Crimea."

Genevieve's eyes were grave as they rested on the monument, but there were no signs of tears. "Thank you for putting 'father,'" she said. "But you know that you are more my father than he was, Uncle Atlas."

My husband's smile was almost a grimace. He still sometimes smarted under the associations brought to mind by his old nickname. Seeing how attached to it Genevieve was, I had tried to reconcile him to it, with only mixed success.

Now as we stood there arm in arm, I squeezed his hand and whispered, "You will always be Atlas to Vivi, because you are the strongest man in her life."

His pale blue eyes warmed as he gazed at me, and he whispered back, "Not George?"

I shook my head. George Bertram was a good, kind man and devoted to Genevieve, but he had never been faced with the crises Atticus had been forced to resolve. "In any case, you do more than hold up our world," I told him. "You hold it together—you hold our family together."

At that, disregarding the time and place, Atticus took me in his arms and kissed me for so long that I heard George voice the protest, "You'll have to learn to be more discreet once the baby is born!"

We parted, exchanging complicit smiles, and Atticus commented, "You're setting out to be a strict parent, Bertram. I think the sight of two people in love is one of the healthiest things a child can see."

"Speaking of the child," said Genevieve with uncharacteristic hesitancy, "George and I have something to ask you." She darted a glance at her husband, evidently for courage, because he put his arm around her waist and gave her a reassuring smile. Thus fortified, she addressed Atticus with an air of seriousness that was unusual in her. "We have been discussing names for the baby," she said, "and how we might honor his heritage, as complicated as it is. If it is a boy, we should like—if you do not mind, uncle—to name him Atticus Richard."

There was a moment of profound silence. My husband's face could not be read. To be confronted with an honor and (as he might see it) a slight in a single gesture no doubt evoked complicated emotions indeed. Then he reached out and took one of her hands in his.

"Not only do I not mind," he told her, "I am delighted. Your child can redeem the name of Richard."

Her pretty blue eyes were still anxious. "Are you certain? Because if you would rather—"

"I'm certain, truly. My brother and I were different in almost every respect, but your child will unite us in a way we never achieved." He gave one of her curls an affectionate tug, and added, "If you have a girl, mind you, I hope you come up with something different. It would be cruel to name her Attica Richardine."

Smiling, Genevieve leaned over to kiss him on the cheek. "It shall be so, uncle. Gravesend will welcome Atticus and Richard again, but this time in harmony."

"Ah," said Atticus, and rubbed the back of his neck. I had been waiting for this moment, wondering if he had changed his mind, but it seemed he had merely been waiting for the right opportunity to speak. "As to Gravesend—it won't be the Blackwood home for much longer."

Two pairs of wide eyes greeted this news. "Telford, you aren't planning to *sell* Gravesend?" George exclaimed.

Atticus was shaking his head even before George stopped speaking. "No, nothing of the sort. But Clara and I have discussed it, and we don't need such an enormous place for just ourselves. However, it would be very well suited for a school, don't you think, Bertram? When the women are ready to leave the institution, their children can move to Gravesend and be educated while their mothers gain a foothold in a new profession."

"The gallery will be the perfect dormitory," I put in, "and think how much exercise and fresh air the children will get with all the grounds at their disposal. So much better than a school in some factory town." We had been pleasantly surprised when sounding out Mrs. Threll and Birch about the idea for a school; Mrs. Threll, it emerged, had a soft spot for children and was delighted to be able to put her administrative skills to work on their behalf; and Birch, to our astonishment, had immediately volunteered to coach the youngsters at cricket. Some of the staff would probably elect to take positions elsewhere, but many had already expressed enthusiasm about the plan for Gravesend. "And Vivi, you would make a marvelous instructor of French, since Henriette prefers to remain my abigail."

Genevieve turned her wide-eyed gaze to me. "You are contented that this should be, Aunt Clara?"

"Most contented."

"Even though—?"

She was privy to the news that I anticipated imparting to Atticus, and I knew she was wondering how I would feel if my own child was not to be raised at Gravesend. I said quickly, "I have given it all due reflection, believe me. And the lodge will be quite spacious enough for—for our needs."

"What about the curse, though?" asked Bertram suddenly. "Aren't you worried about, er, exposing children to that?"

His wife gave him a laughing look. "I thought I was the superstitious one, George! I had no idea you harbored such ideas. Shall you tell our child bedtime stories of monsters and dark magic?"

Atticus was more thoughtful in his response. "Gravesend has seen its share of sorrow and tragedy," he said soberly. "Perhaps more than other houses; perhaps not. But it has also seen much joy." He pressed my hand. "What do you think, Clara?"

Taken aback, I could not produce an answer at once. Gravesend had seen me in my moments of greatest happiness—and had been enmeshed in my times of greatest sorrow. When I forced myself to think back, however, the times since my return that I had felt most ill at ease, most certain of some watchful, portentous presence, were the occasions that I now knew when Richard had been hiding nearby and observing me. Not the house at all, nor some malign supernatural presence, just my senses detecting something that had not fully revealed itself and filling in the gaps with my own remembered dread and misery.

Nothing else that had happened—not my dismissal, nor my mother's death—needed a supernatural explanation. Disasters that had befallen earlier Blackwoods, while sometimes harrowing, could simply have been the vagaries of life. As frightening as the idea of the curse had been, I could see now that it had also offered reassurance: a conviction that some intention or design had lain beneath the sorrows of my life.

And indeed, if there *had* been some otherworldly force at work, who was to say that it was for ill? I had lost Richard, yes, as well as the comfort of believing he had loved me. In his place, however, I had gained a man infinitely his superior . . . and at a time in my life when I was more receptive to his sterling qualities than I would have been as an impetuous, heedless girl.

"Since we've been talking of new beginnings, I think Gravesend deserves one as well," I announced. "The best possible future for the place is for a crowd of children to fill it with their energy and innocence—and chase all the old shadows and superstitions away."

That moved Atticus to embrace me again, to renewed laughing protestations from the others. When finally we started back to the house, the soft dusk was overtaking the gardens, and birds were singing the drowsy song of twilight. Our shadows stretched before us over the green velvet lawn . . . but the era of shadows at Gravesend had come to a close.

The End

Book Club Discussion Questions for
WITH *this* CURSE

Warning: contains spoilers!

If you have not finished reading *With This Curse* and don't want to know what happens, stop reading now!

1. How does Clara change after being dismissed from her position as chambermaid at Gravesend? How does she change as a result of her marriage to Atticus? Compared to her position at the start of chapter one, in what ways has Clara grown and matured by the end of the novel?

2. Atticus is nicknamed for the mythological figure Atlas, a Titan who was condemned by Zeus to hold up the world or the heavens. In what ways does this nickname suit Atticus? Is the association negative, positive, or both? Why?

3. Clara comes to realize that she has romanticized Richard in her memories of him. In what ways are her memories of Richard inaccurate, idealized, or warped by her own predilections and wishes? What makes her realize that her memories of Richard differ from the reality? What does Clara gain by recognizing that her memories were inaccurate?

4. The past plays a large role in the story, especially Clara's and Atticus's past. In what ways are Clara and Atticus trapped in the past? When do their memories and past experiences interfere with their lives—including their life together—in the story's present? By the end of the novel, have they freed themselves from the past or learned to move beyond it? How?

5. Genevieve's arrival at Gravesend is a catalyst in some ways. What happens as a result of her presence? What response does Clara have to her? Lord Telford? In what ways does

knowing Genevieve bring Clara greater understanding of herself and of Atticus? What might Genevieve represent in Clara's eyes?

6. In Victorian England, unmarried women faced severely limited life choices, and few ways were open to them to support themselves. How do we see this manifested in the novel? What are the different options available to Clara when she finds that she is losing her job with Sybil Ingram? Is her decision to marry Atticus understandable?

7. Class distinctions were very much in force in Victorian England. How do they come into play in the story? In what ways are they harmful or damaging? Is the boundary line between master and servant ever breached in the story, and, if so, what are the consequences?

8. Parenthood is an important motif in the story. What examples do we see of good parenting and bad parenting? To what extent do the characters' parents shape them? Would you describe Clara's mother as a good parent? Lord Telford? Will Clara and Atticus be good parents?

9. Clara's perspective on life—particularly life at Gravesend— is shaped in part by her experience as a chambermaid. What insight does this experience give her that is not present in other characters? In what ways do Clara's years in service give her an advantage in her life as Atticus's wife, and in what ways are they a disadvantage?

10. Clara reflects at one point that secrets can be "poisonous." What are some of the most significant secrets that the characters in the story keep? What are the consequences of these secrets, both when they are kept and when they are revealed? How might the story have been different if all of these secrets had been revealed immediately?

Don't miss Clara's continuing adventures in

CURSED ONCE MORE

She went in search of her past . . .
and found danger in the present.

Former seamstress Clara Blackwood seems to have found happiness at last. Having defied the Gravesend Curse, she is a blissfully married baroness and mistress of a grand estate. But now a mysterious summons shatters her contented life.

Clara grew up believing that her mother's family had disowned them. But the grandmother Clara never knew is now entreating her to visit Thurnley Hall, the family seat in Yorkshire. The old lady is on her deathbed and anxious to disclose vital family secrets before it's too late—for Clara's unborn child may be cursed with a horrible fate.

Accompanied by her devoted husband, Atticus, Clara arrives at Thurnley to find intrigue brewing. Her boorish uncle, Horace Burleigh, is greedy for her wealth and desperate to protect the family's mysteries. Superstitious fear of Atticus torments the hulking Romanian servant, Grigore, and even the soft-spoken young ward, Victor Lynch, may have secret motives for getting close to Clara and her husband.

When her grandmother dies under suspicious circumstances, Clara feels compelled to investigate. And when Atticus vanishes mysteriously, she must draw on all her strength and determination to find him before his time runs out . . . before her life can be cursed once more.

Follow the adventures of actress Sybil Ingram, Clara's former employer, in

NOCTURNE *for a* WIDOW

Widowed on her wedding night!

Sybil Ingram is at a crossroads. Once she was the toast of the London stage, but now that she's 28 years old—very well, nearly 30—her draw isn't what it used to be, and her theater troupe is foundering. When her trusted mentor asks her to take the blame for his financial misdeeds, Sybil sees no choice but to retire from the life she loves and move to America to marry New York City hotel magnate Alcott Lammle. But her path to happiness is cut short when Lammle dies suddenly—and in financial ruin.

Widowed, nearly penniless, and unable to return to England, the determined diva sets out to stake a claim on Brooke House, an eccentric neo-Gothic manor in the wilds of the Hudson River Valley. She soon finds, however, that a ghostly presence wants her gone. Even worse, her claim is challenged by the most insolent, temperamental, maddeningly gorgeous man she's ever met: Roderick Brooke, a former violin prodigy whose career ended in a dark scandal.

Soon it's a battle of wills as Sybil matches wits—and trades barbs—with Roderick, finding herself increasingly drawn to him despite her growing suspicion that there is a connection between him and the entity that haunts Brooke House. But an even greater threat arises in the form of the mysterious, powerful queen of local society, Mrs. Lavinia Dove. For reasons that Sybil can't imagine, Mrs. Dove is determined to oust Sybil from her sphere . . . and the lengths to which she will go are chilling indeed.

3 1531 00450 7635

CPSIA information can be obtained
at www.ICGtesting.com
Printed in the USA
LVOW01s1632141216
517260LV00013B/1532/P